WARRIOR OF ROME—BOOK FIVE

Wolves of the North

By the same author

WARRIOR OF ROME—BOOK FIVE

Wolves of the North

HARRY SIDEBOTTOM

THE OVERLOOK PRESS
New York, NY

This edition first in published paperback in the United States in 2014 by
The Overlook Press, Peter Mayer Publishers, Inc.

141 Wooster Street
New York, NY 10012
www.overlookpress.com

For bulk and special sales, please contact sales@overlookny.com,
or write us at the address above.

Cataloging-in-Publication Data is available from the Library of Congress

Manufactured in the United States of America

ISBN 978-1-4683-0820-4

2 4 6 8 10 9 7 5 3 1

To James Gill

The so-called Scythian desert is a grassy plain devoid of trees ... Here live the
Scythians who are called nomads because they do not live in houses but in
wagons ... They eat boiled meat and drink the milk of mares ... As regards
their physical peculiarities and the climate of their lands, the Scythian race is
as far removed from the rest of mankind as can be imagined.

–Pseudo-Hippocrates, *Airs, Waters, Places* 18–19
(tr. J. Chadwick and W. N. Mann)

Contents

Maps

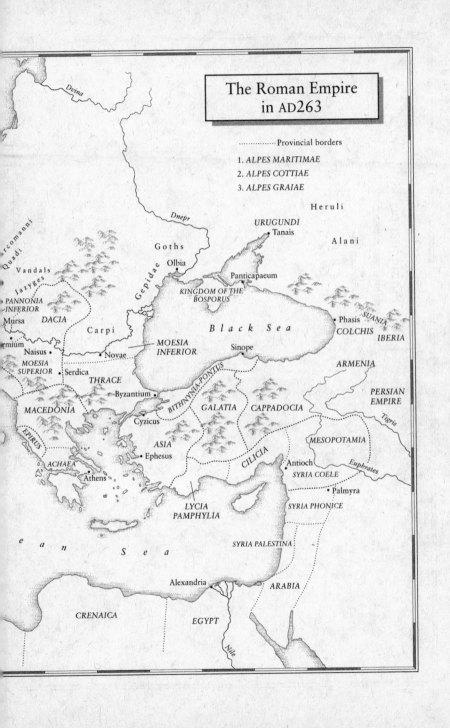

The Roman Empire in AD263

.... Provincial borders

1. *ALPES MARITIMAE*
2. *ALPES COTTIAE*
3. *ALPES GRAIAE*

Dvina

Heruli

Dnepr

URUGUNDI

• Tanais

Alani

Goths

Olbia •

Gepidae

• Panticapaeum

KINGDOM OF THE
BOSPORUS

Marcomanni

Quadi

Vandals

Jazyges

PANNONIA
INFERIOR

• Mursa

DACIA

Carpi

Black Sea

• Phasis

SUANIA

COLCHIS

IBERIA

irmium

• Naisus

• Novae

MOESIA
INFERIOR

• Sinope

ARMENIA

MOESIA
SUPERIOR

• Serdica

THRACE

• Byzantium

BITHYNIA-PONTUS

GALATIA

CAPPADOCIA

PERSIAN
EMPIRE

Tigris

MACEDONIA

EPIRUS

• Cyzicus

ASIA

• Ephesus

CILICIA

MESOPOTAMIA

Euphrates

• Antioch

SYRIA COELE

ACHAEA

• Athens

LYCIA
PAMPHYLIA

SYRIA PHONICE

• Palmyra

SYRIA PALESTINA

e a n

S e a

• Alexandria

ARABIA

CRENAICA

EGYPT

Nile

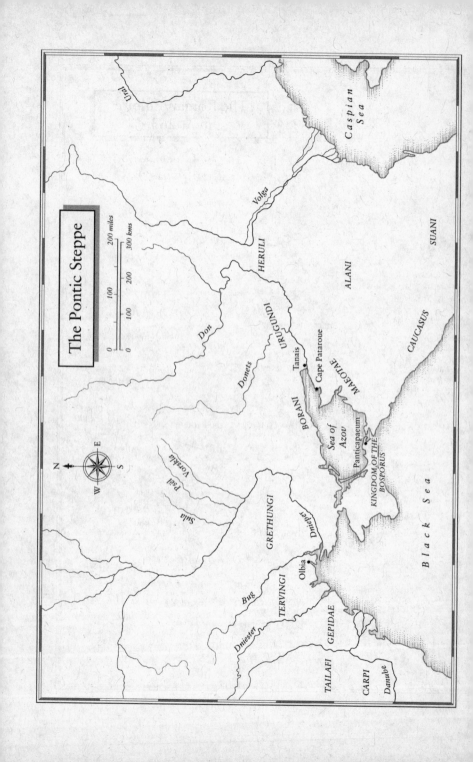

The Pontic Steppe

Prologue

(Panticapaeum, The Kingdom of the Bosporus, Spring AD263)

*This god Death takes many shapes and puts at our disposal an infinite
number of roads that lead to him.*

–Lucian, *Toxaris, or Friendship* 38.

The killer stood in the empty courtyard, sniffing the air, listening.
The smell of charcoal, the distant sounds of metalworking; there
was nothing untoward. The house, like all in the row, was long
abandoned. Yet it had been worth checking; derelict buildings
attracted drunks, vagrants, and – a grimace crossed the killer's
face – lovers with no place else to go.

The sun was shifting down towards the great West Gate, towards
the double walls and ditch which repeatedly had failed to protect the
city of Panticapaeum. In the opposite direction was the acropolis.
There the thin spring sunshine caught the *Pharos* that no one dared
light for fear of the ships it might draw, and the temple of Apollo
Iatros, the home the archer-god had proved unwilling to defend. In
front of these symbols of a threatened Hellenism spread the fire-
blackened, much repaired palace of the King of the Bosporus.
Rhescuporis V, Lover of Caesar, Lover of Rome, styled himself Great
King, King of Kings, and much else. The surrounding barbarian
nomads knew him as the Beggar King. The killer felt nothing but
pleasure in the evidence that evil men brought evil on their own heads.

It would be easy now just to walk away. But night would soon fall. If the necessary actions were not taken, the killer knew only too well what the dark could bring. The self-appointed Hound of the Gods, the Scourge of Evil, walked back into the house.

The corpse lay on its back, naked in the rectangle of light shaped by the door. The killer went to a leather bag, and drew out a piece of string, a scalpel, a knife with a serrated blade and a big cleaver like those used in the meat markets. Hard experience had taught these terrible things were necessary.

The killer laid out the instruments in a neat line by the corpse, and considered them. Better to do the delicate work first. The other way around, and muscle fatigue might cause a nasty slip. There was no point in delaying. The horrible things had to be done. Even in this run-down area of the town, delay might bring discovery.

Taking up the scalpel and kneeling over the body, the killer made an incision the length of the left eyelid. The honed steel cut easily; blood and fluid seeped. The killer pushed the thumb of the hand not holding the blade into the wound, worked it around and down, and drew out the eyeball. It came free with a sucking sound. When the orb was well out of its socket, a neat stroke of the scalpel severed the optic nerve. Although there was a reasonable length of the bloody cord, it proved difficult to tie the string around the slippery, repulsive object.

The Hound of the Gods did not pause, but got straight on with the other eye. Night was approaching, and there was much to be done.

The killer removed both eyes and secured them to the string then exchanged the thin scalpel for the more robust knife with the serrations. The latter were a help. A human tongue was remarkably tough, and there was so much gristle to saw through with the nose, ears and penis. The heavy cleaver came into its own with the butchery of the hands and feet.

It was done, the extremities removed, tied to the string, packed under the armpits. The killer was tired, daubed in gore. Just one last thing. On hands and knees, head right down, the Hound of the Gods licked up some of the blood from the corpse, and spat it out. Three times, the iron taste of blood, disgusting in the mouth, and three times the retching expectoration.

'Barbaric! Gods below, how could anyone do such things?'

Khedosbios, the *eirenarch* of Panticapaeum, did not reply to the new recruit. Instead he looked around the big, desolate room. Shards of amphorae, some recently smashed, lay about. In a corner, an indeterminate pile of sacking and wood was mantled in dust. There was an old mattress in the opposite corner, unpleasantly stained. No other furniture, no graffiti, no clothes, implements or weapons. There was nothing of note except the horror lying on its back near the middle of the floor.

The magistrate turned his attention to the corpse. 'Not barbaric at all. In some ways, fitting.'

The young man of the watch accepted the correction without demur.

Khedosbios crouched down by the body. At least the weather was still cold, and there were not many flies. He took one of the hideously truncated legs in both hands and pulled, manipulating it this way and that. He did the same to an arm. Seemingly satisfied, he lifted the head a little and withdrew the string from underneath. It was stiff with dried blood. Deftly, he unpacked the body parts from under the armpits. They were similarly bloodied, but slimy beneath the dark crust. Stepping back, he ordered the two public slaves to wash the corpse.

As the *libitinarii* got busy, Khedosbios sluiced one of the severed hands with water and carefully examined it. He had been appointed *eirenarch* just the previous year. He was young and only dissimulated his ambition when he thought it served. Since childhood, learning his letters with the *Iliad*, the example of Achilles had always been with him: *Strive ever to be the best*.

The *libitinarii* stood back. The reek of mud and blood was strong in the room now. Khedosbios gave the detached hand to the recruit, and got back down over the corpse. His boots squelched in the newly formed sludge. No matter, only a fool would go to the scene of a murder in anything other than old clothes. Khedosbios scanned the body from the cut ankles upwards. He found nothing of interest on the limbs or torso; the man had been cleanshaven. Khedosbios tipped back the chin and studied the purple groove running around the neck. Then he prised the jaw open and inserted his fingers into the bloody ruin of a mouth, delicately feeling about.

Standing again, he told the *libitinarii* to turn the body over and wash the back.

'Who founded this city?'

Thrown by the unexpected question, the recruit was a moment answering: 'The Milesians.'

'No, before that, in the age of heroes.'

'Medea's brother Apsyrtos. He was given the land by the Scythian King Agaetes,' the boy said with a certain civic pride.

Khedosbios nodded and crouched low. He peered at some small purple blotches on the back of the corpse, wondering at their meaning. Then his fingers traced several rows of tiny indentations. Close inspection revealed they were linked by faint white lines.

The *eirenarch* got up and wiped his hands on his already stained Sarmatian trousers. 'When Medea and Jason had stolen the golden fleece, her father sent Apsyrtos after them. When her brother caught them, they murdered him and dismembered his body. It is in the epic *Argonautica* by Apollonius of Rhodes, although I do not remember anything about the tongue or penis.'

4

'Why?'

'To stop the daemon pursuing them. How can a spirit follow with no feet, or hold a blade with no hands?'

'No, *Kyrios*, why in real life?'

'Is there a difference? Rich, *eupatrid* families forge an ancestry going back to Agamemnon or Ajax. Perhaps the Romans are right: we Hellenes live too much in the past. Reading too many books can be dangerous.'

'He was strangled?' The recruit politely phrased it as a question.

'With a ligature. He was a slave.'

'The rough, calloused hands?'

Khedosbios smiled. The boy was keen. 'Not really; many free men have the like – farmers, stevedores. No, it is the scars of old beatings on the back, and the teeth.'

'The teeth, *Kyrios*?'

'Slave bread is made with the sweepings. It is full of husks, grit – wears the teeth down.' Khedosbios recognized *hybris* as a vice, in himself as in others, but at times the paradigm of Achilles overcame his avoidance of the pride that found expression in the belittling of others.

'As you say, *Kyrios*.'

'How many slaves have been reported missing or run in the last couple of days?'

'Four: a girl, a child and two adult males.'

'Who owned the men?'

'One was the property of Demosthenes, son of Sauromates, the metalworker.'

'An occupation that leaves marks on the hands.'

'The other belonged to the envoy Marcus Clodius Ballista. Shall I send a messenger to tell him?'

'Too late,' said Khedosbios. 'His mission sailed this morning.'

The young man of the watch averted evil, thumb between index

5

and middle finger. 'The gods willing, the murderer did not sail with them. Even being under the same roof as a murderer pollutes, and everyone knows a ship on which one sails comes to grief.'

Khedosbios laughed out loud. 'Not to mention being confined in dangerous proximity to a man who enjoys killing and has a taste for mutilation.'

PART ONE
The Country of Strange Peoples
(Lake Maeotis and the Tanais River, Spring AD263)

He shall pass into the country of strange peoples; he shall try good and evil in all things.

–William of Rubruck, Preface 2 (misquoting *Ecclesiasticus* 39.5)

I

'I did not think Polybius would run,' Ballista said. The tall north-erner spoke in Greek. He turned to look at the other four men.

They were leaning against the stern rail of the big Roman warship. Wrapped in dark cloaks, bulky with covered weapons, the spindrift whipping around them, they looked like gloomy harbingers of some as yet unspecified violence.

A blustery spring wind from the south-west was pushing a following sea under the ship, driving it on. The waters of Lake Maeotis rolled away, very green. A small Bosporan galley bobbed in their wake.

'He never lacked courage,' Maximus replied in the same language. Against the pain of the hangover from the previous night in Panticapaeum, the Hibernian bodyguard had screwed his eyes almost shut. Coupled with the scar where the end of his nose should have been, it gave him an extremely off-putting demeanour. 'Certain, you could not fault him last year when the Goths came to Miletus and Didyma, and he did not disgrace himself in the Caucasus. After all that, a trip to ransom a few hostages from the Heruli should hold few fears.'

The little officer Castricius pushed his hood back from his thin, pointed face. 'Going out on the sea of grass among the nomads might give any man pause. Like all Scythians, the Heruli are not as other men. Despite all their raids into the empire, there may be no one alive to ransom. Some say they sacrifice their prisoners, dress in their skins, use their skulls as drinking cups. Going among the Heruli should give any man pause for thought – even a man such as me, protected by a good daemon.'

'They say they fuck donkeys too,' Maximus said.

'And they say the kings of your island fuck horses,' Hippothous responded. The Greek secretary's shaved head shone in the thin sunshine. 'All nonsense. People place any strange thing they wish at the ends of the world.'

'Well . . .' Maximus looked vaguely embarrassed.

'A serious man of culture' – Hippothous talked over him – 'one who really belongs among the *pepaideumenoi*, should welcome the prospect of travelling among the nomads. Do not forget that one of the seven sages, Anacharsis, was actually a Scythian.'

'I thought he left the tent dwellers to live in Athens,' Ballista said. Maximus grinned.

Hippothous took no notice of either. 'To a student of physiognomy, such as myself, it presents both a challenge and an opportunity. Herodotus tells of many fascinating peoples out there. The Budinians all have piercing grey eyes and bright-red hair. Then there are the Argippaei: bald from birth – men and women alike – with snub noses and large chins. For a physiognomist to see the soul behind such strange faces, that would be a triumph. But most extraordinary of all are the Heruli.'

'Did you not just say people believe any nonsense about the ends of the earth?' Castricius interrupted. 'Herodotus also tells of men with goat feet, whole tribes of the one-eyed, and others who turn into wolves for a few days each year.'

Hippothous smiled urbanely. 'You know your literature, Legate. Men misjudge you when they describe you as an ill-educated soldier, jumped up from the ranks. You have transcended your origins.'

Castricius's thin lips were pressed tight in his small mouth.

'Of course,' the Greek continued, 'most such things may be travellers' tales and myths. Herodotus claimed only to report what others told him, he did not vouchsafe the truth of it. Yet it is universally acknowledged that he was correct to state that climate and style of life shape the character of a people. The sea of grass does not change. So neither do the nomads.'

The fifth man, who had neither spoken nor seemed to have been listening, turned inboard from the sea. He was a strikingly ugly older man; sparse tufts of hair on his great domed skull, a thin, peevish mouth. 'If Polybius discovered the real reason we have been sent, he had reason to run.' At Calgacus's words, the others fell silent. Instinctively, they looked down the length of the warship. There was little privacy to be had on a *trireme*, especially one burdened with an extra thirty-five passengers on deck.

The *trierarch* and the helmsman were some paces away. The commander was talking earnestly to the latter. No one else was particularly near. If the men at the stern kept their voices down, they were unlikely to be overheard.

'Apart from us and the two eunuchs, no one knows,' Ballista said.

Calgacus snorted with derision. 'Shite,' he muttered, perfectly audibly.

Ballista sighed. Since his childhood among the Angles of northern Germania, Calgacus had always been there. When Ballista had been taken as a hostage into the Roman *imperium*, Calgacus had accompanied him. First as a slave then, after manumission, the old Caledonian had looked after him – always complaining, always there. Tolerant *patronus* that he was, Ballista would allow such latitude only to one other of his freedmen. That man spoke next.

'The old bastard is right,' Maximus said. 'The whole boat knows. Eunuchs are like women. They love to gossip.'

'Emperors are fools to trust their sort,' Castricius put in. 'Neither one thing nor the other, they are unnatural, monstrous – like crows. It is an ill omen just to meet one, let alone travel to the ends of the earth with a couple.'

'Neither doves nor ravens,' Maximus agreed.

'Eunuchs or not,' Calgacus said, 'whether there are any hostages to ransom or not, you have fuck all hope of succeeding in the real mission. You will never persuade the Heruli to turn on their Gothic allies. They will take the emperor's gold, little enough as it is, then slit our throats, turn our hides into cloaks, bowcases or some such shite, and no one in our great emperor Gallienus's *consilium* will give a fuck.'

'Not necessarily,' Ballista said. 'Felix and Rutilus will have a worse time in the north trying to get the Grethungi to attack their fellow Gothic tribes, and Sabinillus and Zeno not much better in the west getting the Carpi, Taifali and Gepidae to fight any of the Goths.'

'Good,' said Calgacus. 'We can take comfort in them being as doomed as us. A whole range of men in imperial disfavour will have died serving the *Res Publica*. Of course, the donkey-fucking Heruli may not get the chance to kill us – we have to survive the Maeotae and the Urugundi Goths before we reach them.'

Suitably chastened, the five men relapsed into silence. Ballista judged that Calgacus might well be right, but there was no point in admitting it. Of all the daunting imperial *mandata* Ballista had received from Gallienus and his predecessors, these orders gave him the worst feeling.

The breeze was freshening, cresting the thick, green waves. The little Bosporan *liburnian* forged ahead, its double banks of oars flashing, spray flying. It turned to the south-east. The *trireme* followed, angling across the sea towards the low, dark land. Ballista looked out at the unprepossessing sight, dark thoughts in his head.

The *trierarch*, a short, stubby centurion with a beard, walked to the stern. 'Almost there, *Domini*.' He spoke in Latin to Ballista and Castricius, as the envoy and his deputy. 'We will make Azara in a couple of hours.' He smiled. 'I give you joy of it. Apparently the locals call the place Conopion – Mosquito-town.'

When the ship slipped into one of the many channels of the Lesser Rhombites river, Hippothous was struck by the stillness. The wind was gone. Reeds and sedge pressed in on both sides. The water was black and heavy, glossy in the lowering sun. The creak and splash of the oars, the clicking and chattering of insects and birds, both seemed thin and insubstantial against the oppressive quiet of the delta.

The *trireme* rowed in the glassy trail of the *liburnian*, until both were manoeuvred to rest stern on against a dilapidated jetty at the foot of a low, overgrown rise. The Maeotae were waiting for them in arms. The isolated wooden look-outs they had passed jutting up out of the water obviously gave notice of the arrival of men as well as shoals of fish. These tribesmen belonged to a tribe of the Maeotae called the Tarpeites: fishermen on the coast, farmers inland, said to be brigands in both elements. There were a hundred or so of them, dirty, poorly armed, but obviously dangerous in their barbarian irrationality.

The marines on the *trireme* and the auxiliary soldiers escorting the embassy held themselves very still, weapons to hand. All told, there were about forty Roman fighting men.

The sun was going down, but it was warmer away from the open sea. Hippothous slapped at the insects settling on him and watched the Bosporan ship run out its boarding ladder and the *navarchos* disembark. The grandly titled commander of the fleets of the Great King of the Bosporus talked for some time with the tribesmen. There was an amount of gesticulating. The armed men on the Roman vessel grew bored, put up their weapons, leant on their shields and the gunwales, talked under their breath. Hippothous did not relax. He had not survived a lifetime of violence as bandit, Cilician chief and, for the last few years, *accensus* to Ballista, only by luck. The post of secretary usually did not involve much violence, but in the *familia* of Ballista it was almost the norm.

Finally, the talking ended. Some tribesmen trotted off into the trees which grew up the hill. The *navarchos* waved for those on the *trireme* to come ashore. The herald the imperial authorities had attached to the envoys at Panticapaeum went first down the gangplank. At the bottom, the *praeco* called out in a stentorian voice in Latin: 'The *Legatus extra ordinem Scythica* Marcus Clodius Ballista, *Vir Perfectissimus*, and his deputy, Gaius Aurelius Castricius, *Vir Perfectissimus*.'

Both men had held high prefectures, which had ranked them each as *Vir Ementissimus*. Hippothous noted they had been demoted. The *praeco* had not done that on his own initiative. But Castricius had been Prefect of Cavalry under two pretenders, one of them, briefly, Ballista himself. And it was not Roman practice to send men of the highest ranks as diplomatic envoys to the barbarians, especially not on missions from which they may well not return.

When the envoys had clattered down to the shore with their entourage and eleven-man escort, an individual slightly less grubby than the majority stepped out of the horde of Tarpeites.

'Pericles, son of Alcibiades,' he announced himself in heavily accented Greek. 'Come, I take you to the palace of the king.'

Hippothous did not let himself smile.

Led by Ballista, they followed the barbarian with the ludicrously Hellenic name and patronymic up the path. It was dark under the beech trees, the path narrow. An ideal place for an ambush, Hippothous thought. Surreptitiously, he loosened his sword in its scabbard.

When they emerged from the tree line it was not yet full dark. A sward ran uphill. It was crowned with a rough palisade pierced by a gate with a rustic-looking tower.

'The palace of the king,' Hippothous said.

'Golden Mycenae itself, the strong-founded citadel,' Castricius replied.

The two men smiled, momentarily united in contempt for this place, if in nothing else except their propensity to violence.

'You can quote Homer.' Hippothous managed to sound surprised.

'When I was in Albania last year, it was a bad time. There were . . . few people to talk to, nothing else to read. I have developed a liking for epic poetry,' Castricius ended defiantly.

The hall of the King of the Tarpeites was wooden and thatched. Inside, it was dark, lit by smoking torches. There was a distinct smell of close humanity and smoked fish.

The monarch of all he surveyed sat on a crude wooden imitation of a Roman magistrate's ivory throne. The imperial bureaucracy had provided the envoys with an interpreter from the Bosporus. It was claimed he could speak eight barbarian languages. His expertise proved unnecessary here. The king spoke Greek, the language of diplomacy throughout the east, if in an uncouth way. He and Ballista exchanged what passed for pleasantries. After a less than dignified interval, the king asked for a present. Expecting it, Ballista handed him a *spatha* with an inlaid hilt and fine sword belt. The king examined the gift with ill-concealed avarice. Seeming satisfied, he called for a feast.

Hippothous was placed some way down the hall, with Tarpeites on either side. The one on his left launched into an extended discourse on fishing in execrable Greek. There was no better place in the world for fish than Lake Maeotis. Bream; anchovy by the tens of thousand; given the name of the Rhombites, there were turbot of course; and the finest of all, sturgeon. And it was here that the tunny spawned in the spring. Their migration was interesting.

Despite it all, Hippothous was not unhappy. The last eight months had been hard. Last September, the *familia* had left the Caucasus in a hurry. They had travelled hard down from the mountains to Phasis on the Euxine. There they had chartered a ship to take them to the Kingdom of the Bosporus. As it was late in the season, the owner had charged an outrageous sum of money.

Wintering at Panticapaeum had not been a pleasure. The sights of the town were soon exhausted: the sword with which long ago the Celtic bodyguard had despatched Mithridates the Great, the famous bronze jar split by the cold, the decrepit palace of the kings, echoing of its past glories, the fire-scorched temple of Apollo on the Acropolis, the equally run-down temples of Demeter, Dionysus and Cybele. There had been nothing that passed for an intellectual life in that degenerate outpost of Hellenism, a *polis* where the citizens dressed like Sarmatian tribesmen and as often as not answered to barbaric names.

Come midwinter, Hippothous had never seen snow like it. A wall of cloud had come down from the north-west. The air had been clogged with big flakes like feathers. It had lasted for days, settled everywhere, drifting deep enough to smother a dog or a child. When the snow stopped, it got colder; the sky a clear, unearthly yellow; all frighteningly still. Then the sea froze. At first just by the shore, but soon it stretched as far as the eye could see; a vast white plain, with here and there jumbles of blocks forced up by the pressure. In February, Hippothous had joined Ballista, driving in a carriage across the straits to Phanagoria, the town on the Asian side. Well wrapped, they had watched men dig out fish trapped in the ice. They used a special pronged instrument like a trident. All their winters had to be as bad. Some of the sturgeon they hauled out had been nearly the size of dolphins.

Being quartered in one of the few houses that still had a working hypocaust had been a saviour. Without the hot air circulating under the floor, Hippothous was convinced he would have died of cold.

'After streaming through the Bosporus, the great shoals follow the sun around the Euxine. By Trapezus, they have enough size to be just worth catching.'

Hippothous knew they did not have to be here. The ancients had vastly overestimated the size of Maeotis. They could have sailed from Panticapaeum to the mouth of the Tanais in a long day, especially with the wind set from the south-east. But in Panticapaeum both the king and his *navarchos* had insisted, almost pleaded, they break their journey twice; first here with the Tarpeites, and then with the Psessoi. Long ago, the kings of the Bosporus had ruled these tribes of Maeotae with a secure grasp, their control guaranteed by the might of Rome. Now Rhescuporis V, descendant of Heracles, of the line of Poseidon through his son Eumolpos, hoped the rare sight of a single imperial *trireme* and a handful of regular soldiers in company with one of his very few remaining little *liburnians* might give his claims to local hegemony just a mite of credibility.

In Alexandria, Hippothous had once heard a philosopher from the *Museum* lecturing on power and force. His argument was that they were distinct. Force consumed itself with the deployment of armed men. On the other hand, power was the result of the complex, possibly intangible, calculations the subordinate made concerning the consequences of disobeying instructions. As such, power might last for ever. Sat in this fish-reeking hall, Hippothous knew the philosopher was wrong. With the legions tasting defeat at barbarian hands – the emperor Decius cut down by the Goths, Valerian a prisoner of the Persians – or trapped in endless civil wars, Rome's power was wearing threadbare, the edges of its *imperium* fraying loose.

'Now, when they pass by Sinope, they are altogether riper for catching and salting.'

Hippothous liked fish as much as the next man. The black, salty fish roe he was spooning on his bread – he did not think it had a Greek name – might be poor man's food, but it was good. However, this verbal tracking of tunny from watery cradle to grave was becoming intolerable. He looked around for distraction.

Practising the science of physiognomy did more than assuage boredom. If you got it right, it told you the true nature of those around you, gave you access to their souls. Ultimately, it allowed you to guard against the vices of the bad before you had to experience them. Hippothous let his gaze slide over the body servant Calgacus and the bodyguard Maximus, one too ugly, the other too scarred for clear results; maybe one day he would try to analyse them. The locals were too encased in filth. He suppressed a shudder at the sight of the two eunuchs.

He settled on Castricius. Hippothous had studied the little officer before but, then, his perceptions had been blunted by a raging hangover. Confronted by a grave issue, the Persians discussed it once sober, a second time drunk. Hippothous would revisit the soul of Castricius.

The little officer was seated opposite. He was talking to a young Tarpeites warrior who would have been attractive if he had not been so disgustingly dirty. Their conversation was animated. Hippothous could observe Castricius with little fear of detection.

He no longer cared if his voluble and fish-obsessed neighbour thought him rude.

Hippothous stared at Castricius, emptied his mind, let his training take over. There were good aspects to the man: his protruding lower lip pointed to tenderness, and a love of well being. But the bad far outweighed the good. There was his sharp little nose, thin at the tip. It indicated a great anger. Then there was the short, angular chin, a sure sign of boldness, badness and killing, even entering into evil. Castricius had unexpectedly beautiful eyes. Nothing redeeming about that. Eyes were the gateway to the soul, and beautiful eyes concealed what was there, gave proof of treachery. All the evidence scientifically weighed, Hippothous was as convinced as before that Castricius was a bad man, a bad and very dangerous man.

A burst of loud, unseemly laughter from the head of the hall. It was the king. He was leaning across, roaring at Ballista, patting his leg. The king was drunk. Hippothous considered it unlikely Ballista was having a better time than himself. The big northerner's face was set in an inscrutable mask of polite attention. In the three years he had served Ballista, despite repeated study, Hippothous had yet to reach a definitive conclusion. All the signs had to be considered, and they led to different, mutually incompatible results. The Hellenized barbarian was a complicated subject. His eyes were heavy-lidded, sloping towards the corners. The master physiognomist Polemon judged that this revealed a man contemplating evil. Yet the eyes were dark blue, almost bluish black, and they shone, sometimes like the rays of the sun. Such belonged to a man of compassion and caution, the latter maybe going as far as cowardice and fear.

The king was still laughing. Hippothous watched Ballista sigh and look down at his food. Certainly the big man had reason for melancholy. Ripped from his original home in Germania, he was now also banished from Rome and from Sicily, from his wife and sons – for whom he showed a striking tenderness. Anyone could see this mission was a dangerous fool's errand – the sort landed on the very expendable. And there was the curse. The previous year in the Caucasus, Ballista had taken as a lover a princess of the royal house of Suania, a priestess of the bitch goddess Hecate. It had not ended well. As they left, Pythonissa – a modern Medea – had called up from the underworld the most terrible curse on Ballista:

Kill his wife. Kill his sons. Kill all his family, all those he loves. But do not kill him. Let him live – in poverty, in impotence, loneliness and fear. Let him wander the face of the earth, through strange towns, among strange peoples, always in exile, homeless and hated.

Hippothous thought Ballista might well cast his eyes down and sigh.

The *trireme* had rounded Pataroue point some hours before. They were now not far out from Tanais. The two tribes of the Maeotae – the Tarpeites and the Psessoi – they had been forced to visit were behind them, safely negotiated. It had taken three days. Now the Gothic people of the Urugundi lay ahead, and beyond them the endless expanse of grasslands and the Heruli.

The wind had dropped to a dead calm. The 170 rowers were earning their *stipendium* as they drove the vessel through the thick, oddly opaque water. The triple banks of oars rose and fell like the wings of some labouring waterfowl, never destined to fly. As the blades came free they were festooned with all manner of weeds.

Ballista inhaled the comfortingly familiar smells of a war-galley: the sun-warmed wood and pitch of the decking and hull, the mutton fat and leather of the oar sleeves, the stale sweat and urine of the crew. He was seated in a chair behind the helmsman, towards the stern. He would have been as happy to sit on the planking, but the majesty of Rome demanded a certain *dignitas*. Likewise, her never-to-be-denied *maiestas* insisted her envoy be accompanied by a suitably dignified entourage. Ballista looked down the long deck at them. There was his deputy, Castricius. There was his *familia*: Maximus, Calgacus and Hippothous, and the Suanian Tarchon, who had attached himself to them the previous year in the Caucasus. There also were his young slave, Wulfstan, and the two slaves owned by Castricius and Hippothous. Apart from the *familia* there was his escort sent up from Byzantium: Hordeonius the centurion and his ten men seconded from Cohors I Cilicium Milliaria Equitata Sagittariorum by the governor of Moesia Inferior. And then there was the official staff: the eunuch freedmen Mastabates and Amantius, the interpreter Biomasos, the herald Regulus, two scribes, two messengers, and Porsenna the *haruspex* to read the omens. Six more slaves, variously owned, brought the number of souls to thirty-five.

Ballista looked with particular disfavour at the group of officials around the eunuchs. At least two of these functionaries were bound to be *frumentarii*, imperial agents tasked with spying on him. Unless, of course, one or more of the *frumentarii* were hidden among the auxiliary soldiers. In an age of iron and rust, Roman emperors trusted no one. Once, long ago when they were young, Ballista and Gallienus had been held together at the imperial court as hostages for the good behaviour of their fathers. One father had been an important Roman senatorial governor, the other a barbarian war leader beyond the frontier. Ballista and Gallienus had become close, friends even, despite their origins – Gallienus had always been unconventional. But the elevation of the latter to the purple had banished such intimacy. Any trust that had survived had been killed when circumstances two years earlier had demanded Ballista himself briefly be acclaimed Augustus. That Ballista had set aside the purple in favour of Gallienus within days, and sent any number of letters containing oaths of loyalty since, had done nothing to revive it. Ballista realized he was lucky to be alive. So were all his *familia*, including his sons and wife.

'I am still surprised that Polybius would run.' Ballista spoke to no one in particular, more to take his mind off his wife and sons far away in Sicily than desiring an answer.

'No mystery to it at all,' Hordeonius the centurion said. He rapped his vine-staff of office on the deck in an assertive way.

Ballista came back to his surroundings. Vaguely aware of Wulfstan nearby in attendance, he had not really noticed the approach of the centurion, Maximus, Calgacus and Hippothous.

'No point in asking, *Dominus*,' Hordeonius said. His abrupt, overtly military style of speaking had almost driven out the last vestiges of a North African accent. 'Slaves are all the same – unreliable, untrustworthy rubbish. Every one of the whiplings would run, if they had the courage. Worse than soldiers; they have to be kept down by fear. All slaves are the enemy. Only the shadow of the cross keeps them honest.'

What Ballista had seen of Hordeonius so far had not endeared him. The centurion was of medium height, broad and physically powerful, with a face that promised little understanding but limitless brutality. Hordeonius's men saw him as a petty, short-tempered tyrant. He probably saw himself as an old-style centurion: let them hate as long as they fear.

'Sure, you do like a generalization, Centurion,' said Maximus. 'Consider where they come from. Some are born to slavery, others poor, unwanted babies exposed on dungheaps and raised by heartless slavers for profit. Then there are criminals condemned to the mines and the like.'

'It makes no odds, they are all rubbish,' Hordeonius snapped. 'Slavery makes its mark, and not just whips and brands. It deforms the soul of a man enslaved.'

'Are you saying my soul is deformed?' Maximus spoke quietly.

Ballista watched Hordeonius's face. He could see the retorts rising up, nearly escaping the cage of his teeth.

'I was taken in war. There was a ring of dead at my feet, when I was struck from behind.'

Ballista smiled. It was not how Maximus always told the story of the cattle raid in Hibernia. In more comic versions he was running away, sometimes caught with his trousers down on top of his enemy's wife.

'Slavery is nothing but a roll of the dice,' Maximus concluded.

'Not so, Marcus Clodius Maximus,' Hippothous interjected. The Greek launched into a philosophical discourse. 'What the world calls slavery and freedom are nothing of the sort; nothing but a legal fiction. True freedom, like true slavery, is in the soul. The soul of a good man can never be enslaved. The cynic Diogenes in fetters was a free man. The Great King of Persia, sat in pomp on the throne of the house of Sasan, is unfree if he is a slave to his irrational passions: lust, greed, anger.'

Again Hordeonius was silent. There was no love growing between the North African centurion and the *familia* of Ballista.

'So, my dear Hibernian,' Hippothous continued, 'Marcus Clodius Ballista may have given you a papyrus roll, given you his *praenomen* and *nomen*, and with them Roman citizenship, but, I fear, you remain a slave – a slave to your bodily lusts, to endless amphorae of wine and cheap women.'

Maximus laughed. 'And you? Are you not a slave to pretty boys? I have heard you howl in the baths at the sight of a nice arse. Given his good looks, Calgacus here has not slept at all since you joined the *familia*. Always expecting the invasion, he is. Did I tell you how in his youth, in the bloom of his beauty, he caused a riot in Athens? Very dedicated pederasts, the Athenians.'

As if stirred into action by the mention of his name, the elderly Caledonian spoke. 'The slave Polybius ran from Panticapaeum because he tired of waiting for his freedom.' Calgacus hawked and spat over the side of the ship. Then, in a muttering inflection, but at the same volume, he added, 'Took you fucking long enough to free me, and the yappy Hibernian.'

Ballista became very aware of young Wulfstan at his shoulder, very aware of the tensions in even the happiest *familia* in a slave-owning society.

'Company.' The voice of the *trierarch* rang out.

Ahead, six ships with the distinctive double prows, fore and aft, of northern longships. They were pulling unhurried towards the *trireme*. The Goths were coming to them.

Not by choice, Calgacus had seen the world. He had been with Ballista in Rome, in Arelate, Nemausus and the other fine cities of Gallia Narbonensis, sojourned in Asia at Ephesus and Miletus, lived in Antioch, the metropolis of the east. By comparison, Tanais, most north-eastern of all Greek *poleis*, was a shite-hole. Calgacus's eyesight was not what it had been. Others had spotted the low town before it swam in his vision out of the vast, swampy delta of the river from which it took its name.

First, the *trireme* pulled past an abandoned suburb. It was long abandoned. Trees grew through the remains of houses. What had been thoroughfares were blocked by mounds of rubbish overgrown with patches of marsh grass. The effect was of a juvenile deity's rough plan of a mountain range, set aside through distraction.

The quay was of new, raw-cut timber; the ramshackle build-ings behind the same. The smell of sawn wood mixed with mud, fish and an undertone of burning. Oddly, a huge hill of ash and debris demarcated the harbour from the town proper. Calgacus's eyes, blurred in the spring sun, took it in as best they could, the mean scale of the place. No more than a couple of thousand inhabitants could huddle within its walls. A complete shite-hole.

As they walked up, Calgacus saw that the stone walls were cracked, leaning here and there, in places fallen altogether. Rubble half filled the defensive ditch. Urugundi guards stood, bored, at the fire-scorched gates. They waved them through.

Inside was worse. The street up to the *agora* had been cleared, but the lanes running off it were choked with the debris of collapsed houses. Fire-black beams poked up, mocking man's transient endeavours. Thousands of tiny shards of amphorae crunched like snow underfoot. The town was deserted. The sack had been thorough and recent, no more than a few years.

The *agora* had been scoured clean. Traders had returned; a surprising number of them had set up stalls. They called their wares: oil and wine from the south, hides and slaves, honey and gold from the north. The council house had been repaired. Incongruously, instead of tiles, it had been given a roof of reeds. The Gothic guards at the door told them to wait outside the *Bouleuterion*. They waited. A gang of slaves – Greeks or Romans – was working to repair the gymnasium next door. They were overseen by an architect, who in turn was watched by a Goth.

Ballista stood, feet apart, leaning on the hilt of his scabbarded long sword, head down. Behind him, unconsciously in similar pose, stood Maximus and the Suanian Tarchon. The ruins all around, they looked like penitents of some strange, grim militant sect.

As Calgacus regarded Ballista, he felt a not unfamiliar stab of jealousy. Ballista had been loved from birth. His mother, of course, but also a fierce pride and affection from his father. Isangrim, war leader of the Angles, had other, older children by other women. Politics, not desire nor love, dictated a man of his position in Germania would most likely marry more than once, sometimes concurrently. His relations had not been good with all his offspring, especially with his eldest son, Morcar. Ballista – Dernhelm, as he was called then – the solemn but affectionate, golden-haired child had been another chance, a chance to make things right.

Calgacus had never known his parents. He had been too young when the Angle slavers came. A faint, half-recalled woman's face, a strange tugging at his memory with the smell of a peat fire, that was all he had of a childhood.

The Caledonian cuffed the jealousy down like an unruly dog. He had been with Ballista since the boy was little more than a babe in arms. The boy had suffered too. It was not Ballista's fault, none of it. He had always done his best, tried to do the right thing – by the world, by Calgacus. They could not be closer. Once in a while, they talked openly. Usually, the grumbling on one side, the teasing on the other, both masked and expressed their strong affection. Calgacus loved the man he would always think of as a boy, and knew it was returned.

Calgacus wished he had not made the graceless comment on the boat about freedom. He had been thinking about Rebecca, the Jewish woman, a slave of Ballista's wife in Sicily. Calgacus had grown close to her. He wanted her freedom; hers and Simon's, the Jewish boy she had been bought to look after. If they returned from the grasslands, he would ask Ballista for her freedom, maybe marry her. Ballista would grant it, would feel guilty he had not offered it. Old as he was, Calgacus thought it would be good to have a son of his own. He grunted an obscenity. With luck the child would have her looks.

If they returned from the grasslands and the Heruli . . . The curse lay heavy on Ballista. *Let him wander the face of the earth . . . among strange peoples, always in exile, homeless and hated.* Not just on Ballista. *Kill his sons . . . all those he loves.* The Suanian Pythonissa was a hot bitch. You could not really blame Ballista for fucking

27

her. But what a choice: a priestess dedicated to Hecate. Calgacus had no doubt the dark goddess of the underworld would heed her priestess. You could never tell how, but he had no doubt the curse would play out some way or another.

The time in the Caucasus the previous year had not been good, and not just because of the curse. For weeks, Calgacus had been besieged by a force of the nomadic Alani in a tiny stone tower, just a few paces across. There had been a few others in that close, evil confinement. Most had endured, the eunuch Mastabates, the young Angle slave Wulfstan among them. But it had done Hippothous no good. By the end, the Greek *accensus*'s interest in the nonsense he called something like 'physiognomy' had grown to an obsession. Endless drivel about the eyes as the windows of the soul, peering into your face, him watching you unnervingly in odd moments. It had nearly driven Calgacus mad. After but a few days, he would quite happily have killed the man.

Hippothous was not the only one the mountains had changed. Little Castricius had been away in Albania. The gods knew what had happened there, but he had returned altered. There had always been something about him, something secretive and dangerous. Some undisclosed crime had condemned him to the mines in his youth. Against the odds, he had survived, somehow in the face of the law joined the legions, and since risen to equestrian status and high command. He had always joked that the daemons of death were scared of him, that a good daemon watched over him. But now there was a repetition and an earnestness to these claims that was unsettling, that nodded towards madness.

A tall Goth, taller even than Ballista, walked out. He had long hair, and the muscles of his arms were hooped with finely wrought gold torques.

'I am Peregrim, son of Ursio.' He spoke the language of

Germania. 'If you are minded, the King of the Urugundi would talk to you now.'

It was dark inside the *Bouleuterion*. As his sight grew accustomed to it, Calgacus saw it was roughly square, stone benches running up into the gloom on the other three sides. It reminded him of the council house at Priene. But here there were not just a few Greeks in tunics. The benches were packed with armed Gothic warriors.

Halfway up the opposite side, the benches had been cut away. A large dark-wood throne sat there, two ravens carved on the back. On it sat Hisarna, son of Aoric, King of the Urugundi. He was a heavyset man, broad shouldered, in middle age. Across his knees rested a drawn sword; his father's famous blade, *Iron*. The king's name – Hisarna – meant the Iron One. He was a man to be reckoned with, this Woden-born ruler, as his father had been before him. Thirty years ago, the Urugundi had been no more than a *comitatus* of a dozen or so men who had wandered down from the north, practising brigandage and selling their swords for hire on the shores of Lake Maeotis and the banks of the Tanais. Led by Aoric then Hisarna, they had fought, schemed, negotiated and slaughtered their way to become one of the major groups in the loose Gothic confederation.

'Dernhelm, son of Isangrim of the Angles, why are you here?' Hisarna spoke in the language of the north. His voice was surprisingly gentle, melodious.

Ballista replied in Greek. 'I am here as Marcus Clodius Ballista, envoy of the *autokrator* Publius Licinius Egnatius Gallienus *Sebastos*. My *kyrios* has charged me with ransoming prisoners from the Urugundi and the Heruli.'

Hisarna smiled, and continued in Germanic. 'A thankless task in both parts. The Urugundi hold no prisoners from the empire. When my nephew Peregrim returned from the Aegean last year, outside Byzantium he allowed the official the Romans call the Procurator of the Hellespontine Provinces to ransom all those he had taken. Those Greeks and Romans who lived in Tanais now are my subjects by right of conquest.'

Ballista said nothing.

'As for the Heruli, I wish you well trying to reason with Naulobates and his long-headed warriors.'

From the ranks of the Goths came a deep hooming sound of amusement.

Ballista switched to Germanic and spoke politely. 'Then I would ask your permission to cross your lands, and try my luck with the Heruli.'

'It shall be as you wish,' Hisarna said. 'It may be fortunate for you that you are a guest in my hall. There are men here known to you.'

Some Gothic warriors at Hisarna's right hand stood. Calgacus saw both Ballista and Maximus stiffen. In the poor light, Calgacus did not recognize them.

Hisarna did not take his gaze from Ballista. 'Videric, son of Fritigern of the Borani, also is my guest. No bloodfeud will be played out in my hall.'

Calgacus found he was gripping the hilt of his sword. Some years before, Ballista had killed the entire crew of a Borani longship. They would not surrender, so he killed them – shot them down with artillery from a distance, then, when they were past resistance, used the ram of a *trireme* to finish them off.

'Videric and his men leave tomorrow,' Hisarna said. 'Dernhelm, your men and you will stay in one of my halls by the harbour, until boats are ready to take you up the Tanais river.'

Videric the Borani spoke, hatred tight in his voice. 'I am a guest in the hall of Hisarna, and would not go against my host. It will not be here, but between me and the slave the Romans call Ballista there will be a reckoning. Let the high gods warlike Teiws and thundering Fairguneis bring the *skalks* Ballista before my sword.'

Ballista replied, almost wistfully, 'Wherever you go, old enemies will find you.'

There was nothing to do but wait. Ballista did not much mind. It was an experience he knew well. Over the years, he had become used to its ways. Usually, he had been waiting for bad things to happen: for the centurion to take him as a hostage into the *imperium,* to be admitted into the pavilion of the emperor Maximinus Thrax, to be hauled before a murderous Hibernian chief with designs on the throne of the high kings of that island.

When he was young, he had not been good at waiting. Often, he had prayed to the gods to make it end, or, conversely, to postpone the approaching event indefinitely. In those days, he had had a child's or young man's belief that his life had a purpose and a goal; that its course could be determined by his will. He had seen it like the trajectory of an arrow. If he were not the bowman or the arrow itself, he was at least the breeze that could affect the arc and influence where the shaft fell. Forty-one winters on Middle Earth had disabused him of such juvenile fallacies. His life meandered. He went where he was sent. In Greek tragedy, the characters were playthings of the gods. He was at the whim of the yet more immanent gods who sat on the thrones of the Caesars. There was no point fighting. It was best to accept it, and wait.

There were worse places to wait. The hall was new-built, still clean, roomy enough for thirty-three men and two eunuchs. It reminded him of his father's hall in Germania. There was little privacy, but Ballista knew his desire for it was unusual. The hall overlooked the harbour: both the *trireme* and the Gothic longships were gone. He watched the shallow draught merchant vessels come and go, listened to the scream of the gulls. Early the first morning, he sat looking at the mist coiling up from the broad, silty river. The trees on the far side grew straight out of the water. There were ducks and moorhens over there.

Later that first day, a Gothic priest came. The *gudja* was festooned with bracelets, his long hair braided with amulets and bones and other, unidentifiable things. He was followed by a quite exceptionally hideous old woman, hunched and filthy beyond description. The priest said his name was Vultuulf; much beyond that, he was not inclined to talk. He brought livestock for them – some chickens, two pigs and four sheep – and grain: wheat and rye.

By the second day, they had settled into routines to which their interests led them. The official staff, the herald and his like, kept to themselves; the interpreter apart even from them. The centurion drilled his men, stamping bad-temperedly along the quay. Maximus and Castricius each disappeared separately into the inhabited parts of the town, presumably searching for drink and women. Hippothous likewise, although Ballista assumed the human objects of his desire were different. The two eunuchs remained in the recesses of the hall, cloistered close together. Calgacus sat staring out at the river; Tarchon with him in companionable silence. The Suanian did not care to be far from one or other of Calgacus or Ballista since they had saved him from drowning in the Alontas river the year before. When drinking – for him a not uncommon activity – he was given to swearing blood-chilling oaths in very bad Greek concerning his readiness, eagerness even, to repay the debt by dying for them. All reckoned, Ballista thought he had a reasonable chance of it happening, probably quite soon, somewhere out on the Steppe.

Ballista ate, slept and read. There had been few books for sale in Panticapaeum – little enough of any luxury goods, although the eunuch Amantius had spent some of his almost certainly corruptly acquired money on a gilded brooch studded with sapphires and garnets. Of what books there had been, Castricius had bought all the epic poetry. Ballista did not mind. The north-erner liked Homer and, last year, sailing the Kindly Sea, he had quite enjoyed listening to Apollonius of Rhodes being read to the elderly senator Felix, but, in general, more recent epic was not his choice. Ballista had purchased cheaply all of Sallust's *Histories* and the *Annals* of Tacitus. He had finished the many rolls of the former during the winter. Now he was reading Tacitus's account of the reign of Caligula. The hard-edged, practical pessimism of both authors appealed to him. Most human nature is weak, poli-tics corrupt, freedom unattainable, *libertas* in fact no more than a word.

By the fifth morning, Ballista had had enough of waiting. He called Calgacus and Tarchon to him, and set out to see Hisarna. It had rained in the night. Little rivulets of milky water ran off the hill of ash before the town walls. It steamed slightly in the sun. The Urugundi guards at the gates seemed neither surprised nor interested to see them. At their appearance, however, one of them strolled off ahead of them into the town.

The *agora* was quieter than the first time. The slaves were still working on the gymnasium, but their efforts seemed desultory, unmotivated. There was no one outside the council house. The door was shut.

Ballista pushed it open, walked in. The big room was empty, the untenanted benches stretching up to the gloomy rafters. The throne of the Iron One was gone. Motes of dust turned slowly in the light from the door.

Ballista sat down, thinking. Calgacus sat next to him. Apparently unnerved by the emptiness, Tarchon prowled about, glaring into the shadows, as if expecting the apparition of a threat.

'The Borani were here; now they and the Urugundi are gone,' Ballista said.

'Aye, it could signify something or nothing,' Calgacus responded.

'Bad feeling, *Kyrios*,' Tarchon gravely announced. 'Much malignity.'

With theatrical abruptness, a long shadow was thrown into the *Bouleuterion*. The *gudja* stood haloed in the doorway. The sunshine glinted in the things in his hair. The old woman was behind him.

'Hisarna, son of Aoric, has gone,' the priest said.

'Where?' Ballista asked.

'To another place. The boats will come for you soon.'

'When?'

'Soon. You should go back to the hall.'

'Why?'

'It is safer. Many men hate you. Some of the gods hate you. Dernhelm or Ballista, many would rejoice to see you dead.'

There was no point in denying it, no point in arguing.

He was in a hot eastern city. There was dust everywhere. People were running, shouting. Maximus was with him in the street, looking absurdly young.

The men were running out of the hideous dark mouth of a tunnel.

35

They were Roman soldiers. They were running away. Where was Calga-
cus? The old bastard was over there – thank the gods for that. Soldiers
were rushing past, jostling, panic stricken. If Ballista did not give the
order, the Persians would take the town. But Mamurra was still down
there.

Maximus was shouting something. A soldier knocked into Ballista.
There was no choice. Ballista gave the order. Maximus was yelling – no,
no, you cannot leave him in there. The men with axes moved forward –
the thunk, thunk as they got to work. Calgacus was saying it had to be
done – they would kill everyone.

Soil was sifting down from the roof of the tunnel. A sharp series of
cracks. The pit props gave. The tunnel caved in. A cloud of dust rolled
out.

Mamurra was still in there.

Ballista jerked awake. The dream slipped away like smoke, leaving a feeling of utter dread.

Heart racing, he tried to force his eyes open, fearing what he
would see. He looked towards the opening in the hangings, his
eyes wide now. Nothing. No tall, hooded figure. No grey eyes filled
with hatred. He looked all around the small, curtained-off area.
There was no lamp, but enough light from the main body of the
hall to see it was empty. Maximinus Thrax was not there.

Ballista had had just sixteen winters when he had killed the
emperor at the siege of Aquileia. Maximinus Thrax had been a
tyrant, a savage tyrant. But Ballista had sworn the military oath
to him. He had broken his *sacramentum*. The other mutineers had
decapitated the emperor's corpse. Since then the daemon of that
terrible man had pursued Ballista. The appearances were infre-
quent, but utterly petrifying. Ballista's wife said it was nothing but
bad dreams brought on by exhaustion or stress. It was easy for
Julia. She was an Epicurean. Ballista was not. But he wished she
was right.

Suddenly, like a dam giving way, the dream came back to him, bizarre in its clarity. Poor, poor Mamurra. Ballista had left his friend to die alone in the dark.

The boats did not come the next morning. The *familia* and the rest ate lunch together in the hall.

'Why did Hisarna call the Heruli long-headed?' Ballista asked.

'Skull-binding,' said Hippothous. 'They are the Macrophali of whom Hippocrates wrote. They tie tight bandages around the soft skulls of infants, before they are properly formed. Their heads grow long, pointed, hugely deformed. After a generation or two, nature begins to collaborate with custom. If bald parents often have bald children, grey-eyed parents grey-eyed children, if squinting parents have squinting children, why should long-headed parents not have long-headed children?'

'That is a grand idea,' Maximus said. 'If your nomads turn their enemies' skulls into drinking cups, the bigger the skull the more drink in your cup.'

'You should not joke,' the eunuch Mastabates said, speaking in public for the first time since they had arrived in the town of Tanais. 'They are like no other people. They sacrifice prisoners to their god of war. The first captive in a hundred, they pour wine over his head, cut his throat, catch the blood in a jar, tip some over their swords, and drink the rest. They cut off the right arms of the others and behead them. They skin the arms and use the skins as covers for their quivers. With the heads they make a circular cut at the level of the ears, shake the scalp away, scrape it clean with a cow's rib, sew them together to make patchwork coats. The skull is lined with gold inside and leather outside. When they have important visitors to impress, they bring out these grisly cups and tell their story. They call this courage. The grasslands are a terrible place, inhabited by terrible people.'

Hippothous laughed. 'It should suit you well, eunuch. Hippocrates wrote that because of their moist, womanish constitution, and the softness and coldness of their bellies, nomad men lack sexual desire. They are worn out by riding all the time, so are weak in the act of sex. Rich nomads are the worst. The first time or two they go to their women and it does not work, they do not despair. But when it never works, they renounce manhood, take up the tasks of women, begin to talk like them. They have a special name for them, the *anarieis*. You will fit in well with them.'

Ballista looked up, chewing on a mutton bone. 'They only kill one in a hundred? In the north, when the Angles and Saxons go sea raiding, we sacrifice to the sea one in ten of the captured.'

'No, *Kyrios*,' Mastabates said. 'They drink the blood of one in a hundred, but they kill and decapitate them all.'

'Takes away the point in raiding.' Castricius grinned wolfishly.

'That strange-looking *gudja* is here again,' Calgacus said.

Charms and bones clinking, the tall priest entered; as ever, the old hag scuttled behind him. 'The boats will be here tomorrow. It is the will of my King Hisarna that I accompany you upriver.'

Everyone knew that if an unjustified, unpurified murderer set foot in a sacred place, madness or disease would descend on them. The gods could not be deceived. Nevertheless, the figure standing in the temple of Hecate thought it should be safe.

The small temple was in the north of Tanais. The harbour, the road up from it, the *agora* and the handful of streets leading to the few areas of reoccupied housing might have been cleared, but the majority of the town, including the northern quarter, remained deserted. The sack ten years before by the combined warriors of the Urugundi and the Heruli had been savage and thorough. The homes of mortals had been ransacked and burnt; their occupants enslaved. The homes of the gods had been partially spared. While their contents – statues and offerings, both precious and otherwise – had been looted or smashed, the structures had not been fired.

The figure looked around the dusty bareness of the temple. It was dark, suitably Stygian. The only light was from a small, unshuttered window high at the rear and what leaked around the slightly ajar door. Two columns stood two thirds of the way down the space. Beyond them there was nothing to see except the pitiful remains of some broken terracotta figures. These had been of no value to anyone except the devotees whose piety and trust had been so cruelly disabused.

A squeal of rusted hinges, and another figure slipped through the door. He had come.

'Did you get it?'

The newcomer jumped at the question, his eyes flicking this way and that as he tried to locate the speaker in the gloom.

'Back here.'

Locating the voice, the new arrival stepped forward. In those moments his face was bland and trusting, unburdened by anything except a childish avarice. He smiled placatingly, and hurried to unwrap the parcel in his hands. What else could you expect from a true slave? By nature untrustworthy, they were utter rubbish by definition.

Blue and dark-red stones caught, refracted and seemed to amplify the dim light. The slave handed across the small, heavy object. The other took it, pretended to examine it.

'You said . . .' The slave's voice trailed off.

'Yes, I did.' Tucking the jewelled thing into a belt, the speaker passed over a purse, heavy and loud with the desired chink. The slave loosed the drawstring, tipped the contents in his palm. In the untrusting, unseemly way of his kind, he began counting the coins openly, his mouth moving.

The killer turned away, and drew a sword. The blade came free with a whisper. Lost in who could know what sordid material ambitions, the slave noticed nothing.

In one fluid motion, the killer spun around and swung. As the steel hummed through the still air, startled, the slave looked up. He had time to open his mouth to scream. The blade cut heavy and deep into his left thigh. He screamed now, and fell away like some toppled statuette. He rebounded from one of the columns. The wounded leg dragging, he began to flounder towards the door; blood sluicing out on to the dusty floor.

Two quick steps and the killer slashed the sword into the slave's right leg. He went down. On all fours, leaking blood like a pig at a sacrifice, he crawled forward. The other kept pace; treading carefully, boots avoiding the bloody paste created by the slave's agonized passage.

The slave was pleading, begging, promising anything and everything, things that should not be promised. The Hound of the Gods gazed down dispassionately, rejoicing in the rightness of it. Again, there had been no mistake.

Enough evidence forthcoming for the moral faultlessness of the deed, the Scourge of Evil brought down the sword in a flurry of short, chopping killing blows to the back of the head.

Leaving the body, the killer stepped outside. All was quiet, as expected. Back in the temple, the killer went to the leather bag previously stowed behind one of the columns, and took out a length of string and the favoured implements. What had to be done next were the hard, terrible things. The killer briefly wondered about their necessity. The justly killed leave no visitant against anybody; their daemon does not revenge. But a mistake had once been made. The killer knew the ghastly consequences. Far better to be doubly safe.

Afterwards, the killer wended an obscure, unfrequented way down to the riverbank. It was dusk. The ducks were flighting. Taking out the gilded ornament, the killer looked at its sapphires and garnets, dull now in the gloaming. He thought briefly about vanity and threw the pointless thing out into the dark water.

IV

The *haruspex* Porsenna thrust the steaming liver under Ballista's nose.

'The gods are not well disposed. You can see for yourself, the organs are not propitious. They are all deformed, the liver worst of all.'

Ballista looked at the offal in the priest's bloodstained hands. Witness to innumerable Roman sacrifices, he had never brought himself to study the technicalities of their art. Not that he had ever seriously denied the existence of the gods of the Romans, or that they might indicate their disposition through such signs. Yet, despite all his years in the *imperium*, they were not his gods, and these were not the rites of divination his people employed. But he knew the Romans put much store in such things. The morale of the party would suffer.

'Get another beast to sacrifice,' he said. It was the right thing to do.

The *haruspex* washed his hands carefully in the lustral water. Another sheep was led to the bank of the Tanais river. Scenting blood, it bleated fitfully. At a gesture from the priest the hired flautist started playing again; too late to drown the ill-omened sounds.

This was not good – an irritating delay at the least. The boats were waiting. They needed to start upriver. Ballista wondered how much the hands of gods were in this, and how much the desire of the *haruspex* to assert his importance. The priest, like all his *ordo*, had a well-developed self-regard. Since Panticapaeum, Porsenna had made little secret that he felt generally slighted, and that he cared neither for this mission, nor for serving under what he saw as a barbarian.

The little fire on the portable altar hissed and spat as the offerings of wine and incense were made.

The tall, pointed hat of his calling bobbed as the *haruspex* tipped wine on the sheep's forehead. Unsurprisingly, it shivered; seen with the eyes of faith, it nodded acquiescence at its own sacrifice. The priest sprinkled salted flour on its back, passed the sacred knife over its back, intoned a low prayer.

A slave lifted the beast, smothering its spasmodic movements. The *haruspex* pulled back its tufty head and deftly slit its throat so its lifeblood splashed out on to the altar.

Almost tenderly, the slave laid the sheep on its back on the ground. Despite the breeze from the water, the air was close with the smell of blood and wine and incense, hot animals and men. The *haruspex* slit the belly. The entrails slithered out: large, white and sausage-like, faintly marbled with pinks and blues. Porsenna's practised, strong hands delved inside.

One after another he cut and wrenched free the organs – heart, lungs, liver – a grim parody of a demented midwife.

Ballista watched him turning them over, studying them close, frowning. No mystery how this judgement would fall. He remembered a story of Alexander, or was it the Spartan Agesilaus? Thwarted of good omens, he had inscribed propitious letters on his palm; taking the liver he had impressed them on its underside.

Clever – you would have to write the letters backwards. A cynical trick, or maybe a deity put the idea in his mind.

'No better,' the priest announced. 'Either another animal, or we must wait until tomorrow. One hour, even a moment, ruins those who start too early against the will of the gods.'

'No,' Ballista said. 'We are far from Rome. In this time of troubles the Roman gods have many pressing concerns in the eternal city, the provinces, with the legions. We are in the north. We will follow the rites of the north.'

'But . . .' The *haruspex* looked stunned. 'That is barbarity.'

'We are in *barbaricum*,' Ballista said. '*Gudja*.'

Nothing seemed to surprise the Gothic priest. This was no exception.

'The rites of the Urugundi Goths are not far from those of my birth people, the Angles. Tell me the will of the gods,' Ballista said.

'No,' the *haruspex* erupted, 'you cannot get this skin-clad savage . . .'

'I am the one holding imperial *mandata*. I will answer to the emperor and the gods.'

'You endanger the whole expedition. The natural gods will turn against us. You will bring their anger down on us. The Augustus Gallienus will hear of this.'

'I do not doubt it,' Ballista said, and indicated to the Goth to carry on.

From his sable cloak, the *gudja* produced a rolled, white cloth. The old woman who attended him spread it out on a dry place on the jetty. She scuttled away. Then the *gudja*, turning his face to the sky and raising his arms, began to call the gods in a song whose words ran together.

The summoning of the deities of northern forest, marsh, sea and river was not quick. There were many of them; their names and epithets numerous. Most of the Roman party looked askance.

Ballista thought the Gothic holy man magnificent; more than a little frightening, as he should be. The wind shifted his long hair, chiming its amulets and bones, its very movement pointing to his otherwise hierarchic stillness.

When he felt the attention of the gods, the priest stopped singing. Keeping his eyes to the heavens, he lowered his arms and took out the rune sticks. Without a glance, he dropped the thin pieces of willow on the cloth. Then, his face still averted, he knelt and without hesitation picked up three of them. Now he bent over them, scrutinizing the markings on them.

With an air of certainty, the *gudja* looked up at Ballista.

'There is much danger. Men will die. But not today. It is in the future.'

'How far?'

'The runes do not say.' The priest swept up the sticks.

Ballista nodded. He felt confidence in the old ritual of his youth. The Goths used willow, the Angles wood from a nut tree. It made no odds.

'Load the ships. We sail as soon as everything is stowed.' Ballista turned to the slaves by the two carcasses. 'Butcher them, cook the meat. We will eat on the boats.'

As men bustled about, the two eunuchs approached Ballista. For once, it was Amantius, the one who had been with Castricius in Albania, who spoke.

'*Kyrios*, would you order some of the soldiers to search the town? My slave is missing. And . . .' the eunuch looked close to tears '. . . my brooch, the one with the sapphires and garnets I bought in Panticapaeum, is gone.'

'I am sorry for your loss of them,' Ballista said, 'but there is no time. He may well have fled the town; more than one merchant vessel has already put out this morning. If he is hiding in the ruins, there are not enough of us to find him easily.'

Amantius was going to say more, but his colleague Mastabates laid a hand on his arm. Led him away.

A slave, his forearms plastered with gore, made a subtle noise. Ballista indicated for him to speak. '*Kyrios*, what should we do with the gods' share?'

Ballista looked at the organs set aside from the unsuccessful sacrifices of the *haruspex*. 'Throw them in the river. If the gods do not want them, the fish will.'

At Lake Maeotis, the waters of the Tanais thickened to become a huge, swampy delta. The mission was distributed haphazardly between two long Gothic ships. Maximus sat amidships in the leading vessel, with Ballista. The Gothic warriors at the oars pulled them out from the quayside and up the quiet branch of the river that served it. On either side was a thick, feathery-topped wall of reeds. The occasional willow grew down by the water. There were more trees – oaks, ashes and limes – running in ranks along low rises in the mid-distance. There was nothing else to see, except the big sky above.

The eunuch Amantius was still very upset. 'I would have given him his freedom. And he knew how much the bracelet meant to me.'

'Why you Romans free so many slaves? In Suania is not our way,' Tarchon said. 'Oh no, with us, you will die in your bonds; no hope whatsoever. We are most exemplary in cruelty.'

Maximus chuckled. 'The Romans would tell you it is from their innate generosity, the greatness of their soul. Maybe for some, but for most it is just another way to display their wealth; like owning villas or fish ponds, or breaking precious things when drunk. Look at what a great man I am; material things mean nothing to me; I cannot count the number of slaves I have freed.'

'Aye, for once you are not totally wrong,' Calgacus said. 'But, as always, you miss the real thing. Granting freedom is the carrot that goes with the sticks of beating, irons and branding, crucifixion. If you run or rebel, boy, you will end on a cross, but if you are a good little *puer*, you might, just might, one day be given freedom.'

'Only a fool expects loyalty from a slave,' Hordeonius said.

Maximus looked away as the centurion settled into another lengthy diatribe against the servile; tactless at the least, given the life story of several in earshot. Some movement beyond the southern bank caught Maximus's eye. It was gone before he could take it in.

'The only argument against branding all of them is that the bastards would realize their numbers. Even cowards draw audacity from numbers.'

There it was again – something moving on a low hill among the trees. More than one thing, keeping among the shadows well back from the riverbank.

'The old Spartans had the right idea with their helots – let the young go out and hunt some of them down; kill a few, and keep the rest in perpetual fear.'

A break in the cover, and Maximus saw them clearly for a moment. Three riders, clad in furs and pointed hats, trotting their nomad ponies.

'Yes, I have seen them,' Ballista said softly. 'Alani?'

'Alani – three of them, shadowing us.' Maximus's eyesight was sharp.

'The *gudja* has seen them too,' Ballista said.

The Goth was looking out over the black water.

'He does not appear too concerned,' returned Maximus.

'No, not at all.'

On the benches behind them, Castricius was arguing with Hordeonius. 'Slavery changes nothing, Centurion. A fool with any education knows there is a spark of the divine *logos* in all of us.

Now, me, when I was in the mines, my good daemon did not desert me.'

Maximus leant close to Ballista, spoke in his ear. 'Now let me get this right. We are on our way to deal with the chief of the bloodthirsty Heruli. To get to him, we have to travel for days past the grazing lands of the almost equally bloodthirsty Alani, whose king's invasion of Suania we defeated last year at the Caspian Gates.'

'Safrax,' Ballista said. 'The name of the King of the Alani is Safrax.'

'Fine,' Maximus said. 'Now, I am thinking, your man Safrax, when not bothering his herds, will be sitting in his tent brooding on the horrible revenge he will be taking, should his gods be kind enough to put us in his hands.'

'Most likely.' Ballista nodded.

'And in the tent with him will be that nasty little shit Saurmag, dripping poison in his ear. For, by the look of him, the Suanian princeling is unlikely to have forgiven us for removing him from the throne of his native land.'

'The Suanian royal house do not appear much given to forgiveness,' Ballista said.

'And just beyond the Alani, up in the mountains of Suania, will be Pythonissa, the priestess of Hecate you fucked and left, and who cursed you and all you care for in no uncertain terms.'

'Delicately put.'

'And then we have just run into Videric and his Borani, who are very hot for their bloodfeud against you. And now are who knows where.'

Ballista put an arm around Maximus. 'Never fear, little one, I will keep you safe from the nasty men.'

'Grand.'

'Anyway, think how the fates favour us. The other Gothic tribe who hold bloodfeud against us are nowhere near – the Tervingi live hundreds of miles away to the west.'

'Excellent,' Maximus said. 'I feel wonderfully reassured. Looked at in that light, what on earth or below could possibly harm us?'

Publius Egnatius Amantius to Lucius Calpurnius Piso Censorinus, Praetorian Prefect, Vir Ementissimus.

If you are well, Dominus, it makes my heart rejoice.

Your agent found me as we were leaving Panticapaeum. Thank the gods, he was discreet. Indeed so discreet that at first I took him for a most importuning sutler. He gave me your new instructions, and departed with the confidential reports I compiled for you last year in Albania and Suania. I had the temerity to include an unasked-for account of conditions as I found them in the Kingdom of the Bosporus over the winter. As argued there, I believe Rhescuporis V could be returned to complete obedience to Gallienus Augustus for but a modest stipend. After all, it was nothing but money that attached that impecunious monarch to the pretenders Macrianus and Quietus – may their names be forgotten. Yet I must stress again both the powerlessness of Rhescuporis externally and the suspicion of intrigue within his own house.

As it was last year in the Caucasus, I have no way of despatching these reports to you from the field, so will keep them safe until our return. I must confess that when I received your new instructions I prayed to all the traditional gods that you were ordering me home. Although I was born in the wilds of Abasgia, I have lived in Rome since my early childhood. I know no life except that of service at the sacred court of the Augusti. Consider too that I am a eunuch, and our condition renders us less robust than other men. It is my earnest request that on our return from the sea of grass, I be summoned by your magnanimity back to the safety of the Palatine to bask in the glory of our Augustus Gallienus.

Amantius put the stylus aside. He smoothed out his voluminous white robe and stretched out his feet in their soft slippers. Was the request too blatant? Did it come too soon in the letter? Should he sweeten it with an allusion to Homer? Censorinus often quoted Homer – but as often got the poetry wrong. Censorinus was a suspicious man, and if he thought he detected mockery the consequences would be too horrible. Amantius left it as it was, took up the stylus and wrote at some length his impressions of the embassy's meetings with the two tribes of Maeotae and with Hisarna of the Urugundi.

Amantius could not stop himself ending the missive with complaints:

> The *Legatus extra ordinem Scythica* does not keep the discipline looked for among an embassy of Rome. When we left Panticapaeum it was discovered that one of Marcus Clodius Ballista's personal slaves had run. At Tanais, my own slave ran, taking with him a most valuable brooch. The Legatus turned down – and in public, in the hearing of all – my just and reasonable request that a search be made for the runaway. Furthermore, when the haruspex found the entrails were not propitious, the legatus had them thrown in the river, and instructed the Gothic priest sent by Hisarna to embark upon some dreadful barbaric ritual.
>
> In camp, the second night on the Tanais river, fourteen days before the kalends of June.

Mastabates watched some of the Urugundi warriors constructing a tent. They had cut six saplings and were trimming and stripping them. The *gudja* was overseeing the work. For once, that hideous crone was not with him. Other Goths were feeding an already blazing fire. The smells of fresh-trampled earth and woodsmoke were strong; still exotic, faintly unsettling in the sheltered nostrils of the palace eunuch. A life in the scented corridors and colonnades of the palace was not easily abandoned.

It was the third camp they had made on the banks of the Tanais; the first one on the southern bank. It was not easy to judge how far they had travelled in those three days. The longboats were sleek, and Hisarna's Goths skilled oarsmen. But they had rowed with little urgency, and the river meandered extravagantly, its slow but implacable waters ever against them.

There had been a great sameness to their voyaging. The twists in the river conspired with the dense reed beds and the sparser trees to hem in lateral vision. Now and then, smaller branches joined or left the channel, opening glimpses of overhung, still backwaters, hazy with insects. Skeins of geese flew across the sedge. Once, a herd of wild horses had appeared on the floodplain, their chestnut coats so blazing in the evening sunlight as to become indistinct. Several times they passed blackened, abandoned settlements. Vegetation had almost completely overwhelmed those on the southern bank.

The Goths had planted the ends of the poles in the ground, angled them in and tied them together at the top. On this edifice they set about draping felted blankets. The *gudja* evidently was urging them to take care to overlap the woollens, tie them tight. Nearby, fresh wood on the fire cracked and sputtered.

Although almost everything about the nomads and the sea of grass filled Mastabates with revulsion, usually mixed with dread, the eunuch was glad the Urugundi Goths had adopted some nomadic ways. He was delighted to have been asked to join in a Scythian vapour bath. It was like stepping back into the past, like becoming a character in the writings of Herodotus. And Mastabates was not displeased for the excuse to be away from Amantius. Eunuchs were expected to keep together. After all, unable to start families of their own, they had no one else, except maybe the transient favour of a ruler. Who should know better than Mastabates that his colleague was not totally to be blamed for his high, effeminate voice, his blushing and sweating, even his womanly hips and breasts? All too often these things came with the condition. But Mastabates could not see that being cut must lead to an abandonment of all striving for male virtue. The relentlessness of Amantius's tearful, womanish recriminations addressed to his runaway slave boy, the endless complaints about his stolen brooch, were beginning to sicken Mastabates. A eunuch did not have to give way to female lack of control or avarice. It would be good to be away from him for a few hours.

The *gudja* walked around and inspected the tent. It was complete. The outlandish priest signalled to the Goths at the fire. They kicked away the burning branches. Clouds of sparks swirled up in the heat, threatening the foliage overhead. From the shimmering heart of the coals, using long metal tongs with precision, they took up white-hot stones. These were placed in a metal dish raised on four legs. A Goth wearing leather mittens gripped the birch-wrapped handle of the dish. Most carefully, he carried it to the tent, got to his knees and manoeuvred his scorching burden and himself through the low opening.

With a courtly wave, the *gudja* requested the guests to enter the vapour bath. Ballista went first, his great barbarian bulk almost blocking the entrance. Maximus slipped through more easily. *Dignitas* suspended, Mastabates crawled in after him. He was glad he had adopted a normal man's riding costume for this expedition: boots, trousers, short tunic. He even wore a short sword and dagger. Some might snigger to see a eunuch so accoutred, but it was both practical and made him feel a little more complete.

It was dark in the tent. Nervous of upsetting the smouldering dish in the centre, Mastabates clumsily crawled around to the right. He came up against the Goth who had carried the thing in, and tried not to show his uncertainty as he composed himself in a similar cross-legged pose. Ballista and Maximus sat beyond the Goth. Two or three more Urugundi entered, before the *gudja* brought up the rear. He placed a small Greek lamp by the cauldron, and laced shut the opening.

Straight away, the air in the tent was hot and close. Mastabates felt the perspiration pooling in his armpits, his crotch, running down his back. The stones, or the dish itself, ticked with the intense heat. Lit from beneath by the little oil lamp, the faces looked suitably out of the quotidian world.

The *gudja* produced a bag. It contained seeds. Mastabates knew what was coming. The seeds came from a plant which looked like flax, except that it was thicker stemmed and taller, much taller in

Scythia. Mastabates knew more than Herodotus. But knowing is not experiencing. He stilled his nerves. There was a first time for everything. There must have been such a moment for the Goths. Since then, they had taken such a liking to the seeds one of their chiefs had rejoiced in the name Cannabas.

The *gudja* threw handfuls of the seeds on to the glowing stones. Dense, aromatic smoke – once smelt, impossible to mistake – billowed out; much more than any vapour bath in Greece. The thick fumes stung Mastabates' eyes, caught in his throat, made it hard to breathe. Across the tent, the *gudja* was talking in the language of the north. Nodding – obviously following instruction – Ballista leant over the cauldron and sucked in great billows of smoke. The northerner held his breath for an unlikely time. Letting it out with a whoosh, he grinned. The Goths laughed. Maximus was next. An amphora of wine began to go round.

Mastabates inhaled in his turn. Holding the cannabis deep in his lungs was not unpleasant. When he exhaled, he coughed. It was surprising how little smoke emerged. A Goth patted him on the back, somewhat gingerly. Mastabates took a swig of wine – a strong, sweet Lesbian – and felt pleasantly numb.

On the other side of the tent, Ballista and Maximus were laughing. The Goths were laughing with them. Even the stern *gudja* had unbent a fraction. Mastabates envied their strong congeniality; their ease as men amongst men. He had not chosen to be a eunuch. Castration was illegal in the empire. Yet emperors, and some other rich Romans, desired eunuchs in their homes – to look after their women, among other, less salubrious things. Abasgia was not in the *imperium*. Its kings profited from the need: castrating and selling the boys most conspicuous for beauty among their subjects. To avoid revenge, they killed all the male relatives of the boys. Mastabates had not wanted to be a child cursed with beauty; not for himself, not for his family.

The man on his left passed Mastabates the wine. The Goth smiled. He was attractive. He looked like those statues from Pergamon of dying Gauls: barbaric, wild and frightening but rugged and virile, all man.

Mastabates smiled back at the Goth, drank, inhaled more of the smoke. He felt light-headed. Time had overflowed its channels, spread wide. Mastabates seemed to have been in the tent for hours and hours. He wondered if it would have been very different if he had been one of those castrated after puberty, or one whose stones had been crushed rather than cut. Some of them could get an erection. Certain women sought them out. Eunuchs of that sort could give pleasure without the danger of pregnancy. His friend Eusebius had been such a one. Poor Eusebius had not liked women. Poor Eusebius – he had returned to Abasgia, had been man enough to seek vengeance. He had not succeeded. He had just found death, a lingering, dreadful death.

Mastabates took more of the drug. If his sword had been able to stand erect, would he have played Ares rather than Aphrodite in bed? He could not help but giggle. It seemed ridiculous. He enjoyed taking the woman's part in sex with men. It was not a physical failing that dictated his pleasures. Suddenly, the etiquette of the court washed out of him, and he laughed out loud. The whole idea of anyone ever worrying over an erection appeared absurd. How could such a momentary pleasure bear such weight of expectation, such a freight of concern and meaning? Mastabates let the fumes of wine and narcotic coil pleasantly through his mind.

The figure sat on a fallen branch down by the waterside. In the moonlight, the Tanais shone silver and tranquil. The camp was some way off to the east. It had been surprisingly easy to slip away. Despite lying at the very end of Urugundi territory, where the disputed grazing of the Heruli and Alani began, no guards had been posted. Everyone in the encampment was drunk on alcohol and hemp. Intermittent bursts of inebriated, witless laughter tore at the quiet of the night.

The solitary individual watched and waited. The river slid by nigh on imperceptibly. Thoughts of insanity and purity and danger ran in the figure's mind. The gods sent madness and disease to an unjustified murderer who had the temerity to set foot in a sacred place. The killer had dealt justice to the eunuch's slave in the temple of Hecate, the dark goddess of revenge herself. He had never been in better health, felt no tinge of the deranged. Yet, recently, in the dead of some dreadful nights, the daemon of a small girl had come to stand close by the bed of her killer. She had met her end far away the previous year. In that one instance the Hound of the Gods must have been in error. The rituals of purification were messy, yet an acceptance had to be made that now they were necessary. Somehow the appurtenances and privacy would have to be found.

An owl hooted, stilling the scurrying of the small things of the night. The killer regarded the river rolling by, and thought about water, and Medea and her brother Apsyrtus.

There was no wind, and the noise of another making his way to the tall stand of oaks on the riverbank was easy to hear. The watcher sat on. The other blundered nearer, twigs snapping, reeds rustling. A night bird took wing. Some things have to be, thought the one waiting.

'Where are you?' The voice was low and anxious.

The watcher remained silent, reflecting on the retribution of the gods.

'Are you there?'

'Over here.'

The slave emerged, furtive, from the shadows.

'Over here.' The watcher stood up, face bland.

The slave came over, smiling. 'I was not sure you would be here.'

'You would do well to trust me.'

'Yes, of course I do. I do. But it is just so hard to believe – that you will buy my freedom.'

'Hard to believe, but true. You will be free, more free than any man alive.'

A purse, weighed down with coins, passed from one to the other. Holding it reverently, like a token of salvation, the slave got down on his knees. He kissed the other's hand. 'I cannot begin to thank you.'

'No, it is best you do not. Others should thank me – but would they, even if they knew?'

Not understanding the gnomic utterance, the slave looked up. The other gripped his throat, thumbs driving into his windpipe. Taken unaware, the slave could do nothing but scrabble at the hands throttling him, ineffectually beat at the arms. The slave tried to wrench away. The killer, arms locked with the effort, held him. Slowly, the slave was bent backwards – almost double. And the remorseless pressure mounted.

In the bright moonlight their struggling shadows were a hunched parody of some act of love. The efforts of the slave were weakening. His face was suffused, eyes bloodshot and protruding. Of a sudden, there was a sharp tang of urine.

At length, the life choked out of him, the slave convulsed then was still. The killer got up stiffly, breath coming in short gasps. Stretching an aching back, flexing sore fingers – at least three fingernails broken – the killer went over to the bag and removed the accustomed instruments.

Breathing more controlled, the killer stopped to listen. The faint sound of a lyre, some muted hubbub from the camp. Nearer, the timid rustling of nondescript small creatures disturbed by the murder from their nocturnal activities. The plop of a fish or something out on the river. Nothing at all to worry about. The killer sniffed – the river mud, dead reeds, the voided contents of bladder and bowels; soon to be joined by blood, a great deal of blood.

The killer regarded the corpse. He had been a slave as evil, as full of vice, as any. The deed felt right, justified. The gods approved of this wild justice, the justice of the Steppe.

This time, the killer started with the heavy work: the big cleaver and the feet. It went much better with a piece of fallen wood under the ankles. Two, three heavy chops, and the left foot was severed. This was an acquired skill. As the blood pooled black in the moonlight, he picked up the foot, and stood considering Medea and Apsyrtus. In some tellings, when her father's men were overhauling her, she delayed their pursuit by casting the dismembered parts of her brother on to the waters. The killer threw the foot out into the river. As the ripples spread out, he hefted the other leg on to the makeshift butcher's block. If the water was good enough for the age of heroes, it would more than serve in an age of rust and iron.

VI

In the morning, there was much fog. It hung a few feet off the water, slowly coiling up through the spars of the ships and the trees. Colour had leached out of the world, and everything was reduced to muted shades of grey. The camp was unnaturally quiet.

'Where is it?' Ballista asked as he buckled on his sword belt.

'Downstream,' the soldier said.

They set off, two other troopers and Maximus and Wulfstan following, through the tents and shelters. Most of the fires had gone out. Amphorae and wine skins were scattered in the trampled grass. A few revellers lay, insensible, where they had fallen. Apart from the lack of blood and sobbing women, it resembled the aftermath of a sack.

Following the Cilician auxiliary, Ballista concentrated on putting one foot in front of the other. The going was uneven. His head hurt, and there was an unease in his stomach. The cold sweat on him was only partly due to the fog. The Goth that told him cannabis left no hangover had been lying. But, he had to admit, he had drunk a fair amount of wine as well.

Beyond the encampment, the grass was longer and very wet. Ballista's boots were soon sodden, his trousers to the knee no better. The fog seemed denser out here. The far side of the river could not be seen. Only a faint lightening, a hint of warmth, indicated the presence of the risen sun.

Past a stand of tall oaks, the soldier cut off down to the river. They pushed through a bank of reeds and stopped at the edge of the water. A tall elm had been submerged, and the thing was entangled in its stripped, white branches.

'What were you doing out here?' Ballista asked.

'Taking a shit, *Dominus*.'

'You went out to it?'

'Only to pull it in out of the current, so it did not drift downstream.'

Ballista studied the reeds and mud. He was half aware of more men arriving behind him. There was a clear trail where the soldier had waded out and back; no other disturbance. The killing had not been here. The body had floated down the river. There was no way of telling how far. Turning to the other two auxiliaries, he told them to bring it ashore. They looked back at him, crapulous and dubious.

'That was an order,' he snapped.

'We will do what is ordered, and at every command we will be ready,' they muttered.

The water would be cold, and they were undoubtedly suffering from the night before, but the discipline of the soldiers detached from the first Cilician cohort of mounted archers was poor. Ballista would have to speak to Hordeonius, although he was unsure what good it would do; the centurion was already a martinet.

Reluctance, bordering on dumb insolence, in every movement, the auxiliaries went down the slippery bank and splashed out into the shallows. The water came to their thighs. With high, exaggerated steps, they retrieved the bulky, unpleasant object and manhandled it to the side, dragging it the last part, up to where Ballista waited, backed by the newly formed crowd.

The corpse was naked. Where not streaked with fresh mud, it was pallid from its time in the water. Its extremities had been cut off: feet, hands, penis. Its face was a ruin: ears and nose gone, eyes gouged out. Liquid ran viscous from its orifices and wounds. The eunuch Amantius reeled away and threw up noisily. The rest looked on queasily. Still more men were arriving from the camp, drawn by the macabre news.

Ballista put a reassuring hand on young Wulfstan's shoulder and asked those around the obvious question: 'Who is it?'

No one replied. Anyone would be difficult to recognize in such a condition.

Shifting his scabbard to one side, Ballista crouched down and began to scrutinize the mutilated corpse. He remembered examining another cadaver years ago in a tunnel in the city of Arete. He had not been hungover then, and he had been thinking clearly. Today, every little thing would be an effort, let alone something like this.

Irritatingly, some fool in the crowd was intoning an apotropaic prayer in Greek. Too late to avert evil now, Ballista thought.

There were bruises on the neck, punctures and short rips in the skin where fingernails had caught. With a grunt of effort, Ballista half turned the body. Wulfstan bent down to help – the boy had spirit. There were no other obvious killing wounds. The man had been strangled.

They laid the corpse back. The thought struck Ballista that the man might have been alive when he was mutilated. Ballista felt his gorge rise. Do not be ridiculous, he said to himself. Of course he was already dead; he had been strangled.

'Short hair, and dark – a Greek or Roman, not a Goth.' The

gudja had appeared behind Ballista. As always, the crone formed an unlovely retinue of one.

'Yes.' Ballista manipulated an arm. He could not remember how quickly a corpse stiffened after death, nor the time when it relaxed again. Being immersed in cold water probably altered things anyway.

'I thought nomads like the Alani only scalped or beheaded their victims,' Hippothous said.

Obviously, he too had noticed the horsemen stalking them for the previous three days. Neither Ballista nor, as far as he knew, Maximus, had mentioned it to anyone. The *gudja* was unlikely to have spoken. But Hippothous had been a bandit. He must be experienced in the fieldcraft of pursuit and evasion. Still, it was odd he had not reported the followers. Perhaps, like Ballista himself, he had not wished to dishearten the party.

'No, they always cut off the right hand or arm,' the interpreter cut in. 'They make the skin into trappings for their horses.' Biomasos was warming to his self-appointed role as local expert. 'They tear out the eyes as well, but usually only of living captives. They blind not only those they keep as slaves but even those they intend to ransom. They are the most barbaric race on earth, except for the Heruli.'

'And many say we Suanians are savage – next to this we are very gentle people, most eirenaic as could be termed.' Tarchon spoke in a voice of vindication.

Ballista felt sick again. He had just discovered that the tongue was missing. He breathed in through his nose, out through his mouth; in through his nose, out through his mouth. Sensing his discomfort, Wulfstan passed him a leather bottle of water.

'This reminds me of something in poetry,' Mastabates said. 'Maybe from an epic.'

Knowing his liking for the genre, Ballista looked up at Castricius. The latter just shrugged, keeping silent.

'Not epic, but tragedy,' Biomasos announced. 'Aeschylus, the *Choephoroi*.' The interpreter was rapidly becoming insufferable. 'After she has got Aegisthus to murder Agamemnon, Clytemnestra mutilates the body of her husband.'

Ballista was sure he was not the only one to be thinking of another wronged woman with murder in her heart. Pythonissa was not far away in Suania, just beyond the Alani; and her brother Saurmag was with the nomads.

'You will find it is better known from the *Electra* of Sophocles,' Mastabates stated. 'But I still think there is something more pertinent somewhere in epic.'

Ignoring the bookish Hellenes, Ballista concentrated on the mutilations. The cuts and slices were neat, as if done with practice. That was not at all good.

'Someone must know who he is,' Maximus said. 'Who is missing from the Roman party?'

'My slave was not in the tent just now, when the noise woke me,' Castricius said. 'I have not seen him yet.'

'Is this him?' Ballista asked.

The short Roman put his sharp, pointed face very close to the ghastly face of the corpse. 'It could be.'

The fog did not lift that day, nor the next. Under it, the camp was subdued, out of sorts. The clammy entrapment was part of it, but more was down to the after-effects of the debauch. There was much idle speculation, but the death of the slave secretary seemed not to weigh that heavily on most, not even on his owner, Castricius. Urugundi guards were posted, and most felt the death was not their concern. Slaves often died – of disease and deprivation, at the hands of their owners or each other; the free were above such things.

Wulfstan was in attendance on Ballista. Both days, the big

warrior mostly remained in his tent, Maximus and old Calgacus with him. As men with hangovers do, they ate and drank vast amounts, shifted about desultorily. Maximus moved on to wine mid-morning of the first day – a hair of the dog, nothing like it to straighten you out; the other two did not join him. Conversation in the tent was disjointed, rambling, but, like a dog returning to its own vomit, always circled back to the killing.

'It is not the style of the Goths,' Ballista said. 'Videric and his Borani would come straight for me. They would think less of themselves if they did not pursue the bloodfeud openly.'

Maximus belched. 'I am thinking it is more likely the Alani, or that evil Suanian bastard Saurmag, or maybe his poisonous sister. The mutilation would appeal to your girl Pythonissa. As the Greeks said, you could see a woman's spite there.'

'Loving a woman is like setting out over ice with a two-year-old colt, restive and unbroken.' Calgacus was sometimes given to wheeling out the proverbs of the north. 'Of course,' he added, 'it may be nothing of the sort. The slave was in Albania with Castricius, his fate could have followed him from there – it is not that far. Your little Roman has not been the same since. It was after that he started claiming to be Macedonian, and we all know the little shite is from Gaul; and all that bollocks about daemons – the good one that sits on his shoulder, and the spirits of death being shite-scared of him. He is as gone in the head as Hippothous with his physiconom . . .'

'Physiognomy.' Ballista wondered if Calgacus could say the word if he chose. He picked at some chicken. 'And it could all be something else altogether.'

Wulfstan was up before dawn on the third day. In the night, a north wind had torn the fog away. There were spits of rain in the air. He prodded the fire back to life, cooked breakfast for

Ballista and the other two: bacon, lots of it, fresh bread, and thin ale.

When a weak sun came up he went down to the river to wash the mud and blood from Ballista's clothes. The water was still, like a black, polished stone. A carp flashed out in the stream, the ripples of its passing spreading wide. A big Urugundi warrior on guard watched it in a bored way

This was not the life Wulfstan was born to live. As he pounded a tunic on a stone, poetry of his childhood ran in his mind:

> There is no one still living to whom I dare open
> The doors of my heart. I have no doubt
> That it is a noble habit for a man
> To bind fast all his heart's feelings,
> Guard his thoughts, whatever he is thinking.

If the Langobardi slavers had not come, if they had not burnt his village, slaughtered his family, he would have grown to be a warrior, not a drudge. And those dreadful things would not have happened to him.

> The weary in spirit cannot withstand fate,
> And nothing comes of venting spleen.

Wulfstan was young – just thirteen winters, not yet a man; he did not agree. If he got his freedom, he would vent his spleen on all those who had owned him before Ballista. It should not be impossible to track them down. He had been traded one to another down the great rivers from the Suebian Sea to the *imperium* and Ephesus. He would retrace his steps; from Ephesus north through the Aegean and across the Kindly Sea, then up the Amber Road. Wulfstan's return would be charted in blood and burning. The

Taifali, a tribe loosely connected to the Goths in the west, were said to do to their own young men the shameful things which had been done to Wulfstan. A Taifali youth washed away the stain on his reputation when he killed a boar or a bear. Wulfstan would find redemption in blood; not in the blood of animals, but of man, and of many more than just one man.

The lowing of beasts, a deep rumbling and the high-pitched squeals of wood broke into Wulfstan's consciousness. There was a massive cloud of dust approaching from the west.

'The wagons are here,' said the Urugundi guard.

VII

Ballista watched the long line of ox-wagons. There were ten of them, each drawn by eight bullocks. Slowly and very noisily, half hidden by the dust raised, they pulled into a wide circle. The drivers unspanned the beasts and began to herd them down to water in the river. There seemed no end to the animals.

'Ho, Sarmatians, where are your women?' one of the Urugundi called.

From under their caps, the drivers cast dark looks at the Goth.

'Driving wagons is women's work,' the Urugundi said to Ballista in the language of the north. 'Once, the Sarmatians were lords here. Now they are our *skalks*. These Sarmatian slaves try to keep their women away from us.' He laughed. 'They are right to. Their women are a good ride – big tits, good fat arses. They have no interest in their husbands when they have had a Goth between their thighs.'

The *gudja* silenced the warrior with a curt gesture then spoke to the drivers in a language Ballista did not know, presumably Sarmatian. It could be the tiresome interpreter Biomasos might have a use after all. The Sarmatians grudgingly acknowledged whatever the *gudja* had told them and carried on seeing to the oxen and hobbling the dozen or so horses which had travelled tied to the rear of the carts.

'Now the wagons are here, my Goths will take the boats downstream to Tanais.' The *gudja* spoke to Ballista in the language of Germania. 'I will remain to guide you to the Heruli. Their winter pastures are not far from here, but they left for their summer ones some time ago. It will be a long journey east and north before we overhaul them.'

'Thank you,' Ballista said.

'I doubt you will when we reach them. As everyone will have told you, they are not as other men, and their ruler Naulobates is the worst of all. The superstitious say he is not a man at all but a malignant daemon.' The *gudja* smiled, as if in anticipation of the encounter.

'I have no choice in the matter.'

'No, I suppose you do not. The Sarmatians can help your slaves load your baggage. I will keep one wagon for myself and my servant.' At the mention of her, the priest's ill-favoured acolyte gave a one-toothed, senile grin.

Maximus leant close to Ballista. 'Thank the gods we will not be without female company. Do you think the old Goth will share her?'

The next morning, the Goths were gone not long after first light. By midday, the remainder had gone nowhere. Ballista had allocated the wagons, apart from that already claimed by the *gudja*. The meagre money for ransoms had been divided into two. The soldiers loaded the gold into the carts in which Castricius and Ballista himself would travel. Hordeonius then officiously ordered his auxiliary archers to stand guard over them. It was a rare command of the centurion's with which his men were perfectly happy. As it transpired, no one seemed to want to trust the Sarmatians with handling their property; conquest and cuckoldry were thought to do something to a man. So the tribesmen sat and scratched themselves as seven slaves tried to break camp and manhandle everything into the wagons. Biomasos the interpreter, Porsenna the *haruspex* and the other imperial functionaries, let alone the eunuchs, knew such manual labour to be far beneath their *dignitas*.

To get somewhat out of the chill north wind, Ballista and the freemen of his *familia* sat in the shelter of some willows. Castricius, Biomasus and the two eunuchs joined them. They talked in a random, inconsequential fashion as they watched the uninspiring scene.

'If I was the sort of man to fuck another man's wife,' Maximus said, 'ideally, I would like to see him disarmed.'

They all looked at the nearest Sarmatian. He was leaning in the lee of his wagon; a big man, blond, handsome. From his boots to his cap, his clothes were embroidered nomad-style. Everything about him was surprisingly clean. On his hip was a long, straight sword, suitable for a mounted warrior. A long dagger was strapped to his thigh. He had a coiled bullwhip thrust through his belt.

'The Urugundi might have told more than the truth,' Ballista said.

'It could be a Sarmatian cares more if you take his sword than his wife,' Hippothous said. 'His chief god is worshipped as a sword, and he swears his most solemn oaths on his sword. On the other hand, if he comes home to his tent and finds another man's quiver hanging outside, he wanders off until the stranger has finished with his wife.'

'Marvellous,' Maximus said. 'A whole tribe of complaisant husbands.'

'Oh no,' Hippothous said, 'no good even for you. You see, nomad women are quite hideous. Because they breathe the damp, thick air of the Steppe, drink water from snow and ice and do no hard work but sit in wagons all the time, their bodies are not hardened. They are heavy and fleshy, their joints covered, watery and relaxed, their cavities very moist. Not being swaddled as children, they are disgustingly flabby. Their very obesity prevents them receiving male seed easily.'

'I do not know, it does not sound too bad,' Maximus said. 'I sometimes like my women carrying a bit of weight – warmth in the winter, shade in the summer – moist cavities and little danger of getting them pregnant. Did I ever tell you about the time –'

'Nonsense.' The interpreter cut him off. 'The promiscuity of nomads derives from an outdated story in Herodotus about one tribe, the Agathyrsi. The Sarmatians, like their cousins the Alani, are polygamous. Having several wives does not mean they are happy if another man tries to lie with them. Doubtless the Heruli are the same.'

'It is Strabo the geographer who claims that nomad women in general are available,' Hippothous said. 'Anyway, they smell, never wash.' He addressed the latter to Maximus.

'I heard they kept their virginity until they had killed three men in battle,' Castricius said.

'And cut their right breast off,' added Ballista.

'Their mothers are said to *burn* them off,' the interpreter pedantically corrected.

The wind had got up, whipping the branches above their heads. The sky was dark, threatening rain. Down by the river, bitterns boomed, deep and resonant.

'Gods below, it is getting cold,' said Maximus.

'Not as cold as it will be out on the Steppe,' remarked Castricius. 'Winter is near continuous all year round. The north winds are charged with bitter rain, chilled with ice and snow.'

'Mules and asses die in the cold, and cattle lose their horns,'

Mastabates joined in. 'Only animals small enough to live underground can survive.'

'And summer lasts but a few days. Even then there is mist. On the few occasions the sun does appear, it has little warmth,' Castricius said.

'That is not what Strabo says,' Hippothous put in. He seemed to be attempting to outdo the interpreter in pedantry. 'According to the geographer, the summer heat is too severe for those unaccustomed to it. Anyway, as a man of culture, I look forward to seeing strange and wonderful creatures – the tarandos, which changes its colour, and the colos, which runs swifter than a deer. It drinks through its nostrils and stores water in its head.'

'Fat and smelly? Well, I do not really care, as long as they are willing,' Maximus mused. 'Actually, even if they are not all that at first . . .'

A violent gust of wind ripped across the river, bringing the first of the rain. It was not yet heavy, but squalls flurried across the ground where the camp had stood, around the wagons. The beasts stood in what shelter they could find, heads down.

'Enough of this. Everyone on their feet,' Ballista announced. 'Help get your things into your wagons.' The company scattered, heads cocked into their shoulders against the rain.

Ballista walked over to where the auxiliaries were sheltering in and around the wagons with the gold. 'Where is your centurion?' Hordeonius stuck his head out from under the felt canopy, half sketched a salute. 'Leave half your men on guard, and send the others to load the wagons,' Ballista ordered.

'But . . .'

'Yes, Centurion?' Ballista's voice was icily polite.

'Nothing – we will do what is ordered, and at every command we will be ready.' The centurion set about rousting out his men with needless harshness, a swing of his staff here, a kick there.

Ballista stamped through the weather to the wagon where the *haruspex* and the staff were. He climbed up on to the tailgate and stuck his head through the hanging. Pale, sullen faces gazed at him from the gloom. 'Everybody is to help load the wagons.' The others looked to the *haruspex*. After an insolent pause, the latter nodded. Ballista got down. Led by the priest, the occupants clambered from the wagon and went off unhappily.

Ballista stood, the still centre of squelching activity. The rain ran down his face. His long hair was wet on his shoulders. He felt eyes on him. The *gudja* was standing on the driving box of his wagon. In his rain-slick sable cloak, he looked like a ragged carrion crow. The *gudja* smiled, obviously enjoying the disquiet among the Romans.

The first day's travel was not good. There were only a few curtailed hours of daylight left when the wagon train finally moved out. Curtains of rain swept in from the north. Water sluiced off the felt canopies, darkened the hides of the oxen. The horses on their long leads plodded after, heads and tails down. Occasionally, one snickered its displeasure. The unsprung wagons jolted along at a snail's pace. The noise was deafening. As the inexperienced occupants had not properly secured the coverings, they leaked. The Sarmatian drivers out in the elements, caps pulled down to meet their cloaks, only their eyes and noses showing, seemed impervious. Everyone else, huddled and jarred in the body of the carts, was thoroughly miserable.

When it became fully dark, they made camp. It was a protracted, chaotic affair. The fires did not want to light. Some of the provisions had got wet. Their patience worn thin, men cursed, cuffed the slaves. They had not travelled above three miles – four at most.

The next morning, things were much improved. Hippothous had slept well. He and his slave, Narcissus, had been assigned a wagon with Castricius, Biomasos and Hordeonius and their two slaves. When not in motion, the wagons were comfortable; snug, yet agreeably roomy.

Climbing down, Hippothous saw that the rain had blown away south. A line of trees marked the Tanais to the left. Above, the sun shone from an enormous, washed-out blue sky. They ate breakfast – rye bread, dried meat, salted fish – and set about getting ready.

Having checked Ballista had no need of his services as *accensus*, Hippothous asked if he could exercise one of the horses. There were only twelve, and he was delighted when Ballista assigned one permanently to him. The bandit-turned-secretary tacked up, slung his weapons and kit and rode out across the Steppe. Apart from the trees marking where the river ran, a flat sea of grass spread in all directions. None of the spring grass came up to the soles of his boots. There were some low mounds in the far distance, oddly regular in shape, but nowhere else could he see anything which offered concealment. The bandits – Alani or whatever they were – who had trailed them up the Tanais were nowhere in sight.

From a distance, the great wagons and oxen looked like a row of toys laid out by a serious-minded child. Hippothous watched Ballista riding up and down the train. The order of march was the wagon of the *gudja*, that of Ballista and his *familia*, the two containing the soldiers, that of the *haruspex* and functionaries, three wagons with the stores, the eunuchs', and Castricius's at the rear. Hippothous assumed Ballista's thinking was to have the Goth at the front as the guide and the two senior officers at either end of the rest. Given his past profession, Hippothous was unsure it was wise to have half the gold in the last wagon.

When Ballista must have considered all was vaguely in order, the whole was got under way. The cracking of whips, the complaining of beasts and the squeal of the axles travelled clearly to

Hippothous. With the breeze behind them, sounds could travel a long distance out on the Steppe.

Back in the town of Tanais, Ballista had encouraged those who considered themselves fighting men to purchase local bows and quivers. Now, Hippothous took his out and began to practise shooting from horseback. To his irritation, he found it almost impossible. At a canter, let alone a gallop, the string bounced out of the notch of the arrow. On the rare occasions he managed to keep it in place long enough, the shot careered off nowhere near where he intended. It proved impossible to find some of the wayward shafts in the grass.

After a time, Hippothous gave up. He stowed the recalcitrant weapon back in its *gorytus*, and fished in his saddle pack for a book. Other riders were about. Castricius, Hordeonius and Biomasos all galloped separately across the Steppe, exercising their mounts. Hippothous ignored them. With the morning sun on his shaven head, he unrolled the papyrus and read the *Physiognomy* of Polemon. His horse ambled along, the reins loose on its neck.

At midday, Hippothous cantered back. They were to take lunch on the move. At the lead wagon, Hippothous found a difference of opinion between Ballista and the *gudja*.

'It is asking for trouble,' said Ballista.

'We are too many for casual bandits, and it could draw the unwanted attention of others,' the *gudja* advised.

'There should always be outriders,' responded Ballista.

'This grazing is disputed between the Alani and the Heruli. Both send out raiding parties of young warriors. Scouts and the like would draw them down on us. Remember, we Urugundi know these Steppes and these tribes. You do not.' The Gothic priest was not to be contradicted. Reluctantly, Ballista gave way.

The second day went better. The wagon train made at least eight miles. By the third, they were getting into a routine. Although some dark clouds scudded across, the weather continued fine. Hippothous rode alongside Ballista's wagon, where the northerner's young slave, Wulfstan, was sitting up front alongside the Sarmatian driver. Hippothous had approached him before, the previous year back in Byzantium. The boy had turned him down flat, using words the servile should not utter. Hippothous had not taken much offence, none of it to heart. He knew the reason. The youth had been forced and mistreated by several owners before Ballista. Still, time had passed. His own slave, Narcissus, was getting past his first bloom. The young barbarian was more than attractive; he was beautiful.

Hippothous put himself out to be charming. It was hard to make yourself heard over the cacophony of the wagon. Although studiedly polite, the boy quickly made it abundantly clear he was uninterested. Rejection never sat well with Hippothous, especially dished out twice by a slave. Outwardly maintaining an affable demeanour, talking lightly about trivial things, he turned the searching eye of a physiognomist on Ballista's pampered pet.

The boy did not have the form of a typical northerner. While he was tall for his age, with the expected red-blond hair and blue eyes, his skin did not look rough to the touch, nor did his ankles appear thick. In some ways, he was close to a pure Hellene: erect posture, beautiful in face and appearance, a squareness to the face and a slimness in his lips. His head was finely proportioned, between small and large, from which one could judge intellect, perception and clemency. His ears also were evenly proportioned, which showed alertness. His hands were well made, with the broad white nails of understanding and memory. He was heavy in his speech, a sign of sadness but also of long-lasting ambition and strong desire. But, as ever, it was the eyes that were the key. The eyes are related to the heart, and it is through them you look to the conversation of the soul.

The youth's beauty would blind many, but to the close scientific study of a trained physiognomist his eyes revealed the terrible story of his soul. His cow-like blue eyes inclined downwards and had a shade of green; the eyes of one vehement in thought and force, a lover of killing, a lover of blood. His eyes were flurried, with much movement – the eyes of one governed by a rebellious and angry daemon; a vengeful daemon which will visit harsh trials upon him and all those around him.

'Ahead! Heruli!' The voice of the *gudja* broke Hippothous's concentration. The wagons were grinding to a halt. Reaching for his sword, Hippothous reined his horse away from the column to see.

About half a mile away, a line of six horsemen were silhouetted on a low rise. Immobile, the Heruli looked like black sentinels to another world.

PART TWO
The Wolves of the North

(The Steppe, Spring–Autumn, AD263)

The Heruli observed many customs not in accord with other men.

–Procopius VI.14.2

VIII

It was true. The Heruli were not as other men. Ballista tried not to stare. The six Herul horsemen were identical, and like nothing he had seen before. Each had bright, dyed-red hair, moustaches and goatee beards. Almost every bit of skin visible – faces, necks, hands and wrists – was covered in red tattoos like heraldic symbols or letters from some outlandish script. But it was not any of this, and not their clothes – bulky nomad coats – which made them so very strange. It was their heads: great, pointed skulls, nearly twice as long as they should be, slanting up and back like those of antediluvian predatory beasts or creatures from the underworld.

'We are sorry we are late,' one of them said. He spoke politely in the language of Germania; his accent close to that of Ballista himself. 'We would have met you at the river, where our grazing lands begin, but my brother Philemuth was unwell.'

Now he looked, Ballista saw there were differences of age and physique. The one indicated looked old. He was slumped forward in his saddle. Behind the dyed hair and tattoos, his face was pale and drawn; there were blue-green smudges under his eyes. He looked deathly ill.

'It is you again, *Gudja*' – the first Herul spoke warily – 'and as ever the *haliurunna* is with you.'

The Gothic priest nodded slightly, but the old crone at his side cackled and made fast, strange movements with her hands.

Making a quick gesture of his own, the Herul turned away from the Goths towards Ballista. He placed the palm of his right hand flat on his forehead. 'I am Andonnoballus, and the brothers that ride with me are Philemuth, Berus, Aluith, Ochus and Pharas.'

Ballista bowed. 'I am Marcus Clodius Ballista, *Legatus extra ordinem Scythica*, sent by Imperator Publius Licinius Egnatius Gallienus Augustus. To my own people I am known as Dernhelm, son of –'

'Son of Isangrim, son of Starkad, of the Woden-born house of the war leaders of the Angles. A Herul would forget his own name sooner than your lineage and the name of your grandfather.' The Herul did not pronounce the words fondly.

Ballista ignored the reaction of the Roman party around him. All looked at him in surprise, except old Calgacus.

'That was then; two generations ago,' he said.

'We Heruli keep some of the old ways.'

'As do we Angles. Trust me, we have not forgotten the things done then.' Ballista smiled, as if putting the subject aside. 'Let me introduce my deputy, Gaius Aurelius Castricius.'

Again, the Herul placed his right palm flat to his forehead. Castricius dipped his head and saluted in acknowledgement.

'But you have not honoured us with the names of your fathers,' prompted Ballista.

'Only the gods might say. We are Heruli, all brothers.'

'The father of your King Naulobates was Suartuas, and his father before him was Visandus,' Ballista said.

The Herul laughed. 'We have not held to all the ways of our

ancestors in the north. Many things are different on the sea of grass. It changes men. We are not the people Starkad knew.'

'I can see that.'

'Our camp is to the east. If it pleases you, we will go there. Our slaves are preparing food, and the vapour baths we are told you enjoy.'

The Heruli rode ahead, and the others followed after. Ballista studied the nomads. Biggish men on small, rough horses. Each had a combined bowcase and quiver, decorated with patterns akin to their own tattoos, although in different colours, a long sword and a dagger on their hips and a round leather shield hung from their saddles. They wore voluminous sheepskin coats; no helmets or armour. They were equipped as typical light-horse archers.

Maximus nudged his horse alongside Ballista. 'You will be noticing their splendid trophies?'

Horsehair pennants fluttered from their reins and horse furniture. Ballista looked harder. No, not horsehair – human scalps, some dark, some lighter; all too many of them. And their quivers were not painted or embroidered, they were tattooed human skin.

'What exactly is a *haliurunna*?' Maximus asked.

'A Gothic witch. They commune with the underworld, mate with unclean daemons. It is said they can see the future, change the weather, raise the dead,' Ballista answered.

'And do you want to tell me how come you and the Heruli know so much about each other?'

'Not now; another time.'

'Another time then.' They rode in silence for a while, before Maximus spoke again. 'Who was it told them we liked the cannabis?'

Ballista did not answer.

Maximus looked thoughtful. 'That witch – rather the daemons than me.'

The Steppe spread all around them. The grass was enamelled with bright flowers: tulips, irises. Up above, below the white clouds, four rooks circled, harrying a lone vulture.

Slowly, very slowly, a line of round, grassy mounds drew nearer.

'*Kurgans*,' said Biomasos. 'The tombs of long-dead warriors and chiefs of the grasslands. At night, lights can be seen within; the sounds of ghostly feasting drift out. The gods strike down any who disturb them.'

The lumbering ox-wagons clanked and squealed between two of the larger *kurgans*. Beyond was the camp of the Heruli. There was but a handful of tents, and four or five of the smaller shelters for inhaling hemp. Half a dozen slaves stood waiting for their masters. The slaves were dressed just like the Heruli, but they had no tattoos, their hair was not dyed and their skulls appeared completely normal. On the far side was a herd of animals: sheep, camels, mainly horses. There had to be over a hundred horses; mainly chestnuts, and some light greys. They were all hobbled and grazing quietly; an immense number for so few men.

Mastabates felt light-headed, and a little sick. The vapour tent was close, oppressive; the laughter too loud in his ears. It was not the amount he had inhaled or drunk but the strange alcohol the Heruli had dispensed. Although clouded in his thinking, he was quite adamant on that point.

Still, bizarre as they looked, you could not fault the hospitality of the nomads. No sooner had the wagons been circled and the beasts seen to than a feast had been ready. It had been completely without ceremony. There were no sacrifices or prayers beforehand, not even the most cursory libation. Men sat in no order, where they pleased, on rugs or on the grass. When they had served the food, the slaves of the Heruli joined their masters. And the slaves talked – not only to each other, loud enough to be heard by all, but they even addressed the free men unbidden. It was like an impromptu rustic *Saturnalia*.

There was no bread of any sort, but more than enough food: mutton stew, sausages – Mastabates enjoyed them even after he was told they were horsemeat – and a good, strong cheese. But the drink was another matter. When handed a leather skin, he had incautiously taken a long draught. The effects had been instant: a sharp stinging on his tongue, a sweat breaking out all over his body as the liquid went down. The Heruli had laughed as he spluttered. One who had a little Greek told him it was fermented mare's milk. Not wishing to give offence, he had persevered with small sips. It was not totally unlike a thin yoghurt, but sharper; a Hellene would always sweeten his *oxygala* with honey or cut it with oil. Once he had got accustomed to it, he began to quite like its aftertaste of bitter almonds.

Just when Mastabates had begun to relax, one of the Heruli had jumped up and grabbed his ears hard, tugging vigorously at them. Thinking he was being attacked, he had scrambled backwards to his feet, making ineffectual slapping gestures of defence. This had provoked uncontrolled mirth. His assailant had begun to clap his hands and dance. Ballista had come over, slapped Mastabates on the shoulder and explained that the Herul was doing him honour, was inviting him to drink with him.

Prodigious quantities of food consumed, they had split up and gone to the cannabis tents, taking many skins of alcohol with them. Mastabates was in a shelter with Ballista, Maximus and old Calgacus. The *gudja* was there; inscrutable as ever. Andonnoballus and another three Heruli crowded in with them.

One of the Heruli started to play a martial air on the lyre. As he began to sing, Ballista and Calgacus stopped laughing. Maximus's hand went to his hilt. At a sharp word from Andonnoballus the singer stopped. He smiled, obviously apologized, and his plectrum picked out a different tune. Although unable to understand a word, Mastabates could tell this new song was a sentimental love ballad. He found himself giggling – as the singer was a Herul, most likely it was addressed to a donkey.

As the lyre player drifted into a lengthy instrumental passage, men began to talk again. The conversation, like the songs, was in the northern tongue.

The Herul to Mastabates' left – the sickly-looking one, Philemuth – spoke some Greek. He exhaled and smiled sadly. 'King Cannabas that guides our King Naulobates.'

Unable to think of any response, Mastabates asked him about the *anarieis*. The men who took a woman's part, were there many of them, and were they really regarded with reverence in Scythia? It soon became apparent the Herul had no idea what he was talking about, and seemed set to take offence.

'How did you learn Greek?' Mastabates changed the subject. At the imperial court, you failed to learn tact at your peril.

Philemuth brightened. 'I went' – he used a barbaric word – 'into the Kingdom of the Romans with the Borani and Urugundi. We were at Trapezus. There were many Roman soldiers. They were drunk, lazy. They had no courage. We placed tree trunks against the walls. The Romans fled. We sacked the town. It was good; much gold and silver, much wine, and women, many women. I took many slaves home.'

Unsure how to respond, Mastabates made a noncommittal noise.

'One girl – a Greek, her name is Olympias – very beautiful.' Philemuth coughed. The old Herul looked sad. 'I took her as my fourth wife. She gave much pleasure; to me, to my brothers. But now I am ill. If I need to die, it will not be good for her.' The Herul began to weep; openly, without shame.

The tent suddenly seemed very small to Mastabates. The fumes were suffocating. The elongated skulls of the Heruli were becoming ever more daemonic. Calgacus's misshapen head was no better. The taste of almonds was cloying. Mastabates felt his gorge rising. He had to get out.

Stumbling over legs, muttering apologies, he crawled to the opening. He heard laughter; assumed it was mocking.

Outside, the air was cool. He could breathe. He gulped down big lungfuls. He steadied himself against a guy rope. It was a still, cloudless night. Overhead, the panoply of stars wheeled.

'Too much mare's milk?' The voice was inebriated, but kindly. Mastabates had not noticed anyone approach.

'Here' – the man passed an amphora – 'this will take the taste away, cleanse your palate. It is Arsyene. Not a noble wine, but light and clean.'

Mastabates drank. He felt better. He was surprised at the consideration shown him.

'Thank you.'

'Think nothing of it.' The other took back the wine, took a long swig. He swayed slightly. 'A beautiful night.'

'It is.'

'A night of endless possibilities, a night for wild feasting. Come, walk with me.'

As if in a dream, Mastabates fell into step beside him. They had a torch to light the way.

'One of the *kurgans* has been opened – tomb robbers, I suppose. Let us go and see if it is true that the ancient chiefs feast by night.'

'No, I am not sure . . .' Mastabates had no wish to do such a thing.

'Afraid?' The other grinned, his teeth very white. 'Me too. Come, unless you are not man enough?'

Again, Mastabates walked with him. There was something strangely attractive about his companion, as there often was with rough men.

Away from the camp, it was dark beyond the light of the torch. The mound loomed, massive and rounded. At its side was a black opening, like a door to Hades.

Mastabates followed him inside. A passage sloped down. After a while – twenty, thirty paces? – it opened into a hollowed-out circular chamber. They stepped over the worm-eaten remains of a wooden cart.

Inside, the chamber was large; twenty paces across. It was empty, except for some scattered bones and a large leather bag. Everything of value had been looted. The place smelt of earth and old decay.

Mastabates regarded the bones. There were a lot of them – at least fifteen skulls; a couple were horses', the rest human.

'They killed many of the chief's servants to accompany him to the underworld,' Mastabates said.

'Maybe, but one of the Heruli told me these *kurgans* are often reused.' He held up the torch, and Mastabates saw two entrances other than that by which they had entered. One was blocked, one open. 'Sometimes there is more than one chamber. Robbers often dig more than one tunnel.'

'What about their daemons?' Mastabates asked.

The man took another drink. He seemed more sober now. 'Not all daemons are bad. Anyway, only the ghosts of those unjustly slain harm the living. The gods let them walk to punish those who robbed them of the divine gift of life. It was the Scythians' custom to sacrifice the servants, so they were killed justly.' He passed the amphora to Mastabates. 'Is it hard being what you are?'

Mastabates drank, trying to arrange his alcohol- and narcotic-fuddled thoughts. 'Yes, it is not easy. Men – normal men, whole men – see us as things of ill omen: like eastern priests, cripples, like monkeys. They turn away if they meet us. No, it is not easy to be thought of as a monkey.'

The man considered this. 'I went to a dream diviner once – probably a charlatan. He told me the kinds of men one should never believe if they spoke to you in a dream: actors, sophists, priests of Cybele, the poor and eunuchs. They all raise false expectations.'

'Why did you bring me here?'

'Nor should you trust Pythagoreans, or prophets who divine from dice, from palms, from sieves, or from cheese. But the dead are always worthy of credence.' He put out a hand and touched Mastabates' face.

'I thought you were one of those who saw my kind as ill omened. I thought you did not care for my company,' Mastabates said.

'My likes and dislikes are of no importance. It is the will of the gods.' He trailed the back of his fingers down Mastabates' cheek as if measuring him. 'Do you know what you are?'

Mastabates stepped back. The man's eyes were odd. This was all becoming strange beyond measure.

'I think you really do not know.' The man's eyes were flecked red in the torchlight. He stood between Mastabates and both the unblocked tunnels.

'We should go.' Mastabates heard the anxiety in his own voice. He had been a fool; a drunken, womanish fool.

The man drew his sword. In the flickering light, the steel seemed to ripple.

Mastabates took another step backwards, panic rising in his throat.

The other watched him.

'You killed the slave in the river,' Mastabates said.

'And many others.'

Mastabates went to draw his own blade. He had forgotten the amphora. It slipped from his grip and shattered loudly. Wine splashed on to his boots.

The man made no move.

Mastabates fumbled his short sword clear of its scabbard. *No need to abandon all attempts at manly virtue,* he thought. *A eunuch can still be a man.*

The other flexed his sword arm.

'Why?' Mastabates said.

The man paused, as if he had been waiting for the question, had been asked it before under like circumstances. 'For your own good, and the benefit of others. Because the gods . . .'

Mastabates thrust forward, sword aimed at the body.

Caught unaware, the man was late blocking. Mastabates' blade was only a hand's breadth away when a clash of metal deflected it. The eunuch's momentum carried him. He crashed into the man, who staggered backwards.

Mastabates was clear. He was past the killer, was at the entrance tunnel. He went to hurdle the remains of the cart. A bone turned under his foot and his ankle twisted. He went down, crashing among the papery, dry baulks of timber. His sword slipped from his grasp.

The wind was knocked out of him, and his ankle hurt abominably, but Mastabates was up in a moment. He scrabbled on his hands and knees, groping in the dirt for his sword. Noises behind him. His fingers closed on the hilt. He rolled over, bringing the blade up.

A flash of burning light, a jarring impact, and Mastabates' sword was smashed from his hand. The steel went spinning, skittering across the floor of the tomb to its dark further reaches.

The killer stood over him. He held the torch in one hand, his long sword in the other. The sword was pointed at Mastabates' throat.

No, not disgrace myself. No, not beg, Mastabates thought. *Be a man.*

He was panting. So was the killer. Apart from their breathing, all that could be heard was the hiss of the torch.

Be a . . . The sword thrust down. Pain like nothing Mastabates had known. His body arched. He could not scream; could not breathe. He was choking on his own blood. Dimly, he noticed his own legs drumming on the ground. Blackness in all the corners of his vision. Horribly swiftly, the dark edged in, and closed over him.

IX

'The same killer,' Ballista said.

None of the men contradicted him. There were eight of them in the tomb: five Romans, Castricius, Maximus, Hippothous, the centurion Hordeonius and Ballista himself, the Gothic *gudja*, and two Heruli, Andonnoballus and Philemuth. There had been many more, a packed crowd, gawping. Ballista curtly had told Calgacus to herd them out. Ballista knew his temper was short, and he knew why: thousands of tons of earth poised above his head, and the only ways out two long and narrow, obviously unsafe tunnels dug by robbers. He would have given a lot to be able just to leave.

The scene in the chamber did not help. It was infinitely macabre. The freshly mutilated corpse lay among the bones of ancient violence. In the torchlight, the shadows of the living shifted on the rough walls as if souls already halfway to flitting like bats in Hades. All too easy to imagine being trapped here for eternity.

'Why stuff the body parts under his armpits?' Maximus asked.

'Offerings to the infernal gods,' Hordeonius replied. 'As we offer the heart, liver and organs of a sacrificial beast. The murderer turns his victim into a sacrifice; turns away the anger of the gods, buys their protection.'

'Or something more practical,' Ballista said. 'A daemon cannot accuse you with no tongue, cannot harm you with no hands.'

'And cannot fuck you with no cock,' Maximus added. 'Although that might not be too much of a problem with a eunuch.'

'The murderer will kill more than just slaves,' Ballista said.

'Possibly not – the eunuch was a freedman,' the centurion said. 'Once a slave, always a slave. You can always tell. I remember being in the baths at Byzantium. It was in the *apodyterium*, I was just putting my clothes in a locker.'

Ballista let Hordeonius run on. The fumes of cannabis and alcohol were still in his head. It was easier to think without having to talk. Both bodies had been found outside the camp. The first could have been killed anywhere. It had drifted down the Tanais. The blood showed that this one had been killed in the corridor of the tomb. Mastabates was unlikely to have ventured outside the camp on his own. He had to have been lured out.

'The man barged past me, almost knocked me over. Not a word of apology.'

Mastabates would not have left the camp with a stranger, certainly not to this ghastly place. The killer had to be travelling with them. But who?

'So I punched him to the ground. His slave came at me, so I knocked him down too. Beat them both like dogs; used my fists, feet, a wooden clog.'

And why?

'You see into a man's soul when you beat him.'

Of course, the killer might be in the pay of an outsider. Not the Borani. Somehow, it was not the way of the Goths, not the northern

91

way of doing things. It could be Safrax, the King of the Alani. Certainly, he would hold a grudge from his defeat at the Caspian Gates. But, on such grounds, it was much more likely either Saurmag or Pythonissa; a prince denied a throne, and a woman scorned. The Suanian royal family were brought up in a world where murder was common currency. They prided themselves on their ingenuity in killing: poison, steel, drowning, suffocation. And Pythonissa had cursed him with that terrible curse.

'He was nothing but a dirty little freedman from Lycia who had made some money.'

Yet the killer's motives might have nothing to do with the outside. Like his person, they could be contained inside this strange caravan plodding across the Steppe.

'Even naked, as we all were, I could tell what he really was.'

Ballista thought of his own slave, Polybius. Had he run back in Panticapaeum, or had something worse happened? If the latter, the killer had been with them from the beginning.

'It is just a eunuch,' Andonnoballus said. 'Easy to replace.'

'He was a brave . . .' Somehow, Ballista could not say 'man'. 'He did not lack courage. Last year, when our ship was being chased by pirates on the Euxine, he stepped up to fight. He did not deserve to die like this. No one does.'

'You do not like them any more than anyone else,' Maximus said. 'The other year in Cilicia, when we captured the Sassanid king's harem, you killed two of Shapur's eunuchs out of hand, just because they were crying and it annoyed you. What was it you said? Something like, *We never cared for their sort in the north*.'

Ballista suppressed a flash of anger. He had been out of his mind then, maddened with grief. He had been convinced his wife and sons were dead. But he was not going to voice that excuse; did not want to be reminded of that time at all. Fuck Maximus for bringing it up.

'Look at the eunuch's head; the killer cleaned his blade on his hair,' the *gudja* said in heavily accented Greek.

It was true. There was much blood from the wound at Mastabates' throat and the various mutilations, but none of it seemed to account for the clotted hair. From his youth at the imperial court, half-remembered lines of poetry came into Ballista's mind. He recited hesitantly; losing the metre, missing words altogether.

Think . . . is it likely the dead in the tomb will take these honours well,
who mercilessly slew him . . . armpitted him, and for ablution wiped off
the bloodstains on his head . . .

'What is that?' Maximus asked.

'Lines from Sophocles' *Electra*. Clytemnestra tried to avoid the blood guilt of killing her husband, Agamemnon, by wiping the murder weapon in his hair. On his own head be it. It was his fault for sacrificing their daughter, Iphigenia. Mastabates mentioned the lines when we were looking at the body of Castricius's slave. Now, Mastabates is the dead one.'

Ballista paused, thinking.

No one else spoke.

'Mastabates said he was sure there was something more about mutilation, not in tragedy but in epic.' Ballista looked at Castricius and Hippothous.

Neither the enthusiast for epic poetry nor the self-styled man of Hellenic high culture reacted.

Suddenly, the weight of the earth above was very heavy on Ballista. He was tired, hung over, oppressed. He had to get out of this tomb. Abruptly, he turned to Hordeonius. 'Organize the burial,' he said.

As he neared the surface, Ballista could hear the wailing of the other eunuch, Amantius.

★

The tunnel was almost pitch dark. Men were screaming. The sounds of fighting were coming nearer. The flickering of distant torches gave it the look of Hell.

Mamurra was down, wounded. He was shouting something. Ballista could not hear. He felt the crushing weight of the earth above them. It was hard to breathe. He was choking. Far away behind him was the faint light of the outside world, the light of safety.

Mamurra shouted again. His hand reached out to Ballista. The Persians were getting closer. Earth drifted down on to Ballista's head, like flour on a sacrificial animal. He felt as much as heard the thunk, thunk of axes biting into the pit props. He had to get out. He took a last look at Mamurra. His friend's eyes were wild. Ballista turned and ran.

He stumbled out into the light . . .

The dream scrambled and retreated.

Ballista lay in the darkness. Poor old Mamurra. Poor square-headed old bastard. A man you could trust. A man who had trusted him.

Ballista had not been in the tunnel at Arete. But he had given the order. What in Hell else could he have done? Spare one and let the others die? He had given the order, and left his friend entombed in the dark for ever.

The Steppe was like nothing Calgacus had ever seen. It was another world. The ox-wagons had rumbled east for four days since the discovery of Mastabates' corpse. They must have covered forty miles. But it could have been four hundred, or no distance at all. The Steppe gave no indication of having any beginning or end.

Many found it monotonous. But Calgacus was comfortable with the sameness. Although there were occasional bursts of rain – it was still May – most of the time, the sun shone. Calgacus enjoyed each day's travel. The plain spread flat in all directions. There were spring flowers in the grasses: blue, lilac and yellow. There were milkwort and wild hemp, and tall candelabras of mullein flowers. And everywhere was grey wormwood; everywhere the bitter aroma of wormwood.

Not all was monotony. Groups of rounded barrows of the dead came and went. Then, abruptly, the convoy would come upon small watercourses. Hidden in their own declivities, the streams sparkled, refreshing the eye. Snipe flew up, and there were chub, tench and pike, even crayfish, to be caught. Mice and larger rodents dived into holes and burrows. Maximus claimed to have seen all sorts of other animals – wild asses and goats, a vixen playing with her cubs – but Calgacus's old eyes were not sharp enough to catch them. The Hibernian was probably lying.

The days were one thing, but the nights were another. In the day, unless you rode away from the din of the caravan, you could not hear the Steppe singing. But, at night, when men and beasts slept, there was no escaping it. The wind – and there was almost always wind – sighed through the fresh spring grasses. The sibilant whistling and whispering insinuated thoughts of regret and loss, instilled a feeling of trepidation. Nightingales and the call of owls added to the melancholy. On those nights when there were no clouds, the moon was bright enough to illuminate every blade of grass. The unfathomable immensity of the sky made Calgacus uneasily aware of the fleeting insignificance of man. He thought of Rebecca and the boy Simon, of his own hopes of comfort and domesticity. If he survived this – and in the face of such alien vastness it seemed somehow implausible – he would marry her. Ballista might hanker for a return to the north, at least in half his heart, but Calgacus wanted none of it. He had been a slave there. In the south, he had freedom. He wanted nothing more than to live out his days under the hot Sicilian sun, a son of his own playing at his feet.

On the fifth morning, Calgacus rode with Ballista and Maximus away from the others.

'So, would now be a good time for you to be telling me how you and the longheads are so well informed about each other?' Maximus asked Ballista.

'You might as well know,' Ballista said. 'Once, the Heruli lived in the north, on the island of Scadinavia, across the Suebian sea, north-east from my people. In my grandfather's time, the Heruli killed their king, for no better reason than they did not want to be ruled by him any more.' Ballista smiled.

'We Germans do not exalt our rulers like the Persians or Romans, but among the Heruli their kings enjoyed practically no advantage over any other warrior; all claimed the right to sit with him, eat with him, insult him without restraint.' Ballista smiled again.

A brace of partridge flew up, their whirring wings making the horses skitter. Ballista soothed his mount, and took up the story once more.

'They chose a new king, Sunildus. He was more to their taste. They were numerous and warlike. They soon conquered most of the thirteen neighbouring tribes on Scadinavia. Both the powerful Gauti and the savage Scrithiphini fell under their sway. Their king tried to call a halt, but they reviled him, called him effeminate, a coward. Their natural avarice was aroused. He did not dare try to curb them. They crossed the sea. The Eutes were subjected. The Heruli moved south, raided far and wide. The terrible things they did roused the other tribes against them: the Varini, Farodini, Reudigni, Saxones, Aviones and the Angles.'

Ballista stopped. Calgacus was half listening; he knew the tale of old.

'And?' Maximus prompted.

'And, my grandfather had been away when the Heruli came.

They raped and killed his first wife, their two daughters. It was Starkad who formed the tribes into alliance against the Heruli, persuaded their subjects to revolt. He killed their king Sunildus with his own hands. The Heruli were driven from their lands. Sunildus's son, Visandus, led them into exile. Many of the Eutes went with them. Now they are here.'

Maximus laughed, and turned to Calgacus. 'Did you know this?'

'Aye.'

'And you both thought telling anyone might cast a further blight on the spirits of your companions?'

'Something on those lines,' Ballista said.

'I can see your point,' Maximus said. 'Being tracked by an unknown murderer through a wilderness utterly forsaken by the gods but seemingly crowded with your enemies; that I am sure they can take in their stride. But should they discover that if, by some miracle, we are lucky enough to reach our destination alive, we will have delivered ourselves into the hands of a people who have good reason to want to see your entire family, and probably anyone connected to you, dead, now that might depress anyone a little.'

'Like hunting bear across ice with a cracked bow and a torn hamstring,' Calgacus said.

The other two ignored him. He wheezed his own amusement.

Then, for a while, they rode in silence.

'Who do you think it is?' Ballista said, breaking into their thoughts.

'A man who does not like slaves or eunuchs,' Maximus said. 'It could be me.'

'So you do not think it is the old witch?' Ballista asked.

'Sure, you can never tell,' Maximus said. 'She is a villainous-looking old bitch.'

'Never succumb to the soft words of a witch, or her snaring

embraces; every sweetness will turn sour, you will take to your bed broken with sorrow,' Calgacus said.

'Stop it,' said Ballista, smiling. 'When you get happy enough to start quoting northern aphorisms, it always depresses me.'

'Aphor-what?'

'Sayings.'

'Are you sure it is not the Borani?' Maximus asked.

'Quite sure. They want me dead, not some slave and an imperial eunuch.'

'Pythonissa cursed you and all you love. Now, unless your girl thinks you have taken to loving eunuchs, it is not going to be her behind it. Come to that, it is not going to be her brother Saurmag or the Alani either.'

Ballista nodded in acceptance.

'I have been wondering if it might be the King of the Urugundi,' Maximus said. 'He will not be wanting to be attacked by the Heruli, and he has that old *gudja* on hand, and he is a nasty piece of work.'

'If Hisarna knew we are meant to set the Heruli on him, he would not have let us cross his lands. He could have sent us back, or just had us killed.'

Again they rode in silence. Another group of barrows was looming.

'But you might be right that it is political,' Ballista continued after a time, as if he had not stopped speaking. 'We are in the middle of nowhere, cut off from all news. But out there the dance of emperors and kings goes on, and for all we know we may be a small part of it. The Persians do not want the Urugundi fighting the Heruli. The easterners want them and the other Goths free to raid the *imperium*. As *Corrector* of the Orient, Odenathus of Palmyra has been taking the fight to the Persians. They would rather he was distracted chasing northerners around the southern shores of the Euxine. There again, Postumus the pretender in the west must know Gallienus is preparing to attack him. It is better for him if Gallienus has to deal with Gothic raids in the Aegean and Greece.'

'How is killing a eunuch and a slave going to make the embassy fail?' Maximus asked.

'If the Heruli think there is a killer with us, they might not want us coming too close to their king,' Ballista said. 'It could be politics.'

Calgacus hawked and spat. 'Was it politics drove you to kill those two eunuchs in Cilicia?'

Ballista shot him a fierce, unhappy look.

'You were out of your mind,' Calgacus continued. 'Same here; no politics, no deep reason – it is the work of a madman.'

'Who?' Maximus raised the question.

'Of course,' Calgacus went on, 'it might not be a man at all. No one has seen the killer. Maybe not a man, but a daemon.'

They rode past the first of the tombs. From its summit, an ancient stone effigy of a warrior holding a sword gazed down.

Hippothous felt like a character in a novel. Not one of those centred in the Hellenic world, but an adventure story that roamed to the ends of the earth; something like *The Wonders Beyond Thule*. Certainly, this journey was tough, brought its dangers: *Numberless are the challenges which lie before you on your outward journey and on your return. But I am destined by the hateful decision of a god to die far away*, as Idmon had prophesied to the crew of the *Argo*. Hippothous was sure the first line was the one that was relevant to him.

The sea of grass was a constant delight. That afternoon, they had ridden into camp across a carpet of hyacinth and tulip. The scent of the thyme crushed by their horses' hooves mingled with the intoxicating tang of wormwood. The customs of the Steppe were fascinating, well worth study. Hippothous was not one of those Hellenes who, no matter where they went, just found Hellas. He saw himself more like Herodotus; interested in other peoples for their own sake, not in a hurry to judge, prepared to accept that, everywhere, *custom is king*.

Like Herodotus, like those men of culture who accompanied

Alexander, he was venturing beyond the known, opening new fields of enquiry. That was why Hippothous was so pleased to be able to attend the ritual that was to unfold after the feast.

The fire was sawing in the perpetual wind, tongues of flame drawn away into the night. The air was pungent with mingled woodsmoke, animal dung and roast lamb. Philemuth, seated on the left of Hippothous, knew some Greek. As the participant in the forthcoming ritual, it was unsurprising the sickly Herul did not want to talk. On the other side of the fire, Ballista was talking to Andonnoballus; Maximus and Calgacus with a couple of other nomads. They were using one of the languages of the north. Hippothous, of course, could not understand a word.

Unable to join in the conversations, Hippothous ate his lamb quietly and sipped his drink. He was very sober; the significance of the evening did not encourage heavy drinking or much levity. With nothing else to do, as so often, he gave way to his passion for physiognomy. He was not in the mood to study the Heruli. Although they *were* interesting. Once you looked beyond their artificially distorted skulls and pale, rough, northern skin, they were surprisingly normal; some even evidently of good character. But they could wait until they reached the court of King Naulobates. Now Hippothous wanted to practise on two subjects he had put off for far too long, for three years – four, if you counted inclusively.

Calgacus was in direct view, well lit by the fire, and caught up in discussion with his neighbours. It was an ideal moment for prolonged scrutiny. The test of skill would be to penetrate behind the natural ugliness of the subject; to tear that unlovely veil aside and reveal the soul. No squeamish feelings of revulsion should be allowed to stand in the way.

The old Caledonian had a large head. Usually that was good, indicating intelligence, understanding and high ambition. But

Calgacus's head was too large; a horrible great dome-like thing. That must mean the opposite: a lack of knowledge and understanding, and a complete indifference. And his head was crooked, pointing to a failure of modesty and a dissolution of covenants. Not a man to be trusted, but nothing too bad so far.

Calgacus had a big chin. Which should denote the ability to suppress anger, but the tendency to talk at the wrong time. The latter rang true to Hippothous, but he was unsure about the former.

Calgacus shifted, scratched his crotch. From various trips to the baths, Hippothous knew Calgacus possessed a very large penis. Maximus often called him *Buticosus*, the 'big-stuffer' in Latin. Calgacus was the sort of man the *frumentarii* would have kidnapped in the reign of the pervert Heliogabalus to give the emperor pleasure. Although Hippothous could remember nothing at all in the *Physiognomy* of Polemon or that of Loxus about penises – an odd omission – a big cock was obviously a very bad thing. Everyone knew a small penis was the mark of a civilized man. The opposite was barbaric irrationality and loss of self-control.

The eyes are always the truest witness. Hippothous peered across at Calgacus. The northerner's eyes were somewhat bleared. That was nothing but old age. They were an indeterminate shade of blue. Little to be made of that. They were small. That was more revealing – small like kinds of snakes, monkeys, foxes and the like. They most resembled the eyes of a serpent: malicious, intelligent, tyrannical, wary, timid, sometimes tamable, quick to change, and bad-natured. Hippothous thought the last obviously correct.

Calgacus was oblivious, still deep in conversation. His eyes were still, fixed, but his forehead and eyebrows were contracted as he listened to the Herul. It was the revelation Hippothous needed. As Polemon had written, when you saw eyes of such a type, *Know that he is a hated man and an enemy*, and, if they were combined with a frown, *Judge him for perfidy and cunning*.

Hippothous leant back. At last his judgement was made, scientific in its exactitude. He took a drink. He felt rather drained, but it was no time to rest.

Despite the subdued, even apprehensive, mood of the meal, Maximus was yapping away; hands moving, bird-like head nodding. Hippothous found it difficult to get past the missing end of the Hibernian's nose; the scar was distractingly reminiscent of a cat's arse. He took another drink, tried harder.

What was left of Maximus's nose implied that it had once spread. That sign of fornication and a love of sexual intercourse could not have been more apt. The hair on his head was black, cropped short but thick. Its darkness indicated cunning and deception, in thickness it resembled that of a savage wild animal. The hair of his eyebrows was long, almost touching the temples, signifying much desire and the nature of a pig. Maximus wore a short beard, little more than stubble, but it was more luxuriant on the neck. The untrained viewer might think this nothing more than an indolence in shaving. The physiognomist knew better. It showed power, strength, even magnanimity, like a lion. But, as ever, the eyes were the key. They were never still, always moving fast, and that pointed to lack of truth, to wicked conjecture, and all the way to true evil.

A Herul slave came out of the darkness to Philemuth. It was time for the scapulimancy. The slave carried the shoulder blades of three sheep; he passed them to the nomad. Everyone, even Maximus, was quiet. The bones were very white; scraped, possibly boiled clean. Philemuth turned them in his hands. Everyone knew the question Philemuth was putting to them. He was asking his gods: *Should I die?*

At length Philemuth handed the bones back. Using tongs, the

slave placed them one after another in the heart of the fire. The flames licked white around them. The shoulder blades would crack in the heat. If but one cracked cleanly lengthwise, the answer to the question was yes.

No one spoke as they waited. Beyond the sounds of the wind and the fire an owl called in the immensity of the Steppe. Hippothous wondered what deities drew near across that dark ocean of grass. The Heruli worshipped many gods; none gentle or mild.

'Hunh.' Philemuth grunted, then coughed. The slave went forward and retrieved the bones. They were black now. He placed them on the ground to cool.

Philemuth sat cross-legged. His fate was decided, waiting to be discovered, but he showed no impatience. Once, he doubled up coughing. But he forced himself upright again, motionless.

A horse snickered out in the darkness. Philemuth gestured. The slave gave him the first shoulder blade. Philemuth peered close at it, lips moving as if reading a book. He took his time, then he put it aside. Three fine cracks were discernible running across the bone.

A gesture, and the slave gave the next one into Philemuth's hands. The Herul spent less time studying it. Before he put it down, Hippothous could see the round flakes that had burnt off, the fine patina of cracks covering the whole surface.

Philemuth seemed to barely glance at the final shoulder blade. He put it down on the grass, and stood up.

Hippothous saw the clean break running lengthwise.

Philemuth walked out of the circle of firelight into the darkness.

'No, no.' The young Herul Aluith was laughing, although not unkindly. 'You draw the arrow like this.' He leant out of the saddle, across between the horses. Wulfstan could not understand how he did not fall.

Aluith again guided Wulfstan's fingers in the strange nomad draw: the thumb pulling the bowstring back, right forefinger locked against the thumbnail, the whole hand twisted to the left so the knuckle of the forefinger held the arrow in place.

'Now, try again.'

Wulfstan booted his mount into a canter. Although gripping as hard as he could with his legs, the young Angle bounced precariously. It felt very unsafe with no hands on the reins. The horse picked up speed. The Steppe rattled by all too fast. The sack stuffed with straw came nearer. Wulfstan nudged the horse on to a slightly different approach. Concentrating hard, as Wulfstan nocked the arrow, he remembered to place the shaft to the right of the bow. The string cut into his thumb as he drew – everything about this nomad way of doing things seemed wrong. He tried to aim. The motion of the horse made it impossible. He was almost on top of the target. He released. The arrow flew well wide. Grabbing both the reins and the tuft left low down on the mane for that purpose, he pulled the horse around in a wide circle. He trotted back again, dispiritedly.

As soon as the wagon train had got going that morning, Ballista had asked the Heruli if they would teach him and some of his men how to shoot at the gallop in the nomad style. Andonnoballus, Pharas and young Aluith had agreed, seemingly delighted to demonstrate their skills. Seven had assembled for instruction. The centurion Hordeonius had claimed his auxiliary light-horse bowmen were already more than well trained. The *gudja* had smiled disdainfully. No one had suggested asking the Sarmatian drivers.

Irritatingly, Ballista, Maximus and Hippothous had grasped the basic technique in a reasonably short time. Castricius and Calgacus had taken rather longer. The latter never came anywhere near real proficiency. The Suanian Tarchon had given up altogether. Now, only Wulfstan was still trying. He was very hot and tired. He had been at it all morning.

It was good of Aluith to remain behind, good of him to teach a slave in the first place. When the idea was raised that morning, Wulfstan had been prepared to beg Ballista to be allowed to use a horse and try. No opportunity to learn was to be spurned. When free, he would need all the killing skills he could possess. Wulfstan had been pleased Ballista had granted his request without demur. He had ridden ponies often before he was enslaved. The big Sarmatian warhorses – and he was on his third this morning – were very different. Guiding a horse just with your legs was difficult, but drawing a bow with your thumb, not your fingers, and trying to aim the arrow all at the same time was quite impossible.

'You must relax. A horse trained by a Sarmatian is not as good as one trained by a Herul, but it still knows what to do. Just point it in the general direction. Pull the bow back smoothly, try to hold the position I showed you earlier; think of it as an extension of your arms. Let me demonstrate again.'

In one fluid motion, Aluith pushed his mount into a gallop and withdrew bow and arrow from his *gorytus*. He made high *yipping* noises as he raced across the Steppe. The bow curved back. An arrow sped towards the target. As it thumped home, another left the bow, then another. Aluith spun the horse around in its own length. Thundering back through the dust of his own making, he shot another three shafts into the sack.

Wulfstan spat. The bitter taste of wormwood was in his throat. He grinned ruefully. 'How?'

'It comes naturally, when you have learnt as a small child. Now you try again.'

Gamely, Wulfstan nocked another arrow. His thumb hurt. The blisters had burst, and they were bleeding. He squeezed the barrel of the horse with his thighs. As it set off, Wulfstan felt momentarily light-headed. The grass accelerated under him; bright flowers flashed by. The sack seemed to blur in his vision. The pressure of the string cut into his thumb. Wulfstan felt dizzy. He released the bow. The arrow went nowhere near the target. He reined the horse back to a standstill.

In the distance, the horizon shifted. It and the sky ebbed away. They were retreating faster and faster, dragging the Steppe after them. The grasses, the wormwood shrubs, the bright dots of flowers were racing away. Wulfstan felt it pulling at him. There was a great heaviness in his body, behind his eyes.

'Are you hurt?'

'No, I do not think so.' Wulfstan was on the ground.

Aluith cradled Wulfstan's head, put a flask to his lips. Wulfstan coughed it up.

'I am sorry. I forgot some outlanders do not like fermented mare's milk. I will get something else.'

Wulfstan lay back, closed his eyes again.

'Try this.' Aluith lifted Wulfstan's head once more, put another flask to his lips. It was watered wine. Wulfstan drank. He sat up, opened his eyes. The Steppe had stopped moving.

'You have been out here a long time. I should have made you drink more,' Aluith said.

'No, it was not that. It was . . . strange. The Steppe seemed to move.'

'Yes, it can do that; even to those born here. The spirits try to pull you to them. Many die from it.'

Aluith, squatting on his haunches, took Wulfstan's hands, looked at the deep cut on his thumb. 'You have tenacity. You put aside the pain. You would make a good Herul.'

'How? I am a slave.' There was no disguise to the bitterness in Wulfstan's voice.

'Herul just means warrior. Our slaves fight alongside us.'

'You do not blind them?'

Aluith laughed. 'You have seen them. Why would we do something so stupid? If a slave shows courage, he wins his freedom. Of course, he cannot become one of the Rosomoni, but he becomes a Herul.'

'Rosomoni?'

Aluith touched the bright-red hair on his elongated head. 'You are born one of "the Red ones", the brothers. But several of Naulobates' leading Heruli warriors were slaves. One was even a Greek slave taken out of Trapezus – imagine that.'

Wulfstan drank some more.

'We should get back,' Aluith said.

Wulfstan went to remonstrate.

'We will practise more tomorrow. I will get you a ring for your thumb.'

The Herul helped Wulfstan to his feet, on to his horse; whistled for his own, and jumped into the saddle.

They rode back together in silence. Wulfstan's thoughts were full of new ideas of slavery and freedom.

XI

Ballista was riding with Calgacus and Maximus, as he had been for several days. Always travelling, never arriving; the Steppe stretched on without limit. Time stagnated. It took an effort to remember it was only eleven days since the discovery of Mastabates' body, only fourteen since they set out on to the alien world of the Steppe.

As they trudged into the east, *kurgans* would appear in the distance. Slowly, the barrows got closer, were passed, and left behind. Watercourses were stumbled upon, each one somehow a surprise. The ox-wagons were braked down hard into the streams, hauled up the other side. Occasionally there would be a glimpse of white up ahead in the distance, a fixed point in the shimmering sea of green. Not until they were on top of it could the travellers tell if it was a boulder or a blanched skull. A lot of cattle and other creatures had died out here.

Ballista watched a lapwing swooping and diving around the head of the column, screaming outrage and distress at the threat to its unseen nest.

'At least we have not seen hide nor hair of the Alani since the river,' Maximus said.

'That means shite,' responded Calgacus. 'The dust, the camp-fires; making only ten miles a day – we could not be easier to follow. There could be any number of the bastards out there tracking us.'

'Child's play,' Ballista agreed. His mood was as glum as any. 'The main body could hang back miles away. Have a couple of scouts watch our dust cloud from over the horizon; nothing to stop them riding in to have a closer look in the dark.'

'Not at all,' Maximus said. 'A couple of horsemen on their own would not last a night out there alone – the daemons would get them.'

Both Ballista and Calgacus gave him a dubious look.

'The plains are crawling with daemons and other foul, unnatural creatures. Ochus the Herul told me so.'

'And you believed him,' Ballista said.

'And why not? Your long-headed fellow was born out here. He should know.'

Calgacus made an unpleasant grating, coughing sound – what passed for laughter.

'Go on, laugh, you old fucker,' Maximus said. 'See if you are still laughing when one of them is pulling your guts out, drinking your blood.'

'Like a retarded fucking child,' Calgacus muttered.

'Ochus said that your Gothic witches, like that old bitch with the *gudja*, go out and copulate with them, breed more of the things. At Ragnarok, a whole horde of them – daemons, half-daemons, all sorts – will come out of the Steppe, kill everything in their path.'

'I think they might be one of the lesser things to worry about at the end of days,' Ballista said. 'Especially once the stars have fallen, the sun has been devoured, and the dead risen – there will be a lot on our minds.'

'Say what you like, you would not catch me out there at night on my own.' Maximus was reluctant to give up the otherworldly threat of the Steppe. Something about the strangeness of the landscape encouraged credulity.

'Fine bodyguard you are,' Calgacus said.

Maximus rounded on him. 'You miserable old bastard, only the other day you said the killings might be the work of a daemon.'

'Aye,' Calgacus agreed, 'but I was thinking of a real one, not a silly story. You know as well as me, ever since Ballista here killed Maximinus Thrax, he has been haunted by his daemon. When the other mutineers cut off his head, denied him burial, they condemned the dead emperor to walk. It might have been half a lifetime ago, but Maximinus has eternity.'

Ballista considered this. He had told very few people of the terrifying nocturnal apparitions: Calgacus and Maximus, his wife, Julia, his one-time secretary young Demetrius, and a friend, Turpio. The last was dead.

'I do not think so,' Ballista said. 'It has been months since Maximinus troubled me. When he appears, the daemon offers no violence – just the threat he will see me again in Aquileia. We could hardly be further from northern Italy.'

'It might be the two of you have forgotten, but we have been cursed by a priestess of Hecate,' Maximus said. 'Pythonissa summoned the dark bitch goddess and all her creatures up from the underworld against us.'

'And you are frightened she might set an *empusa* on us; one of those nasty shape-shifters that frighten small children. I remember Demetrius mistook a man for one once in Mesopotamia – terrified the little Greek, it did.' Calgacus's amusement turned into a coughing fit.

'Actually, I was thinking more of the Kindly Ones. Dog-headed, snakes for hair, coal-black bodies and bloodshot eyes;

you do not want to meet them. Any fool knows the *eumenides* are relentless.'

Ballista noticed even Calgacus surreptitiously put his thumb between his first two fingers to avert evil. Live long enough in the Roman empire, and it seemed even a Caledonian became a little bit Hellenized.

'Someone else has been in my thoughts,' Ballista said. 'Well . . . in my dreams really – old Mamurra.'

'It was not your fault,' Maximus said, quick as a flash.

'Aye, you had to do it,' Calgacus agreed.

They were both far too quick to exonerate. The three rode in slightly awkward silence. Some clouds were coming down from the north. An inevitable vulture was riding the wind very high above the caravan. Below it, a couple of rooks circled. The Steppe ahead was somewhat less flat, beginning to roll just a little.

'Do you think he could have survived?' Ballista asked.

'No,' Calgacus said. 'If the collapse of the tunnel did not kill him, the Persians would have finished him off.'

'No chance at all. For all we know, he was dead before the tunnel came down.'

'If he had got out, he would blame me,' Ballista said.

'There is absolutely no fucking possibility he survived,' Maximus said. 'A man could not be more dead.'

'No one down there would have given him an *obol* for the ferryman,' Ballista said.

'In that case, as I think your Greeks and Romans have it, he would just spend forever waiting by the banks of the river Styx.' Maximus was waving his hands around to emphasize his point. 'So he would not be roaming around these empty grasslands chopping up people he had never met.'

'Shite, you two are as bad as each other,' Calgacus grunted. 'Retarded fucking children both of you, imagining things to scare yourselves. It is just where we are. This gods-forsaken shithole of endless grass is unlike anything we have known, and it is preying on our minds.'

'Well,' Maximus said, 'that and the two dead, horribly mutilated corpses.'

'I still think it could be three or four,' Ballista said.

'Someone is coming,' Calgacus said.

A Herul was cantering out from the line of the wagons. It was Andonnoballus. He looked very serious.

'Dernhelm, son of Isangrim, I have a favour to ask.' The Herul put the palm of his right hand to his forehead. 'It is on behalf of my brother Philemuth.'

Ballista woke to the *thunk*, *thunk* of axes chopping wood. The Heruli and their slaves were using the oxen to drag the timber up from the banks of the small river. The Sarmatian drivers had been deputed to help. The beasts lowed as the whips lashed across their backs.

The pyre was going up fast. Already the framework was assembled, and both the platform and ramp put in place. Now the trimmed branches were being added, doused in oil and other flammables.

Ballista watched and thought of old age and debility, and death.

> *. . . Today and tomorrow*
> *You will be in your prime; but soon you will die,*
> *In battle or in bed; either fire or water,*
> *The fearsome elements, will embrace you,*
> *Or you will succumb to the sword's flashing edge,*
> *Or the arrow's flight, or terrible old age;*
> *Then your eyes, once bright, will be clouded over;*
> *All too soon, O warrior, death will destroy you.*

If the *norns* had spun him that long a life, what would his clouded eyes regard in old age? He thought fondly of the villa in Tauromenium. He saw himself sitting on a bench in the garden down by the gate, a fruit tree shading him from the Sicilian sun. Isangrim and Dernhelm were with him, full grown, tall and clean-limbed. Their golden hair shone in the shadows. The Bay of Naxos spread out below them. Perhaps their sons played at their feet.

No sooner was the idyll in his mind than it was replaced by another image. He saw himself seated on the great throne in his father's high hall. The smoke from the fire drifted among the eaves. His warriors feasted and drank on the benches; their arms glittered with the rings he had given them. A bard sang of his grandfather Starkad, of all the war leaders of the Angles back to the Grey-eyed Allfather, Woden himself.

Yet it was hard to see his sons in the north they had never known. Impossible to imagine Julia, the daughter of a long line of Roman senators, being content as the wife of a northern chieftain. And, of course, he had older half-brothers. Morcar would die rather than see Ballista in their father's place. If Ballista had not been taken as a hostage into the empire, they would have fought.

Ballista's thoughts shied away to generalities of old age. The ancient Spartans had given the condition high accord. They had been guided in everything by the *Gerousia*, a council of ex-magistrates serving for life. The life of their *polis* had been dictated by a small group of elderly men, a strange, decrepit gerontocracy. The Romans also seemed to hold old age in high esteem. Many of them chose to have their portrait busts looking lined and wizened, showing them grown aged in hard service to the *Res Publica*. Some were given a senility in marble that they lacked in reality. But not all Romans wanted to appear old, and Sparta was not what it once had been. Perhaps neither the Greeks nor the Romans had ever lived up to their ideals of respecting old age. If they had, what need would there have been for countless philosophers to advocate the virtues of such veneration?

The pyre was almost finished. The Heruli were setting out rich brocades and cushions on the platform, carrying up food and drink, and weapons. Their slaves and the Sarmatians were busy spreading kindling. It would not be long now.

Among Ballista's own people, advanced age got a man a voice in the assembly. Yet only if his younger deeds were remembered as worthy. Powerful kinsmen aided the esteem given to the elderly, but mainly if their kin were young warriors. Things were worse with other peoples. Apparently, among the Alani, those men who did not die in battle but reached old age were confined to the wagons. There they lived the lives of women or children; the objects of bitter reproaches, despised as degenerate and cowardly.

Ballista, however, had never encountered anything quite as terrible as the practice of the Heruli. Certainly, the *gymnosophists* of India did much the same. Calanus had mounted the pyre in Babylon under the eyes of Alexander. Zarmarus had done the same in Athens, watched by the emperor Augustus. But the Indian philosophers had acted as their own wisdom and conscience dictated. Their euthanasia had been voluntary, not enforced by social expectation. And no one had been assigned the awful task of assisting them.

It was time. Philemuth was brought out of his tent.

Ballista wondered if he would rather have remained inside, even if it meant being reviled.

Philemuth walked unsteadily to the foot of the ramp. Two other Heruli helped him up it.

Andonnoballus came over to Ballista. The northerner felt sick. 'You know what to do,' Andonnoballus said.

Ballista knew. It had been explained to him. It could not be done by a kinsman or a slave, and all the Heruli present were Rosomoni or servile. Andonnoballus had said it was an honour to be asked. When they reached his camp, Naulobates would think well of him for doing it. Ballista knew he had no real choice.

When the other Heruli had descended, Ballista walked to the ramp and climbed to the top of the pyre. He had killed many men, but none like this.

Philemuth lay, slightly propped up on the expensive cushions. His hands rested on the hilt of his sword on his chest. His whip and *gorytus* were close by him. His shield and other arms, jugs of drink and bowls of food were placed around. The Herul's face was waxen, his eyes fixed on the sky.

Down below, the Heruli began to clash their swords on their shields. An insistent chant rose up. There was a smell of fresh-lit torches.

Philemuth said something.

Ballista could not hear. He leant down.

'It takes courage,' Philemuth said.

Ballista was unsure to which of them he referred.

Philemuth spoke again. 'I will not trouble you – now or later. Tell Ochus and Pharas I will see them soon.'

Ballista nodded.

'Make it quick and clean.'

Ballista drew the dagger from his hip. *Do not think, just act.* The often repeated mantra ran through his thoughts. He had killed many, far too many, men. One more made little difference. *Do not think, just act.*

Ballista knelt by Philemuth's head. He passed his palm over the Herul's head, hoping he would close his eyes. As gently as he could, he lifted Philemuth's beard and chin. *Do not think, just act.*

Ballista cut the old man's throat.

Philemuth's hands grabbed for the blade. His body jerked up. The blood pumped, thick and very red.

After a time, Philemuth stopped moving. The flow of blood slowed. It seeped from the dark wound, down the tattooed neck and on to the sodden brocade.

Ballista disengaged the hands from his own. He stood up.

When he reached the bottom of the ramp, Ballista walked over to his *familia*. Calgacus put an arm around his shoulder.

Still chanting, the Rosomoni approached the pyre, torches in hand.

Despite his care, Ballista noticed there was blood on his clothes. The dagger was still in his hand.

The pyre was burning strongly. Great clouds of grey smoke from the green wood billowed high into the sky, visible for miles across the open Steppe.

The eunuch Amantius sat back and pulled his robe free where it was caught tight across the protuberance of his stomach. He shifted his soft haunches, and reread what he had written. It started conventionally and calmly enough.

> *Publius Egnatius Amantius to Lucius Calpurnius Piso Censorinus, Praetorian Prefect, Vir Ementissimus.*
>
> *If you are well, Dominus, I can ask the gods for no more.*
>
> *After three days in the third camp on the river Tanais the ox-wagons promised by Hisarna arrived.*

Amantius scanned the bulk of the letter. It contained a brief description of the caravan provided by the Goths, and a lengthier discussion of early impressions of the Heruli, the latter far from good. With something of a flourish, it conveyed the more surprising information of the murderous family history between

Ballista and the Heruli. As he neared the end, Amantius began to read more closely.

So while the Heruli have so far shown no overt hostility, two extremely disturbing developments must be brought to your attention. First, the collapse of disciplina which I mentioned in my first report has gone much further. Many members of the embassy pass much of their time in drunkenness caused by consuming vast quantities of the fermented mare's milk of the nomads and in inebriation brought on by adopting the barbarians' habit of inhaling cannabis. I regret to inform you the lead in this is taken by none other than the Legatus extra ordinem Scythica himself. With every day Marcus Clodius Ballista appears to be sloughing off his acquired layers of Romanitas and reverting to his barbaric nature. Early today he went so far as to kill a man in some ghastly nomad ritual of enforced euthanasia. The maiestas of Rome could be brought no lower.

Of the second development I am almost too frightened to write. While we were still in camp on the Tanais, twelve days before the kalends of June, the body of a slave owned by Gaius Aurelius Castricius, deputy to the Legatus, was found in the river. It had been horribly mutilated. Just six days later, the morning after we encountered the Heruli, my colleague Publius Egnatius Mastabates – my only amicus in this cavalcade of savagery – was discovered in an ancient barbarian tomb. He too had been cruelly killed and his body desecrated. One of the barbarians laughed and said it was just a eunuch, easy to replace. Some bloodthirsty killer or daemon preys on this caravan and, as the victims are but slaves and eunuchs, no one cares. May the gods hold their hands over me.

In camp on the Steppe, by my reckoning seven days before the ides of June but, on the Steppe, even time becomes uncertain.

XII

Maximus was glad he had not had to kill the old Herul Phile-muth. It was a couple of days ago but, oddly, still on his mind. It had not done Ballista any good. Maximus remembered Calgacus talking one night when they were drinking. Where had it been? In Ephesus? No, before that. Maybe it was one of those small, ravaged towns in Cilicia. No, it was Cyprus; Keryneia in Cyprus. It was in the small bar with the blonde with the generous mouth. What was she called? Callirhoe, or something like that; claimed she was a high-born virgin who had been kidnapped. Likely story, she went at it like a sparrow when you got her going – and everyone in the world knew how depraved sparrows were; worse than quails. When Maximus had come back from his first bout with her, Calgacus had started going on about how Ballista was not a natural killer, unlike Maximus. The old Caledonian was drink-taken, but he might have been right.

Killing had never bothered Maximus. It was what warriors did. If you did not want to be a farmer and shovel shit, or a slave and be fucked up the arse, you learnt how to fight and kill people.

There had been little call for sophists or philosophers in Hibernia, and Maximus was hardly cut out to be a priest.

Most of the men Maximus had killed had been trying to kill him. And the others? Well, most men were vicious bastards. Probably, they were better off dead. It could be he had done them and those they would have run into a good turn. Anyway, Calgacus was on thin ice – he had never shown any inclination towards turning the other cheek, like one of those demented Christians.

Cutting the elderly Herul's throat seemed to have upset Ballista. He had not been himself since Pythonissa cursed him the year before. Having to kill Philemuth had made him worse. He could still make the odd joke, but something boyish in him had been lost. He looked withdrawn, glum. He rode along with the expedition like a passenger, caught up in it by mistake, rather than the leader it required. He needed something to take his mind off the Herul. Maximus was worried about Ballista. He could think of nothing better than a fight to bring Ballista out of his passivity, to bring him back to himself.

Of course, part of it was that Maximus owed a great debt to Ballista. The Angle had purchased him from a gladiatorial troop. Most would consider that a good turn beyond price. But it was not all that. Maximus had not minded fighting as a gladiator. Actually, he had enjoyed the applause of the crowd. Killing men in the arena, on a battlefield; what difference did it make? He had slaughtered people in all sorts of strange places. His mind wandered to the enormous aqueduct outside Nemausus in Gaul. Nasty, long way down for the fellow.

It was nothing to do with the arena or any of that. The debt was more recent. It went back to Africa. Ballista had saved his life there. Maximus could still picture the moment clearly – losing his footing on the marble floor, his sword jarred out of his reach –

always attached it by a wrist loop since then – the fierce brown face, the raised sword, and Ballista cutting the man down.

Maximus had sworn he would not take his freedom until he had repaid Ballista. Yet he had accepted manumission anyway, on a burnt hillside among the remnants of a defeated army. They had all thought they were going to die. But that made no difference. They had not died, and the debt still existed. Maximus would settle it with Ballista one day. They were bound together, and, if truth be told, Maximus loved the man. It was that simple.

They were riding, the three of them, with the Suanian Tarchon tagging along behind. They were well to the north of the dust and noise of the column. Young Wulfstan and Ochus were yet further out. The Heruli were still trying to help Wulfstan master the nomad draw from a galloping horse. Ochus now took over when Aluith was needed elsewhere. The Steppe spread all around. It was less flat here. There was a wind. The grass rolled in waves. Flowers flashed on the dark-green surface. The Steppe looked like an ocean when the sun was on it, but the storm was swelling.

Ballista and Calgacus were banging on the same drum about the murders.

'It was a lone madman,' Calgacus said.

'If I were you, I would not be so sure,' Maximus put in.

'Not more daemons,' Ballista said.

'Yes, lots of daemons. It is not just your male daemons fucking horrible Gothic harridans. Hippothous told me about the nomads. They descend from Heracles mating with a female daemon out on the Steppe. And her relatives are still out here. You are riding along, in the middle of nowhere, and there is a beautiful woman. She shows you her tits – fine, they are. She gets you all stirred up. You jump off your horse, ready to jump on her. And what do you find? Not a nice warm delta ready for the ploughing, oh no. From the waist down, those daemons are snakes. And they crush you to death. Your body starts to go rotten in an instant.'

Calgacus rolled his eyes in comic exasperation.

'I hear the same thing happens quite often in Libya,' commented Ballista.

'Hippothous may be off his head, but sure he has prodigious learning,' Maximus said.

'The killings are the work of a madman.' The Caledonian addressed himself to Ballista. 'You say it is all in some old Greek books, but only the insane would mutilate men like that in reality.'

'Who?' Ballista asked.

'There is no shortage of probable lunatics among our travelling companions,' Calgacus said. 'That *gudja*; bones in his hair, muttering incantations all the time, claims he talks to the other world. Come to that, there is the hideous *haliurunna* with him.'

'She looks a bit old and feeble to be strangling and stabbing grown men, even if it is only eunuchs and slaves,' Maximus said. 'And there is all the effort of cutting them up afterwards.'

'If she really is a witch, maybe she gets one of your endless daemons to help her,' Calgacus replied. 'And what about that centurion Hordeonius? Nasty bit of work, and he hates slaves and eunuchs with a vengeance.'

'We do not know anything about the interpreter Biomasos, the *haruspex* Porsenna, or any of the official staff,' Ballista said. 'And the same goes for the auxiliaries. Apart from it is a certainty there are a few *frumentarii* among the two groups.'

'It could be Hippothous,' Maximus said. 'Always peering into your face, he is, going on about seeing people's souls. Or Castricius – do not get me wrong, he has been through a lot with us – but all that stuff about the good daemon on his shoulder scaring off the spirits of death. And who knows what happened to him in Albania? If you ask me, they are both as mad as each other; as demented as a follower of Bacchus or Cybele, or whoever it is who cut their own balls off.'

'They do both read a lot of books,' Calgacus conceded.

'The Goths think reading books cuts your balls off, metaphorically speaking,' Ballista said. 'They could have a point.'

Something caught Maximus's eye; an unexpected movement way off to the south, beyond the dust of the wagons.

'Castricius and Hippothous have changed – got stranger – since we were in the Caucasus,' Ballista continued.

There it was again: tiny black shapes rising up out of a line of trees by one of the hidden watercourses. Ten, twenty of them – more – moving north.

'Over there.' Maximus pointed.

Calgacus squinted short-sightedly. But Ballista saw them. Tarchon had seen them too. He clattered up to join the others.

Forty or more horsemen, riding hard towards the caravan.

Hippothous was out front of the caravan, riding with the four Heruli. The nomads did not talk much, and when they did it was in the language of Germania. Hippothous did not mind. A couple of them, Andonnoballus and Berus, spoke Greek. He passed the odd comment with them, but most of the time he was happy to ride in silence.

The long column stretched away behind. The wagon of the Gothic priest came first, the other nine, strung out in single file, following. Almost lost in the dust behind was the herd of Heruli horses, spare mounts and pack animals. The nomads' slaves cantered around, hazing the horses into order.

Hippothous enjoyed the Steppe. The patterns made in the grass by the strong breeze pleased him. There were clouds chasing south. The big sky was shades of variegated blue, like the most delicate intaglio work, where a skilled craftsman had cut away layers of glass. There was a freedom to the expanse of the Steppe. There was space for a man to be what he wanted. The Heruli might be almost the antithesis of Hellenic civic life, but there was something strangely appealing about them. They offered opportunities. It was true they were ruled by a king – and from what he heard, Naulobates was attempting to set himself up as a tyrant – but at the same time they still seemed to have something approaching a rough, barbaric democracy. Clearly, men could say what they thought. Hippothous liked the fact that a man could rise on his merits. One of Naulobates' chiefs had been a Greek slave in Trapezus. A man achieved status among them by his deeds in war and his words in council. Aside from the Rosomoni, birth did not count; nor, seemingly, wealth. Unlike in the *imperium*, a man's past did not weigh him down. Hippothous thought he might do well with them. He was not bound to Ballista for ever. Ballista seemed to have less and less use for him as an *accensus*. As things were turning out, he might have to leave the northerner's *familia* soon.

A corncrake took off in front of his horse. The following wind puffed the bird's feathers up, giving it the size and appearance of a startled chicken.

One of the Heruli – Aluith – called out, his tone urgent. Hippothous looked to the south, where he was pointing. Horsemen, fifty or more, on small Steppe ponies. They must be Alani. They were over half a mile away, but closing fast.

A burst of guttural talk among the Heruli was cut short by Andonnoballus. He issued what had to be orders. Aluith wheeled his mount and set off in the direction of the leading wagon. Andonnoballus spoke some more. Pharas and Berus hared off towards the tail of the column. They kept to the far side of the approaching Alani.

Andonnoballus was about to leave when he remembered Hippothous. 'The Alani are after your Roman gold and our horses.

We are going to circle the wagons. You should choose a place to fight.' He spoke in Greek. He grinned. 'Try to stay alive.' He booted his horse, and clattered off after Aluith.

Hippothous wondered what to do. He circled his horse. There was no sign of Ballista and the others to the north. Where in Hades had they gone? The first wagon was turning. The Sarmatian driver was plying his whip; the oxen shambling into a run. The Alani were still a way off. Hippothous could see them clearly now. Big men on small horses – they seemed top-heavy. It might have looked funny, if they were not so dangerous. They were all unarmoured. No banners flew above them. They were splitting up. The largest group – twenty- or thirty-strong – was angling towards the rear of the wagon train and the Heruli horse herd. Another, smaller bunch was aiming at the centre of the column. The final group, a dozen or so, was going to skirt around the front. They were coming straight towards Hippothous.

What to do? Hippothous considered riding away to the north. If the Alani were just after loot, they might not chase him. But then he would be alone on the Steppe. He was not ready for that. And he wanted to impress the Heruli. He might well need them. His own possessions were in the last wagon. His books – his precious copy of Polemon – and armour, his money and his slave, Narcissus; he was not about to let the nomads have them. He sawed on the reins and kicked his horse into a gallop in the tracks of Pharas and Berus.

Hippothous cut across the lead wagon. It was obvious at a glance the circle would not be complete in time. The Alani would reach it in a few moments. He could hear them whooping.

As Hippothous raced past the third and fourth wagons, he saw the Roman auxiliaries peering out. They looked baffled. Gods below – he ought to do something. He skidded his horse around alongside.

'Where is your centurion?'

The soldiers looked blankly at him.

'Where is Hordeonius?' This time, he remembered to put it in Latin, the language of the army.

'No idea, *Dominus*.'

Hippothous cursed. What should he do? Fuck. He swore like the lowest plebeian. His life as a bandit chief told him they should all just run. Maybe sacrifice someone so the rest could get away. He had no real experience of commanding troops in battle. The auxiliaries were looking at him expectantly. What would Ballista do?

'You lot in the first wagon, protect the gold in the legate's wagon ahead of you.' He had to bellow to make himself heard. 'The rest of you, follow me.'

The soldiers looked irresolute.

'Now!' Hippothous roared.

The auxiliaries tumbled out of the moving wagons, falling, tripping, dropping their weapons, their *disciplina* a thing of ignominy.

'Follow me!'

Hippothous set off again towards the rear. He kept to a slow canter, trying to give the five soldiers on foot a chance to keep up. He looked over his shoulder. They were running, but falling behind anyway.

The Alani had reached the rear of the caravan. There was fighting amidst the herd of horses. The two Heruli and their six slaves had to be outnumbered at least three to one. Horses were trumpeting, stampeding in all directions. A thick pall of dust swirled over the chaos. A little nearer, some of the Alani were swarming around the rear of the wagons. Hippothous dug in his heels. With luck, the auxiliaries would follow him into the fight.

The Sarmatian driver of Hippothous's wagon stood straddle-legged on the box. He wielded his whip with a will; lashing across the backs of his oxen then sending the vicious, knotted bullhide snaking out at any Alani horsemen who got too near. But he could not cover the rear of the wagon. Two Alani rode there, one of them leading a riderless horse.

Hippothous dragged his mount around so that he was going alongside the wagon. He lifted himself by the twin horns at the front of his saddle and wedged his left boot against the near-side one. His horse was only cantering, to keep pace with the wagon, yet the evident danger of falling under the wheels made the speed appear greater. Hippothous checked that his sword and weapons were not caught on the saddle. He steeled himself to jump. There was a burst of whooping behind him. An arrow shot past his head. He felt the wind of its passing and jumped.

Hippothous's timing was all wrong. His shins barked against the side of the wagon. He was thrown head first on to the box and collided with the driver. It was like hitting a tree. Hippothous rebounded. Hands flailing, fingernails scrabbling on the wood, he was slipping, face down, back off the wagon.

A hand grabbed his shoulder. He was hauled up on to the box. Holding on for dear life, he struggled to his feet. The wagon was lurching and bumping like a mad thing. Hippothous started to thank the Sarmatian. But the driver grunted something and jerked his head back towards the enclosed body of the wagon. Above the clatter and squealing, Hippothous could hear screaming.

The Sarmatian flicked the long bullwhip out as one of the Alani pressed up from the rear. The rider ducked, and reined back. He was reaching for his bow.

Still clutching at one of the uprights, Hippothous drew his sword. He pulled back the felt hanging with his sword hand and stepped into the tent.

It took a time for his eyes to adjust to the gloom. He kept his blade out in front. There was sobbing, shouting, the clash of steel.

Two slaves – one of them Narcissus – were huddled down to his left. They were crying, their hands up in futile supplication.

Another figure was standing with his back to Hippothous. It was the interpreter Biomasos. He had a sword and was desperately fending off the attack of an Alan. There was a body on the floor behind the nomad. There was a reek of blood, and an acrid stench of urine and fear.

Hippothous went to aid the interpreter. He moved to his right. The floor of the wagon punched up under his feet and he staggered forward.

The Alan lunged. The point of his sword was aimed at Hippothous's chest. Boots scrabbling for purchase, Hippothous got his own sword in the way. Sparks flew. The Alan retrieved his weapon, regained his balance, readying himself to strike again.

For a few frozen moments, the three men stood swaying. Pots and pans, any number of things, rattled and rolled around the dim interior.

The Alan feinted at Hippothous, then twisted and cut at the interpreter. The sword hit the interpreter's forearm. A howl of agony, and Biomasos reeled away. Clutching his injury, he lost his balance and went crashing into the side of the tent. He went down, curled up in pain.

Hippothous struck. The Alan somehow wrenched his body out of the way. The momentum of Hippothous's blow drove them together, chest to chest. The nomad's beard rasped Hippothous's face. Crushed together, boots shuffling and stamping, neither could get his sword into play. Their breath mingled, hot and foul.

Hippothous clawed with his left hand at the man's eyes. The nomad got a grip on Hippothous's throat, then shoved him away.

Fighting for balance, both men got their weapons up. As the wagon jolted along, they rolled like sailors in a storm; both searching for an opening. The eyes of the Alan were black, blazing with bloodlust.

The wagon lurched. Some instinct warned Hippothous. He half turned, putting his back to the side of the wagon. With his left hand he unsheathed the dagger on his right hip and brought it up to guard his left.

Another Alan was climbing into the wagon from the front. Hippothous made to thrust at his first opponent then swayed back, driving the dagger at the newcomer.

The wagon suddenly yawed to the left. All three fighting men went staggering across to the opposite side of the tent. The wounded interpreter underfoot threatened to trip Hippothous, but he pushed himself back upright off a wooden strut. The two Alani also recovered. On either side of him, the steel in their hands glinted wickedly. Hippothous realized this could end only one way.

The Alan on his left yelled. His sword clattered to the floor. His hands clawed at his left leg. A small knife – something innocuous like a fruit knife – was embedded in his thigh. Narcissus was scuttling back out of the way.

Hippothous and the first Alan swung at the same moment – each hoping the other was distracted. Hippothous dropped to one knee. The nomad's blade thrummed just over his head. It cracked through an upright, and tore a gash in the side of the tent. Hippothous's sword took the man at the right knee. The man collapsed like a punctured wineskin, blood gushing.

Bright light poured through the rent in the coverings.

Hippothous rounded on the other Alan. The man was doubled up, long hair hanging down. He had wrenched the knife from his thigh, and dropped it. Both his hands were pressed tight to his wound. Sensing Hippothous, the nomad's head came up. His open mouth was a wet, red circle in his beard. Hippothous smashed the hilt of his sword into the man's face. Teeth and bone shattered.

The Alan went down, Hippothous landing on top of him. Releasing his sword, he seized the man's chin, yanked it up. He sawed his dagger across the exposed throat. The Alan's blood was hot, soaking Hippothous's clothes.

Rolling off the man, Hippothous looked for his sword. It was gone somewhere out of sight. There was debris strewn everywhere, all of it bloodied. Hippothous still had the dagger. On hands and knees, like a beast red in tooth and claw, he hurled himself down the wagon at the other nomad.

The Alan had lost his sword. Too slow to draw his dagger, he tried to fend off the attack with his bare hands. Hippothous slashed and stabbed with his dagger. The nomad's arms were no defence. Hippothous pinned one down, hacked the other aside. Again and again he plunged the eight inches of steel into the man's chest and stomach. It took a long time for him to stop moving.

Hippothous dragged himself to his feet. The wagon had come to a standstill.

Snatching up a sword – not his own – Hippothous stumbled over the scattered belongings and dead bodies to the rear of the wagon. Pulling back the hanging, he saw three more Alani galloping towards the immobile wagon.

Gods below, this had to be the end.

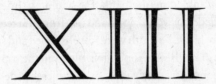

XIII

Ballista led them along the bed of the small river. The bottom was firm, and the water came only up to the hocks of their horses. There were no trees flanking the stream, but there were dense patches of reeds. The vegetation on the banks was very green. A brace of snipe flew up, and winged around them.

As soon as Maximus had seen the Alani, Ballista had called Wulfstan and Ochus in from the north. Before the Alani had reached the convoy, Ballista had taken his men down into the stream, out of sight.

Above the plugging hooves, the rattle of harness and the wind sighing in the reeds, they could hear fighting. Ballista knew they were heading in the right general direction, although the high banks prevented them seeing anything. Ballista looked over his shoulder. They were all there, in single file: Maximus, Calgacus, Wulfstan, Tarchon, and the Herul Ochus. He kept them down to a very careful canter. The water splashed up like a spray of diamonds in the sun.

The river turned to the east. Ballista thought this was as near as the cover would get them. He held up his hand to halt them, and reined back his mount. Jumping down, he got water in his boots. He handed his reins to Maximus and made the universal signal for silence – a finger to the lips – and an impromptu palm-down motion to indicate that no one was to move. The horsemen nodded.

Ballista scrambled up the bank. He had no helmet or hat, and hoped his blond hair would not stand out from the reeds. His cloak and tunic were black, but both were travel-stained and sun-bleached, so might not draw the eye too much. Nearing the top of the bank, he got down on his stomach and, parting the reeds delicately, wriggled forward. Probably he was exercising too much caution: the fight must be at least two hundred yards away.

Ballista was good at fieldcraft. He had been well trained. First, by his father's people, the Angles; then by those of his maternal uncle, the Harii; finally, by everything that could be thrown at him during twenty-five years with Roman armies. But he was surprised. He had misjudged their progress. The nearest Alani were only about fifty yards away. Their attention was on the wagon train, and so away from him.

The wagons were motionless, the defensive circle incomplete; more of a Latin 'C', with a lengthened and straight upper curve. Ballista could see at a glance why: a dead ox in the traces of the second wagon. At the lower left of the 'C', just in front of Ballista, three Alani were exchanging arrows with the occupants of the lead wagon. Ballista spotted the *gudja* at its rear, the Sarmatian driver at the front, and the long, red head of one of the Rosomoni aiming through a slit roughly hacked in the side. It was clear the Alani were not pressing home their attack but merely keeping the men in the wagon occupied.

A little further to the left, half a dozen or so Alani horsemen were riding away from the second wagon. A couple of loose horses ran with them, and there were at least three of the nomads left behind dead on the ground; an assault had failed. That was Ballista's own wagon. In it was half the gold and other gifts intended for Naulobates.

There was little to be seen of the rest of the fighting from Ballista's position. Nothing really, apart from Alani in the middle distance racing here and there, and a huge swirling cloud of dust beyond the wagons. That was back where the Heruli herd had been. It seemed to be the scene of the worst fighting.

Could five men and a boy make a difference? The whole was a messy, large-scale fight. Maybe they could, if they had surprise on their side. The Alani being closer than he had thought might help. Ballista wriggled and slid back down to the others.

Taking his reins back from Maximus, he swung back into the saddle. He gestured the others to come close, and quietly explained what he had seen. He outlined his plan, such as it was, in the language of the north. He spoke slowly so Tarchon could follow.

'With the exception of Ochus, they will all be better horse archers than we are. So we have to get in close, try to trap them against the wagons, fight hand to hand. With luck, we might break them with our impetus. It is a pity we are not armoured, but our horses are bigger. Wrap your cloaks around your left arms to act as a sort of shield. We will charge in a boar's snout. I will be at the apex. Wulfstan, you will tuck in behind.'

The boy bridled, but Ballista silenced him with a look.

'Now, we need to get the horses out of this stream.'

About fifty yards further along was a break where largish animals – maybe deer or wild horses – came down to drink. They scrambled out on to the Steppe and formed up.

The three Alani were still skirmishing with the men in the first wagon. Four of the others had dismounted. Their horses were being held by their remaining mounted comrade. The ones on foot were preparing to storm the second wagon. They were about a hundred yards away.

Ballista arranged his cloak, unsheathed his long sword. As so often over the years, Maximus had taken station on his right; Tarchon fell in beyond the Hibernian. Calgacus was on Ballista's left, Ochus beyond him. Ballista noticed the Herul had his bow in his hands. That was fine; it was the weapon of his people. Young Wulfstan's horse was just behind, screened by the older riders. He would be safe in the first clash.

As Ballista took them straight from a walk into a controlled gallop, one of the Alani duelling with the first wagon saw them coming. The nomad yelled, pointed. As he did so, an arrow pitched him off his horse. But he had alerted the two men with him. Now they shouted warnings to the others. But they did not stop to fight or see if their yells were heeded. They wheeled their mounts and raced off between the two wagons.

Ballista angled the arrowhead of horsemen towards the remaining Alani. The ground thundered under the charge. The nomads hurled themselves on to their ponies, yanked their heads round and set off after their fleeing kinsmen. They did not even shoot back over the tails of their mounts.

Ballista slackened the pace, roaring for everyone to close up. He heard the blood roaring in his ears and laughed out loud. For the first time in months, he felt exhilarated, intensely alive; a man who could influence his own destiny.

As they cantered between the wagons, auxiliary soldiers stuck their heads out of the second one. They gave a thin cheer. Maybe they were not as bad as Ballista had thought. Maybe their centurion was not such a useless martinet after all. The *gudja* and Andonnoballus popped their heads out of the other wagon. Ballista waved. Andonnoballus placed the palm of his right hand to his forehead. The *gudja* did not respond.

Emerging into the centre of the part-formed wagon-laager, Ballista saw the seven retreating Alani approaching another group of about ten nomads. The latter were caracoling in front of one of the central wagons, against which they had trapped a small knot of the Cilician auxiliaries. The nomads galloped in, shooting as they went. About thirty paces out, they spun their mounts around then galloped away, shooting more arrows behind them. They were operating as individuals, but the combined effect was that there were always a lot of arrows hurtling towards the Roman soldiers.

You could not fault the Alani horsemanship, but Ballista thought they were poorly led. Where they were in the centre of the semi-circle of wagons, they were enfiladed by half a dozen of the wagon drivers. These Sarmatians were shooting fast. There were a couple of Romans on the ground. But there were also a few loose Steppe ponies, and at least two Alani were down and looked unlikely to get up.

As the fugitive Alani riders reached those manoeuvring, they all whooped and, bending low over the necks of their ponies, melted away through the gaps between the wagons. In a moment, they had vanished off to the south.

Ballista brought his small group to a halt. Horses and men were blowing hard. So far, it could not have gone better – provided those Alani did not rally and return. He dismissed the possibility from his thinking. Long ago, on the Danube, his old general Gallus had told him that a vital element of command was the ability to put things out of your mind. Ballista had to concentrate on the real test that lay ahead.

Three Alani horsemen were galloping towards the last wagon. It was slewed out of line. Its driver lay dead some way off. Ballista could see movement inside. The remaining half of the gold and presents were in there. Should he intervene? No, if they were to survive this, they had to break the main body of the Alani.

Beyond the wagons, to the west, was utter chaos. Dozens of horses were stampeding and fighting; some in groups, some individually. Biting and kicking, white-eyed, mouths streaming, their flanks were thick with roped sweat. Most were riderless. Through the kicked-up dust and turf, some warriors could be seen hunched and twisting in the saddle. Many more of the riders wore the embroidered tunics and full beards of the Alani than the bulkier coats of the Heruli. Just one, possibly two, elongated red heads of the Rosomoni showed for a moment and were gone.

Ballista looked at the scene as a weak swimmer would look at a river in spate. If they went into that vortex, how could they hope to escape?

To Ballista's left, Ochus shifted posture. His brothers were fighting, probably dying. It was no time for reflection.

'The same as before,' Ballista said. 'We keep together, pin them against the loose horses, fight hand to hand. When we come out the other side, we wheel as one, go back in.'

They all nodded.

'Are you ready?'

'Ready.'

'Time to go.'

The same as before, Ballista thought. But it was not. This time, the Alani would not obligingly run away. Ballista knew that none of them was likely to come out the other side.

As if to prove his prescience, a line of Alani formed at the edge of the maelstrom. There were ten or so, grim-faced, bows drawn.

The wedge of horsemen gathered speed, Ballista at their apex. He saw the arrows released and crouched forward, trying to make as small a target as possible. If only he had armour, a helmet. The grass sped past. No arrow touched him. The smell of hot horse was strong.

The horse on his left stumbled. The feathers of an arrow

protruded from its chest. The horse lost its rhythm. Its front legs folded and it tipped forward, like a ship pitch-polling. Ballista saw old Calgacus frantically trying to push himself out of the horns of the saddle, trying to throw himself clear. Allfather, the thing was going to crush him, bury him with its weight.

Ballista heard the crash behind him. He could not see it. An arrow whipped past his face. Wulfstan was attempting to close up on his left. Ochus forced him back. The Herul was knee to knee with Ballista.

The Alani facing Ballista had drawn his sword. Ballista set his mount straight at the nomad. The animals ran into each other, chest to chest. The impact threw Ballista half out of the saddle, up on the neck. His horse was jarred to a standstill. The Alani Steppe pony had been knocked back on its haunches. Its rider was only just clinging on. Ballista recovered his seat, kicked on. His mount gathered itself, sprang forward.

He went to cut down to the left, across the neck of his horse. Another Alani swung at him from the right. Ballista brought his blade back, blocked the blow. The swords sang as they slid edge to edge.

A space opened, and Ballista was clear. No rider in proximity. He wheeled his horse around. It felt lame on a foreleg. Two Alani were flanking Wulfstan. The young Angle fended away the first blow. He ducked. The second narrowly missed his scalp.

Ballista booted his horse towards the fight. Wulfstan caught another thrust on his sword, but his left side was exposed. An Alani blade flashed. Ballista's shouted warning was lost in the uproar.

From nowhere, an arrow took the Alani in the neck. He toppled as his pony ran on.

Ochus backed his mount, seeking a clear shot at Wulfstan's other opponent.

The Alani saw Ballista coming, turned his mount on its toes.

Ballista cut to the head. The nomad's blade came up. Ballista altered the angle. His sword cut deep into his opponent's forearm. The man howled. Ballista withdrew the weapon, and thrust it into the nomad's chest.

A blood-splattered Maximus surged alongside. Ballista circled his horse. The animal pecked as he did so. He was not sure it would stand long; it was in the hands of the *norns*. He put it out of his mind. Maximus was here, so too Wulfstan and Tarchon. The four were alone – Ochus had vanished, Calgacus was fallen.

A half-circle of Alani ringed them.

'Close up!' Ballista shouted. 'Fight our way out together.'

As they jostled into line, the Alani backed their mounts. Then, without a signal, the nomads turned and rode off into the thinning battle.

Ochus galloped up.

'They are going,' the Herul said. 'They are driving off most of our herd, but they are going. It is over for now.'

Hippothous watched the smoke from the pyre. Its lower stages were silver-grey, gnarled and massive, like the trunk of an ancient olive tree. Higher the wind took it, and plumed it away to the south. Hippothous was still surprised to be alive to see it.

When he had seen the three Alani galloping towards the wagon, he had gone back into the body of the vehicle. He had ordered Narcissus to his feet. The boy was shaking. Hippothous told him he had done well with the dagger. He picked up an Alani sword from the floor, put it in the slave's hands. Hippothous sent him to the rear opening, told him to hit anyone who tried to climb in. If he did well, he would have his freedom. Narcissus had stumbled to his post.

Hippothous had tried to do similarly with the other slave, the one owned by the centurion. It had done no good. The whipling just cowered, sobbing. Hippothous kicked him hard.

The interpreter had staggered up. He had tied a makeshift tourniquet on his arm. He half fell as he bent to get a sword. Hippothous had told him instead to find a bow and bring it to him. Hippothous's own spare *gorytus* was somewhere in the tent, and he was sure he had seen another. But the gods knew where – things were scattered all about. The interior was like the end of a Macedonian drinking session.

Hippothous had taken his own station at the front. He had peered out of the hanging. An arrow had winged towards him. He had ducked back.

The sounds of fighting, the whooping of the Alani and the higher yipping of the Heruli came from outside. In the gloom, Hippothous waited, trying to master his breathing, trying to fight down his fear.

After what seemed an eon, the noise lessened. Hippothous had peeped out again. The Alani had gone.

Hippothous had emerged into the ghastly aftermath. There were loose horses, some still running; others were wounded, either head down standing still, or limping. There were broken bits of weaponry in the grass, and arrows sprouting on unlikely surfaces. And, wherever you looked, there were dead men strewn. Ten were dead from the caravan: three auxiliaries, two of the Heruli – Aluith and Beras – and two of their slaves, the slave of the interpreter, and two Sarmatian drivers. Three others were severely wounded: old Calgacus, another auxiliary, and one of the Roman scribes. Mysteriously, two men were missing: Castricius and Hordeonius the centurion. No one had seen them during the fighting, and no one could remember where they had been before it started.

The Alani had left twelve of their number dead on the trampled grass. Hippothous was not squeamish – far from it – but watching the Heruli scalp and skin them had been unsettling. The Heruli were skilled; their long knives flicked and sliced quickly. They took extra trouble over where the skin of the Alani was tattooed. Andonnoballus assured him the tattoos made the best trophies; wearing them made certain the dead men could not escape serving their killers in the afterlife. Hippothous knew most Hellenes would be both shocked and revolted by both deeds and belief, but as Herodotus had written everywhere, custom was king. Who was he to judge their habits? The mutilated corpses – repulsive pink-blue things, no longer human – were thrown out on the Steppe for the birds of the air and the beasts of the Steppe to eat.

Now, the next day, their own fallen – Heruli, Romans and Sarmatians – were consigned to the flames. It was not the elaborate and measured cremation of Philemuth. There were too many bodies and there was too little time. But you could not fault the Heruli for offerings: gold, furs, unguents, all sorts of expensive goods. Hippothous was impressed. Such disregard for the things of this world could allow the freedom to concentrate on the things that really mattered: on the souls of men – your own and others.

It was a large pyre. It had taken the remainder of the day of the ambush and the following morning to build. Two of the wagons had been dismantled to add to its bulk. Again, Hippothous was full of admiration. It exhibited a ruthless pragmatism, providing more firewood while also shortening the baggage train. After all, they were now two drivers short.

The pyre had more than enough room for Aluith and Berus to be placed a little apart. All the others would be interred here where they fell. The bones of the two Rosomoni, however, were to be carried back to the summer camp of the Heruli. Andonnoballus said there were further rites to be done. Everywhere, custom is king.

The smoke streamed out, high and long across the plains. It would be visible for many miles.

'Will they come again?' Ballista put the question that all the survivors had been thinking, but none had asked.

'They might not,' Andonnoballus said. 'They had no banners, and none of them had armour. There were none of their nobles riding among them. It might be they were just a raiding party of young warriors out to prove themselves, maybe even from the Aorsoi or the Sirachoi or some other tribe subject to the Alani. It could be they were just bandits.'

The older Herul, Pharas, shook his elongated head. 'I do not think so, *Atheling*. They were well informed. They knew which wagons held the Roman diplomatic gifts. But more than that – they fought too hard. Bandits never want to leave twelve of their own behind.'

Hippothous knew that was true.

'They could have left their banners and armour off, hoping we would think them just a party of bandits,' Pharas continued. 'Safrax, the King of the Alani, is cunning. He could hope to get the Roman gold and our horses, maybe to kill the man who defeated him last year at the Caspian Gates, and then if your . . . if King Naulobates threatened him with war, Safrax can deny it was any of his doing.'

'If they come, next time we will be ready,' Andonnoballus said. 'We have pickets out, a well-formed wagon-laager. Tomorrow, we will keep proper march discipline.'

Hippothous noted what he did not say. There were only just over twenty fit fighting men left with the caravan: Andonnoballus and Pharas themselves, their two Heruli ex-slaves, six Roman auxiliaries, eight Sarmatian drivers, the Gothic *gudja*, and Ballista, Maximus and Hippothous himself.

'How long before the two messengers you sent yesterday will reach the camp of Naulobates?' Ballista asked.

Straight after the retreat of the Alani, even as the dead were being numbered and collected, Andonnoballus had presented the four surviving Heruli slaves with the shields of freedom. Two of them were immediately sent to get help. Thoughtful of encirclement, Andonnoballus ordered them initially to ride in different directions; one to the north-east, one due north.

'It is some distance to the summer camp,' Andonnoballus replied.

'How long before they get there, and how long before Naulobates' men will reach us?' Ballista was insistent.

Andonnoballus and Pharas looked at each other. Pharas shrugged.

'Riding hard – and they each have four spare horses – they might get there by nightfall today.' Andonnoballus stopped.

'And how long before we can expect relief?' Ballista was not going to be deflected.

'It might take a couple of days for King Naulobates to gather a large war party. After that, three days to ride down here.' Andonnoballus smiled. 'But, of course, we will be moving towards them ourselves.'

'Four days at the minimum, more likely five, and it could even be six,' Ballista said. 'That is, if your men got through.'

'If they got through,' Andonnoballus agreed.

XIV

Calgacus was being trampled and kicked. The hooves were coming down so hard the ground was bucking, throwing him from side to side. The worst was the horse stamping on his right shoulder and arm. It was quite deliberate. The pain was unbelievable. He cried out. Someone was lifting his head. A flask was put to his lips. Liquid ran into his mouth and throat. It tasted bad. He choked, coughing it up. The flask was back at his lips. A familiar voice was talking some soothing but insistent rubbish. *Swallow it, swallow it.* He swallowed the stuff. They laid his head down. The noise and movement and pain receded. The darkness came back.

They were back in Sicily, out on the estate on the lower slopes of Aetna. Maximus had bought a horse. It was a big bay Sarmatian, called Akinakes. Anyone but the half-witted Hibernian could see it was unbreakable – cunning as a snake, vicious beyond reckoning. The thing was even named after some eastern weapon. Ballista had been holding the twitch when Maximus put the roller on its back. Feeling the unaccustomed weight, the mad animal had reared. Ignoring the pain of the twine twisted tight around its upper lip, it had torn the wooden handle of the twitch clean out of Ballista's hands.

The pain was white, then a dark red. Figures moved in its murk. One had bones in his hair. He was talking quietly to Ballista. It was the *gudja*. More of the unpleasant liquid at Calgacus's mouth. Everything slipped away again.

Somehow, the Hibernian had got a saddle on the horse. They were in the big stone barn. It was always cool and dark in there. The Sarmatian was standing, ears back, showing a lot of white of eye. *Sure, I will be fine*. Maximus vaulted on to its back. For a moment, nothing happened. *Let go the bridle*. Ballista let it go. The horse took off. Ballista dived back over the gate out of the way. Rearing, plunging, the horse careered around the confined space. Maximus clung on like a monkey.

The horse stopped. It was snorting. Maximus grinned. The horse backed towards the wall. Maximus booted it forward. The horse ignored him. Maximus booted it some more. The horse reared high on to its back legs. Maximus clung on. The horse threw itself over backwards. It smashed Maximus against the wall. It slid down. Maximus was trapped, the immense weight of the horse grinding him against the rough stonework.

The horse scrambled up. Maximus lay unmoving. Long whip in hand, Calgacus jumped off the gate, Ballista with him. Quite deliberately, the horse kicked out at Maximus's prone body – once, twice, three times. Then, careless of the lashes, it trotted to the far end of the barn. Bastard animal, utterly evil; as bad as any man.

The dark receded. The pain was back; the jolting, the thumping, the deafening noise. Gods, it all hurt. Calgacus opened his eyes.

Ballista was leaning over him. The lad smiled. He was trying not to look worried.

Maximus peered down at Calgacus. 'You are not dead then.'

The Hibernian handed some coins to Ballista. He looked at Calgacus with grave disappointment. 'I had a bet you would die.'

Ballista helped Calgacus sit up a little, gave him a drink. Watered wine, no hint of anything else.

Calgacus was in their wagon. It was rattling along faster than he had yet known. They had put lots of cushions and rugs under and around him, but they were still being jarred around. The motion was agony. His arm was splinted, and his shoulder strapped.

'How long?' Calgacus said.

'Bugger,' Maximus said. He handed more coins to Ballista. 'I said your first words would be a more traditional *Where am I?*'

'Three days inclusive,' Ballista said. 'You came round later that day. We gave you the poppy and a lot of drink, kept you near-unconscious all yesterday.'

'My arm?'

'Broken. The *gudja* set it. He is not happy with your shoulder either.'

'Nor am I.'

'You remember what happened?' Maximus asked.

'Of course I fucking remember. A horse buried me.'

'Actually, no,' Maximus said. 'You jumped clear. You just fell awkwardly, bust your arm, knocked yourself out; all very clumsy.'

'Wulfstan?' Calgacus asked.

'Fine,' Ballista said. 'He has cooked you some food, been keeping it warm on a brazier, nearly set fire to the wagon.'

'Chicken soup, sure it is finer than your mother made,' Maximus put in.

'Anyone else?' Calgacus said.

'No one that matters; except Castricius is missing. So is the centurion,' answered Maximus.

'Missing out here is not good,' said Calgacus.

Wulfstan came into the covered part of the wagon with the food. The other two left. Wulfstan helped him eat, gave him more wine and more poppy. Calgacus fell into a narcotic half-sleep.

When next Calgacus woke, Tarchon was staring at him.

'I am most pleased you did not die,' the Suanian said.

'So am I.'

'If you have been dead, I could not have repaid my debt.'

'No, I suppose not.' Calgacus was not sure he was ready for this sort of conversation concerning Suanian honour. He gestured for Tarchon to pass him a drink. 'And would you open the hangings?'

'However, *Kyrios*, if you have dead, I still can repay Ballista.'

'Will the Alani come again?' Calgacus asked.

'Most likely. But we are running away as fast as the wind – well, as fast as oxen go. Also, the longhead Andonnoballus and the *kyrios* Ballista have been busy, most thorough.'

'Huhn.' Calgacus made a noise indicating he doubted it, but Tarchon should explain anyway.

'The Heruli are out on all sides as . . .' Tarchon said something in Suanian. 'How you say in Greek? *Kaka* . . . something.'

'*Kataskopoi*,' Calgacus said. 'And apart from the scouts?'

'It is highly thorough. The wagons goes in two lines; the first and the last ready to turn in to form a laager. That is right – laager?'

'Yes, laager; a northern word, a camp or temporary fort.'

'Good – laager. Anyhow, there is just eight wagon now. The stores ride in two not three, and the soldiers haves one not two. Other soldier ride in the one with the eunuch Amantius, and another with the' – a Suanian word, obviously not flattering – 'mans of the staff, as well as a soldier in with each of the stores. The spare horses runs in the centre.' Tarchon grinned, proud of his grasp of things. 'See, we are most highly prepared.'

Calgacus made a sound expressing profound misgiving. 'How many fighting men are left?'

Tarchon started counting on his fingers. 'Do I count also the wounded?'

'No.'

'And not mans missing?'

'No – definitely not mans missing.'

'The Sarmatian drivers?'

'Yes.' Calgacus found it hard work, even without the pain.

Tarchon began counting again. 'Twenty-four.'

'We are fucked,' Calgacus said.

'Yes, we are most fucked.'

Calgacus lay back watching the sun arc up over the Steppe. It was hotter now they were into June. With every slight jolt, sharp stabs of pain shot through his shoulder and arm. His head ached dully.

'Where is Ballista?' Calgacus said.

'I get him for you, *Kyrios*.'

Calgacus rested as still as he could, swallowing the pain, trying to think through it.

Ballista and Maximus climbed into the wagon with Tarchon.

'How are you?' Ballista asked.

'We have changed direction,' Calgacus said.

'We are heading north-east to the camp of Naulobates,' said Ballista.

'Why now?' Calgacus's voice sounded weak and peevish to him.

'Because he is our only fucking hope,' Maximus said.

'You mean, why not before?' Ballista asked.

Calgacus grunted.

'Why did the Urugundi land us on the southern bank of the Tanais?' Ballista was frowning with concentration. 'Why not the northern side, head north-east, then cross the river higher up?'

Maximus and Tarchon had assumed thoughtful airs that failed to hide their incomprehension.

Ballista continued, thinking out loud. 'Why did first the *gudja* and then Andonnoballus lead us due east, through the grazing disputed between the Alani and the Heruli?'

Calgacus wheezed and muttered, 'Fucking clever now.'

'A deliberate provocation,' Ballista said. 'They both wanted the Alani to attack.'

'Maybe,' Calgacus grunted.

'Fuck,' Maximus said.

'Oh yes,' Tarchon put in brightly. 'As I was saying to the *kyrios* Calgacus, we are most fucked.'

'Why?' Ballista said.

A high call – *yip-yip-yip* – cut off any answer. Wulfstan stuck his head around the awning. 'Horseman approaching from the south-east.'

Everyone rushed out. Calgacus listened to them mounting, riding a little ahead.

After a time – hard to judge when he hurt that much – Calgacus rolled on to his good left arm, and painfully crawled to the front. He looked out over the right shoulder of the stolid Sarmatian driver.

A lone rider was coming. Even at a distance, it could be seen that his horse was dead beat. The man himself was slumped forward in the saddle.

A small knot of horsemen were waiting to one side of the wagon train. They were all gazing at the man approaching, except Ballista and Andonnoballus, who were looking all around, everywhere else.

'Not as fucking stupid as some,' Calgacus said to himself.

'Castricius,' Maximus shouted, 'you little bastard.'

The Roman let his horse stop next to the others. It looked ready to drop.

'What happened?' Ballista asked.

'I was out for a ride, bumped into a group of Alani warriors coming from the south. About a dozen of them chased me. I went off east. They followed – persistent buggers. Finally slipped back through them last night.' Under the ingrained dust, Castricius's face was pale.

'You are hurt,' Ballista said.

'It is nothing, a scratch.' Castricius put his hand to his left leg. 'The spirits of death are still not ready for me.' His small, angular face creased into a smile. 'And now, my good daemon has saved not just me, but all of you as well.'

Narcissus heard the commotion outside. He clambered through the cluttered wagon to see. It was time for the evening meal. A horse was loose in the camp. Something had spooked it. Unable to escape the encircling wagon-laager, it careered around, sending things flying, overturning cooking pots. Men ran after it, shouting, making things worse. The other horses were getting stirred up.

Let someone else deal with it. Narcissus had his orders. He went back into the empty wagon to continue sorting out everyone's jumbled possessions. He moved a heavy leather bag. A papyrus roll fell out. Narcissus had been educated to be a secretary. He unrolled the first sheet and went nearer the lamp to read. *Taking my start from you, Phoibos, I shall recall the glorious deeds of men of long ago who propelled the well-benched Argo* . . . It was the *Argonautica* of Apollonius of Rhodes.

A memory came to Narcissus, then the realization tumbled in: Mastabates asking about epic poetry, the denials that had been uttered, the killings and mutilations that had haunted the caravan, the ritual mutilations that followed that of Apsyrtus by Jason in the poem.

A noise outside. Without thought, Narcissus stuffed the roll into his tunic. He must tell someone, must tell Ballista.

Narcissus jumped down from the tailgate of the wagon. The camp was still in uproar.

'What have you got there?'

The voice was behind Narcissus. He spun round. 'Nothing.'

'Give it to me.'

Narcissus fished the roll out. 'I was just tidying, doing my duty.'

'Of course.'

The left hand held it out.

As Narcissus passed it over, the other's right fist closed on his throat. The papyrus fell to the ground. Narcissus clawed at the hand choking him. He could not break the grip. He could not shout. He was being dragged into the darkness out beyond the wagon.

The man got both hands on his throat. Blackness crowded Narcissus's vision. The terrible pressure increased.

'Just a dead slave' were the last words he heard.

XV

A Sarmatian driver answering a nocturnal call of nature had found the body. It lay outside the line of wagons, but not so far as where the sentries patrolled out in the dark. No attempt had been made to conceal it.

In the grey light before true dawn, there was no time to lose. Torches fizzed and spluttered. The oxen were put under the yokes, the laager broken, the two lines of wagons arranged, the scouts sent out. While all that was going on, men – subdued by the time of morning, the news of the body, and their own fears for the coming day – took what breakfast they could. Out where the corpse had been found, the two slaves owned by the auxiliaries dug a shallow grave.

Ballista and three others paused to inspect the remains of Narcissus. The light was gathering.

'Throat cut and strangled, very thorough,' Maximus said.

'Strangled, then throat cut,' Ballista amended. 'No point in strangling someone if you have already cut their throat.'

'What would be the point the other way around?'

'Make sure he was dead, not just unconscious, or' – Ballista pointed to the dried blood in Narcissus's hair – 'so that you had a blade to wipe the blood on the victim's head: "On his own head be it."'

'And you say the Greeks and Romans think that this might stop the dead man coming for revenge?' Maximus spoke in tones of incredulity at the childlike beliefs of the southerners.

'Poor Narcissus,' Hippothous said. 'He served me well.'

'Although, surely he was getting a bit long in the tooth for your tastes,' Castricius said. 'I thought your sort liked them young: downy cheeks, tight arses and such like.'

Hippothous did not react. 'I had promised him his freedom after the way he behaved when the Alani attacked. He was braver than you would expect from a slave secretary.'

'You should know,' Castricius said.

Hippothous half turned, hand going to hilt. 'What do you mean?'

Castricius grinned, his face all wrinkled amusement, not all of it false. 'Nothing deep. He was your slave. You were there. You should know.'

A high calling came from the front of the caravan; a high *yip-yipping* that was picked up by the other Heruli outriders. The wagon train was ready to move.

Ballista relaxed. They would not come to blows.

Maximus appeared oblivious, captivated by the flight of a bird far out over the Steppe. Ballista knew it was a pose.

'Time to go,' Ballista said. 'That will have to do.'

The two military slaves climbed up out of the grave. They had already removed Narcissus's boots, belt and purse. Now one of them removed a small coin from the purse and placed it into the dead slave's mouth. They offered the rest of the possessions to Hippothous. He told them to keep them. The slaves thanked Hippothous, then, with no ceremony, rolled the body of Narcissus into the hole, and started shovelling back the earth. It might be enough to keep off animals.

Ballista took the first watch as outrider to the north-west. Two of the Heruli always rode on the more likely approaches of the Alani to the south. The nomads knew the Steppe, knew how to recognize the signs. After four hours, Maximus cantered out to relieve him. Ballista had seen several vultures, a flock of crows, and some big mice, which scuttled away into holes. Away from the wagons, the grass sang and occasionally an invisible bird of prey screamed. With the blatant exception of the caravan, and some distant burial mounds, the sea of grass was devoid of human trace.

His watch over, Ballista went and hitched his horse to the wagon, unsaddled it, and clambered inside to be with Calgacus. The old Caledonian looked stronger, but his temper was no better than ever.

'You know this is the twentieth day since we left the Tanais river,' Ballista said.

Calgacus grunted.

'By my reckoning, it is two days before the *ides* of June.'

'Not rained for days, getting hotter; fuck me, it could be summer,' Calgacus muttered.

'I got married in June. You remember?'

Calgacus gazed balefully at him.

'I was told by Julia's family it was unlucky to marry before the *ides* of June. Not until the Tiber has carried the filth from the temple of Vesta down to the sea – that was what they said. Except they expressed it in Latin verse, very sonorous. It took me months to find out it was Ovid.'

Still, Calgacus did not reply.

'Marriage is not for everyone. I miss the boys. Do you want to talk about Rebecca?'

'No.'

'It is your choice.' Ballista nodded. 'Did you know the wife of the Roman priest they call the *Flamen Dialis* will not touch him until after the *ides* of June?'

'I could not give a fuck,' Calgacus said.

'No, nor could I,' Ballista said.

'You have that look on you.' Calgacus peered myopically. 'What did you really want to talk about?'

'Rebecca.'

'Apart from her.'

Ballista smiled gently at his old friend. 'You remember back in Arete, the messenger from the Subura on the staff; the one who took a Persian arrow in the collarbone?'

'Died slowly,' Calgacus said. 'They found the *Miles Arcana* disc of a *frumentarius* hidden on his body.'

'Yes, that one.'

'And there will be *frumentarii* on our staff now,' Calgacus said. 'There always are. Emperors do not trust people. Gallienus does not trust you. So what?'

Ballista sighed. He did not want Calgacus to dismiss his idea out of hand. It had seemed much more plausible earlier, when riding alone. He decided to come at it obliquely.

'When we were in Antioch, before the battle of Circesium, I read a lot of a Greek writer called Lucian.' Ballista smiled. 'I was reading his satire *The Dance* just before I was attacked by those assassins wearing pantomime masks – odd coincidence.'

'Pretentious fucker,' Calgacus muttered, perfectly audibly.

'One of the satires is set out here on the Steppe; well, some of it.'

Calgacus let his breath hiss through his teeth.

'There is a Scythian,' Ballista said. 'A blood-friend of his is insulted by the King of Bosporus when he asks to marry one of

154

the king's daughters. So the Scythian says he will bring his friend the head of the king.'

'Bollocks,' Calgacus snorted.

'So the Scythian,' Ballista ploughed on, 'got himself sent on an embassy to the Bosporus. They dealt with normal things: the payment of tribute by the king, grazing rights, the punishment of criminals. The Scythian said he had some private business to discuss with the king.'

'Utter fucking Greek nonsense.' Calgacus was not being carried along.

'Anyway' – Ballista realized he would have to end the story quickly – 'the Scythian persuaded the king to go into a temple with him on his own . . .'

'Stupid fucker.'

'. . . and they locked the door behind them.'

'Of course they did.'

'When the Scythian came out, he had something under his cloak, but he called back into the temple that he would return in a moment.'

'And,' Calgacus interrupted, 'he jumped on his horse, and took the king's head back to his friend.'

'Yes,' Ballista said.

Calgacus wheezed his amusement. 'I thought you hated Greek novels.'

'I did not say I believed the story. It is more that it points to a –'

'A way of doing things.' Calgacus finished the sentence for him.

Ballista nodded.

'You did not have to retreat into the fiction of the *Graeculi*.' Calgacus turned his domed head towards Ballista; suffering had not improved his looks. 'Not that long before our time – when things were just threatening to go bad for the Romans – the emperor Septimius Severus wanted rid of the man he had appointed

Caesar. He sent five envoys to Albinus in Gaul. They asked to speak to Albinus alone. The Caesar was suspicious, and had them arrested. Concealed knives were found. Under torture, they confessed they were *frumentarii* with orders to kill him.'

'How did you know that?' Ballista asked.

'I have been in the *imperium* of the Romans as long as you. I just do not parade my knowledge like you.'

Ballista accepted the rebuke with a smile.

'You think it may be we are being used as a screen for a *frumentarius* to get close to Naulobates and assassinate him,' Calgacus said.

'Yes.'

'And this *frumentarius* is getting his hand in early.'

Put like that, Ballista thought it sounded particularly unconvincing. 'Some men develop an unhealthy taste for killing.'

'You were out riding in the sun too long. The killer is just an insane individual.'

'*Just* an insane individual?' Ballista said. 'He has murdered at least three, if not four or five.'

'Two slaves and a eunuch, that we know; maybe another couple of slaves – none of them fighting men. He poses little threat to the likes of us.'

Ballista laughed. 'You are getting better; more like your old, heartless self. In no time you will be back to bothering the baggage animals.'

Calgacus told his *patronus* to fuck himself.

They sat in silence, having to cling on in the jolting, rocking wagon. It was all very amicable.

'*Atheling.*' Wulfstan came in. 'There is a cross up ahead.'

Ballista went to look. There *was* a cross, a simple 'T' shape, planted on top of a tall burial mound. Even at a distance, it was obvious there was a man on the cross.

Ballista had to put the saddle back on his horse. By the time he reached the tumulus, there were several riders at its foot. They parted to let him through. On the cross was the missing centurion Hordeonius.

Dismounting, Ballista automatically hobbled his horse. He walked up the steep, grassy slope. The wind sang in his ears. You could see for miles from the top. The plain shimmered in the sunshine.

The centurion was nailed to the crossbeam through the fore-arms. His ankles were nailed to the sides of the upright. His body was twisted, head hanging forward. He was naked, and his legs had been broken, their position grotesque. All over his body were small cuts. Below the body, the wood of the cross was stained with his blood and filth.

Ballista had not liked Hordeonius, but it was a slow and horrible way for anyone to die.

A horrible way to choose to die. For nine days, the Allfather had hung on the tree of life, pierced by the spear. No one had comforted him. No man had offered him a drink. Thus he had won the wisdom of the dead. He had died and risen again: an offering of himself to himself. Ballista did not know how long the god of the Christians had lasted.

The wind moved the centurion's hair.

Behind Ballista, someone spoke of getting Hordeonius down.

'No' – Andonnoballus's voice was hard – 'he stays up there. The Alani crucified him here not just to terrify but to delay us. We keep moving. They will be close.'

The centurion's head moved. His eyes opened.

'Gods below, he is alive!'

There was a babble of voices. Men were scrambling off their horses, starting up the slope.

The arrow missed Ballista by a palm's breadth. It thumped into Hordeonius's chest.

Andonnoballus was holding his bow. He was still mounted. There was silence, apart from the wind in the grass.

'He would not have lived,' said Andonnoballus.

XVI

It was just before sunrise. Wulfstan sat on the box by the driver. The long whip of the Sarmatian cracked loud above the backs of the oxen, and they put their weight against their harness. With a groan, the wagon shifted, paused, then gathered way.

Behind, in the covered body of the wagon, Calgacus cursed. All the others – Ballista, Maximus and Tarchon – had already ridden off into the near-darkness to take their posts. The old Caledonian had not liked being told by the *gudja* yesterday that he must continue to rest. The enforced inactivity was making him even more than usually vile-tempered.

Wulfstan would have liked to ride. Yet after the depredations of the Alani, and the two Heruli messengers each taking four spare horses, only fifteen mounts were left, and these were assigned now only to men of fighting age. Wulfstan had survived the charge with Ballista, but he knew he was not yet a warrior. He had not killed an Alani. He had not killed anyone in the fighting. He had not even struck anybody. But he had survived. Wulfstan could not wait to be a warrior. Another two winters and he would be the age Ballista was when he first stood in the shieldwall of their people, first killed a man. Maximus had been even younger, just a winter older than Wulfstan.

It was not too bad sitting up front. The driver had a smattering of the language of Germania – his people had been subject to the Urugundi for some years. Already Wulfstan had quite a few words of Sarmatian. They could converse. Now and then, they did so, but mainly the Sarmatian was silent. Wulfstan did not mind. The young Angle had a *gorytus* on one hip, a man's sword on the other. He had to think himself into the man's role he must play when the Alani caught them. And he had a lot of other things to think about.

Presently, the sun came up.

> *Time and again at the day's dawning*
> *I must mourn all my afflictions alone*

The raking light gilded the tops of the grass, but threw deep shadow into every hollow and made forbidding black boundaries of any watercourses. The intense clarity of the light made every shrub of wormwood, every lonely tree stand stark.

Now it was light, they quickened their pace. All around whips cracked, pots rattled, axles screeched, and right behind Wulfstan the old Caledonian swore, voluble and exceedingly foul.

Wulfstan thought of the stark cross yesterday. He had enjoyed seeing the centurion nailed there. It was especially good he had still been alive, good he had suffered for a long time. Hordeonius had been a cruel man, with the soul of a tyrant. You only had to look at the weeping, broken slave the centurion had left behind to know the latter's endless tirades against the servile had been more than just words. Wulfstan admired the matter-of-fact way Andonnoballus had despatched the centurion. Allfather, there was much to admire about these Heruli.

There were many other men – evil, bad men – Wulfstan would love to see despatched. From the brutal slave dealer in Ephesus to the merchant of Byzantium, to the sea captain from Olbia, to the traders along the Borysthenes and Vistula rivers all the way back to the Suebian Sea and the Langobardi raiders. Not the quick arrow or the clean steel for any of them. The things they had done called for much worse; called for the cross – a slow, agonizing death in their own piss and shit – or the stake thrusting up their arses and into their bowels. It would not be quick. It would take Wulfstan months, maybe years, to carry his vengeance the length of the Amber Road.

The wagon hit a rut, pitched violently. Wulfstan shot out a hand to hold on. The Sarmatian grinned sardonically. From behind, Calgacus let loose a torrent of repetitive obscenity.

Wulfstan's mood lightened a little. Old Calgacus had been good to him. So too, although less overtly, Maximus and Ballista. The latter would have made a fine treasure-giver to the warriors of the Angles had the *norns* spun differently. And there was Tarchon. The Suanian had done him no harm. Indeed he made Wulfstan laugh: the absurd, touchy pomposity, and the bizarre formality as Tarchon mangled languages – that of Germania, Greek and Latin, and his own native tongue. The *familia* was not home – it would never be – but it was the first place since the Langobardi came where Wulfstan had felt almost safe.

He laughed at himself. To feel *almost safe* as they raced across this endless alien wilderness, pursued by a horde of nomads and haunted by a malignant killer, had to be a reflection on the terror he had felt before, rather than any sensible estimate of his relative safety.

And even in the *familia* not all was good. The little ferret-faced Roman officer Castricius with his endless stuff about daemons good and bad was unnerving. But he was not the real problem. It was that odious secretary Hippothous. Back in Byzantium, Wulfstan had sent him away in no uncertain terms when the *accensus* had made disgusting suggestions. Here on the Steppe, the *graeculus* had approached him again, if in a more subtle way. After rebuffing that attempt, Wulfstan kept finding Hippothous staring at him. It was probably just something to do with his ridiculous obsession with trying to read people's faces, but it was disconcerting. There was much about the shaven-headed Greek with the pale eyes that was disconcerting. Wulfstan would shed no tears if a stray arrow, Alani or otherwise, found Hippothous. As Wulfstan had learnt from the ambush, battle was chaos; almost anything could happen undetected.

Wulfstan ran a hand over the nomad bowcase on his hip. The *gorytus* was covered in decorations. Prominent among them was the personal emblem of Aluith. The *tamga* took the form of something like the Greek letter *Chi* or the Latin X with a curling line across the top. After Aluith had fallen, Andonnoballus had given the *gorytus* to Wulfstan. The young Herul leader had said it was fitting, as Aluith had taught Wulfstan to shoot from the saddle.

Aluith had been the closest thing to a friend Wulfstan had made since Bauto the young Frisian he had met in slavery. Bauto had looked after him; looked after him in the worst of times. Bauto had been lost overboard in a storm in the Euxine the year before. Wulfstan mourned both Aluith and Bauto.

> So this world dwindles day by day,
> And passes away; for a man will not be wise
> Before he has weathered his share of winters
> In the world.

Still, Aluith, with some help from the other Herul Ochus, had finally taught Wulfstan to master the nomad release. The Angle was nearly as proficient as Datius and Aordus, the two ex-slaves now become Heruli who still rode with the caravan. How Wulfstan had envied them and the other two slaves; the ones gone north as messengers. Straight after the ambush, the three remaining Rosomoni had presented them with the shields which marked their freedom: just reward for their courage. As free Heruli warriors, the four inscribed *tamgas* of their own choosing on the small, round bucklers. What a contrast from Narcissus, promised his freedom by Hippothous but murdered before he was awarded it. Would it have been granted had he lived? And what a contrast from himself, riding in the charge which turned the day yet promised nothing, and given nothing.

Wulfstan himself would have given much – even an eye, as the Allfather had – to be Datius or Aordus. If Ballista eventually manumitted him, in the *imperium* he would remain reviled as a freedman. His subjection, the unthinkable things done to him, would be commented on and sniggered about. It would forever be a stain that could not be washed away. No Greek or Roman ex-slave could become a magistrate or serve in the legions. None of them could become a free warrior proudly bearing his own *tamga* on his horse and arms, like Datius or Aordus.

The smug self-satisfaction of the inhabitants of the *imperium* infuriated Wulfstan. The way they liked to equate the whole inhabited world with the part they tyrannized. The way they divided the world into their *humanitas* and all other peoples' *barbaritas*. The way they understood all other peoples through writings hundreds of years old about totally different peoples who happened to inhabit vaguely the same part of the world. This lazy, retarded thinking would betray them one day. Wulfstan snorted. For all their literary ethnographic posturing, men like Hippothous and Castricius, or the dead eunuch Mastabates, would never understand the Heruli. Wulfstan doubted they would ever hear the names of Datius and Aordus, let alone understand what motivated them.

Aluith had said Wulfstan would make a good Herul warrior. Should he approach Calgacus? Ask the old Caledonian to intercede with Ballista for his freedom? If he were manumitted now, out here on the Steppe, he could ask Andonnoballus for permission to join the horde of Naulobates. He would happily submit to re-enslavement, if that was what it took. He would rather be a slave of the Heruli than of the Romans. Among the former, valour could win true freedom and a future untainted by the past. Among them, he could rise to the right hand of a king.

Such a course, however, entailed letting go his revenge. It meant men like Potamis, the trader at the rapids of the Borysthenes, and the others like him would go unpunished. And that could not be. Revenge was an honourable motive; none more so. Wulfstan would have his revenge. Afterwards, he might think of joining the Heruli.

Yip-yip-yip. Wulfstan now recognized the different tones of the Heruli calls. This one was the alarm.

Yip-yip-yip. It was coming from the rear of the twin column. From his place in the lead wagon of the right-hand line, Wulfstan could not see anything. He leant way out to the side, hanging by one hand, the grass racing beneath him. Still, the following wagons and the dust obscured his view.

Pharas the Rosomoni cantered up. He gave concise orders to the driver in Sarmatian. The whip flicked out above the oxen. They broke into a shambling flat-out run, their great dewlaps swinging. Pharas spurred ahead, towards where Andonnoballus rode at point.

'What is it?' Calgacus's misshapen old head appeared through the hangings.

'Alarm from the rear.'

The Caledonian treated him to a withering look.

Wulfstan turned to the driver. He had to yell to make himself heard. 'What trouble?' Wulfstan dredged out the words in Sarmatian.

The driver was standing now, the better to ply his bullwhip. He jerked his head backwards. 'Much dust . . . many riders . . . Alani.'

Riding well out to the front, Maximus was worrying about women and about the feelings of the Heruli towards him. Wearing his mailcoat – everyone was wearing their battle gear now – he was sweating heavily in the hot sun.

Maximus had not had a woman since the night before they left the town of Tanais. Three days up the river, three days waiting for the ox-carts and horses, and this was the twenty-first day out on the Steppe. Twenty-seven days without ploughing a field. That was nearly a month. He should have been ready to jump on anything; one of those female daemons with the nice tits – to Hades with the snake lower half, he could avoid going downstairs and concentrate on stopping her talking – or maybe even that hideous old Gothic witch. But, worryingly, he was not that desperate. He was almost used to the abstinence. Was this how the decline into impotence started? You just got used to not having it. He remembered Ballista and Demetrius talking about some old Greek writer who, when he could not get it up any more, described it as like being freed from a cruel tyrant. Maximus did not want that sort of freedom.

There were some *yip-yip-yip* sounds a long way to the rear.

Maximus was concerned if things would improve when they reached the camp of Naulobates. He had discovered that not all nomad tribes had the same attitudes to sex; far from it, indeed. One of them – he forgot which – would kill you if you fucked their women. But their wives might give you a view of the cave.

165

Their explanation was that it was better other men could see it but it was unattainable than it was covered but easily reached. The men of another tribe – some eastern subjects of the Heruli – did not mind you sleeping with their wives, if they did not actually witness it. The Alani turned out to have many wives, but would disembowel you if you so much as looked at them. Now, the Heruli, or at least the Rosomoni among them – and they were quite open about this – had adopted the custom of one of the tribes they had subdued. Like the Agathyrsi, they now shared their women in common. They said it abolished jealousy; made them a true band of brothers.

The *yip-yip-yipping* had not stopped.

With true Steppe hospitality, the Rosomoni had no objection to honoured guests enjoying their women. Ochus, laughing and looking hard at Maximus, had said everything was good, provided the women did not find you too ugly. Which Maximus considered rich coming from a man with a head the shape of an upturned amphora. Anyway, he had already discovered from Andonnoballus that visitors were usually offered slave girls, whose opinions on male beauty were of no concern to anyone.

It was not female rejection that was troubling Maximus. If you propositioned almost every woman you met – and he had made it his life rule to do almost exactly that – you got used to a high rate of refusal. Although, of course, it only needed a low percentage to agree to get you a grind or two a day. No, what was bothering Maximus was practice. If you had not spoken a language for a long time, it was difficult to just pick it up again. Maximus could not remember going this long without sex. Would that prove as difficult as, say, speaking Greek after several months of not?

The *yipping* was closer, louder, more insistent. Maximus looked back towards the caravan. The wagons were moving much faster, probably as fast as the oxen could pull them. Dust was billowing up. In front and to one side of the two lines of wagons, a group of horsemen were talking. One or two more were galloping up.

Something was wrong. There was a threat Maximus could not see.

Before turning to ride back, Maximus automatically gazed all around. The plain rolled gently here, but not enough to hide more than one of those big mouse-like animals which had their burrows everywhere. The Steppe was empty, except for a group of three low *kurgans* a couple of hundred paces off to the left, and, about a mile and a half or more ahead to the north-east, a straggly line of dark trees. The latter had to mark an otherwise hidden stream of some sort. Beyond the trees, a line of lilac clouds rose on the horizon like a range of distant mountains in an otherwise perfectly blue and empty sky. As he wheeled his horse, Maximus saw movement among the trees. It ceased before he could focus.

Maximus reined his horse around again. He pretended to gaze off to the south-east, while watching the trees intently out of the corner of his eyes. Only the foliage moved in the north wind. It had not been that before. The movement had been lower, gone further than one tree. It had been too big for one of those mouse-things. It could easily have been a wild horse, deer or ass. Nothing moved except the leaves and branches. His horse dropped its head to graze. He pulled it up again. Still, nothing moved. He galloped back to the others.

When Maximus reached the other riders, he saw the problem straight away. No longer masked by the dust of their own wagons, another tall column of dust showed three or four miles behind. It was solitary, and went up straight until the wind took it off to the south. An experienced eye could read it like the *gudja* could read runes. It was raised by a compact body of cavalry moving fast. That much dust meant a large body of cavalry; most likely a hundred – or more, maybe a lot more.

'The barrows offer some protection, but there will be no water there.' Andonnoballus was countering the proposal of another Herul. Maximus fell in with the cavalcade. The mounted conference was conducted at a fast trot to keep ahead of the wagon train.

'The *atheling* is right,' Ochus said. 'It may be several days before Naulobates' men reach us. We may have to hold out until then.'

'We must reach the watercourse ahead,' Andonnoballus said with finality. 'Use it as one side of the laager, and have the wagons coming off it in a semicircle.'

The others made noises of agreement.

'I do not want to be upsetting anyone,' Maximus said, 'but there may be a problem. Something moving in the trees. We could be riding into an ambush.'

The jingle and creak of harness, the stamp of hooves were loud as they rode, digesting this unwelcome news.

Ballista was the first to speak. 'I will take the four Roman auxiliaries who have horses, and those of my *familia* who are mounted. We will go ahead. It may be nothing. If there is a trap we will spring it. We may be able to fight through to the riverbank. If not, you form the wagon-laager in the open, and we will fall back to you.'

Andonnoballus and the Heruli agreed with no debate. The nomads spun their mounts and raced back to their stations around the caravan. Ballista explained the plan in Latin to Castricius, and asked him to call up the auxiliaries. The little Roman rode off, shouting and beckoning the troopers from the Cilician cavalry unit.

Maximus nudged his mount up on the left of Ballista. Hippothous had already taken the post to his right. It seemed strange not to see Calgacus there. Tarchon was close behind.

As they trotted forward, waiting, Maximus untied the helmet from one of the horns of his saddle. Once it was settled on his head, he took the small buckler from the pack behind him and strapped it very tight to his left forearm. He liked this new shield; it gave some protection, while leaving his left hand free for the reins or a bow. Next to him, Ballista ran through his pre-battle routine. Left hand to dagger on right hip, draw it a couple of inches, snap it back. Right hand to sword on left hip, same motions, then touch the healing stone tied to the scabbard.

'Helmet and shield,' Maximus reminded Ballista. The latter nodded acknowledgement and began to get his accoutrements into place. Ballista's fingers fumbled with his chin strap. Maximus grinned.

Ballista was always nervous before combat; always had been. Once, lacing his boots, he had thrown up through sheer nerves. Maximus found it hard to understand. He felt the familiar feeling in his chest, hollow and tight at the same time, and the slight tremble in his arms, but that was nothing but excitement.

The others caught up. Castricius reined in next to Hippothous, two auxiliaries outside him. Ballista waved Tarchon alongside Maximus, the remaining two auxiliaries flanking the left of the Suanian.

A final glance along the line, and Ballista led them out across the front of the wagon train. He set a fast canter towards the river.

Ballista appeared the epitome of calm competence. Under his bird-of-prey-crested helm, his face looked fierce, ready to fight. Maximus knew Ballista would be fine when the fighting started. He also knew that, now, Ballista would be a tangle of apprehension.

The hooves rattled across the dry plain, stamping down the grey wormwood and the brown knotgrass. So far nothing moved in the line of the trees, not above half a mile off.

Maximus and Ballista craned their heads around to see the wagon train and beyond the dust raised by their pursuers. The latter was closer, but still a couple of miles away. The Alani riders were in sight; so far, a dark, undifferentiated mass at the foot of the cloud.

'If nothing delays them, the wagons will reach the watercourse just before the Alani catch them,' Ballista said. The words were perfectly audible. He was used to making himself heard on the field of battle.

'If there is nothing hiding in that stream to hold them up,' Maximus said.

'If there is nothing there.'

A brace of partridges whirred out from a patch of longer grass. One of the Cilician troopers had to whip his mount back straight. Still no movement from the trees.

Maximus slid the bone ring on to his right thumb. He pulled back the felt cover of his *gorytus*, took out the recurve bow, notched an arrow to the right of the bow nomad-style. They all had their bows to hand. The soldiers were from a unit of mounted archers. Maximus wondered if they used the nomad thumb draw, wondered how good they would prove against nomads.

They were about two hundred paces from the covert, just beginning to relax, when they saw the riders. Pointed caps, drawn bows, embroidered tunics and trousers, boots, long swords at their sides, coming out of the trees. The Alani were there with the complete suddenness of an apparition.

They whooped, all ragged and uncoordinated. There were less than twenty of them. None were armoured, no banners flew above them. There were no obvious leaders.

They must be what is left of the original ambush party, Maximus thought. The rest must have driven the Heruli horses off south or gone away as messengers. Now the remainder will try to delay us long enough for their more numerous kinsmen to catch us.

'Get in close, hand to hand, break them, make them run,' Ballista roared. 'We must not let them get at the wagons.'

The Alani were cantering forward. The first arrows flew from their line. The Romans replied. A shaft came at Maximus, deceptively slow, then terrifyingly fast. It sliced past a hand's breadth or two away: a black line, hard to see. Maximus drew, aimed and released. The Alan was unhurt. He had missed. Bugger. He nocked another. The distance was fast diminishing. Arrows thrummed through the air. To the right, Hippothous pulled up; his horse lame. One of the Alani was swept backwards off his mount as if by an invisible hand. An arrow thumped into Maximus's *gorytus*. Gods below, far too fucking close. Tarchon had gone. Maximus drew hard, the bone, wood and sinew of the composite bow groaning. In front, an Alani horse went tumbling, the bright fletching of an arrow in its windpipe. That's the idea, Maximus thought. This time he aimed low, released. He missed again.

No more time. Maximus shoved the bow back into the *gorytus*. He slipped his hand through the loop of his sword, felt the sweat-worn leather of the hilt. It was snug in his hand. Two Alani were closing on him. He dropped the reins. Using his knees, he guided the horse towards the nomad on his left.

The three came together in a moment; many things happening at once. A strange clarity descended on Maximus, the battle calm that gave him time and made him such a killer. He blocked a downward cut from the left with his buckler. A splinter of wood cut his cheek, nearly took his eye. His left knee struck something hard. A surge of pain. The other man grunting in pain too. A sword cut from the right. Maximus caught it on his blade, rolled his wrist left to right – forced the other's steel forward – rolled his wrist back, thrust overhand with much of his weight behind it. The point punctured the tunic, and deep enough into the flesh under it. The Alan howled, dropping his own weapon. Blood darkened the nomad embroidery on his flank. He was of no more account.

Left hand gripping a saddle horn, Maximus pulled himself back. Using his momentum, he swung overhead at the back of the man to his left. The Alan twisted, got his own blade in the way. They were still knee to knee, no room for manoeuvre. Their swords were locked together; their horses circling. The nomad had a long Sassanid blade with no hilt. Maximus beat aside a hand clawing at his throat. He forced his sword to scrape down. Edge to edge, the steel rang. His fingers moments from being cut, the Alan jerked away. Maximus dived inside his guard. The sword sliced across the front of his tunic. It was not a clean blow, but enough to double him up in pain. Maximus finished him with a downward chop to the back of the neck.

A respite – no Alani very near. Maximus searched for Ballista. The Angle was but a few horse lengths away. He was trading blows with a nomad. Maximus went to help. Before he arrived, the Alan crashed from his mount. Castricius drew up with two of the auxiliaries. Tarchon was scrambling on to a nomad pony. Hippothous was further off. He was on foot, despatching a wounded man. He was laughing. A third soldier appeared. The final one had vanished. There were only a couple of loose ponies and some dead Alani near by. The living nomads, no more than ten of them left, had ridden through the Roman line and continued on.

'They are running,' a soldier said.

'They are making for the wagons,' Ballista said. 'Close on me. We must stop them.'

In a loose line, the seven riders set off after them. Ballista took his party straight to a flat-out gallop. Yet it was obvious they would not catch the Alani before they reached the caravan.

The wagons were still careering towards the watercourse, and thus towards the ten Alani. The five Heruli were now fanning out in front of the double line of wagons.

Ballista's men thundered on in their futile pursuit.

Arrows ripped through the air between the Heruli and the ten Alan. The strong sunshine glinted on the vicious heads, flared the bright colours of the feathers. An Alani pony shied off to one side. Its rider slowly slid from the saddle. A Herul fell sideways. His horse trotting around in a circle to nuzzle him. He was trying to rise. Another Alan clutched his thigh, and yanked his mount off to the south.

All the remaining Alani were racing off to the south. But as they sped across the face of the caravan, they loosed repeatedly at the leading caravan of the southern column. The oxen were hit. They were pulling up.

'Calgacus and Wulfstan are in there,' Maximus shouted.

The following wagons drove past it on either side. The stricken wagon was lost to sight.

'We must get to them,' Ballista called.

XVII

Tarchon was riding holding on to the front horns of the saddle. He was holding on for grim death. Raised in the high mountains of the Croucasis, a Suanian warrior but not a nobleman, he made no claims to horsemanship. It was a pity the big Sarmatian horse he had got used to had been shot out from under him. The stray Alani pony he had caught was skittish and snappy.

Ballista and the other five were drawing some lengths ahead. Tarchon wanted to drive his mount on with shoulders and arms like them. Yet he knew if he let go of the saddle horns, at this pace, most likely he would take a fall.

It had been a good little fight back there. Tarchon laughed out loud. The Alani had been lining up Ballista's back, composite bow at full draw. Tarchon had cleaved the nomad from the shoulder to the saddle. A mighty blow. The blow of a hero. Tarchon had saved Ballista's life. He had repaid the Angle. But did it count, as no one seemed to have witnessed it? As he posed the question, Tarchon was furious with himself. What was he thinking? This was the sort of chiselling reckoning of some fat Greek merchant. This was unworthy of a Suanian warrior. Honour was not to be measured out like olive oil or salt fish.

Old Calgacus was injured in the abandoned wagon. It was Tarchon's duty to save him, or die in the attempt. It was very simple. Tarchon let go of the horns, began shaking the reins, pumping his elbows, making strange noises intended to speed the pony. The effects were other than what he had hoped. His ungainly bouncing seemed to be upsetting the animal's balance. It started to crab. Tarchon felt his seat shifting. Long-suffering Prometheus, he was going to fall off. He abandoned his ill-conceived urgings, and grabbed hold of the saddle again. Better he got there a little slowly than broke his neck without aiding the other man who had saved him from the Alontas river.

They were passing the seven wagons coming the other way. Ballista veered a little, so they skirted the southern line of three wagons. The oxen were bellowing their pain and fury at being harried with the whip into such unaccustomed alacrity. The wagons themselves were screaming; innumerable joints of wood under stress. Sometimes, one of the great heavy things would lurch into the air, one or more of the four wheels off the ground. It was a wonder on landing they did not break apart.

Andonnoballus the Herul was riding alongside the wagons. He called to Ballista. It was lost in the kicked-up dirt and pandemonium. Tarchon could not even tell what language it had been. Ballista shrugged and drove on.

They burst through the dust cloud as if into another world, one marked by the passing of the convoy, but not yet vitiated. The lone wagon stood in the warm sun not far off. The oxen, injured and unharmed alike, were head down and placid.

Tarchon's heart lurched. There were nomad horsemen already around the wagon. How could they be too late? By all the gods and men, it was not possible. They would all have to die to avenge

175

Calgacus. They and all their families. And poor young Wulfstan; they would suffer for his death.

The nomads turned and started to trot after the other wagons. As they came towards him, Tarchon saw the bright-red hair, the very long heads of the first two riders. It was Ochus and Pharas. The ex-slave Aordus was with them. Each rider had a man up behind him. There was Calgacus. And young Wulfstan. And the Sarmatian driver. Prometheus and Hecate be praised, the Heruli had ridden back and rescued them all.

Ballista slackened the speed to a walk as the two little cavalcades came together.

'You had better not delay, if you want to save any of your possessions,' Pharas said as they passed. 'Be quick. We will see you at the riverbank. We will need every man.'

The Heruli and their passengers trotted on. The arm of one, Ochus, was soaked in blood.

Ballista sat looking about. The caravan was vanishing in the obscurity of its own making in one direction. The main horde of Alani were approaching from the other. Tarchon could begin to make out individual riders among the latter. It meant they could only be a thousand paces away.

'Castricius,' Ballista said, 'take the three troopers, and go after the wagons. Screen their right flank, in case those other few Alani to the south try to interfere or shoot any more oxen.'

The Romans hastened away.

'Maximus, Tarchon, come with me.'

At the wagon, Ballista handed his reins to Tarchon and told Maximus to do the same. Tarchon, uneasily sitting his pony and controlling their horses, watched them climb into the back. He was puzzled. This seemed most unlike either of the northerners. Material things never seemed to trouble them.

After a few moments, they reappeared, lugging towards the

176

tailboard the heavy wooden box which contained half the gold for the ransoms and the diplomatic presents. Ballista broke the seals and wrenched the lid open with his dagger. Tarchon watched in something approaching dismay as the two scooped up handfuls of golden coins and, to save time bothering to open their wallets, tipped the *specie* into their boots. Then, at a word from Ballista, they hefted the box high, swung it, and – one, two, three – threw the whole thing over on to the ground. The wood split. Shining coins tipped out and lay glinting in the trampled grass.

'Tarchon, are there any of your possessions you particularly want?' Ballista called.

'Tarchon is warrior. Possessions mean nothing to him,' the Suanian replied stiffly.

Annoyingly, the Hibernian laughed as they ducked back under the covering.

Both re-emerged a moment or two later. Each carried his own saddlebag. Ballista had Tarchon's as well. He threw it across. The Alani pony chose that moment to sidle and try and bite one of the horses. Tarchon nearly slipped off. Somehow he managed to hang on to the saddlebag, and let go neither the others' reins nor his own dignity.

Ballista and Maximus swung easily into the saddle. As they secured their baggage, they looked at the approaching menace. The heads of the Alani were visible, distinct round balls. It meant they were no more than seven hundred paces distant.

Ballista looked at the gold. 'The oldest trick in the book. It worked for me once in a riot in the Hippodrome in Antioch. You scatter rich things and hope your attackers are greedy enough to be distracted.'

They wheeled their mounts, and kicked straight on to an in-hand gallop. Getting on for half a mile start over the Alani. They should reach the watercourse just after the wagons, comfortably ahead of the nomads.

Soon they were overhauling the swaying, jouncing wagons. The handful of Alani out to the south had not attempted to intervene, and the main body, if anything, seemed to have fallen back a little.

A deafening, splintering crash, followed hard by high screaming; human as well as bestial. An enormous cloud of dust and debris mushroomed ahead. One of the wagons of the northern four had crashed. The last wagon in the line manoeuvred desperately around it, and did not stop.

From behind came the distant whooping of the Alani. Nothing could encourage them more. The gold might seem less tempting. Now they would drive their mounts all the harder.

'Come on.' Ballista booted his animal towards the wreck.

The north wind was blowing away the murk. A tangle of wood and felt and leather traces, of scattered possessions, of fallen oxen and twisted men was revealed. It had been the conveyance of the Roman staff: Porsenna the *haruspex*, the herald, the two scribes and the two messengers. One of the lead oxen appeared to have caught its leg in the hole of one of the big mouse-like things. It must have brought the rest of the team down and the wagon had ploughed into them. An upturned wheel still rotated.

'Maximus, take the driver on your horse, unless he is badly hurt,' Ballista said. 'Tarchon, take any one of the staff; not an injured man though.'

Tarchon dismounted carefully. He was not going to let the pony loose and be stranded here himself. The Alani were coming. He had seen what they did to the centurion.

Several crumpled bodies were scattered in or near the wreckage.

'Ballista, the Sarmatian is dead – broken neck,' Maximus called.

'Take someone else.'

A survivor tottered up to Tarchon. 'Help, I am hurt; my leg.' It was one of the scribes. There was a terrible gash in his right thigh.

Tarchon roughly pushed him aside. The wounded man fell. He whimpered with pain.

'You.' Tarchon led the pony to a man standing overwhelmed by the calamity. 'Are you injured?'

'No, I do not think so.' It was Porsenna, his voice flat and dull. With difficulty, Tarchon helped the diviner up behind the saddle. The wretched pony tried to bite him. He hit it hard on the nose. It laid its ears flat back and began to circle.

'Come on,' Ballista called. The big northerner and Maximus were already back in the saddle, a passenger behind each.

With the encumbrance of the *haruspex*, and the pony turning, Tarchon could not remount.

The light-coloured dots of the faces of the Alani, the *draco* and some other banners snapping above their heads, the colours of their tunics, all could be seen clearly. Not more than five hundred paces at most.

Tarchon made another jump. The pony side-stepped away. He slid down its side.

The Alani were whooping. The rattle of their horses was loud.

Tarchon went to make another attempt. The pony skittered sideways.

Ballista rode up. Without ado, he grabbed the *haruspex* by the scruff of his tunic and hauled him off the pony. There was a yell of pained outrage as he hit the ground.

Ballista took the pony by the bridle, wedged his own horse against it so it could not sidle away. 'Get up, quick.'

The horrible *whisp-whisp-whisp* of the first incoming arrows. By Prometheus, they were less than two hundred paces away.

Tarchon struggled, ungainly and urgent, into the saddle.

179

'You cannot leave me.' The hands of the *haruspex* clasped Ballista's boot.

A shaft sliced through the air past Tarchon's ear. Hurriedly, he gathered the reins.

'I am sorry,' Ballista said.

'You faithless barbarian,' Porsenna spat. He was clinging to Ballista's leg, as if trying to unhorse him.

Ballista leant down and took him by the throat, breaking Porsenna's grip. Ballista pushed him back, then kicked him in the face. The *haruspex* fell.

'He is a fighting man, you are not,' Ballista said. 'I am sorry.'

'Sacrilegious barbarian filth!' The voice was high-pitched with pain and hatred and fear. 'Curse you! May all the gods of the underworld . . .'

The venomous Latin was drowned by the sound of their horses, by the sound of the Alani.

They pushed their mounts as fast as they could. With two up on Ballista and Maximus's mounts and Tarchon no great horseman, and with three or four hundred paces to the riverbank, things did not look good.

Unwittingly, the *haruspex* and the remaining staff bought them the necessary time. The Alani seemingly had not stopped for the gold and the first abandoned wagon. But the second was too tempting. It had people to be taken prisoner or killed. The pause was brief, but enough.

Tarchon held tight to the horns on the saddle. He let his pony have its head. Obeying the instinct of its kind, it raced after and alongside the other horses. As they neared the riverbank, they had to swerve aside to avoid the herd of oxen released from their traces and driven out of the forming wagon-laager. It was good thinking on someone's part. The stampede was impressive, frightening even, out on the wide Steppe. In the confines of a small, enclosed camp, it would have been devastating.

They clattered into the semicircle, and the last two wagons were drawn together behind them.

Tarchon was grateful to slide from the back of the ill-natured, wilful pony. He stood by its head, blowing nearly as hard as the animal. He smiled happily. In Tarchon's Suanian terms of understanding, Ballista had proved himself a Sceptre-bearer worth following. The trick with the gold had not worked, but it was cunning; worthy of the great ancestor Prometheus himself. And the northerner's good sense when it came to warriors and those who dare not lift a weapon was exemplary. He had shown a fine lack of care for the latter. Ballista was a fine *sceptouchos* to follow, Tarchon thought. The pony swung its neck and sank its big, yellow teeth into his arm.

Ballista looked for Andonnoballus in the chaos of the laager. Men shouted, and horses called. A surprising number of domestic animals had escaped from the wagons and now darted about between the river and the semicircle of the laager. It was as well the oxen had been driven out.

The young Herul was in the centre of it all. Still on horseback, his long head rose above the confusion. Turning, he called out orders, encouragements and reprimands. He pointed and men ran to do his bidding.

'Where do you want me?' Ballista asked.

Andonnoballus saw him and smiled. It struck Ballista the Herul would have been a handsome northern warrior were it not for the deformed skull and the tattoos.

'Down by the watercourse. Hold the bank. How many men do you have with you?'

'Just Maximus and Tarchon.'

Andonnoballus looked at the other two.

'They are just members of the staff,' Ballista said. 'No use in a fight.'

'Take them anyway,' Andonnoballus said. 'I will try to send you one or two more – if we can spare them.'

Ballista summoned the others to his side. The two members of staff shuffled up. They would not hold his gaze. They were terrified; they would be no use. Maximus trotted his horse over. He was holding a chicken by its feet. He wrung its neck, and tied it to a rear horn of his saddle. Tarchon had to be called several times. The Suanian, a wistful look on his face, was standing holding his pony at arm's length. He seemed lost in some barbaric other world. Seeing him made Ballista feel guilty about Porsenna. That he had disliked the pompous *haruspex* made it worse.

There were about forty paces of riverbank between the end wagons of the makeshift fortification. Half a dozen mature limes grew in quite an evenly spaced line. Ivy curled up their lower trunks. There was some thorny undergrowth between them and the lip of the watercourse.

The whooping of the Alani was growing louder.

Ballista and Maximus dismounted. They hobbled their horses, bringing the reins over the head and tying them around a foreleg. Tarchon did the same, although with some difficulty, and getting nipped in the process. They each took their bowcase from their saddle. Ballista told Maximus to take the right, Tarchon the left. He would take the centre. Use the limes as cover.

Both the staff had disappeared already. As if hiding among the baggage would do them any good if the Alani broke into the camp. Inconsequentially, Ballista realized neither of them could be *frumentarii*. In just this one instance, it was a pity. All *frumentarii* were trained soldiers before they were seconded. They could not have known it, but they had saved the wrong men. Yet Ballista doubted if the *haruspex* could have been a *frumentarius*. It was impossible to imagine he had ever been a legionary.

Pushing through the shrubs, Ballista quickly inspected the river.

There was a steep drop of some ten, twelve paces down to the water. The soil of the bank looked quite loose, friable. The river was about twenty paces across. The far bank, if anything, was higher. You could get a horse up and down, but it would not be easy. All that was very good. Not all aspects were as encouraging. The water was not deep, not above knee level at any point. The bed of the river looked solid. The vegetation on the far bank matched that on the side of the camp, giving the Alani the same cover as the defenders until they attempted to cross the river. Yet, all in all, it could have been far worse.

The howls and roars of fighting came from behind Ballista. The Alani were attacking the wagons. The noises told him it was not yet hand to hand. The Alani were pressing close with a storm of arrows. Ballista went back, thorns plucking at his clothes. Overshot arrows were plunging to the ground all around. Ballista sheltered under the branches of the central lime, back against its smooth, grey trunk. He kept an eye over his shoulder on the river and what he could see of the Steppe beyond. He devoted the rest of his attention to holding his small buckler out ready to deflect any arrows that made it through the foliage.

Ballista looked up through the leaves at the sun. It was early afternoon. He was hungry. They had missed lunch. It was going to be a long day.

XVIII

The first Alani outriders were no time in appearing. They came splashing down the bed of the stream from the right, moving at a high-stepping trot. They must have climbed down the bank somewhere off to the east.

Ballista took a dozen or so arrows from his *gorytus* and pushed them point down into the soil at his feet. They would be easy to get at there. Some said the dirt poisoned the wound. Ballista did not care about that, he just needed them to hand. He leant the bowcase back against the tree. There were about forty arrows left in it. He selected one. Waiting, he ran his forefinger and thumb down the shaft to check it was straight and true, he felt the feathers, and finally he nocked it.

The noise of combat rolled across from the wagons.

Maximus was taking his time. Ballista was dry-mouthed with apprehension, but he admired the Hibernian's control. So far, there were only six Alani riding in line. Let them get well into the killing ground. The foremost rider was bareheaded; a strip of scarlet cloth holding back his long brown hair. His upper body was encased in bright scale armour. He must be a nobleman. Those following were unarmoured, in patterned tunics and trousers. Ballista knew what was in Maximus's mind.

An arrow hissed across from the left. It narrowly missed the head of the Alani noble. That fool of a Suanian, Ballista thought. All the Alani brought up their bows, scanning both banks for targets. The leader went to kick on. An arrow punched deep into the shoulder of his mount. The warhorse plunged, half unseating its rider. Ballista stepped out, drew and released. His arrow sank into the injured horse's flank. It reared. The Alan went sprawling. As it landed, the warhorse sank to its knees.

Alani arrows were whipping through the branches. Ballista drew again. The rear horse he had intended as his target was already out of control, maddened by the pain of the arrowhead embedded in its neck. Maximus was doing well. Ballista calmly shot an Alan in the centre of their line out of the saddle.

With the riverbed ahead and behind partly blocked by dead or dying animals, the Alani realized their dreadful position. Almost as one, those still mounted set their horses at the far bank. An arrow from Tarchon took one in the shoulder. The Alan somehow clung on as his pony scrambled up the almost sheer incline. You could not fault their horsemanship. And you could not fault their courage. They were only intended to scout.

A flash of silver, like the belly of a fish. The Alani nobleman in the scale armour was out of the water, hauling himself up the opposite bank. An arrow from Ballista's left missed him. One from the right did the same. Hand over hand, he scrabbled, the soil landsliding behind him. The other Alani, having forced their horses through the sharp bushes, had turned and were shooting to cover his escape.

Ballista stepped clear of the tree. As he closed one eye and drew, an Alani arrow screeched close past. Part of him noticed he had reverted to the normal European two-finger draw. Another

185

incoming shaft snapped a twig a foot or two away. He released, and stepped back into cover. He heard the splash as the body fell back into the water, and the babble of angry foreign voices. At twenty paces, even metal armour offered little guarantee of protection.

When he had stilled his breathing, Ballista peeked out; the other side of the tree, low down and quick. No arrow thrummed at his face. As far as he could see, the Alani outriders had gone. The noise of the skirmishing along the line of the wagons at his back must have masked their hooves. Below, down in the water, were two dead horses and three dead men. Ballista had not noticed the third die.

For a little time he debated whether to climb down, and, like some Homeric hero, strip the Alani noble of his fancy scale armour. The Romans had a very special award for a general who defeated the enemy commander in single combat, the *spolia opima*. He thought better of it. He was neither an Achilles nor a Romulus. And the Alani would return in numbers at any moment.

'You hungry?' Maximus had jogged over. He tossed a bag of air-dried meat across to Ballista. Wherever they were, the Hibernian would produce the stuff. It was a good job Ballista liked it. He took a handful and threw the bag back.

Maximus nodded at the wagons. 'Company.' He walked off.

Ballista got a wine flask from the saddle of his horse. The animal was cropping the grass, seemingly oblivious to the surrounding drama. As Calgacus came up, Ballista embraced him and gave him a big kiss on top of his balding head.

'Get the fuck off me,' Calgacus said. 'I am not a fucking Greek.'

Ballista punched Wulfstan's arm, ruffled his hair and shook Hippothous by the hand. He was grinning with pleasure at their survival, with pleasure at still being alive himself.

'Wonderful reinforcements,' Maximus called over. 'A child, an old cripple and a pederast secretary. Nothing can touch us now.'

'Half-witted Hibernian shite.' Calgacus's mutter was, again, perfectly audible above the none-too-distant sounds of battle. 'Brain in his prick.' Calgacus, like the other newcomers, was armoured. He was carrying a heavy axe in his left hand. His right arm was still in splints.

Ballista wondered where Wulfstan had got his too-large mail-coat. It was a wonder the boy could stand, let alone move in it. He must be stronger than he looked.

'Castricius is coming,' Hippothous said. His voice echoed oddly from behind the 'T' opening of an antique Greek helmet he had acquired a year or two back in Ephesus, or Miletus. 'He should be here in a moment.'

'And so will the Alani.' Ballista was still laughing. With an effort, he calmed himself down. 'Hippothous, take a position between me and Tarchon. When Castricius comes, he can go between Maximus and me. Calgacus, go and watch Tarchon's back. Wulfstan, stay here with me.'

'Will they come again?' Wulfstan asked.

'Yes, but they have travelled a long way,' Ballista said. 'They and their horses are tired. If their next attack does not break through, they will draw off until tomorrow.'

No sooner had the others started moving off than Ballista could hear the thunder of approaching cavalry. It seemed to be approaching from both sides. He very much hoped he was right about the Alani.

The Alani did not make the mistake of approaching along the riverbed again. They must have forded the river up- and down-stream. From both sides, a large band of riders swept around to link up on the Steppe to the north of the watercourse. They pulled up, a couple of hundred paces away, out of most effective bow range.

Castricius ran up. Ballista waved him over to where he wanted him to stand.

The Alani waited quietly behind two standards. One was an abstract design on cloth, a nomad *tamga*, the other a horsetail on a pole. In all, Ballista estimated about a hundred warriors. Maybe one in ten armoured. They seemed to be waiting for something; most likely a signal.

Ballista noted that there was no battle din from the wagons behind. Earlier, he had seen a big *draco* standard. The nomads were showing themselves disciplined enough to wait for the word of the chief who rode under the dragon. They would all attack at once. That was not good. Nor was the fact that down here by the river – good defensive position though it was – Ballista's *familia* was outnumbered to the order of twenty to one.

The wind soughed through the lime trees, fretted at the thorn bushes. Out beyond the river, it raised little dust devils. They were the first Ballista had seen on the Steppe. The summer sun was drying the plains.

The nomad standards snapped in the breeze. Ballista wished he were standing under his own white *draco*; hearing its bronze jaws hiss and seeing its body writhe with menace. Ballista wished he were out there at the head of a confident troop of men, look-ing in, waiting to finish an outnumbered huddle of enemy. He pulled himself up. The Alani could finish the men in the wagon-laager, and do so quickly – if the nomads were well led, if they wanted it enough and, above all, if they were prepared to take the casualties. Ballista knew what he would have his men do if he were the Alani chief. They should ride up to the tree line, dismount, force their way through the scrub, some should provide covering shooting, the rest rush down the far bank, cross the stream, and storm the near bank. But Ballista also knew that, while they were doing it, his arrows would drop at least four or five of them; and then he would hope to take one or two with him in the final hand-to-hand struggle. Maximus, Hippothous, Castricius and Tarchon should do no worse than him. Wulfstan with his Herul bow and old Calgacus one-handed with his axe might take a few more. The Alani could kill them all, wipe them from the face of Middle Earth, but thirty or more of the nomads would not see the end of the day.

Thinking about the final moments, Ballista glanced over to where his hobbled horse grazed. A cowardly thought, the thought of a *nithing*, insinuated itself through his mind. No, he would not disgrace himself in his own eyes, or those of others, or those of the Allfather. When the last moments were close, he would get the boy Wulfstan on the horse. In the confusion, he might just have a chance to get clear. He could go north. Bearing the arms of Aluith, once Wulfstan told his story, the Heruli were likely to welcome him.

Ballista wondered what his own boys were doing, far away in Sicily. Would they ever hear of his death? He pushed down the self-pity. Allfather, if I fall, let your shield-maidens choose me for Valhalla; and then, and none too soon, many years from now, let them bring my sons to me there. Let us feast together through the long ages until the coming of the winter of winters, until the icy cold of *Fimbulvetr* brings on *Ragnarok*, and it is the end of all of us; gods and men.

The deep boom of a drum broke Ballista's reverie, made Wulfstan next to him start. The beat was slow, deep, menacing.

'The Persians do the same; it signifies nothing.' Ballista made his voice sound dismissive. Wulfstan looked a little reassured.

Ballista stepped out from the cover of the lime and gazed out at the Alani host. The trees on the far bank did not altogether obscure his view. A warrior moved his horse out in front. A conical, gilded helmet on his head, silvered mail on his body, the nobleman shone like the sun. The Alan removed the helmet, hung it on a horn of his saddle. Bareheaded, he raised his arms, presumably to address some high god or martial deity the Alani believed might bring them fortune in the grim work ahead.

'Stay here.' The decision was made on an instant. Bow and a couple of arrows in hand, Ballista brushed through the undergrowth. He slid on his arse down the bank. Holding the bow high, he splashed across the stream and launched himself up the far bank.

At the lip, he slowed, careful to rise up in the shelter of a tree. He could hear his *familia* calling – Come back; what the fuck are you doing? Ignoring them, he pushed through the bushes until he had a clear view.

He nocked, raised and drew in one motion. There was a warning shout from the ranks of the Alani. Ballista aimed, allowed for the wind from the north – a little higher and a shade to the left – and released.

Ballista knew he should run, but he had to watch. Two hundred paces – a very long shot indeed – the arrow seemed an age in flight. Alerted, the warrior in the gorgeous armour turned his head but did not desist from summoning the god of his people. The arrow took him in the thigh. The deity had rejected his importuning.

A roar of fury from the Alani. Ballista turned and ran. Fear and triumph added wings to his feet. He flew, like Hermes, down one bank, across the water, and up the other, behind the coming thunder of several hundred hooves, the yells of outrage, fury at the sacrilege.

Ballista ducked behind the tree. He doubled up, fighting air into his lungs. Wulfstan and the others were already shooting. The range was still long, shifting branches in the way. They would not hit many yet. But there were plenty of arrows. Let them carry on. It gave them something to do in the face of the charge, made them feel better.

'Fuck me, have you annoyed them!' Maximus shouted. He was laughing now. 'You did not kill him, mind, just nailed his leg to his saddle.'

The Alani were whooping, shooting as they rode. Their arrows were falling thick, like winter snow. But the spreading lime trees gave cover overhead and, lower, the shrubs took some.

Ballista steadied his breathing, put an arrow on the string and leant out, looking for a target. The Alani were almost at the tree line. Off to the right, a pony bucked, an arrow in its foreleg. Ballista chose and shot. Without looking, he reached for another arrow, drew and shot again.

The nomads were driving their mounts through the thorny undergrowth. Scratched and bleeding, the ponies were jibbing and refusing. They were getting in each other's way. Their very numbers were against them. The Roman arrows were adding to the confusion.

Ballista sent a shaft deep into the neck of a pony. It stood for a moment, then fell, as if sacrificed. Its rider jumped off its back. The pony behind ran into him, sending him spinning. The pony stumbled, its rider half up its neck. Ballista put an arrow in its haunch. It spun, kicking out. Its hooves caught another animal in the barrel. This leapt sideways, and went crashing – legs scrabbling – over the bank and down into the river.

All along the lip, among the sharp brambles, nomad ponies were barging into each other, tripping, falling, their riders powerless against the elemental confusion. Only a few animals had got down the bank on their own feet and with a rider still on their back.

Ballista dedicated his arrows to these. Without the need of an order, so did the other bowmen of the *familia*. It was like shooting fish in a barrel. In the riverbed, the ponies made big, unprotected, almost stationary targets. Once one or two were hit, they thrashed around, hopelessly impeding the rest. A river running red was not merely a poetic fancy.

One of the Alani – surely a hero among his people – had negotiated all the disarray. Like a centaur, he and his mount breasted the Roman side of the bank. As hooves scrabbled over the top, and the rider was motionless against the sky, Ballista shot him in the chest. He toppled back. The pony ran on into the wagon-laager. It almost seemed a pity to snuff out such extravagant courage.

Another of the Alani reached up over the bank. This one was on foot. Ballista shot him. The arrow hit him in the left shoulder. He spun around. Then he straightened, drew his sword with his right hand, and came on. Ballista shot him in the stomach. He doubled up, left hand around the shaft. He was on his knees. Somehow, he forced himself up again, took another shaky step forward. He had not dropped his sword. Ballista shot him again. In the chest, this time. Finally, the warrior went down.

On the far side of the carnage, a horn sounded a clean note that cut through the sounds of exertion and pain. The Alani snagged among the undergrowth began to hack and fight their way out. The few alive in the river rushed back up their own bank. Dispassionately, Ballista shot a couple more in the back as they fled. They made no odds. In a fight like this, it was not about the number of attackers killed, but about their will to fight. In a sense, it was always like that.

Wulfstan was exhausted but, still, hours later, his excitement kept him going. He was a warrior. He had killed a man. And not just one man, but three, maybe four. He would never forget the sheer, untarnished pleasure of his first kill. The Alani pony had refused at the lip of the far bank. The nomad was kicking in his heels, urging it down towards the water. The steep, untrustworthy-looking slope, the smell of blood, the squealing of others of its kind in pain and distress, all combined to make the pony reluctant. The Alan was silhouetted. Wulfstan drew the bow. And something happened; something very strange. His hands were guided. It was as if he had done this before, many times before. It was as if Aluith were alive, guiding his hands. Wulfstan released. The arrow shot straight and true. There was never any doubt it would take the Alan full in the chest. The nomad fell, a look of indignant surprise on his face.

That Alan was just the first. The others were easier still. Wulfstan wielded Aluith's bow as if he had the strength of a grown man, as if the bow had been made for him. Wulfstan was a warrior now. Killing a man was a greater deed than killing a boar or a bear. If he had belonged to the Taifali, all the unclean things he had submitted to would have been washed away in the blood of the men he had killed that afternoon. He was not of the Taifali. He was an Angle; maybe destined to become a Herul. But now he was a warrior, a man-killer. Now, he had the skills to exact his revenge, to wash himself clean in the blood of many, many men.

When the horn sounded, the Alani had pulled back from the river. Soon after, they had broken off their assault on the wagon line. It was mid-afternoon. They had asked for no truce to reclaim their dead but had ridden off in silence. They had established a main camp some three or four miles away to the south. Ballista had been right, both nomad man and beast had been tired from hard travel.

Yet not all the Alani – and there had to be around three hundred or more of them – had retired to their camp. A large troop – a hundred or so led by the noble with the *tamga* standard from earlier – camped out half a mile to the north. And while the Alani made no more all-out assaults in the rest of the day, small parties kept feinting attacks all along the perimeters. Sometimes, they carried fire pots with them, from which they would kindle flaming arrows. With the wagon-laager by a stream, there was little danger of serious conflagration. But it all added to the strain.

There was no rest between the feints. Under the joint direction of Andonnoballus and Ballista, the defenders were kept very busy. Every member of the caravan, even the slaves and staff found cowering in the bottom of the carts, even the old Gothic witch, was put to work. Ropes were dug out, and the wagons tied tight together. As an added precaution, each was staked down in place. Furs, skins and felt were stretched and tacked between wheels and across gaps to keep out arrows and hinder attackers. The whole assemblage was doused from the stream, and butts and cauldrons brimming with water were placed along the inside of the line. All the baggage was laboriously hauled out. Sacks, boxes and barrels were piled up to complete the barricade. Bales of delicate silks, diplomatic presents from the Roman emperor to the King of the Heruli, were piled with amphorae of pickled fish.

It was no more peaceful to the north, by the river. Ballista had them tie ropes from one lime tree to another. He then showed them how to construct a barrier of entwined thorn bushes, like the *zereba* the tribes of North Africa built. This *zereba* was reinforced with assorted belongings and ran along the front of the fighting position.

When released from improvising field fortifications, the defenders scurried about collecting undamaged arrows. Some might find an ironic pleasure in sending the Alani shafts back.

Darkness brought no relief. Bands of Alani continued every so often to canter up to the defences. There was a big moon, and few clouds. The nomads were perfectly visible, their shadows sliding across the Steppe like black souls escaped from Niflheim. Some again brought fire pots, lit flaming arrows and sent them arcing into wagons. The others who did not were the more frightening. Shot at a high trajectory, the swift black shafts fell nearly vertical inside the laager; hard to see at all, and almost impossible to judge where they would strike. Some of the Alani used special hollow arrowheads which whistled or screeched as they fell.

Those down by the river who could sleep despite the Alani still got little rest. Ballista had divided his command of six men into three watches. Only two were to stand down, while the other four remained on watch, and the rest period was just two hours. Wulfstan, with Castricius, had been the first off duty. The little Roman had pulled his cloak over him in the shelter of one of the lime trees and started snoring almost instantly. The continued work on the *zereba* did not disturb him in the slightest. Wulfstan, however, had been too excited to sleep. He had killed a man; his first man. Now, much later, some time after midnight, and with his next period of rest postponed, he wished he had had more self-control, wished he had at least shut his eyes.

Wulfstan was pleased he had not had to prepare food for everyone. Maximus had plucked and gutted the chicken he had acquired earlier and put it to boil in a pot suspended over the big campfire lit by the Heruli. Old Calgacus had scrounged or stolen various bits and pieces to add to the stew. With some dry, army-style biscuit and washed down with rough wine, it was not too bad. Once he had started eating, Wulfstan realized he was very hungry. He had even eaten the core of the apple he had been given. Calgacus had said they may as well eat most of their stores tonight, because by the end of tomorrow there would be fewer alive needing a share. Wulfstan had looked at the others and thought, You poor bastards, you poor, *old* bastards.

Ballista did not seem to rest at all. He disappeared back to the wagons for a time. Not long before midnight, he came back lugging two shovels and two big bundles of staves of wood. He roused his men out and quietly gave them his instructions. They were to tie dark scarves or cloths around their helmets, sword belts and scabbards. They were to smear mud on their armour and any exposed skin. Shield ornaments likewise were to be covered, if not prised off. Finally, if there were hobnails in their boots, they should muffle them with rags.

When the seven dark figures, reeking of river mud, were assembled, Ballista checked them over and then outlined what he intended. Three – Castricius, Calgacus and Tarchon – would remain behind the *zereba*. They should provide cover, if things went wrong. The other four were going to cross the river. Ballista himself, and Maximus, would work through to the edge of the scrub and keep watch on the Alani out on the plain to the north. Hippothous and Wulfstan were to take a shovel and a bundle of wood each. To make it as difficult as possible for the Alani in the morning, they were to dig shallow holes in the soft soil of the riverbank, plant the staves Ballista had sharpened point up in the bottom and cover the traps over with some brushwood. They would only be able to do a couple of short sections of the bank, but everything would help.

Crossing the stream, the four of them together, Wulfstan had not been unduly fearful. The bodies of the Alani caught in the reeds did not bother him, and the babbling of the water was somehow homely. Even the splashing of their passing did not make him think it would warn the Alani. Then Ballista had waved Maximus and Hippothous off to the left. Soon they had been lost in the undergrowth downstream. Ballista indicated where Wulfstan was to start digging. The big warrior then climbed the bank and, with no sound at all, was gone.

Wulfstan was alone. He had been alone for – he guessed from the stars – about an hour. To begin with, he had not minded too much. But now he was very tired, and the night and the isolation were growing oppressive. The scurry of small nocturnal animals no longer sounded reassuring. The play of shadows as clouds chased across the moon began to presage something dire. Every sound in the night, every plop as a rat or its like took to the water was enough to make him jump. When an owl called from one of the trees, he had to fight down an urge to run. His nerves were stretched, creaking like an over-drawn bow.

The scrunch as his spade bit into the moist soil was unfeasibly loud. The Alani were but a few hundred paces away; it must carry to them. He tugged aside a reluctant root with his bare hands. Allfather, he was tired.

Something splashed behind him, upriver off to his right. He forced himself to ignore it. Warriors – Angle or Herul – did not jump at the slightest sound. All these Steppe streams were full of fish – chub, gudgeon, pike – then there were all those mouse-like creatures: voles, marmots, all sorts of rodents.

Wulfstan bedded in another stake: *tap-tap-tap*. His hands were coated with dirt. It stung where the thorns had cut him. The wet riparian smell was strong in his nose. He reached for the spray of undergrowth he had already cut. The scratch of it was loud as he dragged it over the fresh-dug hole, arranged it just so.

Again, a splash behind him. This time, there was something more; a sucking sound – the sound of something moving through the water. Something, or someone, was moving downstream towards him.

Wulfstan flattened himself against the bank. He listened as hard

197

as he could. Nothing, just the river. The hoot of a distant owl. Nothing out of the ordinary. Nothing made by man.

Wulfstan breathed out; almost a sob. His nerves were cracking like spring ice. He went to move. And there was the sound again. Closer now. Much closer now.

Allfather, Deep Hood, Death-blinder, hold your hands over me.

Wulfstan forced himself to look. A sombre, hooded figure maybe thirty paces away. A man was coming cautiously down the stream towards him.

If he moved, Wulfstan would be seen straightaway. If he did not, the man would stumble across him in no time. Wulfstan's fingers dug into the earth. He began to pray.

In the milk-white light of the moon, the man came on. Twenty paces, less.

Nerthus, Earth Mother, do not desert your child.

An amorphous shadow detached itself from the bank behind the figure. With no sound, it entered the stream. Only faint ripples on the water's silver surface betrayed its corporeality.

The hooded man came on. Silently, the shadow closed behind it. Steel glittered in the moonlight. An arm snaked around the hood. The steel flashed, cold and without pity, sawing across a pulled-back throat. Legs thrashed, churning the stream; impossibly loud after the silence.

The shadow lowered the dead man into the water, cleaned the blade on his clothes, pushed him aside into a clump of reeds. All was quiet again.

The shadow removed its muddied headgear. Its long hair shone white in the moon.

'Come, time to go.' Ballista held out a hand.

Wulfstan took it, let himself be helped down.

They both looked at the dead man.

Do not fear, and let no thought of death be upon you.
But come, tell me this thing and recite it to me accurately:
Where is it that you walk alone to the ships from the army
Through the darkness of night when other mortals are sleeping?

Wulfstan gazed up at Ballista, uncomprehending.
  Ballista smiled. 'An old Greek poem. Come, time to go.'

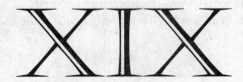

XIX

Although he had never been more deeply asleep, Ballista woke easily, without a sound, and was calm feeling the pressure on his neck. He opened his eyes. He saw one of the two men whom he had known he would find looking down at him.

Calgacus removed the fingers he was pressing below and just behind Ballista's left ear. The northerner smiled. The waking gesture was one of many signs he, Calgacus and Maximus had evolved over the years. Sometimes, he thought these signs amounted almost to a private language. It was something to be used when words would not do: in the din of battle, among the intricacies of a court, or in the dead of night.

Calgacus's face moved. In the light of the low, central fire, it lost much of its ugliness and assumed a delicacy it lacked by day. It wore a sad, tender expression.

Ballista rolled out of his cloak and painfully levered himself into a sitting position.

'Maybe half an hour to dawn,' Calgacus said.

Ballista had slept for a couple of hours. In that time, the wind had dropped altogether, and it had clouded over. The moon was hidden. The sky now was a uniform blue-black, except for a few rents in the clouds where it was a translucent yellow-tinged blue. With no wind, the Steppe grass had ceased to sing. Other sounds had come to the fore: the lapping chuckle of the stream, a background chirring of insects – it was a warm June night – and the strange whistling of those large mouse- or squirrel-like rodents that seemed to inhabit every hollow in the Steppe. Now and then, a horse stamped or coughed.

With difficulty, Ballista got to his feet. Allfather, he was too old for this. Forty-one winters on Middle Earth; far too many to be sleeping on the ground in a war shirt of mail. He walked, stiff in every joint, to the thorn fence. He pulled up his mail, fumbled with the clothes under it and pissed on the *zereba*.

When finished, he walked back and sat down heavily next to the old Caledonian.

Calgacus passed him a beaker of warmed, watered wine.

'Thank you.' The northerner sipped. It was too hot to drink. Calgacus passed him some dry biscuit and a hunk of cold fat bacon. Ballista put the bacon on the leg of his trousers; it was no time to be over-fastidious about grease. He dipped the biscuit in the drink and, as each bit softened, nibbled it.

'Anything?' Ballista asked.

'Horsemen moving from the little camp over the river, about an hour ago.'

'How many?'

Calgacus shook his head. 'It had already clouded over, black as Niflheim.'

'And they were leaving the camp opposite us?'

'It sounded like they went to the big camp to the south.'

'Any sign of men withdrawing from there?' Ballista asked.

'No.'

They sat in silence. Beyond the wine and the bacon were other smells. The Alani dead had not started stinking yet. There was the scent of clean water, of leaf mould, of crushed grass. Against the bitter aroma of wormwood were other, sweeter scents of those flowers not yet scorched by the heat of summer. The smells of horse and unwashed humanity may have been there, but Ballista could not tell; he was inured to them. The smell of the bacon was there. It came to dominate. Ballista started to gnaw at it.

The Alani had not asked for a truce to reclaim their dead. That was not good. It meant they were going nowhere. They had moved some horsemen from the camp opposite Ballista to the main one. It might help Ballista's men, but was not good for those holding the wagons.

Ballista could not see how the main defensive line might be improved. The wagon-laager would be near impossible to move or burn, and it would be slow and difficult to get across. Its real weakness had no remedy: there were too few defenders. In each of the six wagons were a Roman soldier and one of the Sarmatian drivers; except the third from the left, which had two Sarmatians but no soldier. In four of the five fortified gaps between the wagons, one of the Heruli was stationed; two of them, Ochus and Datius, were carrying wounds. In the last gap on the right, the *gudja* had taken post, thus freeing Andonnoballus to move about as the commander.

Andonnoballus had with him the two slaves owned by the soldiers to act as runners. The arrangement was the product of much thought and discussion. It was the best they could do. But it was desperately inadequate. There was no reserve. There were just far too few men.

Behind the clouds, the eastern sky had lightened a little. A lone bird began to sing. Almost inconspicuously, others – dozens, then hundreds, if not thousands – joined, until, before the listeners really noticed it, the air was full of birdsong.

'Do you think the Sarmatian drivers will fight to the death?' Calgacus asked. 'They are kin to the Alani.'

Ballista did not reply at once. He was still listening to the dawn chorus, trying to hear any sounds beyond it that signified danger.

'The Urugundi have their families. While the *gudja* lives, they must fight.' Calgacus answered his own question.

'Even if the Gothic priest falls, and the old witch too, it is too late for the Sarmatians. They have no more freedom in the matter than we do,' Ballista said.

With the coming day, the wind returned. The rents in the cloud were ripped wider, revealing a sky turned pale, silver-gold. Soon, all that was left of the blanket of the dark were isolated clouds fleeing south, the tattered survivors of some celestial rout.

As the light improved, Ballista, Calgacus and every man in the beleaguered laager peered out across the Steppe. Rather than serried ranks of Alani, their mounts literally champing at the bit, there was nothing to be seen except the quiet, dark shapes of the two nomad camps and the smoke rising above them.

The defenders watched and waited. The Alani presumably took their breakfast. The mingled smells of woodsmoke, dung burnt as fuel, and food drifted over.

'After yesterday, they are reluctant to attack,' Wulfstan said. He sounded at once both hopeful and disappointed.

'It may well be,' Ballista said. 'But it also means they think they have plenty of time.'

'And that means Naulobates' ugly fucking Heruli were nowhere fucking near by last night,' Calgacus said.

'They are nomads; they travel fast. They could outrun the news of their coming.' Ballista felt he had to say something encouraging.

When Arvak and Alsvid, the horses of the sun, hauled the bright chariot over the horizon, the Alani stirred. A dozen outriders rode out of the camp in front of Ballista and formed a screen. The rest followed, forming up into a compact body under the *tamga* standard, out of bow shot. There did indeed seem fewer of them than the day before.

The Alani standard bellied out in the north wind. The *tamga* looked a bit like an upside-down Greek *omega* with a stylized bird perched on top. Ballista wondered if it had any meaning beyond signifying this particular nobleman.

A messenger, one of the soldiers' slaves, ran up and told Ballista that much the same was happening at the other camp. There, the Alani had split into three divisions; one aimed at each end of the wagon-laager, one at the middle. There were fewer riders in the latter group.

Ballista thanked the messenger, told him what little news there was and sent him back to Andonnoballus. The main attacks would come here across the river, and at either end of the line of wagons.

The Alani across the river remained where they were.

Maximus started laughing. 'Keeping out of harm's way today,' he called. Ballista and Wulfstan joined in the laughter.

'Why are you fuckers giggling like girls?' To Calgacus's eyes, the Alani were an undifferentiated blur.

'The priest or nobleman Ballista shot in the leg yesterday is summoning their gods again,' Wulfstan said. 'He is rather further away, and hardly in front of the others at all.'

The deep percussion of the nomad war drum carried across the plain. It reverberated in every man's chest. High, peeling horns rang out. The enemy trotted forward.

The Alani set to with their customary whooping. The handful of Heruli answered with their high *yipping* sound.

'Are you ready for war?' Ballista's battlefield Latin carried across the martial sounds of the Steppe.

'Ready!' The *familia* and the auxiliaries huddled in the wagons shouted back. The voices of the latter were muffled and faint.

'Are you ready for war?' Three times the call and response rang out. Yet it was a thin and insubstantial thing against the nomadic uproar. Ballista wondered if the traditional Roman battle call had ever been heard so far out beyond the frontiers. This was not the *imperium*, but another world. This was *barbaricum*, and it demanded something else. His youth in Germania told him a battle can be won or lost in the shouting, before a blow is struck.

'Out! Out! Out!' Ballista bellowed the age-old war cry of the Angles. Wulfstan, Calgacus and Maximus picked it up. 'Out! Out! Out!' Tarchon shouted something similar. Ballista wondered if the Heruli behind him heard, and if it held any folk memories for them.

The ground rang under the drumming hooves of the Alani ponies. The nomads had accelerated into a fast canter. They were shooting as they came. The arrows whistled full of menace through the air. But the trees on both banks and the reinforced *zereba* rendered them ineffective.

Ballista and his men, steady on their own two feet, and presented with a large, dense target, released fast and accurate. Three, four horses crashed to the ground, riders thrown tumbling into the dirt. When the Alani reached the opposite tree line and reined in, there were five riderless horses turning and boring amongst them, causing confusion.

The majority of the Alani swung down, throwing their reins to the few who remained on horseback. The latter wheeled and kicked back towards their camp, four or five ponies galloping behind each on lead reins.

Ballista kept shooting: pluck arrow from ground, nock, draw, aim, release. Nomads continued to fall. Ballista half noted one staggering with an arrow protruding from his eye.

A shaft ricocheted off the lime next to Ballista's face. It left a weeping, sappy scar on the bough. Ballista drew and released again. The incoming arrows were getting closer. About half the dismounted Alani had remained on the far bank. Scattered among the trees and undergrowth, they were pouring arrows into the defences.

The other nomads – twenty, twenty-five of them? – were rushing down the bank.

A nomad suddenly collapsed, clutching his leg. Another tripped, tumbling face first down into the water. Further along, off to the left, one seemed to half sink into the earth and screamed a terrible scream as if some chthonic deity were dragging him down to the underworld. Others shied away from those areas of the bank. The pits dug by Hippothous and Wulfstan were channelling the Alani, making them bunch up, making them yet better targets.

'Shoot the ones in the water.' Ballista doubted if all would obey his order. It is almost impossible to shoot at someone else and not the men shooting at you. Fighting the urge to target the embroidered coat of a bowman pulling an arrow from his *gorytus* on the bank directly across from him, Ballista closed one eye, allowed for the man's movement and sent an arrow smack into the chest of a man splashing through the river.

The attacking party reached the southern bank. Two nomads climbed over the top. Both toppled back, skewered by shafts from Ballista and Wulfstan. Ballista's vision of the world shrank to just those few feet of muddy riverbank. Three more nomads hurled themselves over. Ballista missed. Wulfstan hit another. Four more followed over. They were at the *zereba*; wielding their long swords, trying to hack a way through the thorns. Ballista shot one in the shoulder; higher than he had intended.

Two of the Alani crouched to hoist one of their kin over the *zereba*. Ballista shot the one on the right in the side. He collapsed, dropping the nomad half in the air. The man screamed as he landed amid the sharp, tangled thorn bushes. He thrashed around, becoming more embedded. Red gashes of blood blossomed where his clothes were torn. Ballista drew his *spatha* and brought it down on the man's head. The long, heavy blade crumpled the skull like an eggshell.

The Alani who had survived the ill-fated attack were scrambling back across the riverbed, up the opposite bank and into the shelter of the trees and undergrowth. The ones who had remained there were still shooting. They continued to pose a threat. It was best to keep your head down. Yet the intensity had gone. An Alan would pop out, shoot a wildly aimed missile and duck back. Given Ballista and his men were helmeted and armoured, to come to serious harm they would have to be either unlucky, slow or stupid.

Ballista leant his back against the sticky bark of the lime tree. There was a gash on his left forearm. Not serious, but he had no idea how it had got there. Now he had noticed it, the thing stung abominably. He wiped something else sticky off his face. A mess of blood and brains came away on his hand; from the man he had killed with his sword. It tasted as if some were in his mouth. He took a drink of wine, rinsed his mouth and spat. He stoppered the flask and checked on the enemy. Nothing new. He nocked an arrow. With more incoming than outgoing, there was no need to conserve arrows. He scanned for a target, found one, waited and shot. He missed, but it was good to keep their heads down.

'Keep shooting,' he called.

One of the messengers puffed up to Ballista and sketched a Roman salute. He was a slave of the military and had a sword in one hand. '*Dominus*, Andonnoballus asks for help. The Alani have got into the laager. They have taken the wagon at the eastern end. They are throwing in men. They will roll up the whole line.'

Now that the fighting on his own front was not so pressing,

207

Ballista could hear clearly the din of battle behind him. Some of it was hand to hand. Thinking, he released another arrow. It shaved past the head of an Alan in the bushes opposite.

'*Dominus?*' The messenger was shifting on his feet in his impatience for an answer.

Ballista stood, turning it over in his mind. Could he make a difference with but a few men? And if he did strip his own defences, would the Alani recover their spirit and overrun the *zereba*?

The interpreter, the one who had done well in the fighting in the original ambush, came from the opposite direction. He skidded to a halt, doubling up. He was very out of breath. He had a blade in his left hand and his right forearm was heavily bandaged.

Ballista could not remember the man's name. 'What is it?' He could wait no longer. It was not going to be good news.

'The Alani have dismounted.' The interpreter's chest was heaving. It was not that far to run; he must have been fighting. 'They are assaulting the wagon of the *gudja*. The Goth needs more men.'

'Fuck.' Ballista swore monotonously as his mind raced. The Alani over the river had taken casualties. They had been held by the *zereba*. Perhaps it would be fine if he went with some men. And – the thought struck him – the Alani had taken riders from over the river last night. Perhaps the river was never anything but a diversion. He would take Maximus, Tarchon, the injured Calgacus and young Wulfstan with him. It would leave only Castricius and Hippothous. Two men to hold off forty or more. Ridiculous.

Ballista looked at the expectant faces of the messenger and the interpreter. Fuck! Where to go? To the *gudja*? To Andonnoballus? He turned to the interpreter – Biomasos, that was his name.

'Had the Alani actually got through the defences when you left?' The interpreter shook his head. 'But they were . . .'

Ballista motioned him to silence. A plan fully formed – as in some improbable, queasy-making Greek myth of the birth of a divinity from a parent's head – had appeared.

Ballista turned to the interpreter, and pointed west. 'Biomasos, you see the last of the limes, where Tarchon and Calgacus are fighting? Go and send them both to me here. You will take their place; use Tarchon's bow.'

'But *Dominus*, I am a poor shot, and my arm is wounded.'

'No matter, just show yourself now and then, take the odd shot, let them know there are still men defending the *zereba*.'

'We will do what is ordered, and at every command we will be ready.' It was good the interpreter had done a great deal of work for the military.

As Ballista waited, he took another arrow and aimed very carefully at an Alan lurking in a thick patch of brambles across the stream. He took his time. He dismissed from his mind a nomad arrow that came from nowhere and crashed through the foliage not far from the right of his head. Gently, he released. The arrow sped away. Like a striking hawk, it flashed over the water. A foot or two from the chest of its prey, a briar deflected it. The tribesman yelped, and dropped hurriedly out of sight.

Tarchon and Calgacus arrived.

'The best hunting is the hunting of men,' the Suanian said. He was beaming. The mountaineer liked killing people. 'There is no boar nor lion that can compare.'

'Fucking half-wit,' Calgacus muttered.

'You all follow me,' Ballista commanded.

Running, bent low, they reached Maximus at the right of their line without mishap. There was something comical about six of them attempting to find cover behind one tree, broad though its trunk was.

Ballista addressed the slave. 'You will take the place of Maximus here. You heard what I said to the interpreter.'

The slave looked aghast.

'If you play a man's role here, I will purchase your freedom – if we survive,' Ballista said. He saw that the bracing effects of his words were somewhat undercut by the last phrase. 'If I fall, one of these men will buy your freedom.'

'We will do what is ordered, and at every command we will be ready.' The slave took the bow and *gorytus* that Ballista passed over.

'Let us be men,' Ballista said in Greek. 'Maximus and Tarchon with me. Calgacus, watch our backs, finish off any wounded. Wulfstan, use your bow, try to keep out of the melee. Ready?'

'Ready.' Maximus, Calgacus and Tarchon gave a quiet, personal acknowledgement. It had none of the bravado of the Roman call and response. Wulfstan said nothing.

The five of them checked their swords, hefted their war gear.

Ballista spoke in his own language, two lines of epic poetry.

> *Wyrd will often spare*
> *An undoomed man, if his courage is good.*

Calgacus spat. 'If you are doomed, no courage will change the course of events.'

'You really are a miserable old bastard,' Maximus said.

They were all laughing, except Wulfstan. The young Angle's face was clouded.

Ballista drew his dagger, snapped it back; drew his sword, snapped it back; touched the healing stone on his scabbard. All the time, he looked at Wulfstan, thinking. Then he cursed himself for not realizing more quickly.

'Wulfstan' – Ballista spoke in their own language – 'if you live through this, I will give you your freedom. If I fall, these men can witness, I wish you manumitted in my will.'

The boy's face broke into an enormous smile. 'Thank you, *Atheling*. No doom can touch us now.'

'Huhn,' Calgacus snorted.

They pushed through the undergrowth away from the river, up to the tailgate of the wagon at the eastern end of the semicircle. It was deserted. There was fighting in and around the wagon beyond.

Ballista waved Wulfstan out into the open centre of the laager and led the other three along the inner side of the wagon.

The defences between the two wagons had been breached. A Herul and a Roman soldier lay dead there. Alani were treading on them as they clambered through. All the attention of the tribes-men was on the wagon where there was still resistance.

Ballista caught the eyes of the others. He held up three fingers. They nodded. One – two – as he lowered the third finger, they hurled themselves around the corner of the wagon. The first Alan looked round. Ballista's *spatha* sheered half his face away. Maximus darted past Ballista's right shoulder and thrust his shorter *gladius* deep into the chest of a second. Tarchon moved up on the left. A third, climbing through the gap in the barricade, opened his mouth to scream, threw up his arm to shield himself. The sound never came. The arm was severed at the elbow. The nomad looked at the stump stupidly. It was fountaining blood. Tarchon drove the point of the blade into his throat, then pushed him away with a boot. Another Alan had been clambering into the wagon with the fighting. He turned, went to shout a warning, and an arrow took him in the neck. He turned slowly, as if taking a last stock of the sunshine of the mortal world, and fell off the wagon. Four Alani dead in about as many heartbeats.

Ballista gestured for Wulfstan to come close. Calgacus was making sure the downed Alani were dead with the point of a sword. Another one, blissfully unaware, appeared through the gap in the fortification. With a wild yell, Tarchon smashed him backwards. Cries of consternation arose from outside.

'Tarchon, Wulfstan, stop any more getting through here.'

They moved into position, Wulfstan sending a couple of arrows whipping out, to leave no doubt in Alani minds that the defences were manned again.

Ballista and Maximus jumped up into the rear of the next wagon. Calgacus, his right hand still near useless, slowly hauled himself up after. Bodies were strewn across the floor of the wagon; six or seven of them, defenders and attackers, piled indiscriminately. Otherwise, it was empty. The fighting had moved on. The three followed through the body of the wagon, stumbling over the corpses.

Outside on the Steppe, over the boom of the war drum, horns blared out afresh. Most likely they were telling of the closing of the breach, Ballista thought. But were they summoning reinforcements or admitting defeat? *Wyrd will often spare an undoomed man, if his courage is good.* The lines ran in his mind.

There were half a dozen Alani preparing to storm the third wagon. They had their backs to Ballista. As he saw them, two slipped off around the inside of the wagon to outflank the defenders.

Side by side on the tailgate, Ballista and Maximus looked at each other. They both mouthed, 'One-two-three.' Together, they jumped down. The Alani heard them, glanced back, expecting their own. Horrified, they started to turn. Ballista staggered a little on landing. Rather than try to regain his balance, he carried on forward – half running, half falling – blade first, at the Alan on his right. The nomad was wheeling around, bringing his sword across to guard himself. It was all too late. The tip of Ballista's steel sliced through the side of the nomad's tunic and on into the delicate flesh. It grated on rib, and kept going. Ballista used the impact to halt his momentum.

Ballista heard Calgacus curse as he dropped from the tail of the wagon behind.

Pushing the incapacitated, probably dying, man away, Ballista turned to face the one to his left. He used his shield to parry a wild swing to his neck. Both stepped back. Ballista got into an ox guard; shield parallel to the fighting line, sword held overhand, sticking forward from the side of his brow like the beast's horn. The Alan held his shield in the same way, but had his sword down by his right thigh. Both shifted on their feet; waiting for the other to move, waiting for an opening.

Ballista could hear the clash of steel, stamping footfalls and grunts to his left, heavy feet and Calgacus swearing to his right. No time to look; both his friends were still alive.

With no warning, Ballista thrust at the face. His opponent brought his shield up. Ballista rolled his wrist and changed the blow into a downward slice to the left leg. The Alan withdrew the leg, stepped forward on to his right, and made an inside-edge thrust to the head. It was the obvious response; the one Ballista had expected. With a speed that belied his size, Ballista twisted his entire body, bringing sword and shield up and across almost together. The impact ran through his left arm as the shield blocked the Alani's blow, but he more heard than felt his own sword cut into the nomad's exposed right arm. It was like a knife in cabbage. The man shrieked, dropped his weapon, reeled around. Quite calmly, Ballista chopped his sword down into the man's right thigh. He could be ignored for now.

A glance to his left. One Alan down, Maximus driving the other back. Ballista looked to the right. The two outflanking Alani were coming back, heading for Calgacus. They were moving cautiously, swords and shields well up. Ballista edged over towards Calgacus;

close, but not so close they would get in the way of each other's swordplay.

A strange quiet seemed to descend as the four became isolated in their minimalist, deadly dance – a half-step here, a slight change of balance there. Sunlight flashed on the questing steel. Ballista only part registered a lithe shape drop softly from the wagon behind the Alani. An elegant lunge, and the Alan in front of Ballista dropped like a poled beast. A movement like a mere tremor in the hot air, and the other pitched forward, coughing out his lifeblood.

'Thank you,' Ballista said.

'Think nothing of it,' Andonnoballus said. 'And thank you for coming.'

Maximus had killed his man. Calgacus shuffled over and finished the second Ballista had felled. The four men stood, panting.

'They are withdrawing.' A voice could be heard from somewhere. As if in confirmation, there was a diminishing thunder of hooves and a bray of distant horns. It took a moment to realize the war drum was silent.

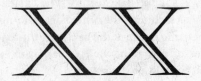

Calgacus had taken longer than the others to get up on to a wagon. It was not just the splint on his right arm impeding him; when he moved, things deep in his shoulder grated together painfully. None of the demented running, clambering, jumping or fighting had helped. And he had long accepted he was far from young.

Finally achieving a point of vantage, Calgacus peered out across the plain. He was not going to admit either to the pain, or that he could see little apart from a blurred cloud of dust that marked the retreating Alani horsemen.

'Quite a few of them are carrying wounds,' Maximus said.

'But, again, they are leaving their dead,' Andonnoballus said. 'They will return.'

As they watched the Alani ride away, Ballista and Andonnoballus discussed what had happened, re-creating in detail the ebb and flow of events.

Calgacus had no patience with such futile endeavours. The face of battle was no stranger to him. Battle was nothing but chaos, every man isolated in his own few yards of fear and exertion. Every participant saw a different battle. Yet, afterwards, some primal urge forced the survivors to impose a pattern, to tell a clear, linear story. It was as if their own memories lacked the necessary validity unless they could be placed within something generally agreed.

'Their plan was sound,' Ballista said. 'They made two diversions; one across the watercourse, the other some mounted skirmishers looking like they might attack the centre of the wagon line. These tied down some of our men, while their two main assaults came in on foot at either end of the laager.'

Calgacus watched three vultures coast in just outside the laager on their feathery wings. All their grace was lost when they came to earth.

'And it nearly worked,' Ballista continued. 'At the western end they were fighting hand to hand around the wagon of the *gudja*. Here in the east they got inside the defences. If we had not blocked the breach and killed the few already inside, it would have worked.'

'But it did not work,' Andonnoballus said. 'There is nothing nomad horse archers hate more than trying to storm a wagon-laager, even if it is defended by only a few desperate men.'

'It is not just on the Steppe,' Ballista said. 'There is nothing harder in the world than taking any fortification manned by just a handful of brave, well-equipped men who will obey orders and dig in their heels. The casualties of the attackers will always be horrendous.'

The Alani had indeed suffered many casualties. No fewer than thirty-nine nomadic corpses were counted. Luckily for the prospects of the majority of these Alani in the afterlife, the three surviving Heruli were too tired and too busy to scalp and strip the skin from the right arms of more than a couple each.

Only eight of the defenders had fallen: the Heruli Ochus and

Aordus, three soldiers, including the one who had been lying already close to death in their wagon, and three Sarmatians.

For the moment, all the corpses were given the same treatment. Defenders and Alani alike were merely rolled and thrown out beyond the defences. Lack of manpower, time, even energy, precluded anything more elaborate and either denigrating or respectful.

Calgacus felt that at this place – Blood River, as it was in his mind – the spirits of death hovered close. He knew Ballista's people saw the choosers of the slain as beautiful young women. These white-armed, white-breasted girls would carry the chosen to Valhalla, and there in the golden hall of the Allfather they would serve them mead, maybe take them as lovers. For Hellenes like Hippothous, or Romans like Castricius it was different. For them, two grim-eyed warriors, Sleep and Death, bore them away to the underworld, where all but a tiny few would flit and squeak like bats in the dark and cold for an eternity. Calgacus had no idea of the views on the afterlife of his own native tribes in Caledonia. He had been taken too young. He hoped a lifetime among the Angles and serving one of them in remote places would make him eligible for Valhalla. You had to die in battle. There were worse ways to die. Your passing would be one of pain, but that might seem a low price to enter one of the better afterlives. Although the many willing virgins of Manichaeism – was it seventy or more? – also had a strong appeal. And it might be you did not have to die a violent death to get there. Maybe, if he lived through this, he would find out more about the strange new religion.

At any event, Calgacus hoped the souls of those killed had departed, for there were any number of vultures arrived. Ungainly in their haste and greed, they set up a flapping uproar as they squabbled over this sudden, rich bounty. Things would get worse later, when the darkness allowed the scavengers of the earth to overcome their fear of living men and slink out to devour the dead.

The majority of those being consumed were Alani. The losses of the defenders had been light, but they could ill afford them. Ballista and Andonnoballus rearranged the defence. The river remained held by Hippothous and Castricius. Each was as skilled a killer of men as the other, Calgacus thought, and each as dangerously insane as the other. They were aided by the interpreter and the soon-to-be-freed slave of the soldiers. A reserve of six was to be held back. It consisted of Ballista, Andonnoballus, Maximus, Tarchon, young Wulfstan, and Calgacus himself. It would be certain to be called upon. The actual wagon line now was held only by the *gudja*, two Heruli, three Roman auxiliaries, four Sarmatians and the other military slave. The latter had also been promised his freedom, conditional on both his martial valour and his survival. The latter seemed the larger impediment to his manumission.

It all looked hopeless. Twenty-one men to hold out against still easily more than ten times their number. The majority of the defenders were carrying some wound or other. Several of these were seriously incapacitated; the Herul Datius, the interpreter, one of the Sarmatians, young Wulfstan, who had picked up a nasty gash to his right arm right at the end of the fighting, and, of course, Calgacus himself.

For certain it was hopeless. They were all doomed. Calgacus wondered if he was afraid to die. Certainly he did not welcome death; neither the probable pain of the thing itself, nor the uncertainty of what might come after. And he wanted to live. He wanted to go back to Sicily. He wanted to marry Rebecca, to look after Simon, to have a son of his own. But if all that was to be denied him, if the *norns* had spun that he was to die out here on the Steppe, then he might as well die bravely. He might as well die out in the open by the side of Ballista and Maximus. As Ballista often said in Greek – some poem or other – death comes to the coward as well as to the brave. And if, by chance, any of them survived, what a song this doomed last fight would make.

'Three riders coming from the main Alani camp,' someone called out.

Wearily, Calgacus dragged himself to his feet, along with everyone else whose station allowed them to see.

'*Zirin! Zirin!*' One of the horsemen had a good, strong carrying voice.

'The call of an envoy or herald,' Andonnoballus said. He stood high on a wagon, and waved them to approach.

The three rode abreast, very close together. They rode slowly. The outer two seemed to be supporting the one in the middle. As they got closer, the latter could be seen to be slumped in the saddle.

At about the distance an arrow might still penetrate armour, a bit over one hundred paces, Andonnoballus called that it was close enough.

The three stopped. One of the flanking men slung a leg over the neck of his mount and nimbly dropped to the ground. As if it were a sack, he roughly pulled the one in the middle from the saddle. The man feebly put out an arm but crumpled in a heap. The other hauled him to his feet, hung something around his neck and pushed him in the direction of the wagon-laager.

'He will give you the message. It is his calling,' the one on foot shouted in the language of Germania. He vaulted back into the saddle. 'Let him smell his way to you.' The Alan and his companion laughed, spun their horses and raced away.

There was something strange about the man. He walked like a man in a thick fog; arms out in front, stepping hesitantly, as if he suspected the ground might betray him. And he was not walking

219

straight towards the camp but off at an angle that would take him past its southern extremity.

'By all the graces,' said a voice in Latin.

'Gods below,' said another.

'Fuck,' said Maximus.

Calgacus saw the man stumble, almost fall. There was something odd about his arms.

'Come on,' Ballista said to Maximus. The two clambered through the protective screens and dropped down outside the laager. Vultures waddled away, loud in their complaints.

Instinctively, Calgacus scanned the plain. He could see the two horsemen. They were more than half a mile away. He could see the smudge of smoke that bannered the big nomad camp in the distance. He could see nothing else. Except along the watercourse, there were no trees. As far as he knew, there were no hidden gullies or deceitful undulations where ambushers might lay hidden.

Ballista and Maximus had reached the man. Solicitously enough, they had removed the thing hung around his neck and taken him by the shoulders. Yet in the act of supporting him they seemed to wish to keep their distance.

'Infernal gods, it is the herald Regulus,' someone said.

'How could they do what they have done?' another said. 'What evil daemon could drive anyone to this?'

When they were about as far as a boy can throw a stone, Calgacus saw, and wished he had not. The horror was beyond all bearing.

There was blood all down the face of the *praeco*, all down his soiled tunic. His arms were stumps. They ended at the wrist. There were no bandages. Instead, the wounds appeared to have been cauterized. But there was much worse, a much fouler disfigurement. His eyes were gone. No one, not the most skilled physiognomist, could read his soul in those ruined, bloody sockets.

'Bear a hand,' Ballista said. 'Bear a hand, and haul him up.'

Calgacus swallowed his revulsion, took the herald under a shoulder and, as gently as possible, helped lift him up into the wagon-laager.

'Get flax and the whites of eggs for his eyes,' Ballista said.

'I will take care of him.' The *gudja* – tall, imperturbable – laid an arm around the shoulders of the *praeco*, and led him away to his wagon as a father might lead a son.

Ballista passed the piece of papyrus taken from the herald's neck to Andonnoballus. There was Greek script on it. The Herul's lips moved as he read it, but he made no sound. Finished, he smiled, but with no humour. He held the papyrus up and read aloud. 'Hand us Andonnoballus and Ballista, and the rest of you can depart unharmed. If not, when you fall into our hands, you will beg for this man's fate.'

A muttering ran along the wagons, as men repeated it and translated it into various tongues.

Laughter – muted, rueful chuckles at first; no one was sure where it started – spread through the laager.

'Fuck you!' Maximus howled. Others joined in: obscenities, curses, vows of revenge, even dark jokes were shouted at the distant Alani camp and at the uncaring vastness of the Steppe.

The *gudja* returned.

'How is he?' Ballista asked.

'At peace,' the Goth replied.

Ballista looked shocked.

'It is best,' the *gudja* said. 'What life would there be for a man with no eyes to see, no hands to feed himself?'

The others were silent.

'They had castrated him as well.' The bones and amulets in the hair of the *gudja* clinked as he turned to go.

'Sure, it is a kindness,' Maximus said, 'but a terrible kindness which will weigh on you.'

The *gudja* walked off without replying.

Calgacus drew a little apart with Ballista and Maximus. They stood in the centre of the laager. 'Are you certain no one will betray us?'

'Certain,' Ballista said. 'No one could be that big a fool. The Alani have lost too many for clemency. Everyone knows they will kill us all.'

'The Alani king is not here, and I have not seen the Suanian Saurmag among them, but still they want you badly,' Maximus said.

'And Andonnoballus,' Ballista added. 'It is interesting they want him, but not the other Heruli.'

'They are moving.' The shout from Wulfstan curtailed further speculation.

There were more Alani this time, but they kept further away. Somewhere near extreme bow shot, approaching three hundred paces, thirty or forty Alani swarmed. Many of them got down from their ponies.

Except for those keeping watch over the other approaches, the entire beleaguered garrison crowded to watch. Hippothous came and stood next to Calgacus and the others. The Greek had left Castricius overseeing the river.

The sounds of hammering drifted across, covering the sighing of the grass and the quarrels of the vultures. The hammering stopped. There were wild shouts and mocking laughter. Then there were screams – at first of fear, then of agony, terrible agony.

> *I dare not see, I am hiding*
> *My eyes, I cannot bear*
> *What most I long to see;*
> *And what I long to hear,*
> *That most I dread.*

Hippothous recited the verse well.

'Sophocles,' Andonnoballus said.

Hippothous was not the only one to look at the Herul with surprise.

Andonnoballus ignored them.

The Alani mounted up, whirled their horses and, whooping, rode a little further away.

Three stakes were left standing in the Steppe. On each a man was impaled.

'Who are they?' Calgacus's eyes were not near good enough to hope to recognize individuals at that distance.

'It looks like the rest of the staff,' Maximus said, 'Porsenna the *haruspex*, and the other scribe and messenger – the poor bastards.'

'Poor bastards,' Calgacus agreed.

'I suppose sending the herald to us was irony,' Ballista said.

A chilling scream cut across the plain.

'At least one is alive, then,' said Hippothous.

'They will all be alive,' Andonnoballus said. 'If he can take the pain and not move, it can take a man hours, sometimes a day or more to die. It all depends how you insert the stake up his arse.'

'You know this?' Ballista said.

'I know this,' Andonnoballus said.

'Alani indeed is the most cruel of savages,' Tarchon said. 'And most terrible ones for thieving. When they cross the Croucasis so their ponies can eat the sweet meadow grasses of Suania, always they are stealing; apples, pears, small children, all manner of things.'

'They have put them out there to dishearten us,' Ballista said. 'If any of us go out to help them, we will be ridden down.'

Another ghastly scream echoed across the Steppe.

'We have to do something,' Maximus said.

'Wax,' Tarchon said. 'Beeswax best in the ears. Next to no sound gets through.'

223

'Something for them.'

'Oh, in that case, we must shoot them.'

'The Suanian is right,' Andonnoballus said.

'It is a long, difficult shot,' judged Ballista.

'I would take it myself, but they are your men.'

'Yes,' Ballista agreed. 'They are my men.'

They brought him his own bow, the one he had loaned to the slave down by the river, and gave him some space to concentrate.

A bright, sunny June day, not much past noon. As hot here as it would be in Sicily. A steady wind from the north. He would have to allow for that. The grass shimmered in the nearly three hundred paces between him and the twisted figures on the stakes. Silkweed and side-oats waved above grass. He drew the composite bow – two-fingered, back to the ear, sighted down the shaft – released, and missed. The arrow slid past the right of the central figure. He had overcompensated for the breeze.

The second arrow missed as well; same side, a touch closer. The third took the man in the leg. Ballista killed him with the fourth. In all, it took nine arrows to kill the three men. It took quite a long time.

When he had finished, Ballista walked alone down to the stream. Calgacus followed him at a distance. Ballista sat and stared out across the water. Calgacus sat not far away and watched him. From things Maximus had said, Calgacus imagined that Ballista might be thinking about hauling the *haruspex* off Tarchon's horse and leaving the diviner to his fate. Right from the start, from the days by the Suebian sea, Calgacus had said Dernhelm was no natural killer. He had always said that. Now, the boy was a man called Ballista, as proficient a killer as varied training and extensive experience could make. Yet, in some ways, nothing had changed.

Maximus walked down to where Calgacus was sitting. 'The Alani are stirring.'

'How long?'

'No great hurry. Their outriders are just leaving the camp.'

Calgacus nodded and levered himself to his feet. Hercules' hairy arse, his shoulder hurt. 'You go back. I will fetch him.'

Ballista was looking away, his gaze fixed a distance upriver. Some birds were darting among the reeds. They were small, fast; maybe a brace of snipe. Calgacus could not tell. 'The Alani,' he said.

Ballista looked at him, a question on his face.

'Plenty of time. The main body is still in the camp.'

Ballista motioned for Calgacus to sit down. 'Herodotus says the nomads blind all their slaves; presumably, to stop them running away. He must have been misled. Having blind slaves would not work. The herald would not have found our camp. It is hard to think of a worse place for a slave to make a run for freedom. There is nowhere to hide on the Steppe, except for the grave mounds that have been opened and in the watercourses.'

Calgacus said nothing. He had long grown used to Ballista's oblique approaches to what troubled him.

'A story in the *Toxaris* of Lucian is set out here, on the Tanais river. The Scythians lose their camp and herds to a surprise Sarmatian attack. A Scythian warrior – I forget his name – is among those who escape. But his blood-friend has been captured. I do not remember his name either. The one who escaped goes to ransom his blood-friend. The King of the Sarmatians laughs in his face. What will he use for ransom, as the Sarmatians have already taken all his possessions? He answers his own body. The Sarmatian king says he will only take a part of the ransom offered – he will take his eyes. The Scythian lets himself be blinded. Somehow, the two swim the Tanais to safety.'

Calgacus sat, waiting for Ballista to talk himself out.

'But does the story end well? Inspired by the sacrifice, the Scythians rally and defeat the Sarmatians. The two friends live out their days honoured by their people. But the one who was ransomed cannot bear to see his friend's sightless eyes. Maybe the empty orbs are a constant reproach to him. Anyway, he plucks out his own eyes. Presumably, they sat out the rest of their lives in the wagons with the women and the children, in their shared darkness.'

Ballista stopped.

'What happened to the staff,' Calgacus said; 'it was not your fault.'

'Not even Porsenna the *haruspex*?'

'From what Maximus says, he was endangering Tarchon's life; all of your lives. You did what you had to do.'

'You always find a path to it not being my fault.'

Calgacus frowned, obviously framing his words with care. 'Not always. The things you did the year before last in Cilicia – those you did not have to do. Torturing the Persian prisoners – or at least your pleasure in the torture – killing the Sassanid king's eunuchs in cold blood, raping his concubine Roxanne; you did not have to do any of those things. But at that time you thought your sons and Julia had been killed by the Persians. Your grief and desire for revenge had driven you mad.'

'So, again, you would say it was not my fault,' Ballista said. 'If you had been a Greek, you could have been a Sophist.'

Calgacus wheezed. 'You read too many Greek books.'

Ballista smiled at his old friend. 'I was reading Euripides back then in Cilicia; I have not read him since.'

'The Alani will not wait for your philosophizing.'

'Euripides was not a philosopher. He was a poet, a tragedian.' Ballista got up, and helped Calgacus to his feet.

'Probably much the same bollocks,' Calgacus grunted.

'In some ways,' Ballista said.

The Alani arrayed themselves in a loose but complete circle

226

around the wagon-laager, all mounted, about three hundred paces out.

'The *battue*,' Andonnoballus said. 'The hunting formation of the Steppes. It drives the game into the centre.'

'So, they are thinking to hunt us down like animals,' Tarchon said.

'No, for us it will be different.' Andonnoballus seemed remarkably cheerful. 'I imagine they will ride in fast, putting a lot of arrows in the air. They will come close, maybe only twenty paces from us. Some will stay in the saddle, shooting. Behind them, the rest will dismount. The ones on foot will move into . . .' He struggled for the right word in the Greek he was speaking. 'Into *chisel* formations – is that right, *chisel*? The pointed thing sculptors use?'

'Yes, chisel,' Ballista said.

'Good. Then they will storm the laager in chisel formations.'

'How many points of attack?' asked Ballista.

Andonnoballus laughed. 'I have no idea. But as there are so few of us, providing they attack in at least two places, they will overrun us.'

Doomed, Calgacus thought, fucking doomed. And it was odd Andonnoballus could recognize the poetry of Sophocles, but claimed he was not sure of the Greek for 'chisel'. Strange people, these Heruli.

'But,' Andonnoballus said, 'I do not think the gods will let that happen. I have been observing the heavens. From the flight of birds, I know the gods are watching over us. And I heard a wolf howl not long ago.'

'And that is good?' Ballista questioned.

'Very good,' Andonnoballus replied.

Not far away, the other surviving one of the Rosomoni, Pharas, was laughing. He seemed at ease, content with the way things were. From the other side of the laager, the last Herul, Datius, looked across with comparable equanimity.

Out of their minds, Calgacus thought. Absolutely fucking out of their minds. Surrounded, outnumbered beyond measure, in the middle of nowhere, and a wolf and a few birds convince them we will be fine. Had they not noticed the Steppe was full of fucking birds, probably lots of wolves too? It was certainly full of fucking Alani warriors. Obviously, having your skull bound into a point as a baby did something to your brain.

'What are they up to now?' Maximus asked.

'They are going to sacrifice some of our oxen,' responded Andonnoballus.

'Sure, I could do with some roast beef myself,' Maximus said.

Ignoring the irreverence, Andonnoballus, who seemed now in an expansive mood, decided to explain the ritual. 'You see the naked sword? It catches the sun, just to the right of the oxen. That is Akinakes.'

'I had a horse called that once,' Maximus said.

'The Alani, like the ancient Scythians, are simple, childish in their religion. They worship but two gods: Anemos and Akinakes. They say there is nothing more important than life and death. So they worship Anemos and Akinakes because Wind is the source of life, and the Sword the cause of death.' Andonnoballus pointed to one of the drivers. 'Their Sarmatian cousins hold the same view.'

'The north wind that quickens their mares?' Ballista said.

'And the wind that is their breath. They are simple people. They build no temples. Nothing but thrust a drawn sword into the ground. See, now they are offering the blood of the oxen to Akinakes.'

'The Heruli do not worship Akinakes and Anemos?' Ballista asked.

'Of course we do.' Andonnoballus sounded surprised. 'But we are

228

not so foolish as to ignore all the other gods: Air, Earth, Sea, Springs, Woden, Orestes, Abraham, Apollonius, Christ, Mithras. There are many, many gods. All must have their due. My . . .' He paused. 'My king is a most devout man. Naulobates has summoned holy men from different religions to his court. This summer, they will debate their beliefs in front of him; Persian *mobads*, Christian priests, Platonic philosophers, Manichaeans. He asked Mani himself, but he could not come. Perhaps it will happen while you are in his camp.'

'A delight to anticipate,' Maximus said, straight-faced. 'If we survive today.'

Andonnoballus laughed again. 'Have I not told you, the gods have their hands over us.'

The great war drum of the Alani began to beat. Akinakes having had his fill of blood, the ring of warriors began to whoop.

'Not long now,' Andonnoballus said.

Castricius ran up from the *zereba*. As he did, the whooping of the Alani faltered.

'Over the river,' Castricius said, 'the Alani are moving. They are riding away.'

'Did I not tell you?' Andonnoballus said.

The war drum lost its rhythm and was silent. Anxious shouts replaced the exultant Alani whooping.

As Calgacus watched, the Alani formation broke apart. In moments, the nomads were dashing away to the south. In no order, individual horsemen scattered like so many terrified animals before a brush fire.

Andonnoballus turned to the north. Like a great wave born in the depths of the ocean, a wall of dust bore down on them. Hundreds, possibly thousands, of cavalry riding fast, bright banners flying in the choked air above them.

'The wolves of the north,' Andonnoballus said. 'The Heruli are come.'

XXI

Maximus checked the girths of his mount and the packhorse. He kicked the latter hard in the stomach. It let out the breath it was holding. As he tightened the strap, it tried to bite him. It was a wilful, cunning brute. The Herul who had handed it over had said as much.

They were all nearly ready to leave. The scale of things, the speed with which everything had happened, had staggered them all, Maximus as much as the others. Less than forty-eight hours before, he had been reconciling himself to death. Not a bad life by his own lights. He had travelled the world, had his fill of drink and women. Not what a philosopher would call a considered life, but he had been a man. All that had remained was to die like a man by the side of Ballista and that old bastard Calgacus. He loved Ballista. There were worse men to die with than the ugly old Caledonian. Maximus had always known it had to come.

Then the ground had trembled and the air had been filled with the thunder of hooves and the *yip-yipping* of the approaching Heruli. A lifetime of experience had allowed Maximus to judge there were almost exactly two thousand of them. They were riding two deep in a line that swept over a mile of the Steppe. Standards alive with *tamgas* and wolves snapped above them.

And then something almost more wonderful had happened. The Alani, the majority of whom had been fleeing south, came haring back. Some fool in the wagon-laager had called out, What were they thinking, had the gods driven them mad! It should have been obvious to a child. The keen eyes of Maximus had looked beyond them and spotted it straight away – the mile-wide cloud of dust coming up from the south. It had been the work of moments to find the matching clouds rolling in from east and west.

The Alani, careless in their good fortune, had been transformed from arrogant hunters of men to the hapless human quarry at the centre of an enormous *battue*. Afterwards, the Heruli said, with much plausibility, that not a single Alan had escaped. Many were killed, shot down in high spirits. Yet 107 survived to be taken prisoner; among them the chiefs with the horsetail and *tamga* banners.

Dismounted, the Alani had been divested of their weapons and portable wealth, often including their belts and boots. Several suffered unpleasant indignities after Maximus had mischievously suggested they hid coins up their arses. That very afternoon, sullen and often a little bloodied, they were put to work. One detail collected the dead. It was a demanding task. There were more than two hundred corpses, spread widely across the Steppe. Around the laager, those killed the day before were becoming noisome in the June sun. After the members of the caravan had salvaged what of their belongings had not been spilt, blood-stained or otherwise ruined by being enlisted as part of the barricade, a second group of Alani was set to breaking up the wagons. As this progressed, the final detachment had moved from gathering brushwood and begun to build pyres. As the

Sarmatians took their dead away for inhumation, there were three pyres. Two were small, one each for the fallen Heruli and the Romans. The final one was for the Alani. Although it was large, clearly it would not be able fully to consume the number to be cremated. No one but the Alani seemed to care, and their opinion had been of no account.

The work had gone on through the night and into the next day. Relays of Heruli wielding their vicious horsewhips had ensured it never ceased. The pyres had been lit at midday. By late evening, they had been able to rake the smaller two. The bones were collected and placed in any suitably sized, suitably reverent vessels that happened to have survived the fighting. These were then stowed in panniers strapped to some of the numerous pack-horses.

It was not at all the same with the Alani dead. Even now, the following day, Maximus could see places still burning in the heart of the big pyre. At the extremities, where the fire had retreated, were half-burnt bodies. These attracted no more than macabre curiosity. Only their kinsmen would have mourned, and the surviving Alani could no longer see the sight.

As soon as their labours were complete, all but three of the Alani had been herded into a line. Surrounded by Heruli, they had been roped together by the neck. One by one, they had been hauled to the block. Each was held down. An *akinakes* rose and fell. A hideous scream. Sometimes it took more than one blow. The Alan's right hand was severed. Another blade was pulled from a brazier, the hot steel pressed to the stump. The next Alan – struggling, kicking – was dragged into place. The *akinakes* rose again.

It had taken a long time, blunted five *akinakes*, but it was nothing to what happened next. Four of the Alani had died; of fear, the shock of it, loss of blood, or – Tarchon suggested – humiliation and despair. The remaining ninety-nine mutilated Alani again had been pulled forward one by one. Maximus had not stayed to watch. He had seen many dreadful things over the years. Before the walls of Arete, the Persian *mobads* had poured boiling oil into the eyes of their Roman prisoners. He had crossed the river with Ballista and Calgacus and ridden north out on to the Steppe to avoid witnessing the blinding of the Alani.

Not all had shown such delicacy of feeling. Hippothous, Castricius and young Wulfstan had stayed to watch. The surviving soldiers had regarded it as a good spectacle, initially. Yet even they, by the time Maximus and the other two returned, had become quiet.

The Alani were haltered together in a long file of mutilated men. They had been ordered to move. Whips had cracked above their heads. In a sightless world of pain, they had shuffled slowly forward in response to the rope around their necks. The Heruli had left one man with a single eye to guide the others.

Maximus was glad it was all over, glad they were about to move from this daemon-haunted place of suffering. As he swung up into the saddle, Andonnoballus and Pharas came trotting over. There had been no opportunity for much talk with them since the relief. Both greeted Ballista and his *familia*. Andonnoballus looked as if he would say more, but he did not.

'How long were your Heruli scouts watching the Alani attack the laager?' Ballista said.

Andonnoballus smiled. 'You knew they were there?'

'I thought there were men upstream in the riverbed,' Ballista said.

'They had been there some hours. They were waiting for the other columns to get into position.'

Maximus had known nothing of the scouts. He watched Ballista's face. It was closed, angry.

'Why did it take so long for the relief column to get here?' Ballista said.

'Naulobates rules over wide lands. It takes time to gather a large force.' Andonnoballus's voice was smooth.

'Naulobates could have sent fewer men sooner.'

'He wanted to ensure he apprehended all the Alani. He decreed their punishment was to be complete and terrible.'

'Nomad horses ride like the wind,' Ballista said.

Andonnoballus paused. 'When the messengers reached the camp, Naulobates was . . . away.'

'Away?'

'Naulobates is . . .' Andonnoballus looked Ballista hard in the eye, daring him to mock. 'Naulobates is not like other men. He communes with the divine. Sometimes he enters the world beyond.'

'Your father travels in the world of daemons?' Ballista said.

At his words a sudden stillness settled on the two Heruli. Andonnoballus looked at Pharas. The older warrior shrugged.

Andonnoballus asked, 'How did you know he is my father?'

'You Heruli pride yourselves on your brotherhood, your equality, but the older warriors all deferred to you. And occasionally one of them would forget himself and call you *Atheling*.'

Andonnoballus laughed. 'You are no fool. But then you would not be, you are a grandson of cunning Starkad.'

'Wait,' Maximus said. 'If you Heruli have your women in common, how can anyone's father be known? I thought that was the point.'

'It is,' Andonnoballus agreed, 'but it is a recent innovation of my father's. Many things have changed in the last few years. Naulobates is a law-giver like Scythian Zalmoxis or Spartan Lycurgus. He is refashioning the customs of the Heruli. Through him, the gods are creating perfection on earth.'

234

'Well, we shall be honoured,' Ballista said, straight-faced. 'It is not every man that gets to enter perfection.'

Andonnoballus gave him a measuring look. 'It is time to go.'

They rode out past the remains of the laager, past the still smoking large pyre, and past the three stakes. The bones of the Roman staff who had once hung there were now travelling in panniers to their final resting place. Three new men were impaled on the stakes. The Alani chiefs were still just about alive. Above them, the horsetail and *tamga* standards flew.

Maximus and the others forded the watercourse, and rode away to the north.

Wulfstan looked up at the night sky. The moon was waning and the stars were bright – the eyes of Thiazi, many thousands of others and, brightest of all, the toe of Aurvandil the Brave; all placed there by the gods to bring comfort, to watch over man.

It was quiet in the sleeping camp. The wind sang softly through the ropes of the tents. Down in the horse lines, beasts shifted and coughed in their sleep.

Wulfstan's arm hurt. He and Tarchon had been ordered to hold the breach that the Alani had hacked in the makeshift defences between the first two wagons back at Blood River. After Ballista and the others had moved on, the Alani had tried to break in again. Wulfstan had dropped the first with an arrow. Tarchon had near-beheaded the second with his sword. But, shields up, the next two had forced their way through. One went for Tarchon. Before the other could attack, Wulfstan had thrust the point of his sword at the centre of the nomad's embroidered tunic. The Alan was too quick, too experienced – just too strong. He had turned aside the blade, as if Wulfstan were a small child, and riposted in one movement. The steel had sliced open Wulfstan's right bicep. Wulfstan had dropped his sword. He had not been able to stop himself. His left hand had clamped to the wound. Doubled up, it would have been all over with him. Tarchon struck with the speed and sureness of a cat. The Alan he had been fighting was still falling when the Suanian cut down Wulfstan's would-be killer.

They had been ordered to hold the breach. They had done that. Wulfstan's arm was the price they had paid. After the fighting, the *gudja* and the *haliurunna* had cleaned, salved and bound the wound. The hideous old crone had muttered strange incantations over it. That had been four days ago. It still hurt like poison. The last two days riding had not helped. Yet Wulfstan almost did not care.

After they had made camp and eaten the previous night, Ballista had summoned what remained of the Roman mission. With his own money, he had purchased the two slaves from the three surviving soldiers at a more than generous price. Good to his word, he handed both his new slaves a papyrus roll recording their manu-mission. One of the soldiers had tacked up some felt into a pair of pointed caps. The new freedmen accepted these symbols of freedom gladly. There was amusement, as neither *pileus* came close to fitting.

Wulfstan had joined in the laughter, but it was what had happened next that still left him near uncaring of his injury, that still had his heart singing. With no ado, Ballista had called him forward and handed him two papyri. One ended Wulfstan's slavery, the other awarded him the *toga virilis*. Wulfstan had found it difficult to comprehend. He had dropped to his knees, kissed Ballista's hand. He was raised up. In a matter of moments, he was both free and a man. The thoughts still rang loud in his head, drowning out nearly all else.

It was a quiet night. Wulfstan knew he should go to sleep. There would be another long day in the saddle ahead of them. But his arm did not make sleep easy to come by, and his heart was too full. He listened to the *peep-peep* of a night bird and the strange whistling of the marmots in their hollows out on the Steppe. Another sound, closer altogether.

Wulfstan whirled around. His hand went to his hilt. The pain made him wince.

A tall figure emerged from the shadows. It pushed the hood back from its long head.

Wulfstan relaxed.

It was Andonnoballus.

'You are up late,' the Herul said in the language of the north.

'As are you.'

'I had to check the sentries,' Andonnoballus said. 'You?'

'I could not sleep.'

'Have you given much thought to what you will do with your freedom?'

'Some.' Wulfstan did not want to say more.

'The Romans would say you still had a duty to Ballista, now he is your *patronus*.'

'I owe him a debt, but I do not care what the Romans might say.' Wulfstan himself thought his tone sounded immature, almost petulant.

'Aluith said you would make a good Herul.' Andonnoballus smiled.

Wulfstan was quiet for a time. 'Before I came into the *familia* of Ballista, things happened which call for revenge.'

'Even if it can be achieved, it will not undo the past,' Andonnoballus said.

'Some things demand revenge.'

'None among the Heruli would know whatever those things might have been. Among us, under the rule of Naulobates, a man can rise high irrespective of what he was before.'

'I would still know,' Wulfstan said.

Now it was Andonnoballus who paused before replying.

'Revenge is a two-edged sword. It can damage the man who takes it as surely as those upon which it is inflicted. It can become a disease that spreads, infecting everything a man does, everything he thinks. It might be you will not be truly free until you are free of the desire for revenge.'

Wulfstan said nothing.

'I gave you Aluith's weapons because he would have wanted you to have them. You have done well; very well for your age. Aluith would have been proud. He would have wanted you to carry his *tamga*, take his place among us.'

Wulfstan did not reply.

The night stilled. The whistling of the marmots and the peeping of the nocturnal bird stopped.

The silver-white wings of a great owl swept over them; silent, spectral.

They watched the darkness into which the hunter had voyaged. After a while, the whistling and *peep-peep* calls of the less fierce denizens of the night resumed.

Andonnoballus turned to go. 'You might take that as a sign. Naulobates would have known. When we reach his camp, ask him.' Andonnoballus walked away.

Wulfstan remained, deep in thought. The poetry of his youth drifted into his mind.

> *The weary in spirit cannot withstand fate,*
> *And nothing comes of venting spleen:*
> *Wherefore those eager for glory often*
> *Hold some ache imprisoned in their hearts.*

Perhaps nothing would come of venting his spleen. He would not change anything. Kill one slaver, another would take his place. He could bind his memories in fetters, confine them in some dark place in his soul. The Heruli offered a new beginning. He could refashion himself into the warrior he would have become if the Langobardi had not come, if they had not sold him to the slavers. No, not quite what he would have become. The slavery, and this murderous, violent journey across this never-ending plain had tempered him into something stronger.

He shivered. The wind was rising, the night getting colder. Up above, thin clouds raced across the eyes of Thiazi, hid the moon from the wolf that pursued him. Hati would not run the moon down and devour him tonight.

Another sound, close by. Wulfstan turned, expecting to see Andonnoballus. It was not Andonnoballus.

The steel shimmered in the weak starlight. It was at Wulfstan's throat.

'Why?' Wulfstan said.

The killer actually smiled. 'You have an implacable, vengeful daemon.'

'I can change.'

'Your daemon will do terrible things – to those around you, to you.'

Desperately, Wulfstan tried to ready himself. The sword at his throat. His own right arm near useless. Next to no chance. But better than dying like a sheep.

'The young Frisian, your friend Bauto, who drowned – he had a bad daemon too.'

The words checked Wulfstan. He remembered the storm; the year before, out on the Euxine sea. He remembered the rogue triple wave hitting the *Armata*. The seeming miracle when the *trireme* righted herself. The half-demented joy, the cheering. Then the shout, 'Man overboard!' And there, over the stern of the galley, alone in the wild, pitiless expanse of the sea, the small head of his friend, the Frisian Bauto.

With an inarticulate cry, Wulfstan pushed the sword away with his right arm – pain as the blade cut deep – grabbed for the throat with his left hand. Wulfstan felt a blow like a punch in his stomach. Winded, he looked down. He saw the fist curled around the hilt of the dagger. He saw the blade withdrawn, saw the black blood flow.

Ballista had been surprised at the reaction of Andonnoballus to the discovery of the body. The young Herul *atheling*, who had displayed no emotion either when his own men had fallen in battle, or when he had ordered the mass blinding of the Alani and the impaling of their leaders, had been visibly upset. He had not hidden his tears. And he had been angry, at times almost to distraction.

For a day, the horde had remained where it was. Andonnoballus had questioned the sentries. They had seen nothing. A painstaking search of where the body lay revealed nothing; trampled grass, and blood, a lot of blood. Wulfstan had not been mutilated after death – just the blade wiped in his bright hair – but the blows that had killed him had nearly disembowelled him. His killer had to have been soaked in blood. Andonnoballus had ordered a search of the camp. Ballista had thought it most unlikely to discover anything. It found nothing; although one Herul half waking in the night had seen a hooded figure drop what he had taken to be some old rags on one of the campfires. No, he could not say anything about the man; not even if he was Herul, Sarmatian or

Roman. Andonnoballus had the ashes sifted. No tell-tale ornament or anything else came to light.

Andonnoballus ordered a pyre built. He had washed and dressed the body with his own hands. He had placed splendid offerings around the dead youth: the weapons of Aluith that Wulfstan had carried, gold and amber ornaments of his own. The other two Heruli who had been with the caravan from the start, Pharas and the ex-slave Datius, added things of their own.

Before he put the first torch to the pyre, Andonnoballus had spoken a eulogy. Wulfstan had been born an Angle, once the enemies of the Heruli. The fates had cruelly taken him from his home, made him eat the bitter bread of exile and hardship. But his own courage had raised him up again, had won his freedom. Before his murder, Wulfstan had asked to ride with the Heruli. Andonnoballus, by the authority granted him by Naulobates, had accepted the young warrior into the brotherhood of the wolves of the north. Let the murderer know, should the gods reveal his identity, Andonnoballus of the Heruli would track him to the ends of the earth to revenge his unjustly and cowardly slain brother.

They had collected the bones the next morning; packed them in a pannier on a packhorse, like the others. The long journey north resumed.

Ballista rode at the head of the horde with Andonnoballus, Pharas and the commander of the relief, Uligagus. They rode in silence. Andonnoballus's mood did not encourage small talk.

Behind them came three great parallel columns of horsemen. The fourth was further back, out of sight, strung across the Steppe as a rearguard. Each column contained two thousand riders, but many more horses. Each of the Heruli had at least three remounts on a line. They rode at a fast canter.

From the charged silence of the vanguard, Ballista looked back and studied the Heruli. Many banners flew above them, most bearing *tamgas*, some with wolves and other fierce-seeming but less determinable animals. Travelling at speed, they all kept surprisingly good order. Aureolus, the emperor Gallienus's own Prefect of Cavalry, would have been impressed. There was nothing of the irrational or the primitive which Romans liked to see in barbarians in this order of march. The scruffy-looking ponies, however, would have been odd to Aureolus's eyes, as would the complete absence of armour. There was not a helmet or mailshirt among them. Some, presumably the unfree, did not even carry one of their small round shields. Slave or free, they relied on no more than a heavy sheepskin coat for defence. Every Herul had a recurve bow and supply of arrows in a *gorytus* on one hip and a long cavalry sword on the other. There were spare bowcases on the remounts. Ballista was impressed. These were true light cavalry, but, as he knew, they were prepared to fight hand to hand. They would not be able to stand up to a charge by Roman *cataphracti* or Persian *clibanarii*. The big men on big horses, all covered in mail, would ride them down. Yet out here on the Steppe, that eventuality need never arise. In these wide expanses, if the Heruli were well handled, the heavy horse should never catch them.

Ballista's thoughts wandered. The grey clouds of dust the columns kicked up drifted behind them to the south. Up above, the wind had shifted and was blowing wraith-like clouds in the opposite direction. Under the immense sky, the disjunction was vertiginous. It was always some such immensity philosophers invoked to try to assuage grief. He thought of the works of consolation he had been made to read as part of his education at the imperial court. Compare your grief with something huge, something without end – the gods, the divine spark in man, eternal Rome, or time itself. See how insignificant is your misery. He thought back to the time when he believed his wife and sons were dead. He remembered how his recollections of the philosophers had offered him nothing but specious comparisons with things that did not touch him, infuriating injunctions to self-control, and leaden platitudes. In the face of the ultimate profundity, the great minds of a Plutarch or a Seneca could come up with little better than the banalities of a nursemaid soothing a child: *There, there, it will feel better in time.* At least in the latter they had been right.

In honesty, the grief Ballista felt for Wulfstan was limited. The boy had been beautiful. There had been good qualities to him. He had served the *familia* well. He had been brave. A capacity for affection had shown in his grief for his drowned friend, Bauto. Occasionally, there had been flashes of humour. But his enslavement, the never spoken of but obviously terrible things that had been done to him, had made him something almost terrible himself. Wulfstan had wanted to kill. Too young to disguise it, he had enjoyed the pain of others. It had disgusted Ballista when Wulfstan had stayed with Castricius and Hippothous to watch the blinding of the Alani. Ballista was sad the boy was dead, but an unpleasant part of him was glad it was not someone he really cared about; not Julia, not one of his sons, neither Maximus nor Calgacus.

Ballista's lack of compassion made him feel guilty. And, of course, there was something more tangible to feel guilty about. He had brought Wulfstan to his death. Unthinkingly, he had assumed that merely purchasing the boy from the slave market, taking him into the *familia*, one day manumitting him would be enough. But he had brought him into the *familia* of a man in imperial disfavour, a *familia* ordered first to the savage Caucasus mountains, then to this murderous journey. And the *familia* was cursed. *Kill all his family, all those he loves.*

'Another day and we will reach the summer camp.' The words of Uligagus brought Ballista back.

Up ahead was a flock of sheep. There must have been a thousand or more of them. They were herded by just two very young Heruli on ponies. One of the shepherds had the long head and dyed-red hair of the Rosomoni. As the sheep were driven out of the path of the horsemen, they bunched into a solid baaing mass; some were forced up off their feet by the pressure. The two herdboys waved. Some of the vanguard waved back. Andonnoballus did not. Lost in who knew what incarnadine thoughts, he paid them no mind at all.

Seeing the young shepherds, so full of life, Ballista's mind turned back to Wulfstan. The northern poem he had heard the boy reciting came to him.

> *Storms crash against these rocky slopes,*
> *Sleet and snow fall and fetter the world,*
> *Winter howls, then darkness draws on,*
> *The night-shadow casts gloom and brings*
> *Fierce hailstorms from the north to frighten men.*
> *Nothing is ever easy in the kingdom of earth,*
> *The world beneath the heavens is in the hands of fate.*
> *Here possessions are fleeting, here friends are fleeting,*
> *Here man is fleeting, here kinsman is fleeting,*
> *The whole world becomes a wilderness.*

They came to the camp of Naulobates incrementally. First they crossed swathes where the grass had been torn and stamped to near nothing. The grey earth showed through, pocked by myriad hooves. Then they saw a drifting cloud of smoke. From a distance it looked like rain. It was as if the natural order had been subverted, as if some elemental force or capricious deity was drawing the water back into the sky. Getting nearer, Ballista smelt the sharp tang of woodsmoke and burning animal dung. Finally, breasting a slight rise, spread before them was the broad floodplain of a hitherto unsuspected river which ran away to the east. On the near side ordered rows of round tents and covered wagons stretched for a couple of miles. In the centre, one tent, dazzling white in the hot sun despite the smoke, was three times the size of any other. Above it was a standard. On it was a *tamga* drawn like three orbs pierced by an arrow being pursued by three wolves.

A messenger came to Andonnoballus and Uligagus. Ballista had been unsure since the relief which was in command. The messenger announced Naulobates would receive the Roman embassy at a place called the meadow. He stressed all members of the party were to attend.

Ballista, Castricius and the others took leave of Uligagus. The Herul led his fighting men off back into the Steppe to the west of the camp. Andonnoballus, Pharas and Datius remained with the Romans. When all, men and pack animals, were mastered, the three Heruli took them down through the camp.

Walking their mounts along a broad thoroughfare running down to the river, Ballista took it in. Small children watched big-eyed as they passed. Some trotted along beside, waving and calling out to the Heruli warriors and the strange outsiders indiscriminately. The women were more circumspect. They sat weaving or spinning in front of wagons and tents decorated with patchwork patterns of trees, birds, animals and many *tagmas*. Others tended the fires or prepared food. None spoke. Everything was hazed and gilded by sunshine and smoke.

Ballista had seen the camps of many tribes on the move; in Africa, along the Danube. Much here was what he expected. Wherever you looked, you met the guarded, solemn gaze of seated women. Some nursed babies. Everywhere ran gaggles of excited small children. Dogs – lean hunting animals – nosed about. Here and there a sickly colt or lamb was tethered. It took him some time to realize what was unusual. There were no men, and there were no old people. Come to that, there were no pigs either.

The river was fringed with stands of timber. It was wide, but shallow. The ford had a good bed of shingle. The water splashed up, refracting the light, as they clattered across.

The meadow was idyllic. It was ringed by trees: oaks, limes, ashes. Through the foliage could be seen a sweep of lush grass jewelled with flowers. Well watered, the meadow had not yet been scorched by the June sun. Evidently it was debarred to the herds. At the far end a group of men were sitting on the grass, at their ease in the shade. Off to one side two saplings had been bent down and their tops tied together to form a rustic arch. It was the sort of place in which Plato might have set a Socratic dialogue – the lovers of wisdom strolling at leisure, their minds freed from mundane cares by the beauty of their surroundings.

They dismounted at the tree line, hobbling their horses. Andonnoballus said there was no need to leave their weapons. It was the custom of the Heruli to come armed into the presence of their king.

The Romans unstrapped and unpacked those diplomatic gifts that had survived the journey. As *accensus*, Hippothous handed Ballista the small golden image of the town walls. Ballista buckled the Mural Crown – the award for being first over in the storm of a town – on to his sword belt. It seemed a lifetime ago he had won it in North Africa.

As Andonnoballus led them through the trees something high above caught Ballista's eye. He had to look twice. There was a man precariously perched in the topmost branches of an oak. Ballista looked about. Another man was clinging high up in an ash. They did not appear armed. There were just the two. It was not an ambush. And they were unlikely positions for lookouts.

'What the fuck?' Maximus said.

Andonnoballus laughed. 'The Allfather hung for nine nights and days in the branches of the tree of life to learn the secrets of the dead. Naulobates is merciful. Those two will learn the error of their ways from just one dawn to the next. And, unlike the Allfather, their sides have not been pierced with a spear.'

'What if they fall?' Ballista asked.

'It is a long way down,' Andonnoballus said.

Hippothous and Castricius joined in the laughter of Andonnoballus and Datius. Ballista noticed Pharas did not laugh.

Naulobates was seated on a simple wooden chair. His courtiers sat in no discernible hierarchy on the ground around him. Naulobates was dressed no differently from them: a simple leather coat, trousers and boots. His hands were in his lap, hidden in a plain leather bag.

'*Zirin*,' Ballista said, as an envoy should on the Steppe. He placed the palm of his right hand flat to his forehead.

Naulobates did not reply.

'*Zirin*,' Castricius said, as Ballista's deputy. He also made the gesture of respect.

Still Naulobates said nothing.

The King of the Heruli had the deformedly high forehead of the Rosomoni. His dyed-red hair was sparse, ill-kempt. His dyed-red beard was thin and straggly. His face was narrow, fine featured under the red tattoos. But it was his eyes that held Ballista. They were grey and possessed the unwavering moral certainty of the zealous convert armed by a fierce deity with complete faith and untrammelled force.

'Dernhelm, son of Isangrim, son of Starkad, the cruel man of blood.' Naulobates spoke in the language of the north. His voice was soft, unexpectedly high-pitched. 'God, in his providence, has brought you across Middle Earth to the camp of your hereditary enemies.'

All there were silent. Birds sang in the trees.

Ballista cleared his throat. 'I come to the Heruli as Marcus Clodius Ballista, *Legatus extra ordinem Scythica* of the Imperator Publius Licinius Egnatius Gallienus Augustus. The emperor of the Romans prays for the health of you and your men. He has sent me with gifts.'

'*Timeo Danaos et dona ferentes,*' Naulobates said. He recited the Latin of Virgil with a northern accent, before reverting to the language of Germania. 'Unlike the Trojan Laocoon, I do not fear the gifts of the Greeks. But then neither do I need them. Should my warriors desire more cunningly wrought silverware for their tents, I shall lead them again into the *imperium* and they will take whatever pleases them.'

'My Lord Gallienus requests to ransom those of his subjects in your power,' Ballista said.

'We took his subjects in war. It was the will of God. If Gallienus desires them back, he should come and put the issue before God on the field of battle.' Naulobates gestured to one of the men seated at his feet. 'Having tasted true freedom and brotherhood among the Heruli, many, like my brother Artemidorus, would not choose to return to the slavery of the *imperium*.'

'We have made a long and dangerous journey so that those who do wish might have the chance to return with us,' Ballista said.

'Dangerous in the extreme.' Naulobates shifted his gaze above Ballista's head. 'I have observed the trials; yours and those of my Heruli. I was with you every step of the way. Brachus, my *tauma*, moved among you.' Naulobates, seeing the word meant nothing to Ballista, smiled. 'You might call it my daemon.'

Ballista could think of nothing to say. He sensed both Castricius and Hippothous stiffen.

'My *tauma* observed everything. The treacherous attacks of the Alani, and the treachery within your own party.' Naulobates was not smiling now. 'The murderer among you is subtle. His daemon hid from Brachus in devious ways. I would let him know his fate should he disturb the peace of my campfires.'

At a sign from Naulobates, a bound man was brought forth. The prisoner struggled wildly. Through his gag he made incoherent sounds. Four young Heruli manhandled him off to one side, towards where the trees formed the rustic arch.

'This despicable criminal is a traitor to the God-given customs of the Heruli. A thief and a murderer, he sought to appropriate for himself what is the property of all. When another man went to the woman, this sacrilegious wretch burst in and struck him at the moment a man can least defend himself.'

The four young Heruli roped the man to the tied-together branches of the two bent trees. Ballista had heard of such things, but never expected to see them.

'Let the murderer among your party see what will become of him should he let his daemon indulge itself in the camp of the Heruli.' Naulobates nodded.

One of the young Heruli swung an axe. It sheered through the ropes binding the trees together. With the vigour of youth, the saplings sprang apart. Where there had been a man, now severed body parts hung like badly butchered sides of strange, unpalatable meat.

XXIII

After the dismemberment, Naulobates had told the Romans to produce their diplomatic gifts. The consular ornaments had survived the vagaries of the journey reasonably well. Naulobates studied the white toga with the broad purple stripe; the nasty bloodstain on the lower hem had come out quite well. He had peered at the boots with their many, complicated laces which were reserved for Roman senators. The Herul had seemed especially struck by the twelve *fasces*; the rods symbolizing the power to chastise, bundled around the axes representing the right to kill. After musing over these *ornamenta consularia* for some time, Naulobates had looked over the heads of the embassy, out beyond the remnants of the dead man in the trees, beyond the things visible to normal men, and had announced with deafening certainty that one day he would indeed be Roman consul; and that not in token but in reality. No one, Maximus included, had so much as smiled.

The silver dinner service, embossed with scenes of Roman heroes killing barbarians, had not held the attention of Naulobates. Sharing it between members of his entourage as gifts, he had dismissed the embassy from his presence. That had been four days before. They had not seen him since.

Andonnoballus had taken them to the lodgings provided. They consisted of four round nomad tents at one end of the camp. These were more than adequate, given there were but seventeen left in the embassy. Maximus was in the largest, situated at the western end of the row. He was in with Ballista, Calgacus and Tarchon. In the next one were Castricius and Hippothous, with the interpreter and the two remaining members of the official staff: a scribe and a messenger. The three soldiers and their two freed-slaves were billeted in the next adjacent. At the far end was Amantius. The two remaining slaves had no say in sharing with the eunuch. That was just as well, because no one else wished to share with him.

Maximus had no trouble settling into the life of a temporary nomad. Given some of the places they had been forced to sleep over the years, this was close to luxury. The tent was about thirty foot across, and each man had ample room for his bed roll. It was constructed of a framework of curved poles, over which felt hangings were stretched. An ingenious arrangement of cords allowed the hangings to be raised independently of each other to admit whatever breeze was blowing. The Heruli had brought food, a joint of mutton, strings of horsemeat sausages, and lots of their fermented mare's milk. Maximus was developing a taste for the latter, and Calgacus, although still hampered by his arm, cooked the former outside.

You could not fault the hospitality of the Heruli. The very first evening they offered their guests some slave girls, attractive ones at that. For whatever reason – they muttered something about privacy – Ballista and Calgacus declined. Which was fine by Maximus. With what he deemed consideration, he took Ballista's along with his own down to the riverbank. He chose what he thought was a secluded spot. Despite his long-enforced celibacy, everything went fine. After a time – a creditable time, if he said so himself – when it was finished, he discovered he had been wrong about the seclusion. A group of three Herul women washing clothes had appeared near by. They had giggled. Far from seeming shocked, Maximus had thought they looked rather impressed.

The following day, things had improved still more. In the tent, Ballista had immersed himself in reading. Unfortunately, he had taken to reading out and elucidating passages from Tacitus's *Annals*. Neither Calgacus nor Tarchon making a particularly receptive audience, the comments had ended up directed mainly at Maximus. After a brief time, to escape the relentless political insights and literary sleights of hand, Maximus had gone out.

Walking quite at random through the camp, Maximus had come to the market. It was surprisingly large. After he had paid some duty to a Herul official, a trader had been authorized to sell him a large amount of cannabis at a reasonable-seeming price. Strolling back, turning over in his head ways to consume it without bothering to build a special tent, he had run into one of the Herul women from the river. He had struck up a conversation with her. She spoke Greek. Nothing ventured, nothing gained, he had decided to test the encouraging stories about the sexual mores of the Heruli. At first he thought he had misjudged things horribly. She had just stared at him, an inscrutable expression on her face. Even he had been surprised when, almost wordless, she had taken him straight to her tent.

Although there had been male belongings – among them a *gorytus*, a hunting spear and a couple of fine swords – they had a packed-away, unused air. Nevertheless, the woman had hung the bowcase outside. She had closed the hangings, spread bedding, removed her clothes and gestured for him to lie down with her. Something about her very brisk practicality – that and possibly her bizarre dyed-red hair – had set him aback. But he had persevered

– thinking about those two blondes in the brothel in Arete had helped – and after a time things went better. Afterwards they had talked a little, but she had looked sad, and told him to leave.

Now, on the fourth morning, Maximus was thinking about her. From the other side of their tent, Ballista was delivering what amounted to a lecture on the moral corruption of living under an autocracy as analysed by Tacitus. Calgacus was outside, cooking, his movements awkward because of his arm. Tarchon had vanished. Unable to account for the woman's sadness, Maximus was wondering if it would be a good idea to visit her again.

Andonnoballus appeared at the entrance. They invited him to enter. Calgacus came in too. Maximus got them all a drink. At least, Maximus thought, it should call a halt to the drone about politics.

'When will Naulobates grant us another audience?' Ballista asked.

'The answer to your request was unambiguous,' Andonnoballus said.

'There are other things, beyond the ransoms, we would discuss, preferably alone with the king.'

'I am sure he will receive you again soon. Although the work of a lawgiver consumes his time. He does not spare himself, and he has been called away the past two days.' Andonnoballus looked serious. 'The *tauma* of Naulobates has brought back word that the deity prefers Naulobates be called not King but First-Brother.'

'It is not an easy thing to change the laws of a people,' Ballista said. 'Solon, the great Athenian, went abroad when his reforms were complete. Sulla, the Dictator of Rome, retired into private life. When he introduced the rule of the emperors, there were attempts on the life of Augustus.'

Andonnoballus shot Ballista a hard look. 'There is no question of such with the First-Brother. The reforms are God-given. All Heruli are united in support.'

'Yet people are accustomed to their old ways, often they resist . . .'

'There is no resistance. Those who objected showed they were not true Heruli.'

'Tell me about the reforms, especially about the women,' Maximus said quickly.

The conversation had been heading into uncomfortable places. It was unlike Ballista to be so tactless. It was almost as if he had been sounding out the loyalty of Andonnoballus to his father's regime. For a nasty moment, Maximus wondered if Ballista had received further instructions from Gallienus's court, instructions beyond the unlikely task of trying to turn the Heruli against their Gothic allies. Something pricked his memory, then disappeared again. 'Tell me about the women,' he said with an open, affable smile.

Andonnoballus laughed. 'Outsiders always want to know about the women.'

'You all have your women in common?' Maximus asked.

'As in Plato's *Republic*,' Ballista said.

'Not at all, it is far better than Plato imagined,' Andonnoballus said.

This was safer ground altogether. Although Maximus suspected that Plato might prove even less entertaining than Tacitus. The young Herul was obviously setting himself for some weighty discourse.

'Plato abolished marriage, the home and the family. He took babies from their mothers. The guardians of his ideal *polis* were to be mated like hunting dogs, although the occasion would be called a festival. Who got to mate was decided by lot. To ensure only the best mated, the lots were to be fixed. It was cruel, unnatural and all based on deceit.'

'And yours is better?' Ballista said.

'Without doubt. What is more natural than the family? The deity instructed Naulobates that men should continue to marry, should have a tent and possessions of their own. How could a warrior live on the Steppes without his herds? Their number are the measure of his valour. But to ensure harmony, to make us a true band of brothers, no husband objects if another man enjoys his wife. As paternity must be uncertain, every Herul regards every child as if it were his own.'

'How do you avoid incest?' Ballista asked.

'It is a large tribe. You do not lie with the daughters of women you had around the time of the girl's conception.'

'So the Rosomoni are descended through the mothers?' Ballista asked.

'Not altogether. Only exceptionally will a Rosomoni woman lie with a man who is not Rosomoni.'

'What sort of exception?' Maximus was interested now.

'If he is a great warrior, or for some other unusual reason.'

Maximus grinned and got up. 'Sure, that helps me make a decision. I will be off to see the Rosomoni woman I saw the other day.'

'What is her name?' Andonnoballus said.

'Olympias.'

A strange look crossed Andonnoballus's face; not disapproving, let alone hostile, more compassionate. 'Enjoy, but always remember, pleasure is fleeting.'

'Not that fleeting,' Maximus said complacently.

Outside, walking between the neat rows of tents and wagons, Maximus remembered the thing that had snagged at his memory earlier. He had meant to tell Ballista the other day, when Olympias had said it. They were the second embassy of foreigners in the camp this summer. King Hisarna of the Urugundi had ridden out two days before they had arrived.

★

He was back in Ephesus. Lost in the alleys of the potters' quarter. It had rained. The stucco on the close, blank walls was running with water. Thick mud squelched under foot. In the band of sky visible the stars raced to their extinction.

He crouched in the shallow recess of a doorway. Doubled up, gasping. The door was barred. He did not dare knock. The labyrinthine alleys played with the sounds. The baying of the mob came first from one direction then another. Each time, it was closer. If only he had not lost his way. If only he could get down to the Sacred Way, achieve the sanctuary of some holy place in the civic agora.

The mob rounded the corner. He could not run. They closed on him, their eyes as pitiless as the dying stars.

He woke, his heart racing, sweating heavily. It was dark in the tent. He forced himself to peer through the gloom into the further recesses. Only the humped shapes of his *contubernales* sleeping like brute beasts. No sign of the daemon. Just a dream then. Thank the gods for that.

He had made a mistake, had misread the signs. Just once, but that was enough. The daemons of those justly slain did not walk. The little girl in Ephesus had been innocent. Since her daemon had appeared to him, he had ensured another such could not happen. The mutilations kept any unjustly killed from seeking revenge. When time was pressing, licking and spitting the blood and wiping the blade on their heads should prove enough. Jason had not been haunted by Apsyrtus. If a murderer of the innocent stood on sacred ground, the gods sent madness and disease. He had been in temples. He was healthy and sane. To rid himself of her, he needed purification. But the ritual called for things he could not obtain. If not a priest, it demanded at least privacy and a suckling pig. Neither had been available as they crossed the Steppe, and neither were to be had here among the Heruli.

He lay thinking about the words of Naulobates. After the

meadow, out of hearing of the Heruli, the others had sniggered nervously. They were fools. He had no doubt the daemon of Naulobates was as real as that of the dead boy Wulfstan. As real, and as deadly. If he continued his work here among the Heruli, most likely he would be caught. His own fate was of little consequence. But if he were killed, his work, the task the gods had entrusted to him, would end. He should do no more while they were under the eye of the daemon Naulobates called Brachus. When they departed it would be different. Then he could act again.

Of course, it would pain Ballista when he killed the man. Ballista did not see the soul of his friend. But it could not be helped. The gods had made their Hound, their Scourge. If he let the man live, much evil would follow. For a long time he had been unsure, but now he knew he needed to kill him as soon as he could. Perhaps there might yet be a chance while they were still here. Some moment of confusion, the chaos of a battle or the turmoil of a hunt, when the daemon of Naulobates would be distracted. No man lives when the gods want him to die.

The day after Andonnoballus's visit, Ballista walked through the ordered tents and wagons up to the market. Calgacus and Maximus went with him. Tarchon again had disappeared on some business of his own.

It was eight days before the *kalends* of July, and very hot. Heruli sat in the shade; some under the parked wagons. There were more men now that the warriors with Uligagus had returned. Camp discipline was good. Each dwelling was a stone's throw apart from its neighbour. There was little rubbish to be seen and, despite the heat, there were none of the noxious smells one might have expected from a camp of this size.

The market was large, busy and tightly controlled. There were Heruli overseers everywhere, inspecting the traders' permits and collecting taxes on their sales. An extraordinary array of goods was on offer. From the Rha river and the north there was honey, wax, wood and arrows, sheep and cattle, slaves, and many types of fur: sable, ermine, marten, squirrel, fox, beaver and rabbit. There was much amber, some an unusual yellow. From the east, caravans had travelled incalculable distances, bringing silks and spices. Out of the *imperium* to the south had come wine and raisins, olive oil and some fancy metalwork, most of it weaponry. Trade was brisk. There was no shortage of gold among the Heruli. Not just the Rosomoni wore silk.

Ballista was inspecting some river fish: how fresh were they, and how far had they come from the Rha river? Maximus was regaling Calgacus with an improbable account of his sexual performance the night before. *And then she asked if I minded if her sister joined us.* They did not see the messenger arrive. He was just there in their midst. The First-Brother wished to see them now.

Walking back down, Ballista reflected it was just as well. The sooner they were dismissed and on their way back to the *imperium* the better. Once Maximus had remembered to tell him Hisarna of the Urugundi had been closeted with Naulobates, it was obvious the Roman mission had no hope of success. Hisarna had got the *gudja* to bring them slowly, by a round-about route, while the king himself had come straight to confer with Naulobates. The alliance between the Heruli and the Urugundi was as tight as it had been when they sacked the town of Tanais.

Naulobates was holding court in the meadow. The place itself was the same, an unsettling mixture of rural idyll and killing field. The cooling breeze that moved the verdant foliage and sweet grass also turned the black, fly-blown hunks of human flesh strung in the branches. No living miscreants were perched in the treetops this time.

Naulobates was in the same wooden chair. His leading men

sprawled on the grass about him. Castricius and Hippothous were standing a little to one side. In front of the Heruli First-Brother, and the object of everyone's attention, was a strange-looking individual. He was swarthy and had curly black hair. He wore a sky-blue cloak, and yellow-and-green-striped trousers. In his hand was a long ebony cane. Ballista had seen someone similar somewhere before.

'The envoy of the Roman emperor, Marcus Clodius Ballista, better known to my people as Dernhelm, son of Isangrim, son of Starkad, of the Angles.' Naulobates waved Ballista to join the other members of the embassy. As the Heruli were seated, Ballista sat down too. Those with him followed. None of the Heruli complained. The elaborate introduction, Ballista thought, had to be for the benefit of the man in the striped trousers.

'This is Mar Ammo.' Naulobates pointed. The First-Brother seemed in an expansive mood, excited even. His eyes gleamed strangely. 'Mar Ammo has come from the domain of Shapur the Sassanid king. He is a missionary from Mani, the self-styled Seal of the Prophets. He is going to tell us the Gospel of Light.'

A snigger ran through the assembled Heruli. Naulobates' tone had been one of disbelief. The missionary seemed unabashed. Ballista was unsure he would have stood up to it so well. Perhaps the man in the odd trousers had not noticed the decomposing body parts, or perhaps his faith sustained him.

Ballista remembered where he had seen a similar man. It had been in the town of Carrhae, four years earlier. A warm spring dawn, on the top of the citadel, Ballista had been hauled before the Sassanid king. Cledonius, the old *ab Admissionibus* of the captive emperor Valerian, had been with him. To Shapur's left, among the priests, had stood another man with an ebony cane and the same clothes.

'You say you speak the language of the north,' Naulobates said. The missionary bowed.

'Tell us how Mani claims to know the truth about the deity.'

The missionary squared his shoulders. 'Mani is the *paraclete* of Truth, the very spirit of truth. When he was a boy, at the end of his twelfth year, his divine twin first appeared to him. The twin, his *syzygos*, drew him aside and told him he must remain unblemished and abstain from desire. Yet the time was not right for him to appear, for he was still young. When the *paraclete* turned twenty-four, his *syzygos* returned. Now was the time for him to appear and call others to his cause.'

Ballista had attended the *consilium* of enough emperors to know how to mould his face into a mask of interested attention, while his thoughts roamed far away. He wondered why Naulobates had summoned him and the others. It could be he wished to demonstrate to them, and through them to Gallienus and the Roman world in general, his piety and the power of his intellect. Ballista had no doubt Naulobates would cross-examine the missionary. Who would – in Naulobates' eyes – win the exchange was not in doubt. It would have all the lack of dramatic tension of a Socratic dialogue as imagined by Plato. Perhaps Naulobates also thought it would nicely illustrate the geographic spread of his power – men came to him from the Sassanid realm.

'Equipped with his five sons, as if in readiness for war, the First Man came down to fight the darkness. However, the Prince of Darkness fought back.'

The missionary had moved on to telling an incredibly complicated story concerning a war between the Father of Greatness of the Realm of Light and the King of Darkness. This struggle between good and evil was ongoing, and fought at a cosmic level and within every man. It had a confusingly large cast and, Ballista thought, would have been much improved with better battle scenes and a good chase sequence. The only sex appeared to be a few cases of daemonic premature ejaculation.

The missionary droned on. The sons of the First Man, somehow or other, had sacrificed themselves into the darkness. But, unsurprisingly, redemption appeared to be on its way.

Perhaps, Ballista thought, this display was all the other way around. Perhaps Ballista and the Romans were the ones on show to the missionary from the Sassanid kingdom. See, you easterners, how the Romans honour Naulobates and the Heruli.

Ballista's thoughts gathered pace. Perhaps they were on show to others as well. It could be that the Roman embassy, above all Ballista himself, had been slowly trailed across the disputed grasslands in the hope the Alani would attack, and thus give the Heruli and the Urugundi a just cause for war. The Alani had broken whatever oaths had secured the peace on the Steppe. In the eyes of the gods, the world and themselves, Naulobates and Hisarna would be justified in their fight. Look, they could say, they attacked the Roman ambassador Ballista. It was sacrilege. Yet here he is in our midst, the living proof of their perfidy and our pious desire for revenge.

'Enough!' Naulobates' high voice cut through the missionary's recommendations of celibacy and vegetarianism and other joyless things that would make God happy.

'Poor Mani,' Naulobates continued. 'He means well. But he is like a promising student who listens to philosophers when drunk. No matter how he tries, the words elide and confuse him.'

Naulobates smiled, with an air of avuncular forbearance. 'And he is naughty, very naughty. He denies he was born a slave boy called Corbicius.'

'That is a calumny spread by his enemies,' Mar Ammo said. 'His father was Pattikios, a citizen of Ecbatana, and his mother, Marma-ryan, a descendant of the Arsacid royal house of Parthia.' The missionary did not lack courage.

Naulobates fixed him with his strange eyes. 'Have you seen the *syzygos* of Mani?'

'No.' The missionary looked uncomfortable.

'I have.' Naulobates sighed. 'How it fled from my Brachus! But no matter where it went in the other world, Brachus followed. Brachus caught him, as the gods caught Loki. For nine nights and days Brachus tried to enlighten him. But the fumes of wine still clouded his understanding.'

'The Seal of Prophets does not touch wine.' The missionary really had the courage of his convictions.

Naulobates wagged a finger.

The missionary subsided into silence.

'You will stay with me,' Naulobates said to Mar Ammo. 'You will learn the truth. Mani has shown you some aspects. All deities are aspects of the One. Mani was right, the Kingdom of Light is in the north, and working the soil is for lesser men. Yet, in his stubborn drunkenness, he failed to see that the kingdom was already to be found here among the Heruli.'

The missionary looked horrified.

Naulobates clapped his hands. 'Tomorrow we will give a practical demonstration of a field where Mani is very misguided. We will go hunting. It is time for a royal *battue*.'

XXIV

Two hours before dawn, Ballista and Maximus got dressed in the
dark. They had laid out their hunting clothes and equipment the
night before. They did not talk and were as quiet as could be
managed. They woke Calgacus anyway. He cursed them as clod-
hopping, clumsy bastards making enough din to raise the fucking
dead. Neither the Caledonian's injured arm nor being told the
previous evening that he was to remain in the camp had done
anything to improve his habitual waspish temper.

It was cold outside, with a chill bite to the wind. Ballista pulled
on a thick leather coat, stamped his feet. Tarchon led up two of
the Sarmatian horses. Working as much by feel and habit as sight,
Ballista and Maximus tacked up and slung their weapons and gear.
The breath of the horses was sweet in their faces. Tarchon held
the bridles as each mounted.

They waited as Castricius and Hippothous emerged from the
next tent. Biomasos brought round their horses. Soon the four
who had been invited to join the hunt were in the saddle. They
said farewell to Tarchon and the interpreter, and reined about to
set off.

The dim form of Calgacus emerged from the tent. 'A creaking bow, a croaking raven, a yawning wolf, a grunting wild boar; never be such a fool as to trust such things.'

'We will take care,' Ballista said.

'A coiled snake, a burning flame, a flying arrow.'

'Enough.' Ballista clicked his tongue on the roof of his mouth, and his horse walked on. He grinned in the darkness. The old Caledonian was getting protective like a nursemaid. He had noticed it in himself: the older you got, the more you worried.

Men were stirring all through the camp. Ballista and the others joined a stream of warriors walking their horses southward between the tents.

Out on the plain, several large fires had been lit. The ceaseless north wind pulled sparks away high into the night sky. Standards flew upwind of the fires, and the Heruli assembled in their stations. The royal hunt was a great undertaking. A division of four thousand riders had already left the afternoon before under the command of Andonnoballus. In all, another thousand would follow this morning with Naulobates.

Ballista and his *familia* joined those under the banner of three wolves pursuing a *tamga* that resembled three circles pierced by an arrow. Ballista greeted Pharas, but the Herul looked distracted and only nodded. It was slightly off hand, but the twenty or so men waiting to ride with the First-Brother were all quiet. The clicking and cracking of the fire sounded sharp over the creak of leather and the jink of bridles.

Naulobates trotted into the circle of firelight. He was flanked by Uligagus and Artemidorus, the former slave from Trapezus. Behind them rode Mar Ammo. The Manichaean looked thoroughly miserable. Naulobates raised his hands to the dark sky and intoned a prayer to Artemis and an eclectic range of other more obscure deities of the chase. Nomads did not make libations. His words ended, Naulobates made the signal, and they moved off south into the Steppe.

The sun was not yet up, but the sky promised a good day. The wind had dropped a little, lost much of its cold edge. To the east, the horizon was a band of pale blue-gold. Above it, fanning out from the south-east, were ribbed, purple-gold clouds, as solid as dunes in a desert. High above, gaps in the clouds showed a heaven of pure aquamarine. A flight of birds, half a dozen black shapes, gave a sense of scale, of the sheer majesty of it all.

They were riding at an easy canter that ate up the miles. At the head of the small column, Naulobates was bare-headed, laughing. Uligagus and Artemidorus also looked happy. Pharas, the other Herul with them, appeared rather more subdued.

The sun came up. Naulobates halted and, bowing in the saddle, blew it a kiss from his fingertips. His *proskynesis* performed, Naulobates called Ballista and his *familia* to ride up with him. The Heruli fell back, but Naulobates indicated for the Manichaean Mar Ammo to stay.

'Everything I know about hunting was taught to me as a child by my father's friend Phanitheus. He spared me no criticism, held nothing back. He was a warrior feared across the Steppe, a mighty hunter, and a stern teacher. His vigour remained in him a long time. It was only two years ago it deserted him, and obviously it was time for him to die.' Naulobates shook his elongated head sadly. 'I still find it hard to believe he did not face it better.'

There seemed little to say to this.

After a while, Naulobates brightened. 'But, just as a good death does not necessarily redeem a bad man, so the reverse must hold true. I remember the time Phanitheus beat me for forgetting the hunting spears. What a beating that was. He did not spare himself.' Naulobates laughed happily.

Again, this did not invite any obvious rejoinder.

266

'Were you beaten much as a child?' Naulobates suddenly asked Mar Ammo.

'No more than is usual,' the Manichaean said.

'Hmm, perhaps you should have been beaten more. When Mani was Corbicius, he was beaten regularly. Did him a lot of good. It might do you some.'

Mar Ammo was entirely unable to shape an answer.

'Most pleasures are corrupting,' Naulobates said. 'Beating men, for example. Even sex and drink, if taken to excess, weaken a man. Reading too much is the same. But hunting is entirely good for one – the body becomes stronger, the soul braver, and it gives exercise in all martial skills. A man must ride, run, meet the charge of big game, endure heat and cold, hunger and thirst, and get used to suffering all hardships. An envoy from Palmyra told me King Odenathus has always lived in the mountains and deserts, facing lions, panthers, bears and other beasts of the wilderness. No wonder the Persians run before him and the Romans have ceded half their empire to such a man.'

An embassy from Odenathus to the Heruli – Ballista thought on that. It was important news; if it were true. He was not going to point out that, in Roman terms, the King of Palmyra was a magistrate governing the eastern provinces on behalf of the emperor Gallienus.

'Hunting does more,' Hippothous said. 'It has a moral purpose.'

Naulobates turned in the saddle and regarded him.

'A hunter sights his quarry, then he loses it,' Hippothous said. 'The repeated experience teaches him to bear the sudden reverses of fortune. Hunting instils self-control better than any philosophy lecture.'

Naulobates' eyes remained unwavering, fixed on the Greek.

Silence, apart from the jinking of bits and the stamp of hooves. The entourage rode stony-faced.

Naulobates laughed, high and loud, with genuine pleasure. He reached across and patted Hippothous on the shoulder. 'You,' he told him, 'would make a good Herul.'

They rode south-east, and by noon were approaching a bend of the Rha river. The Steppe, as if tired of its own flat monotony, rolled gently. It was greener here. There were copses, pools of standing water and small tributaries ran east to where the Rha lay broad and shimmering in the sun two miles or more distant.

Horsemen were waiting for them. Naulobates and his entourage took their place, the rest of the newcomers flanking them. The *battue* was formed. A great line of riders curved away on either side; rising and dipping, and passing out of sight among shaded trees. Five thousand mounted men in a semicircle would drive the game against the banks of the Rha.

It was hot. Ballista rolled his heavy coat and tied it to the rear horns of his saddle. They ate and drank on horseback; strips of air-dried meat washed down with fermented mare's milk from leather flasks. Despite the presence of the First-Brother, an easy congeniality was on them. Ballista noticed it did not include the Manichaean missionary, or, oddly, Pharas the Herul. The latter fidgeted, and looked abstracted. He was sweating more heavily than the weather allowed.

'The *battue* is real hunting,' Naulobates said. 'The Greeks on foot with nets are no better than the primitive forest tribes of the north. The Romans who sit on cushions to watch the slaughter of animals in the arena are too contemptible for words. The rich of the *imperium*, who hunt with horse and hound, are always too few. It is no training for the manoeuvres of war. The Persians are a little better. Yet in their paradises the animals are in poor condition, lacking the heart that comes from true freedom. The *battue* of the Steppe is the only real hunt. No nets, no walls, just the line of riders. It is a true test of horsemanship, of archery, of the courage of man. With luck, we will find wild boar, even bear, down by the riverbank.

'It is time,' Naulobates said. His standard dipped, and a horn rang across the Steppe. All along the line the signals were repeated. 'Remember, you are not Persians waiting for the king to take the first shot. We are Heruli. We are brothers.'

They set off at a walk. Ballista had Maximus to his left, Hippothous and Castricius beyond him. To his right he was separated from Naulobates by Mar Ammo and Pharas. The Manichaean had a bow in his hands. He looked far from comfortable with it. Quite possibly he was suffering some crisis of conscience between his mission to convert Naulobates and the dictates of his religion that as one of its elect he should not kill.

Ballista fitted his thumb ring, chose an arrow, nocked it and part drew his recurve bow. The sun was on his face, the horse quiet and comfortable under him. Naulobates' lupine banner snapped above their heads. The wind was rising again. Ballista noted its strength and direction. He should remember to allow for it. His head buzzed slightly from the drink.

They plodded down a grassy incline. Rabbits and marmots ran from them. Bows thrummed, and the shafts whistled out at their prey. Ballista took a shot and missed. Others had more success. Little animals tumbled and fell, white scuts and bellies displayed to the sun.

A covert of oaks tangled the line. When they emerged, a small herd of wild asses were in front. The Heruli *yipped* happily, automatically closed their spacing and trotted on. They wielded their bows with mastery. Where there had been motion, in moments there was dead game. Again, Ballista had missed.

A crane flew high across them. Naulobates called out something. The others did not shoot. He switched his bow to his right hand, leant far back in the saddle, drew with his left and released.

The crane was transfixed. It plummeted, broken and ungainly. The Heruli applauded. Ballista joined in. It was a very fine shot, and worth noting that Naulobates could use a weapon with either hand.

The disciple of Mani seemed close to tears. Ballista could not understand these pacifist sects that seemed to be springing up: Manichaeans, Christians, Essenes. If god, or the gods, did not want man to hunt, why had he made it so enjoyable? Among the Manichaeans, at least, the non-elect were allowed to kill. None of the Christians were meant to take life; not human life anyway. They would have to change their tune, if any ruler ever were misguided enough to join them. Still, that was most improbable.

They were near the Rha; no more than two bow shots. Ballista could smell the water. He could see the great river here and there through the wide belt of trees and the high reeds on its banks. Naulobates called a halt to dress the line. Again, the order rippled away; banners dipping, horns blowing. The *battue* jostled into order and immobility. Horses swished their tails, flicked their ears. Horses and men were sweating. Gold-tinged horseflies bothered both.

The thickets ahead grew close-packed. They would be full of driven game, some of it dangerous. The riders' formation would be broken. Ballista flexed his fingers and arms, rolled his shoulders. He took a long drink, put away the flask, and readied his bow. His palms were slick, and his thin linen tunic was sticking to his back. It was going to be chaotic in there.

Naulobates threw back his head and called a long, wild call: *yip-yip-yip.*

Like hunting dogs, the Heruli gave tongue: *yip-yip-yip.*

Caught up in the moment, Ballista hallooed. Next to him, Maximus was bellowing. Everyone was yelling, except the Manichaean and Pharas. Ballista saw the latter's mouth open but somehow knew he was making no sound.

Naulobates kicked in his heels. His horse leapt forward. They all surged after.

Ballista dropped his reins, let his Sarmatian pick its own way into the dappled shade. Men and horses flashed through the bands of sunlight. Ballista bent low to avoid a branch. There were many things crashing through the undergrowth.

A boar started out. Its bald, leathery head and shoulders faced the horsemen. The Heruli *yipped*. The boar turned and broke into its scuttling, bouncing run. The hunters raced after. Glimpses of the beast's shaggy, reddish-brown quarters showed through the bushes. Ballista was up by Naulobates. The Manichaean had disappeared.

Ballista took a shot. The arrow missed. Naulobates aimed. At the moment of release, the boar swerved to the right. Naulobates' arrow snicked into the earth. They wheeled after it.

The boar went tumbling, crashing snout first into the fallen leaves. It got to its feet, its tail flicking. An arrow was embedded behind its near-front leg. Uligagus was right above it; backing his horse. Another arrow, then another thumped into the boar's flank. It toppled sideways.

'On, on,' Naulobates shouted.

They were almost at the water's edge. The bank of reeds was seething with wildlife. Splashes could be heard, as those that could swim hurled themselves into the broad river. Ducks flighted overhead. The horsemen slowed, pushing ahead more circumspectly, shooting all the time.

Ballista had closed up on Naulobates. Maximus was on his left. For a moment, the three were isolated. From behind, an arrow hissed between Ballista and Maximus. Without taking their eyes from the swaying curtain of reeds ahead, both yelled warnings.

Something very big was ploughing through the reeds ahead. Feathery tops jerked and vanished. Naulobates was crooning some prayer; willing the beast to him.

A full-grown stag, a noble spread of antlers above, burst from the cover. It turned to run. Naulobates surged upon it, drawing his sword. The stag swung back, antlers lowered to charge. Naulobates' horse side-stepped. Not quite far enough. There was a spray of blood. As his mount passed, Naulobates cut back and down. The long straight sword went deep into the back of the stag's neck. It collapsed like a sack. Naulobates had half decapitated the animal.

'Your Manichaean would be glad he did not see that,' Maximus said.

The feast was held down on the riverbank. The favoured men around Naulobates occupied a low knoll. Ballista and his *familia* rubbed down their mounts, keeping them from drinking until they had cooled down. The Heruli built fires and collected and butchered the game. When Naulobates had washed, salved and bound his own right leg, he saw to his horse, then skinned and broke up his stag. Like a good hunter and a gracious monarch, he dedicated a share to Artemis and the gods and handed the choicer cuts to those around him, keeping just the liver for himself.

They roasted the meat over the open fires. It tasted good; crisp and flavoured with woodsmoke, the juices running. They had salt, but Naulobates' temper flared when he discovered there was no vinegar. The uncomfortable moment passed, and he began to drink. Ballista was glad he was not the Herul who had forgotten the vinegar. Naulobates did not strike him as the sort of man who forgot things himself. Ballista settled to drink with the First-Brother and his companions. Along the banks of the Rha, they all settled to drink copiously.

Full, half drunk, they sprawled in the shade to take their rest. Ballista lay on his back, patterns of light playing over his closed eyelids.

'Fire!' The shout meant nothing to Ballista. 'Fire!' His eyes were bleared. He forced himself up on one elbow. Sleep is the brother of death; for some reason the Greek idea floated among the fumes clouding his thoughts.

A Herul rode up to Naulobates, who was getting to his feet. 'Brush fire, to the north.'

'How long?'

'With this wind, no time at all.'

'Huhn.' Naulobates tugged at his sparse beard. 'The men who let their campfire get out of control will suffer.'

'No, First-Brother, the fire started out in the Steppe, well beyond the sentries.'

Naulobates gave him a sharp look. 'Ride on through the camp, tell everyone to gather their things and ride due west into the Steppe, fast as they can.'

The Herul clattered off.

Pandemonium ensued at Naulobates' words. But it was a sluggish pandemonium. Everywhere, men staggered to their feet. Half asleep, part drunk, part hung over, they stumbled around. The horses were some way off to the west, hobbled to graze beyond the belt of trees. The less crapulous wandered off to round them up.

Ballista got up, buckled on his sword belt. His head ached, and his throat was dry. There was an unease in his stomach. A dozen or so riders were coming up from the direction of the river, urging their mounts through the reeds. As Ballista bent to get his *gorytus*, the Herul next to him straightened up with a flask and meal bag in his hands. The Herul sank to his knees. There was a look of incomprehension on his face. He toppled forward. The bright fletchings of an arrow stuck out from between his shoulderblades. Another arrow thumped into the leaf mould by Ballista's boot.

'Maximus!' *Gorytus* in hand, Ballista ran towards the nearest large tree. Maximus was with him. Together, they dived behind the wide trunk of the oak.

'Fuck,' Maximus panted.

Ballista looked out. The riders were bearing down, shooting as they came. He ducked back. Dropping the bowcase, he unsheathed his sword.

The thunder of hooves got louder. Ballista and Maximus looked at each other. They pointed to each side of the tree, and nodded. The hoofbeats were almost on top of them. *One-two-three*. They leapt out either side, swords arcing.

The nomad pony shied, its rider released. The arrow whistled high. The last few inches of Ballista's sword caught the animal's front leg near the knee. The impact tried to drag the hilt from his grip. Hanging on, the momentum of the falling pony dragged Ballista to the ground. Scrabbling among the fallen leaves, he saw the nomad jump clear. The pony went down in a tangle of limbs.

'Run!' A hand on Ballista's shoulder was hauling him to his feet. 'Run!' Maximus shouted again.

The nomad was on his feet, pulling his sword free. Maximus, almost casually, dropped him with two blows. Ballista noticed the nomad's clothes were sodden.

They ran pell-mell down the slope. The Manichaean was standing stock-still, mouth open. Ballista took his arm, spun him round, yelled at him to run. They did not wait to see if the missionary did as he was told.

Something plucked at Ballista's sleeve and sped on ahead. He swerved as he ran.

At the foot of the knoll was a mass of briars. They fought their way into them. Ballista felt them catch at his tunic and trousers, felt sharp flares of pain as they tore his flesh.

'Over here.' Maximus dived into the space where two elms grew close together. Ballista threw himself in after.

'Fuck,' Maximus said.

Gasping for breath, Ballista looked back. The horsemen were outnumbered, but more Heruli were falling. One of the riders was circling his mount. 'Naulobates and Ballista,' he shouted above the cacophony.

Ballista saw Naulobates. The Herul had a blade in each hand. He was ringed by three riders. He had no chance.

From nowhere, Uligagus threw himself on one of the horsemen, dragging him to the ground. Naulobates feinted towards the opening, then doubled back at the opposite rider. An arrow hit him in the leg. He kept going. The pony reared. Careless of the flailing hooves, Naulobates ducked under its belly, swords darting. He emerged the other side, as the animal collapsed. Its rider jumped clear. Naulobates killed him. The third mounted man shot. Naulobates went backwards. A pack of Heruli threw themselves on the last rider. Pony and man were hauled to the ground and disappeared beneath the hacking blades.

It was over as it started, with no warning.

Ballista and Maximus fought their way painfully out of the thorn bushes. They trudged up to the ring of men around Naulobates.

The First-Brother of the Heruli was sitting up. There was an arrow in his left shoulder, the broken shaft of another in his left leg. He was very pale behind his tattoos, bleeding heavily. His men were cutting away his clothes.

Naulobates opened his eyes, looked at Ballista. 'Three honourable wounds in one day.' He smiled. 'You should be honoured,

Angle. These Alani were prepared to die to kill two men – me and you.'

'We should get the horses,' Ballista said, 'before we all burn to death.'

XXV

Calgacus knew that the details of the fight were lost beyond human comprehension. They always were. Only fools thought different. But now it was seven days later, the *kalends* of July. He had talked to several of the survivors, and the general plan of the Alani ambush of the hunting party was easy to reconstruct. Some had set a line of fires in the dry grasses to the north, knowing the wind would bring it down to where the Heruli rested. In the confusion, a small band had swum their mounts across the Rha. No sentries had been posted on the riverbank. The Alani had got among their enemy with complete surprise. Only the foolhardy courage of the Heruli, and luck – or divine providence, as Naulobates would have it – had prevented them killing the two men whose lives they had come to take.

He should have been there. He was old, and his arm and shoulder were not good, but he should have been there. Calgacus felt sick every time it struck him how close he had come to losing Ballista. All these years together, and now there was the curse on the boy – *Kill all his family, all those he loves* – a curse on both of them. Pythonissa had prayed not for Ballista to die, but to live on in misery. But curses can play out in unexpected and awful ways if the powers of the underworld listen. Who would they heed, if not a priestess of Hecate? Calgacus was not going to let Ballista get killed out here in this alien wilderness of grass. He was not going to leave the bastard's side until they were hundreds of miles away, not until they were safe back in Sicily, safe in the villa in Tauromenium.

As he walked with Ballista and the *familia* through the Heruli camp to the assembly, he turned the ambush over in his mind. It had been well planned. The Alani had struck at the right time, and in the right place. How had they known there were no sentries along the bank of the river? How had they known the *battue* would end there at all? Treachery was the obvious answer. Ballista had to be right; not all the Heruli were happy with the extraordinary reforms of Naulobates. It stood to reason: not every fucker wants his world turned upside down.

The market had been stripped of traders. Its open space was filling with black clusters of Heruli. As guests, Ballista and his *familia* wedged themselves right at the back, up against a wagon. A great drum thundered, and more tribesmen pushed in from the various alleys. The groups of Heruli coagulated into a solid, slightly shifting mass. Yet more surged in, creating small eddies in the crowd.

Naulobates clambered on to an open-top wagon on the far side. He moved stiffly, using a spear as a staff. He sat in his accustomed plain wood chair. He was on his own.

'What is the meaning of this gathering? What do you want?' Heruli called out from the crowd.

Calgacus smiled. The Heruli had not lost all their old equality in the God-given reforms of their king turned First-Brother. There was a spark left of the people who once killed their rulers for no better reason than they did not like them.

Naulobates raised the spear so he could be heard.

The Heruli were quiet.

'I want your counsel.' Naulobates' strange, high voice carried well. It gave no sign of the wounds, or the pain he must still be suffering. Hercules' hairy arse, but that fucker was tough.

'Some years ago,' Naulobates began, 'we exchanged solemn vows of peace with the Alani. Both sides swore by *anemos* and *akinakes*, the only gods the Alani recognize. We spilt the blood of many oxen. Now the Alani have attacked our brothers who were escorting a Roman embassy. Against the laws of all gods and all men, they tried to kill the Roman envoy. Not content with such treachery and sacrilege, they ambushed us when we were hunting. They have broken their oaths. It means war. The gods are on our side. But how should we fight the war? Give me your counsel.'

The assembly buzzed like a disturbed hive. Discordant voices called out the names of those whom they wanted to speak. Calgacus knew some of them: Andonnoballus, Uligagus, Artemidorus. Eventually, the majority were shouting for one Aruth. The rest fell moderately quiet.

Aruth was a stocky man; one of the Rosomoni with a particularly pointed skull. He was fit to bursting with moral outrage. The Alani were scum; cowardly, sly bastards. His address was long for the brevity of its message. The Heruli should saddle their horses now, this very day, and ride south to sweep the fucking Alani shit from the Steppes. What Aruth lacked in oratorical skills was compensated for by his utter foul-mouthed vehemence.

The next speaker was Pharas. In more measured terms, he supported Aruth. There was no excuse for delay; what was needed was immediate retribution. They would be outnumbered, but the gods would hold their hands over the Heruli. There was laughter when someone yelled, Where had Pharas been when the *battue* was attacked? – he had not been so brave then. Pharas turned the laughter to his own advantage. Yes, he had gone to relieve himself. Nothing was more typical of Alani cowardice than to attack a man when he was trying to have a shit in peace.

Clearly, the firebrand and scatological approach initiated by Aruth was not to all tastes. After much bellowing, Artemidorus was summoned to address the assembly.

'At last, my brothers, I must break my silence. Listen to the words of an old man.'

There was much hooting and laughter. It seemed the lines were not new. Calgacus got the latter dark joke. He presumed the former must have something to do with the reputation of all Greeks for talking too much.

When the amusement ebbed, Artemidorus continued in statesman-like mode. 'The Alani have thirty thousand riders. We muster no more than ten thousand. If we go south, their sheer numbers will overwhelm our courage. The gods do not favour reckless arrogance. We should elect a war leader, have him sit on the hide and summon our tributaries and allies. But, we should not forget, that will do no more than double our numbers. We should move the herds and the main camp north. Let the Alani come to us. If we draw them out on to the endless expanse of the sea of grass, our superior discipline and skill will let us isolate and surround them.'

Some roared their approval. Others shouted that it was just the sort of backsliding advice you would expect from a Greek. More speakers followed. None added anything new to the lines of the debate.

Nearly an hour later, Naulobates had heard enough. Leaning on his spear, he rose to address his brothers. For the first time, the silence was complete.

'Brothers, you give me good counsel, all of it expressed with the freedom of our forefathers. I am sure our brother Artemidorus will not take offence when I say the Greeks have nothing to teach us with their so-called democracy.'

The Heruli enjoyed this.

'If you will accept it, my plan takes these trails.'

The assembly listened.

'Artemidorus and those of his mind are correct that we should move our animals, women and children north, as far as possible out of harm's way. Again, they are correct that we must elect a war leader and have him raise all the warriors we can by sitting on the hide.'

There were murmurs of gratification from the more circumspect.

'However, Aruth and the others have the right of it when they say we must not be supine and wait. Our inaction would encourage the audacity of the Alani. We must take the fight to the oath-breakers. When the levies are complete, we must ride south.'

There was a happy uproar. Naulobates rode the noise, letting it play itself out.

'One thing remains,' he said. 'Who do you want as your war leader?'

Men shouted for Naulobates. What surprised Calgacus was that not every Herul shouted for the First-Brother.

'Andonnoballus!'

'No, he has still got his mother's milk on his lips!'

'Artemidorus!'

'He is not up to it – too cautious!'

'Aruth! We want Aruth!'

'No brains!'

'Naulobates! Naulobates!' The name drowned out the others.

'Do you all agree?'

'We all agree!'

Four Heruli climbed up on to the open wagon where Naulobates stood. Each had in his hands a clod of mud from the riverbank. These they placed on Naulobates' head.

As the mud ran through his sparse hair, down over his face and into his beard, Naulobates thanked his brothers for the honour they did him.

It was the day after the assembly, and Maximus knew he should not attend the ritual. But something compelled him. If he had been Castricius, or maybe Naulobates, he would think it was his daemon. Ballista and Calgacus had been so strong against him going, Maximus had lied. He had said he needed to ride out on the Steppe to get far away from it, to make sure he was not tempted to intervene. He had ridden south out of the main Heruli camp but then had circled back, crossed the river and passed the meadow. The burial ground was in a copse. He stopped at the tree line, where the horses were hobbled. Through the foliage, he could see a crowd on foot: twenty or so Heruli, mostly Rosomoni. He could see Olympias.

The day Andonnoballus had come to their tent, Maximus had visited Olympias for the second time. She had seemed pleased that he had come. They had made love. She had seemed to enjoy it. Yet, afterwards, when they talked again, there had been a strange distance about her, some deep sadness in her eyes. It had been the same every time he went to her tent. On the fourth visit, he had asked her what was wrong. She had looked at him with surprise, and simply said she was the widow of Philemuth. It had taken a moment for Maximus to remember the old Herul; the one Ballista had been asked to kill out on the Steppe.

Later that night, Ballista had told him what would happen. Maximus had ranted against the perverse innovations of Naulobates. He would not let it happen. They could not just stand by and let it go ahead. Ballista had said there was nothing they could do. This was not a new thing thought up by the deranged First-Brother. The Heruli had always had customs not in accord with those of other men. They had done the same in his grandfather's day. It had been one of the things that made the Heruli notorious in the north. If Olympias laid claim to virtue and wished to leave a fair name, she would go through with it. It would be her choice. They could do nothing.

Maximus sat on his horse and watched. Philemuth's weapons were spread out on the grave where his bones lay. They were garlanded with flowers. His favourite warhorse was led forward. It was dappled in the sun. The Heruli sang. Maximus was too far away to catch the words. A long blade flashed, and the horse bled and died by the grave.

Maximus heard the riders coming up behind. He did not look round. Ballista and Calgacus reined in on either side.

'Do not fear,' Maximus said, 'I will not do anything.'

Ballista put a hand on his shoulder.

Maximus watched Olympias step forward. She was dressed in white, golden ornaments in her dark hair. She stood straight. She spoke words he could not hear.

Two other women helped Olympias up on to the bench under the bough. She put the noose over her own head. The other women adjusted the knot. Olympias kicked the bench away herself.

Maximus watched her feet kick, until the two women caught her thighs and pulled hard down.

Four days after the death of Olympias, in the meadow across the river, Naulobates, war leader of the Heruli, sat on the hide.

At dawn, a bull was brought forth. Naulobates had killed it with an axe. He had skinned and butchered it himself. His wounds had constrained his movements. Others had built the fire, wheeled out an enormous cauldron, erected it on a tripod and filled it with water. Naulobates had put in the joints, and lit the fire.

While the smoke billowed, Naulobates had spread the hide of the bull. He sat cross-legged on it, his hands held behind his back, like a man bound by the elbows.

The first day, when the meat was cooked, one by one the leading men of the Heruli had come. There were ten of them. Andonnoballus, Uligagus, Artemidorus and Aruth were among their number. Each had taken a portion of meat and eaten it. Having finished, each placed his right boot on the hide and pledged to bring one thousand horsemen of the swift Heruli to the gathering.

The following days had seen the great men of the tributary and allied tribes pledge men according to their numbers and ability. There had been chiefs from many peoples. First had come the Eutes, the grandsons of men who had followed the Heruli down from the Suebian sea. Second had been the Agathyrsi, their swirling blue tattoos as intricate and dense as the red patterns that blossomed on the skins of the Heruli. Next had been the fabled Nervii. They wore the skins of wolves, and were said once a year to change into those terrible animals. After these had come the leaders of tribes along the Rha river – Ragas, Imniscaris, Mordens – all the way to the Goltescythae of the northern mountains.

After the chiefs came less reputable men. These lean, scarred warriors were from no recognized tribe. Each had a *comitatus* of no more than a dozen at most behind him. The uncharitable might call them bandits. Naulobates did not. He spoke to them with courtesy. Their men helped bring the number of his war band to near twenty thousand.

Seven days Naulobates had sat upon the hide. He had not moved from it. On the hide he had slept. On it he had eaten the food men brought him, and defecated in the bowls they took away.

Ballista had been there throughout, watching. Although it might put himself and his *familia* at risk, he had resisted the unspoken pressure to place his right boot on the hide. He was the envoy of the Roman emperor. He was an Angle; the grandson of Starkad, who had driven the Heruli from the north. He may have been used to start this war, but he had no intention of fighting in it.

The sun was sliding down in the west. The ritual would end at dusk. Ballista reflected on it and on the strangeness of the Steppes. *Let him wander the face of the earth . . . among strange peoples.* Some things among the nomads had proved to be exactly as Greek and Latin literature had led him to expect. The Agathyrsi and the Heruli painted themselves and shared their women. Other things had turned out very differently. Herodotus had written that the nomads blinded their slaves. Far from mutilating them, the Heruli offered them brotherhood, if they showed valour.

The sky was the purple of a bruise that goes down to the bone. No one had placed their boot upon the hide that day. But the crowd was not diminished. It had about it a curious, unfulfilled demeanour.

Ballista had read in Lucian of the sitting on the hide. But Lucian had been writing of the Scythians of at least two centuries earlier. Had the ceremony survived on the Steppe, surviving changes of peoples, somehow hibernating and waiting for the Heruli to adopt it? Or had Naulobates himself also read of it? Certainly, he and his son Andonnoballus had read many books. Had Naulobates also read Lucian, and decided the long-dead, maybe fictional ceremony would fit very well into his God-given reforms? It was too simple merely to think how literature reflected life; to judge how accurately a book captured reality. It could all go the other way. Things in books could alter the real lives of individuals and peoples.

A stir in the crowd broke the path of Ballista's thoughts. 'He is come,' someone nearby said, 'the Iron One.' A thickset figure emerged.

Hisarna, son of Aoric, King of the Urugundi, scooped up a little morsel of meat from the stew and chewed it. He unsheathed his father's famous sword *Iron* and placed his right boot upon the hide. In his melodious and gentle voice, he pledged ten thousand Gothic warriors.

Between Hisarna and Naulobates passed the look of men whose deep-laid plan has come to fruition, unspoilt by neither gods nor men.

XXVI

The Steppe was dry by late July, the grass yellowing and beginning to wither. The passage of nearly twenty thousand men and over forty thousand horses could not be hidden or disguised. The dust rose up around them like thick smoke, as if one of the great cities of the *imperium*, Ephesus or Antioch, was burning. The wind arched it high across the southern sky. There was no way the Alani could fail to know they were coming. Even if the gods struck blind every spy and scout they possessed, the noise of the army carried several miles downwind, and a man with any fieldcraft could put his ear to the ground and feel the reverberations further away still.

The army of the Heruli and their allies was spread over miles of grassland. They rode in four units: a vanguard under Uligagus and three parallel columns under Aruth, Artemidorus and Naulobates himself. All the Heruli and the Agathyrsi had a couple of spare ponies. Some of the Nervii and Eutes also had remounts, but very few of the warriors from the sedentary tribes along the Rha river and none of the bandits were so well equipped.

The strategy of the horde, lengthily and furiously argued over in the assembly, in the result could not be simpler. They would ride south-west to the Tanais, follow the river when it bent to the west and, at about the point the Roman embassy had disembarked, join with the levies of Hisarna, King of the Urugundi. The united force would march south to the Hypanis river and on to the Croucasis mountains. As they went, they would spread out and round up the herds of the Alani and burn their tents. Somewhere between the Tanais and the Croucasis, the Alani must turn and fight.

Ballista and his *familia* rode behind Naulobates. It had not been an invitation that countenanced refusal. Ballista had tied a silk scarf around his face. The dust still clogged his mouth and nostrils, gritted his eyes. Riding in his mailshirt, the sweat coursed down his body. The straps and weight of his armour chafed. The heat, dust and discomfort did not lighten his mood. He had no wish to be here.

Once Hisarna had appeared at the ceremony of the sitting on the hide, it was obvious the Roman mission had failed. A few days later, when granted an audience, Ballista had requested Naulobates' permission to return to the *imperium*. For a time the First-Brother had regarded him with those unnerving grey eyes, before saying he was disappointed Ballista had not put his right boot on the hide. Nevertheless, Naulobates considered the Romans should remain to witness the war which had been caused by their presence. Besides, Naulobates had added enigmatically, at some point he wished to discuss with Ballista the old days, the days of their grandfathers. The prospect of discussing Starkad with any Herul, let alone Naulobates, was not encouraging.

Ballista very much wished not to have any part of this expedition. The whole thing seemed ill-conceived. The Alani would know Naulobates and Hisarna were coming. The majority of the Urugundi warriors would be on foot. When the Heruli joined with them, the combined army would move slowly. If he were

Safrax, the King of the Alani, he would move his herds up into inaccessible glens in the Croucasis, and block or set ambushes in the passes through the foothills that led to them. The latter should not demand many men, leaving the majority of the Alani cavalry free to harass the invaders or, more boldly, to counter-strike at their dependants. And, of course, there were said to be some thirty thousand Alani warriors. If they could catch either the Heruli or the Urugundi before they met on the lower Tanais, the Alani would outnumber them by at least three to two.

On the fourth evening, they made camp with the Tanais on their right. At this point, the river still ran south. It was broad here, riffling over wide bars of sand and shingle. After they had seen to the horses and eaten, there was little to do. There was no baggage train to worry about. All the horde, even the First-Brother, did without tents and slept on the ground. Drunkenness, gambling and fighting among the horde were banned on pain of death. Given the well-known inventiveness of Naulobates with capital punishment, the prohibitions had proved highly effective – only about a dozen men so far had had to be staked out, disembowelled or otherwise killed.

As the heat drained out of the day, Ballista went down through the wide band of trees to the river to swim. Maximus and Calgacus did not stir, but Tarchon insisted on accompanying him. Remember the boy Wulfstan, the Suanian said. Ballista would rather have been alone, but did not argue. Sometimes Tarchon respected the desire for silence.

Skeins of geese and ducks were over the river. The water held that strange luminescence which rivers can keep after the sun has gone down. Ballista stripped off his mail and clothes and walked naked into the river. He waded out, relishing the chill, clean bite of it on his skin. When it was deep enough, he swam a few strokes. He dived under the surface and came up blowing and wringing the water out of his long hair. After a time, he climbed out and dried himself with a towel Tarchon had brought. He got dressed, but could not be bothered to put his war shirt back on.

They sat side by side in silence. Ballista savoured the smell of the water and the vegetation, and listened to the wildfowl. Their sounds often reminded him of his youth. He thought of his father and mother. What an age they must be now. They had seemed old when he left, but in reality his mother could only have been about the age he was now, perhaps younger. Would he ever return and see them? He thought, far less fondly, of one of his half-brothers. Morcar would not welcome his return. For the first time in months, possibly years, he thought of a girl called Kadlin.

It was good here down by the river. By this time of year out on the Steppe at night the nightingales no longer sang, and the quails and corncrakes no longer called. If you were away from the noise of a horde of men and beasts, there was nothing but the ceaseless sighing of the wind. It was as if the sun had burnt the joy, if not the life, out of the plains. Ballista very much wanted to get away from the sea of grass.

Ballista fiddled with the straps of his mail. In the old days, if there had been even an outside chance of a threat, he would have put it straight back on. Years before, a centurion had told him – it was back in Novae on the Danube, when the Goths were outside the walls – that almost all soldiers became fatalistic, if they lived long enough. At first it was a good thing; they could look beyond preserving their own hides. But then they stopped taking basic precautions; became a danger to themselves and others. The centurion had claimed there were two ways of thinking behind it. Having run repeated dangers, some soldiers thought their luck had run out, there was no point in caring, because they were as good as dead, no matter what. Others fell under the delusion that nothing could touch them, certainly not kill them.

Ballista had no intimations of immortality. Equally, he saw no reason he should die here, rather than in any of the other bad places in which circumstances had placed him. He thought of his sons, the two best reasons to fight his way back. And he had Maximus and Calgacus with him. He loved the two men and knew it to be reciprocated. There was no reason the three of them would not get out of this, as they had of so much else.

When they did get out, perhaps he might be allowed to retire to his estate in Sicily. The mission had failed – far from attacking the Urugundi, the Heruli were their closest ally again – but there was war on the Steppe. While it lasted, it should prevent the tribes raiding the *imperium*. Unless other tribes intervened, it should free Odenathus to fight the Persians, and Gallienus to march against Postumus in Gaul. That must have been why Gallienus had sent him here. Perhaps the emperor would let him retire at last. It would be good to live in peace. When they were home, he would free Rebecca and the boy Simon. It would please old Calgacus. The things that would please Maximus were all too easy to imagine.

As he stood to get into the mailshirt, he heard the urgent triple rhythm of a horse being ridden fast. A challenge was called by a sentry, and the correct password given. The rider asked and was given directions to Naulobates. Ballista struggled into his war gear, and with Tarchon walked back up into the camp.

Few had found sleep easy after the news the scout brought had spread through the horde. Ballista had slept for a couple of hours. It was strange, being in the camp of an army going into battle the next morning but having no duties and not being involved in anxious last-moment counsels. Yet he still felt bone-tired, and his eyes were scratchy with fatigue.

Ballista had a good view. With his *familia*, and those that remained of the trained fighting men of the Roman embassy – just nine riders including himself – he had been summoned to attend Naulobates. There were other dignitaries present: the *gudja*, as ever shadowed by the aged *haliurunna*, two nobles of the Taifali from the west, and three chiefs of the Anthropophagi from somewhere far in the north.

Naulobates had taken station on a low fold in the ground to the rear of his army. Ballista sat on one of the big Sarmatian horses and surveyed the battlefield. Visibility was improving. The sun was up, and burning off the last of the low river mist. Below and immediately to his front was Naulobates' own unit, acting as a reserve. These were the elite, all Heruli, many of them Rosomoni. The five thousand were strung out, side by side, and just two deep. Each man was backed by at least four tethered remounts. Ballista's view was of lots of standards stirring above a sea of swishing horse tails.

The main army was about two bow shots beyond, divided into three more units of about five thousand each. To the right, their flank on the belt of trees by the Tanais, were the warriors of the tribes from the Rha. The various bandit chiefs were with them, and the whole was stiffened by the nomad Eutes. The Herul Aruth was in command. In the centre stood the rest of the Heruli under Uligagus. The left was held by the Agathyrsi and the Nervii. They were led by Artemidorus. These units were more compact, arrayed five deep in a formation Naulobates had referred to as 'the thorn bushes'.

The Alani were about four bow shots from the main line of Naulobates' force. Their disposition mirrored that of the Heruli: three units backed by a reserve. Ballista could just discern the small, indistinct shapes of their leaders riding about in front, but the groups of warriors were nothing but motionless dark blocks on the tawny Steppe.

As a professional, Ballista ran his eye over the whole. Naulobates had done well enough. The Herul had expected to be outnumbered. He had anchored one wing on the tree line by the riverbank and kept back a reserve to deal with any outflanking; either across the river or, more probably, around the other wing on the open Steppe. Gathering all the remounts behind the reserve might trick the Alani into thinking they were additional troops. Yet the plan was essentially defensive, containing no bold moves. There was nothing unexpected to unsettle or panic the enemy. It relied entirely on the fighting qualities of the warriors.

Ballista studied the enemy. At this distance, it was impossible to judge numbers accurately. Yet there did not appear to be more Alani on the field than Heruli. Of course, enemy numbers were often overestimated. Safrax might have left a force to screen the advance of the Urugundi, or he may have left a sizable body of warriors guarding their flocks. Yet it could be something else. At the battle of the Caspian Gates the previous year, Safrax had detached a force to lie in ambush. Naulobates had issued strict orders against any of his men leaving the line today. If they obeyed, any concealed Alani should not pose a problem. But there remained the danger that Safrax had sent some of his warriors on a wide flank march, sweeping out of sight around the Heruli.

If the Heruli were defeated, most of the broken men would stream away to the north and north-east, running back to their herds or settlements. Ballista looked down to the river in the west. From the previous night, he thought he could get his horse to swim the Tanais, even if he were still wearing armour. All those with him were good horsemen, except Tarchon. They could help the Suanian across then ride hard for Lake Maeotis. It would mean leaving the members of the mission still in Naulobates' camp to their fate. Yet, as far as he knew, the Herul had no reason not to release the eunuch Amantius, three members of staff, two freedmen and a couple of slaves. One thing was certain, Ballista himself had no intention of falling into the hands of the Alani king he had defeated, or Safrax's dependant, Saurmag, the prince whom he had driven out of Suania.

Movement caught Ballista's eye from the Alani. In the raking light, elongated shadows were flitting about in front of their line. The dark blocks of warriors appeared to shift and sway. The wind from the north swept the sounds away. There was something eerie about alien pre-battle rituals which were too far away to be made out with any clarity, and which seemed to be conducted in complete silence.

Naulobates called the high-ranking Heruli on the hillock around him. Among them were Andonnoballus and Pharas. Together they trotted forward down the incline. The First-Brother would ride the lines, calling out the things he considered would put heart into his men.

Ballista and the other diplomatic visitors stayed where they were on the low hill. Ballista noticed that several in his party were looking uncertainly at the triad of chiefs from the distant north. Indeed, all three struck one as oddly unremarkable for a cannibal.

A high, uncanny howling came from the left of the Heruli battle line. It mixed with the wind fretting through the standards. Some of the Nervii had dismounted. They were throwing off their clothes and dancing, bare steel flashing in their hands. They danced wildly, drawing down from the high god the power of his favoured predator, the grey wolf. Soon they would be slathering, bestial, ready to rend and tear. It put Ballista in mind of home. As a young man he had watched his father dance as one of the Allfather's wolf warriors before the shieldwall of the Angles.

All along the line the tribes followed their own practices; the blue-dyed and tattooed Agathyrsi, the red Heruli, the Eutes, Rogas, Goltescythae and the others. Ballista knew as well as anyone that men need all the help they can get to stand close to the steel. He pulled the dagger on his right hip an inch or so from its sheath, and commenced his own private ritual.

He watched Naulobates and his men turn to come back. He could hear the enemy war drums now. The Alani were moving forward, like the shadows of clouds, as if the surface of the Steppe itself had started to shift.

Andonnoballus reined in next to Ballista. 'If the reserve fight, you should fight. I would have you back in favour with my . . . with the First-Brother.'

'I do not see we have a choice,' Ballista said.

He could see individual Alani: the barrels of their ponies, the riders themselves a smudge, the animals' legs flickering through the dust.

Naulobates raised himself on the pommel of his saddle, looked this way and that, weighing things up. Satisfied, he drew his sword and flourished it above his head. The deep war drum of the Heruli beat. The standard with the three wolves and the arrow dipped to the fore. In front, hundreds of banners nodded in acknowledgement. The *yip-yip-yip* of the red warriors rose from the ranks. The three divisions of the front line walked forward, moved into a slow canter.

The Alani were closing fast. Padded and muffled, the riders looked top heavy on the little nomad ponies. Guiding with their legs, they drew their bows.

The air filled with the arrows of both sides. Thirty thousand horse archers were shooting as fast as possible. The shafts fell across the Steppe like squalls of rain. Men and horses went down.

Just when Ballista thought to see and hear the shock of collision, the front ranks of both sides wheeled and raced back, shooting all the time over the quarters of their ponies. The second did the same, then those following. A deadly gap of forty or fifty paces was established. Warriors rode up shooting, spun their mounts, rode away still shooting and turned back again. Advance–retreat, advance–retreat; it had the skill of some long-practised, deadly ritual or dance.

It was not long before the dust largely obscured the scene. All Ballista could see was the rear of the Heruli formations, where warriors swung around to re-enter the fray, the many, many standards jerking and swaying above the melee, and the gusts of flighting arrows.

While the warriors twisted and jinked, the fight was stationary. Ballista dropped to the ground to take the weight from his horse's back. It might need all its stamina later. He wished he had his own charger with him. But Pale Horse was many hundreds of miles away, safe on a friend's estate outside Ephesus.

The Sarmatian would have to do. He stood by the head of the big bay. He stroked its soft, whiskery nose. He talked gently to it, making it listen to him, not to the sounds of its own species screaming in pain and fear.

The others dismounted. Maximus passed Ballista some air-dried meat and a flask. They ate and drank without talking to each other, watching the roiling cloud where men were dying. The north wind was getting up. It tugged at their hair, buffeted their shields.

'Look, Aruth's men,' someone shouted.

The melee on the right was moving. Almost imperceptibly at first, then quicker; the fight there was ebbing south along the line of the trees.

'Sound the recall,' Naulobates ordered.

The war drum beat a different, insistent rhythm.

It went unheeded. A gap was opening between Aruth's division and that of Uligagus to its left.

Naulobates shouted another command, and a messenger galloped down to the river.

It was too late. The Alani were fleeing, and Aruth's men were chasing.

Ballista saw the Alani reserve moving forward. It was well placed either to take Aruth's disordered men in their left flank or storm through the gap they had vacated between the river and Uligagus's division.

Naulobates did not rant and rave. Calmly, he addressed Andonnoballus. 'Take two thousand of the reserve and fill the line where Aruth's men were stationed.'

Andonnoballus trotted down the slope to put himself at the head of his men.

Naulobates turned to Ballista. 'You should go with him. Brachus has shown me that your daemon and that of Andonnoballus are blood-brothers in the spirit world. You should fight together in Middle Earth as you do in the *menog*.'

Ballista got back into the saddle. There was no arguing with Naulobates when his incorporeal twin brought him instructions from the beyond. After checking his girths, and checking the others were with him, Ballista cantered down to catch up with Andonnoballus.

Andonnoballus manoeuvred his troop into place with alacrity. Once there, sitting quietly with bows resting on their thighs, they saw the trap sprung.

Aruth obviously was no fool. He had seen the Alani reserve moving up to outflank him or cut him off. With much waving of flags and blowing of horns, Aruth had managed to bring the majority of his command to a halt, some three hundred paces out. The Eutes jostled, men and ponies out of breath, but ready to obey further commands. Those inexperienced in warfare on the plains and the overexcited had careered on after the routed Alani, oblivious to the recall. Things would go badly for those farmers from the Rha river and the motley followers of bandit leaders. But Aruth had plenty of time to lead the Eutes back to the lines before the Alani reserve reached him.

The first sign was movement among the trees which edged the Tanais to the right. Mounted warriors, banded by sunlight, moving up under the willows and ash trees from where they had hidden down by the water. As they cleared the tree line, many standards were lifted. There were many warriors, several thousand, stretching from well beyond Aruth almost back to Andonnoballus.

'Poor Aruth,' Andonnoballus said.

'Either he was stupid and led the charge, or he was weak and let it happen,' Ballista commented.

'It may be better for him to die,' Andonnoballus said. 'I do not know what my father would do to him.'

'Aruth has led many men to their death,' Ballista responded.

'Pharas and Datius are with him.' Andonnoballus's tone was resigned, as if his companions were already dead. There was no possibility of him flouting his father's orders and leaving the line in a rescue attempt.

The warriors with Aruth were rushing back towards a safety they would not attain. The ambushers swept out, closing around the disorganized Eutes tribesmen. Among the Alani standards, one of the nearer caught Ballista's attention. A broad banner depicting a man on a mountain, it stood out from the nomad horse tails, animal skulls and *tamgas*. Prometheus chained on the peaks of the Croucasis; one of the symbols of the royal house of Suania. Only one man in the horde of Safrax would fly such a banner.

'Andonnoballus, lend me two hundred of your warriors.'

The young Herul looked with surprise at Ballista. 'My father commanded that no one should leave the line.'

'I am not under your father's orders.'

'You would risk your life to rescue strangers?'

Ballista shrugged. 'There must be three or four thousand men trapped out there.'

'Sarus, Amius; your hundreds are to follow Ballista.' Andonnoballus looked at Ballista. 'Take great care.'

'I intend a distraction, no more.'

Ballista paced his horse out of the line and turned to address the men, Roman and Heruli, who would follow him. 'We will ride towards the fighting, shoot off a few arrows, then veer off to the right, down to the Tanais. One of the enemy leaders has an animosity towards me. He may be tempted to follow us. If so, it might open a gap through which Aruth and some of his men can escape.'

His audience regarded him stolidly.

'Remember, we are there to cause a diversion. We want some of them to chase us. We do not want to fight them. Shout my name, get their attention, then we make our way back through the trees and the shallows of the river.'

Ballista realized he had spoken in the language of Germania. He repeated his instructions in Latin. Still in that language, he shouted the traditional cry, 'Are you ready for war?'

'Ready!'

Three times the call and response rang out. The sound of the eight riders from the *imperium* was small but brave against the din of battle. The Heruli looked on calmly.

Ballista laced up his helmet, checked the small buckler strapped to his left forearm, pulled his bow from its *gorytus* and selected an arrow. With the pressure of his thighs, he got his horse moving. On his right rode Maximus and Hippothous, to his left Tarchon and Castricius. Old Calgacus and the three auxiliaries were tucked in behind. The Heruli, two deep, fanned out on either side.

As he moved them to a fast canter, Ballista took in what he could see of the whole battle. The melee where Uligagus fought was passing behind their left flank. Presumably, Artemidorus's men were still engaged somewhere in the dust beyond that. The Alani reserve was still quite a way off ahead. Right in front, the Alani ambushers surged around the dwindling band with Aruth. He aimed for the Suanian royal banner.

'Ball-is-ta! Ball-is-ta!' The shout mingled with the rattle of hooves on the hard Steppe. He wished he had his own white *draco* standard. That would have guaranteed the attention of the man he sought.

They were closing fast. Two hundred paces; less. The enemy had seen them. Some were hauling around the heads of their ponies, ready to meet this new threat. Only a couple of hundred of us – they must think we are mad, Ballista thought.

'Ball-is-ta! Ball-is-ta!'

One hundred and fifty paces. He drew his bow, saw those around him do the same. One hundred paces. He released, took another arrow, drew and released. It did not really matter where they fell.

Seventy paces, fifty. Arrows flew in both directions. All around him was the dreadful *thrum-thrum-thrum* of the incoming shafts, the dull, wooden thuds of them hitting shields, the grunting exhalations when one struck a man.

Ballista steered his mount off to the right. A horse behind him crashed to the floor. The others swerved around it, surged after him. He pushed the bay into a flat-out gallop towards the trees.

Looking back over his left shoulder, Ballista saw the Prometheus banner following, many warriors in its wake. It had worked. The resentment and hatred in Saurmag was pulling him after the man who had expelled him from his native land, from the throne he had killed so many of his family and others to attain. Now, all that was left, Ballista thought, was to escape the murderous bastard.

As they entered the trees, the Alani were no more than fifty paces behind. Ballista leant very low over the neck of his mount to avoid the low branches. A pained cry and the sound of a rider falling indicated another had not been so provident.

Ballista wheeled to the right, back to the north, towards where Andonnoballus waited. Men and horses speckled with sunlight weaved through the trunks of trees. An arrow thrummed past Ballista's ear.

All formation was lost. Men rode for themselves, jinking around thorny undergrowth, jumping fallen boughs. Maximus was still to Ballista's right, old Calgacus now up on his left. The gods knew where the others of the *familia* were. The whooping pursuit was loud in his ears.

The ground fell away in front. Water sparkled ahead. The bank of the Tanais. He kicked on, set them to make the jump.

The big horse did not refuse. It jumped down. There was nothing below its hooves. Ballista leant right back in the saddle, stomach lurching as they dropped. The bay stumbled on landing in the shallow water. Ballista was thrown out of the saddle, to the right, up its neck.

The Sarmatian gathered itself, ploughed on through the river. With hands, arms and legs, Ballista fought to regain his seat. He had lost the reins. Lost his balance. The buckler on his left arm was impeding him. It was no good, he was slipping. Slowly, irrevocably, he was heading for a fall. The weight of his mail was pulling him down.

Come off here, and he knew he was dead. Or worse, a prisoner of that evil little shit Saurmag. Better go down fighting. He felt the last of his grip going.

A sharp pain cut into his right shoulder. He was hauled by the baldric of his sword belt back on to his horse. He grabbed the horns of the saddle, fished up the reins – thankfully they had not slipped over the Sarmatian's head. A quick glance right and he saw Maximus grinning. He grinned back.

They were running fast along a part-submerged spit of shingle. Sliver shards of spray flew. The riverbank here was too high for the horses to jump. They had to find a place where the bank had fallen or where animals had broken it down. He looked along the top of the bank. There were riders up there, bows in hand. Allfather . . .

Ballista saw their red hair and tattoos. He looked over his shoulder – a straggle of his men and Heruli, not any Alani in sight.

XXVII

The most creditable aspect of Naulobates' handling of the battle on the Tanais, Ballista thought, had been the running away. As a professional soldier, you could not fault it.

Ballista's diversion at the height of the fighting had worked reasonably well. Saurmag and the horsemen under his command – exiled Suani as well as Alani – had broken off to chase him. Their pursuit had been curtailed when it reached Andonnoballus's riders on the riverbank. The gap temporarily created in their encirclement had allowed Aruth, Pharas, Datius and some two thousand of the Eutes to dash to the safety of the Heruli battle line. The men under Ballista had returned for the loss of only ten Heruli and one Roman auxiliary. Of course, the rest of the Eutes who had not escaped, along with the warriors from the tribes along the Rha river and the bandits – some three thousand men all told – had been massacred. The Alani ambushers had been very diligent in hunting down those who had avoided the trap.

The main battle had continued for several hours. The Alani reserve had moved up to face Andonnoballus's men. All along the line, the bodies of cavalry wheeled, arrows flew, men and animals suffered and died in the choking dust. But it never came to hand-to-hand fighting. In mid-afternoon, it petered out, as stocks of arrows ran low, ponies tired, despite the use of remounts, and hot, thirsty men lost enthusiasm. The Alani had broken off first. But no one in the Heruli horde was in any doubt of the way the day had gone. The Heruli could fight again, but they knew they had lost.

That night, Naulobates had ordered sentries posted, the camp-fires lit and the evening meal prepared and eaten. Afterwards, in strictest silence, the whole army had saddled up and melted away. All the wounded who could sit a horse had gone with them, supported by their kinsmen. Mindful of the prohibitions surrounding the latter, those too badly wounded to ride had been killed with quiet efficiency by their friends. Most had met it well. To the Heruli, the idea was not alien.

The screen of scouts had followed the main body just before dawn. Later that morning, the Alani would have taken possession of a camp consisting of warm ashes, broken equipment, and the dead.

The march south to the Tanais had taken four days. The hectic retreat was completed in just two, with the loss of only a couple of hundred dead ponies, some of the wounded and a handful of stragglers. While they had been away, the main camp and herds had been driven about thirty miles further north, to near a small tree-lined stream running through the Steppe.

It was now four days since they had ridden exhausted mounts up to the main camp. Naulobates had told them they could rest easy; the Alani would not reach them for another two days. Ballista very much hoped this information had reached Naulobates from intrepid Heruli spies or scouts, and not from Brachus and the world of daemons. In case it derived from a fallible supernatural source, he and the *familia* now habitually went in full war gear, and never far from their horses.

After the midday meal, Ballista went alone to the tent of Andonnoballus. Two Heruli stood guard at the entrance. Although it was one of the bigger structures, it was crowded with armed men. Andonnoballus was supported by the other two survivors of the Heruli who had met the embassy, Pharas and Datius, the two commanders of the bands of a hundred who had followed Ballista at the Tanais, Sarus and Amius, and the great generals Uligagus and Artemidorus. On Ballista's side of the circle were Maximus, Calgacus, Tarchon, Hippothous and Castricius. They were all seated cross-legged on cushions, swords close at hand. Some had been talking quietly, with something of a conspiratorial air, but fell silent when Ballista entered.

Without a word, Andonnoballus got up and unsheathed the *akinakes* from his hip. The colours in the steel shone in the light from the open doorway. A fly buzzed in the stifling quiet.

Andonnoballus pointed the sword at Ballista. 'Are you of the same mind as me?'

'Yes.' Ballista held out his right arm.

With his left hand, Andonnoballus gripped Ballista's wrist. With his right he drew the edge of the *akinakes* across Ballista's hand. The bright blood pooled in Ballista's palm.

Someone passed Ballista a drinking horn. He tipped his hand, to let the blood run into it. His palm hurt. The fly buzzed in imbecilic patterns. The blood dripped. After a time, someone gave him a strip of linen. He gave the vessel to Pharas, and bound his wound. He was glad the material was clean. He did not let his face betray any pain.

Andonnoballus held out his right arm, and the procedure was repeated. When it was done, Pharas poured wine to mingle in the drinking horn with the blood of the two men.

Ballista and Andonnoballus put an arm around the other's shoulder, and each gripped the drinking horn with their free hand. They moved close, almost cheek to cheek. Ballista looked sideways into Andonnoballus's grey eyes, at the moment so like those of his father. Together they lifted the vessel and drank.

'By the sword and the cup, we are brothers,' Andonnoballus said. 'Henceforth, one mind in two bodies; what touches the one, touches the other.'

'Brothers,' Ballista said.

The men in the tent, Heruli and Roman, raised their cups and cheered. They drank their undiluted wine.

Ballista smiled. It would have been a mortal insult to reject the offer. A Herul could have only three blood-brothers. Ballista was unsure why Andonnoballus had done him this great honour. Perhaps it was politics; a move designed to bind him more closely to the Heruli in the fighting to come. It could be that Naulobates had instructed him to do it. Or perhaps Andonnoballus had read too much into the actions on the Tanais. It was hard enough to dissect one's own motivation, let alone that of another from a different culture. Ballista himself was unsure why he had volunteered to lead the diversion. Still, the thing was an honour, and Ballista liked Andonnoballus well enough. At least, he could not prove worse than Morcar, his Angle half-brother.

'Now you are my brother, you will come to the assembly as a Herul,' Andonnoballus said.

Again no choice, Ballista thought. But he was altogether less happy with this aspect.

In every Heruli camp an open space was left clear of tents for the assembly. The third drum of the summoning was beating as Ballista arrived with Andonnoballus and the other Heruli. The crowd was dense, but parted a little for the son of the First-Brother and the great generals. Standing near the front, hemmed in by the elongated heads, dyed-red hair and swirling red tattoos – all so very alien – Ballista wished Maximus and Calgacus had been able to come with him. He felt alone, and the horror of confined spaces was tight in his breathing.

Naulobates climbed on to the open wagon.

Loud, almost truculent cries greeted him. 'What do you want?' 'Why have you summoned the assembly?'

Naulobates raised his spear to quell the uproar somewhat. 'I want your counsel.'

'Ask what you want.' 'Spit it out.' The tribesmen were more than boisterous. There was a hard, impatient edge to them. Many were drunk. Defeat had not improved their amenability.

'Where is Aruth?' Naulobates said.

Aruth stepped into the small open space before the wagon. He moved unwillingly, but he had no choice. If he had not, clearly the crowd, heated by alcohol and self-righteous indignation, would have turned on him. As it was, many of the tribesmen bayed and *yipped* at the sight of him.

Ballista had never really looked at Aruth before. He was a short, stocky man in middle age, with the elongated skull of the Roso-moni. He bore himself well. Only the rhythmic clenching of his right fist, emphasized by the red snake inked on the back of his hand, betrayed any nerves. He looked up, square into the face of the First-Brother.

'Am I the elected war leader of the Heruli?' Naulobates asked.

The crowd bellowed in the affirmative to the rhetorical question.

'At the Tanais, did I command that any man who left the ranks would be killed?'

Again the crowd roared its assent.

'Aruth led his men out of the line against orders,' Naulobates said.

A babble of shouts rose. 'Bastard, string him up!' 'To Hell with him, bend down the trees!' 'Kill the dog!'

Not all were for summary execution. 'Let him speak!' 'He is a great warrior, a Herul; just sit him in a tree for the day!' 'No, he must be heard first!' 'Let him speak, it is his right!'

Naulobates raised his spear. A measure of quiet returned. 'It is his right as one of the Rosomoni, as a Herul.'

Aruth gave a searching look at the front ranks, then fixed his gaze back on Naulobates. 'I did not order the advance. The bandits rode out from the line. The farmers from the Rha followed, then the Eutes. I could not hold them.'

His voice was drowned by shouts. The majority were hostile. 'Cowards blame others!' 'Take responsibility like a man!' 'Kill the bastard!' 'Throw him in the thorns!'

A few persevered for clemency. 'It was not his fault!' 'Spare him!'

Here and there, scuffles broke out, as the tribesmen debated with their fists. The outnumbered adherents of Aruth were soon pummelled into submission to the general will. 'Kill him!' 'Kill the dog!' 'Bend down the trees!' 'Tear him apart!'

Naulobates had the drum beaten. 'I hear your counsel. I will pass sentence.'

The First-brother looked at the sky and brooded dramatically. Ballista wondered if Naulobates was communing with the world of daemons, or, at least, if that was the desired impression. The silence stretched. Aruth's fist clenched and unclenched, the red snake flexing its coils.

Ballista, pressed unhappily against Andonnoballus, Pharas and Uligagus, found himself hoping Aruth would be spared.

'Aruth,' said Naulobates, 'did not disobey the order. But he could not control his riders. Men died unnecessarily under his command. He shall be punished as an unintentional killer.'

'The box, hang him in the box!' the open, red mouths of the crowd chanted.

Crushed in the press, Ballista felt light-headed, slightly sick.

Naulobates waved his spear. 'He shall be hung in the box from the high branches. He shall have three loaves and one jug of water. For nine nights and days he will hang. It is decided.'

The multitude echoed the sentence. 'It is decided.'

Two men shouldered through the throng. They were battered and bloodied. One spoke for both. 'We are Aruth's brothers by the sword and the cup. What touches our brother touches us. We will share his fate.'

Naulobates nodded. 'You are true Heruli.' The assembly murmured its approbation.

The three men stood, shoulder to shoulder, as timber was brought out, and the hammering commenced.

Andonnoballus turned to Ballista. 'For nine nights and days Woden hung in the tree. Sometimes the Allfather succours those who suffer the same.'

Ballista did not answer. His thoughts were roaming far away. The Heruli prided themselves on their freedom. Certainly in their assembly they seemed able to say what they liked. But was it any better than in the *imperium*? In the *consilium* of the emperor, fist fights were not encouraged and opinions tended to be expressed more decorously, but those summoned were meant to speak their mind openly. Yet both the First-Brother and emperor could ignore the counsel they received; ultimately, they made the decision.

A long time ago – when he was young – Ballista had thought freedom unproblematic. You either had it, or you did not. Either you were a slave, or you were free. Either you were a free man in Germania, or you lived in servitude in the *imperium*. His own enforced travels had undermined his childish certainty. Different peoples had different ideas about freedom. Freedom itself over time could change its meaning in one culture. He thought of the histories he had been reading on this mission. For the senators in the *Res Publica* written about by Sallust, *libertas* had meant the unfettered freedom to compete with each other openly for election to high office and the rewards they would then reap from exploiting their position. In the principate, as set out by Tacitus, *libertas* had narrowed down merely to freedom of speech under a monarch in everything but name, and freedom from unjust condemnation and the confiscation of estates. Yet, for both historians, most men had used *libertas* as nothing but a fine-sounding catchphrase devoid of real substance.

Ballista wondered how the vaunted freedom of his own people under the rule of his father would strike him now, if he were ever to return to the far north and the lands of the Angles. Perhaps the philosophers were right: the only true freedom was inside a man.

The hammering had stopped. The man condemned by the assembly, and the two condemned by custom and their own courage, did not have to be manhandled into the rough, slatted boxes. The water and the loaves were given to them and the cages nailed shut.

With much hauling and grunting, the cages were hoisted into the branches of a huge, spreading oak. The mood of the throng had turned to profound admiration. But the three men were left suspended between heaven and earth, their only possible salvation in the hands of a distant, capricious god.

Publius Egnatius Amantius to Lucius Calpurnius Piso Censorinus, Praetorian Prefect, Vir Ementissimus.

    Dominus, I doubt you will ever receive this despatch, or the others I have written. It is said the Alani will be upon us tomorrow. The Heruli lost the last battle, and there is no reason to think they will do better in this, which shapes to be the final one. It is most certainly a judgement of the gods on their disgusting customs.

Faithful to your orders, and in the vain hope that some deity will deliver it into your hands, I am prompted to write this last time to give one final piece of information I have gleaned. From a conversation I overheard between the Legatus extra ordinem Scythica and his Caledonian freedman Marcus Clodius Calgacus I learnt that Odenathus of Palmyra has sent ambassadors to Naulobates and the Heruli. I know neither the timing nor the purpose of this embassy, but it must give cause for concern as to the loyalty of the Syrian our sacred Augustus Gallienus has appointed Corrector totius Orientis.

It has been an honour to serve you, Dominus. I have no real hopes of returning safe to the imperium. Even if by some vagary of war the Heruli prevail tomorrow, it is an inordinate distance back to humanitas. And although the exigencies of war have driven it from all other minds, I have not forgotten the fate of my friend Publius Egnatius Mastabates and the others.

A Herul camp on the Steppe, some time in late summer.

XXVIII

Calgacus was unsurprised when Naulobates' prediction came true. It had been two days since Aruth and his blood-brothers had been hoisted into the trees, where, their cages turning gently in the wind, they remained defiantly alive. The previous evening the scouts had reported that the Alani would reach the camp this morning. It was quite possible a daemon had told Naulobates. He had the look of one haunted by unworldly things. It was a look Calgacus had seen over the years in Ballista.

The torches were beginning to pale as Calgacus walked through the camp with Tarchon. The Heruli horde had ridden out long before dawn, and it was strangely quiet except for the lowing of oxen. Perhaps the beasts could sense the unease in the humans. Things would be decided one way or the other today.

Calgacus had got Tarchon to carry most of the food and drink for breakfast. The Caledonian's right arm and shoulder were still strapped, and both his years and his war gear were heavy on him. It was a long walk. Rather than continue the futile retreat north, Naulobates had ordered the encampment put on a war footing. The hundreds of wagons had been set out in a great circle on the southern bank of the stream. They had been chained or lashed together, and any gaps barricaded. The thousands of draught oxen had been corralled in the middle. The non-combatants had gone. They had driven before them the horses, camels, sheep and goats to join the other herds in more distant grazing. The women and children were scattered in the vastness of the Steppe. Of course, should the battle be lost, it would only postpone their rape and enslavement, or rape and death, by a day or two.

It could be, Calgacus thought, that he was to witness the death of a people; an earthly prelude to Ragnarok, when the sun would be devoured, and the end would come for men and gods. But what could you expect when you travelled to the ends of Middle Earth with a man under a curse? *Kill all those he loves. Let him wander the face of the earth, among strange peoples, always in exile, homeless and hated.*

Since Naulobates had led out the fighting men, there were only a thousand or so souls to defend the two-mile perimeter of the camp. About two thirds were the wounded, the rest boys of thirteen or fourteen, fifteen at most. And, to the surprise of everyone, in the assembly last night Naulobates had ordained they were to be commanded by Ballista.

Many of the tribesmen had seemed deeply shocked. They had complained vociferously. He was not a Herul, not one of the brotherhood. He was the grandson of Starkad, the bloody-handed killer who had strangled their king, Naulobates' own great-grandfather. Strangled him, but not before – gods below! – he had hacked off Sunildus's penis and shoved it down his throat.

Calgacus had not known about the mutilation. He wondered if Ballista had known. He wondered if it was true. Folk memories were fallible. They changed to suit new circumstances, new needs. How could the Heruli have found out? Starkad had left no one alive on that desolate shore. And then it had occurred to Calgacus that he only believed that no one had survived the massacre because the Angles telling the story had said so.

Naulobates had dismissed the objections. It was universally acknowledged that no people were more skilled at defending a fortified position than the Romans. Had Ballista not been – for a day or two – emperor of the Romans? As for brotherhood, Ballista was brother by the cup and the sword with Andonnoballus. And as for the past, Starkad and Sunildus were a long time ago. It happened far away in a different country. As a sop to outraged tradition, he named an injured Herul called Alaric as the second officer of the camp.

Ballista had divided his command: the injured standing guard, spread thinly among the carts; the young inside the ring seeing to the oxen. He kept the Roman contingent with him. After walking the positions most of the night, he had taken his own station on a wagon in the southern arc of the laager. The one he had chosen was tall, and constructed entirely of wood. Come daylight, its roof should command a fine view.

Calgacus and Tarchon reached the wagon in the slate-grey light of the false dawn. There was a ladder. Calgacus climbed it, slow and stiff in his movements. At the top, he saw the dark shapes of five seated men. Muffled in their cloaks, they had the air of hooded crows.

Muttering, Calgacus put down the few containers he had carried. 'It is no trouble at all. You fuckers just sit there. Let an old man do all the fucking work. Do not let it play on your conscience.'

Tarchon lugged up the rest of the things they had brought.

'I thought you would never be back, not with all those baggage animals to bother,' Ballista said.

Maximus got up and helped Tarchon pass around what had been brought.

Calgacus sat down where the Hibernian had been, next to

Ballista. On his other side were Castricius and Hippothous. The second-in-command, Alaric, was beyond Ballista. When they had finished serving, Maximus and Tarchon hunkered down next to the Herul.

They all ate warm millet porridge and cold boiled mutton, drank fermented mare's milk, and waited for the day.

'I hope you do not mind me asking,' Maximus said to Alaric. 'Why have you not got a pointed head?'

'I am not one of the Rosomoni,' he replied.

'Some of your tattoos – and very fetching they are indeed – are not red. I am thinking you were not born one of the Heruli.'

'No.'

'So what race were you?'

'Taifali.'

'No offence, but are they the ones that bugger the small boys?'

Alaric grunted.

'Is that why you left?'

'No, I killed a man.'

'So what? Everyone has killed someone. Your men Hippothous and Castricius over there, they have probably killed dozens.'

'The man I killed was my father.' Alaric paused. 'And both my brothers.'

The statement put a stop to conversation for a time.

It was quiet. The wind dropped and was backing towards the south. Yet it was still there, blowing across the measureless nomad sea, almost below the level of hearing, insidiously scratching and sighing through the dry grass.

Irrepressible, Maximus returned to questioning Alaric. This time his tone was less teasing, the subject perhaps less delicate. Were the Heruli not a fine tribe in which to be a man! How many women had Alaric enjoyed? Maximus had never known a better place for the women. Alaric was more forthcoming, and soon Tarchon joined in. By the tenor of their conversation, it seemed to Calgacus there could hardly be a girl beyond puberty one or more of them had not covered. Liars, all three of them, like most men.

Ballista leant close to Calgacus, put an arm around his shoulder, spoke softly into his ear. 'I am sorry I have brought you all into this.'

'You were ordered here. It was our duty to accompany you.'

'I should have found us a way out before now.'

Calgacus gave a wheeze of laughter. 'Oh, we are deep in the shite, and believe me, I have been looking for a way out, but I have not seen one.'

Ballista squeezed Calgacus's shoulder, then stood, stretching until you could hear his joints crack. The big man sat down again to wait.

Maximus, Tarchon and Alaric moved on to discussing hunting dogs and horses. Say what you like about the Alani – and there was much to be said against them – they bred fine hounds. Maximus thought he would try to take a couple back with him. Hippothous and Castricius remained silent, wrapped in whatever clandestine and sanguinary thoughts motivated men like them.

The sun came up, a burnished plate of electrum on the horizon. The sky above the camp was empty, shining and translucent. But the wind had set in the south, and down there a storm was gathering, big black clouds trailing tentacles of night.

In the slanting clarity of the light, even Calgacus's old eyes could make out the whole battlefield. It was demarked in the north by the camp and the stream. Three miles to the south, he could just discern the dark line of trees bordering a parallel stream. It would all be played out in this wedge of Steppe. It struck him as a small, nondescript place to host any such momentous event.

The horde of the Heruli was easy to see. It was assembled just fifty yards away. Despite all the herdsmen of the outlying flocks having been summoned, the losses from the first battle meant there were no more than fifteen thousand warriors. Unsurprisingly, no further reinforcements had arrived from the subject and allied tribes. The host was arrayed in three equal contingents, each ten deep and five hundred broad. On the left were the Agathyrsi and Nervii led by Artemidorus. The centre was held by Naulobates with the Rosomoni. Pharas on the right commanded what was left of the Eutes combined with the remaining Heruli.

The ponies were in ordered ranks. Through the gaps between the units, Calgacus could see the leaders and their aides walking about, their mounts held by handlers. The majority of the warriors were out of sight, sitting on the ground by the heads of their ponies. Above, banners cracked in the freshening air. Below, innumerable horse tails swished. The latter seemed always to be on the verge of forming some pattern, one that remained tantalizingly beyond comprehension.

Calgacus wondered how hard the Agathyrsi and Nervii would fight. They were not bound to the Heruli by bonds lasting generations like the Eutes. Calculations of flight, or accommodation with the Alani, if not outright desertion, had to have entered the thoughts of their leaders. Defeat bred desertion.

And the ambush of the hunt still nagged him. Someone had to have told the Alani where the Herul *battue* would end that day, and that someone had to have been a Herul. Naulobates was a reformer; in his own eyes, a visionary imbued with the divine. Not all men welcome either reforms or epiphanies.

The thoughts of betrayal pressed on, almost of their own accord. All that remained of the embassy that had left the port of Tanais was gathered around the wagon on which he sat. Somewhere near – no further than he could toss a bean – was the man who had mutilated the eunuch, the cruel bastard who had murdered young Wulfstan. Unless, of course, it had been the *gudja*, who was riding with Naulobates, or the soldier killed in the last battle. Or unless the killer had not been a man at all, but a daemon.

Calgacus was glad he was in full armour and that the big Sarmatian warhorses were hitched near the foot of the ladder.

The sun tracked up into the sky, and they waited. It got hotter, much hotter. So much for those Greek writers poor old Mastabates and the others had quoted who said it was always cold up here, and summer lasted but a few days. Calgacus had never liked the nights on the Steppe. The uncanny scale of it always made you feel insignificant, somehow pointless. But on the journey up in the spring he had enjoyed the days. He had taken pleasure in the bright colours of the flowers, in their varied scents. Now there was nothing but friable earth showing through scorched grass, and depressing clumps of brown knotgrass and grey wormwood. The only smell was dust and the bitter tang of the wormwood.

Calgacus again longed to be back in Sicily, back with Rebecca and Simon. The image of him with them in Tauromenium – under a warm Mediterranean sun, all happy – struck him with the intensity of a dream. Its very vividness made him weary.

A gust of wind advanced on them across the Steppe. It raised dust devils. Tall and swirling, they bore down with mindless ferocity, trailing great lateral branches before being torn apart. Behind them, the storm was building; malignant black thunderheads, pierced by points of flickering flame.

'The scouts are coming in,' Maximus said.

It took Calgacus some time to locate them. Four black dots, well spaced but converging towards the centre of the Heruli line, where the big banner with the wolves and the arrow flew. There was no point in asking the news they brought to Naulobates.

The others on the wagon stiffened then stood up to get a better view. Calgacus took his time.

Down below, the Heruli stirred. Heads popped up in the serried ranks of the horde as men got to their feet. The leaders swung up into the saddle. Messengers galloped here and there with last-moment instructions or words of encouragement.

The first Alani outriders were moving fast, raising occasional, random puffs of white dust which drifted in their wake before dispersing. At the sight of them, Calgacus felt the familiar tension in his chest.

The outriders reined in about half a mile away, strung out across the field in an extended screen of individuals. From away by the far stream, a broad, dark column of riders appeared. Just behind the skirmish line, the main body divided, fanning out at speed left and right.

Calgacus admired the neatness of the manoeuvre. Where before there had been empty Steppe, a solid battle line was formed. The dust raised coalesced into a shifting, opaque mist. Through it, the colours of individual ponies could be seen, but the riders were a vague blur. Standards floated in the murk, apparently unattached to the men below.

The Alani occupied the same frontage as the Heruli, but even Calgacus could see their formation was deeper. Even more than before, the Heruli were outnumbered.

The south wind was bringing the storm up behind the Alani. The hulk of purple-black clouds was lit from within by vivid stabs of phosphorescence. The first clearly enunciated clap of thunder reached the Heruli.

'It is very bad,' Alaric said.

'It is nothing. Another of those storms of thunder and lightning, but no rain,' Ballista said. 'Andonnoballus told me you get them all the time out here in high summer.'

'A dark cloud over your enemy, a clear sky over yourself – on the Steppe there can be no more forbidding portent.' Alaric looked downcast.

'Hercules' hairy arse,' Calgacus muttered, 'this is getting worse by the fucking moment.'

Ballista studied the enemy. The Alani were chanting, brandishing their weapons. The movements and sounds were curiously disjointed. Ballista was searching for the banner with Prometheus on the mountain. He found it in the centre of the enemy line, near that of Safrax.

High, indistinct shouts came across the plain, then the low rumble of hooves and the clatter of equipment. Saurmag's banner and several others were moving behind the Alani ranks. Through the fresh waves of dust, Ballista could see that the enemy were extending their left flank.

Nearer at hand, Naulobates yelled orders. The rear five ranks of the Rosomoni in the central contingent wheeled their ponies and cantered off to the right to form up as a new unit and prevent the horde being outflanked. The elongated, red head of Andonnoballus could be seen getting them into order.

With his narcotic-fuelled dreams of the spirit world, Naulobates might well be considered insane, but he could still manage a battle. He had done the right thing. It left the ranks of the centre and new right wing dangerously thin, but the countermove had prevented the Heruli being overlapped.

Like a festival or a dance, a battle has its own rhythms. A hush spread across the almost motionless field, as if all those thousands of men stood in awe of the deeds they were about to commit. The thunder boomed above them, an unseen blacksmith working at some celestial forge.

The keening note of a trumpet was joined by the whooping of the Alani. The enemy surged forward, and the lines of the Heruli went to meet them.

Watching a battle in which he had no part had an air of unreality for Ballista. He watched the gusts of arrows fall, the ponies racing and turning, the men tumbling beneath the hooves. The choking dust slid across everything. The confused roar of it all was loud in his ears. Yet it had a theatrical quality. It touched him no more than the imperial spectacles in the Colosseum. Men died there; men were dying here. It was almost nothing to him.

A battle confuses perceptions of time. Ballista thought he had been watching the deadly show for hours. Yet when the day darkened as the first storm clouds reached out to smother the sun, he saw it was still early morning. The unseasonable gloom invested the battle with a sombre gravity. The air hissed as the lightning speared overhead, illuminating the black thunderheads from within. The earth shook from the battle. The end would be like this, when the wolf Fenrir killed the Allfather, and the nine worlds would burn, and the gods die.

Ballista wanted it to be over. If, outnumbered though they were, the Heruli won, he would drink and feast with them. If, as must be more probable, they were worn down by exhaustion and the day was lost, he would gather his *familia*. They would mount the remaining big Sarmatian chargers and small Heruli ponies and try to cut their way out of the chaos.

'Fuck,' Maximus said.

Ballista looked where the Hibernian pointed to the west. A pillar of dust, at its base; when the lightning flashed, the glint of metal. A large number of mounted men were riding along the line of the northernmost stream. Still a way off, but travelling fast. They were heading for the camp or the rear of the Heruli line. Naulobates' overstretched warriors had no reserve to check them.

'No chance they are Urugundi?' Castricius said.

'No chance at all,' returned Ballista.

'The daemons of death are afraid of me.' Castricius had a far-away look.

'The portent could not have been worse,' Alaric said. 'Now, we must look to defend the camp.'

'It would be no use,' Ballista said.

Alaric continued to talk.

Ballista did not listen. He was looking all around, thinking. It was difficult to take everything in: the approaching cavalry, the confusion of the battle line, the camp, with the boys looking after the restless mass of cattle, and the pitiful number of wounded guards in the wagons. The noise of the oxen reminded him of something that had happened when the Alani had attacked the embassy on the way out. A stratagem he had read was in the back of his mind.

'The boys with the oxen are herdsmen?' Ballista asked.

'Yes,' Alaric said.

'They could drive that herd?'

'Of course.' Alaric looked exasperated. 'The camp?'

'How many of the injured can still sit a horse?'

'Twenty, maybe thirty. Why?'

'Here is what we will do. Alaric, get the boys and all the men that can ride mounted. Have the others cut free four wagons, drag them out of the laager to make an opening. All of us here, get on horseback.'

Everyone was staring at him.

'I think it was Hannibal, maybe in Polybius. When the Alani outflanking riders get near, we are going to stampede all those oxen into them.'

'The First-Brother was right about you,' Alaric said. 'Loki himself could teach nothing to you. You are Starkad's grandson in your cunning.'

'What if it does not work?' Hippothous asked.

'Then we fall back on my other deep plan,' Ballista said.

'Which is?'

'Which is every man runs as if all the daemons of the underworld were snapping at his heels.'

Mounted, armoured, flanked by his two closest friends, Ballista felt the usual apprehension. Maximus never seemed to feel it, but Ballista always did. No matter how many battles he survived, he always feared he would die, or, somehow even more oppressive, would let down those around him, would disgrace himself. He pulled the dagger on his right hip out an inch or two, snapped it back, went into the vaguely soothing pre-battle ritual of his own devising.

Behind him, the seething mass of oxen bellowed. The herders kept them back from the opening with difficulty. The crack and sting of the long, knotted hide whips added to the frenzy of the animals.

Ballista had led out eleven Roman riders. The eunuch Amantius, the scribe and the messenger, and the two slaves had been left in the laager as being of no use. With twenty wounded Heruli warriors and a hundred herdboys, those Romans considered martial enough were drawn up in a mounted line masking where the wagons had been hauled clear.

The oncoming Alani had seen them and deployed into a deep line, at least five hundred wide. They were bearing down, whooping. As Ballista had hoped, the nomads had proved unable to resist the obvious chance to get among the booty of the camp.

The Alani were closing fast, the bouncing, short-legged run of their ponies eating up the distance. Five hundred paces; four hundred. It had to be judged right. Three hundred. The Alani rode with their bows or weapons held out wide to the right, not to catch the sides of their mounts. Two hundred paces. They were committed. It had to be now.

Ballista made the signal with his bow – the arrow with the bright fletchings shot almost vertical into the dark sky.

Neat as could be, the screen of horsemen parted, making two lanes. There was a terrible sound, like stones being ground by a river in spate. Bucking, kicking, snorting in fury, the first of the near-maddened bullocks thundered past. In moments, there was a solid flood of oxen.

The Alani sawed on their reins, pulled their ponies back on to their haunches as they tried to stop, to get out of the way. Their numbers, the depth of their formation, were against them. Ponies barrelled into each other. Riders fought to stay in the saddle.

The onrush caught the Alani. The solid weight of the close-packed bullocks crashed into and through them. Men and ponies went down beneath the thousands of pounding hooves. Ballista watched with horrified revulsion the body of one of the Alani bouncing off the ground as it was stamped again and again, and was reduced to a broken bundle of blood-stained, fouled rags, the shattered white of a bone protruding obscenely.

It was accomplished almost before Ballista could comprehend the totality. The outflanking column of Alani no longer existed. The Steppe where it had galloped so proudly was dotted with knots of fleeing horsemen and a widening spread of escaping oxen.

The majority of the Alani were running south past the western edge of the battle line.

'With me! With me!' Ballista pushed the big Sarmatian into an in-hand gallop after them.

Already, individuals at the rear left of the Alani main fighting line were turning and slipping away. The sight of their fellow tribes-men routing past them had undermined their resolve, filling their minds with shapeless but awful visions of catastrophe.

A tight group of riders was battering its way across the path of the fleeing Alani. Their arms waved, their mouths were open, shouting unheard reproaches. A banner with a picture of a giant chained to a mountain flew above them.

Caught up in the insanity of the violence, Ballista laughed. Saurmag thought to halt the flight of the outflanking column. The Suanian had no hope of success. Instead, the gods were delivering him to Ballista.

'With me! With me!' Ballista angled through the dust and chaos towards the banner. Memories of a tiny underground cell, himself crouched naked, jagged rock cutting his flesh, overwhelmed him. The man who had had him flung into that place was a few paces away. Revenge was here for the taking.

Saurmag saw him coming. The Suanian pulled up, drew a blade. He was yelling at his men. Would he run? Would he fight? His indecision was evident.

Two riders, braver than their master, pushed past Saurmag.

Maximus reached them first. He went for the one on the right. Calgacus crashed his mount into the other. Ballista urged his mount between the duels. Saurmag was just ahead.

Another Alan surged into Ballista's path. The nomad cut at his head. Ballista ducked under the swish of the blow. He thrust back, missed. He tried to keep moving, but the Alan was persistent. Ballista blocked another blow. Saurmag was pulling the head of his horse around. The little bastard was going to run.

A jarring impact – a searing pain in his right arm. Ballista had paid the penalty for his distraction. He could feel the blood running hot down his arm. The Alan cut at his head. As he took it on his own blade, Ballista felt the broken rings of mail cutting into his bicep.

Hampered by the wound, Ballista could only defend. His arm was stiffening, weakening. *Watch the blade, watch the blade.* He had to put Saurmag out of his mind, summon all his will to survive.

The Alan was pressing his advantage, his steel a living thing seeking Ballista's life. There was nothing in the world except the flickering shine of steel. *Watch the blade.*

325

Another flash of light, from an unexpected quarter. The Alan rocked in the saddle. Maximus struck again, and the Alan – his head a thing of horror – toppled from the saddle.

The sound of the outside world rushed back, an almost physical blow in its confused immensity.

The Alani were fleeing; not just this wing, the whole horde. When panic grips an army, it is over in moments, completely irreversible.

Tarchon was in front of Ballista, grinning like a madman, like a devotee of some ecstatic cult. He was jabbering in his native tongue. He had a bloody sword in one hand, something heavy in the other. He held it out to Ballista like a proud child.

'See, I bring you Saurmag.'

XXIX

Maximus had been drinking for three days. He had stopped the afternoon before, when Naulobates rode back into the main camp. Waiting for the Heruli to return from their murderous harrying of the Alani across the Steppe, Maximus had consumed indiscriminately vast quantities of fermented mare's milk and wine, and had inhaled so much cannabis his lungs ached. And it was not just the drinking. He had never had more sex . . . with the possible exception of one time in Massilia.

He raised himself on one elbow and looked at the Herul girl sleeping. He drank some water and tried to put the events of the last few days in order.

The panic had swept through the Alani like a wildfire. The Heruli had tried to get to Safrax. They had failed. The king had a bodyguard of a thousand or so of his nobles. Unlike the majority of the Alani, they wore armour – mail, scale or lacquered – and rode big horses, some armoured like the men. As their enemies closed around them, they had drawn up in a circle and fought. They had sacrificed themselves to the last man – no quarter had been shown – to win their monarch a start. When the nobles were dead, the Heruli had pursued the fugitive monarch south for days. They had killed many, but Safrax had escaped. It was said he was in the foothills of the Croucasis mountains, rallying his remaining warriors to face the inevitable assault.

Ballista and the *familia* had not been asked to join the chase, and they had not volunteered. With the others, Maximus had ridden back to the northern camp. They had spent two days there while the women and children returned, driving in some of the flocks, then three days moving south to the main summer camp by the river. When they had got there, Maximus had started drinking. Now Naulobates was back, and there would be a feast.

Maximus drank more water. He slid back next to the girl, moved against her until she woke, then took her gently. It was one of the few things that made a man in his condition feel better, if only briefly.

Afterwards, she slept again. Maximus lay on his back with his arms behind his head. He did not feel good. He had slept badly, sweating out the alcohol. Strange dreams had troubled him; the hanged woman Olympias, the other women pulling down on her legs.

Maximus got up and dressed quietly so as not to wake the girl. As he left, he wondered what she was called.

The sun was up, but the heat of the day had not yet come down. The sky was a bowl of pure blue. There was a cool breeze off the water as he walked down to the river.

A gaggle of Heruli boys were playing by the bank. They called out happily. *No-nose, No-nose. Bring me more drink.* He picked up a stone, and threw it at them. It missed. They ran off, laughing. *No-nose, No-nose.*

His clothes and body stank; drink, sweat, women, smoke. There was food spilled down his tunic and a leg of his trousers. His hair was matted, and his head hurt. He felt queasy, his limbs uncoordinated and heavy. He stripped naked and waded out. The water was cold, a fine silt giving under his feet. He swam to midstream, and floated on his back, letting the current take him.

In the altered state after his debauch, he thought about Olympias. The pointlessness of the blur of the last three days oppressed him. He thought about love. Ballista had Julia. Old Calgacus had the Jewish woman. And he had endless women, but nothing near love. Now he was older, he often wondered who would mourn him. Ballista, of course; probably Calgacus; and definitely Ballista's sons. He might have sons of his own, scattered across the world. Perhaps he had fathered a few more in the last three days. He remembered Ballista once telling him how the old Spartans had believed the more vigorous the fuck, the more vigorous the child. Perhaps he would leave behind some strong, healthy young Heruli warriors who would ride the Steppe. Vitality was the only patrimony they would get from him, but it was not to be underrated.

It was quiet, just the remote sounds of the camp audible. The riverbank was deserted. He watched a brace of snipe darting about downstream. Self-pity could creep up on him in this condition. Not all men were made to love women. Some – young Demetrius, the insane Hippothous – found pleasure in other men. That had never interested Maximus. In truth, he could not understand it. But he had to accept that he preferred the companionship of men to the cloying demands of women. Constructing fantasies about a woman he had barely known, and who had hanged herself on the grave of her husband, would do him no good.

He swam upstream, back to his clothes. He regarded the filthy things, then scooped them into a bundle. Naked as he was, the malodorous garments under an arm, his sword belt in the other hand, he walked through the camp up to the big tent he shared with Ballista, Calgacus and Tarchon. As he passed, Herul warriors laughed indulgently, the women and older girls giggled, and the children ran after him, calling out, *No-nose, No-nose; more drink.*

The sun was going down as they rode to the feast in the meadow. They splashed through the ford. A flight of cranes were over the river, the undersides of their wings scarlet with the light of the dying sun. Maximus was alongside Ballista and Calgacus. The rest – Castricius, Hippothous, Biomasos and Tarchon – clattered after in no particular order.

Maximus felt somewhat better. He had persuaded Calgacus to cook, and he had eaten a great deal in the morning. If only there had been some bacon. He had dozed most of the rest of the day. Now, he was little worse than weary. Before they left the tent, he had drunk a cup of unmixed wine to liven himself up.

They came to the trees around the meadow, dismounted and tethered their horses. Even in the heat of August – Maximus made it eight days before the *ides*, but he was far from sure – the meadow was still green. The flowers had gone, but the grass was verdant. There had to be a spring or watercourse just below the surface. A quick look up confirmed that the treetops contained no miscreants, live or dead, to spoil the idyll. Perhaps his overwhelming victory had mellowed Naulobates. Still, they had better be careful. The gods alone knew what insane instructions for the First-Brother Brachus might bring back from the world of daemons.

A broad, roofless chamber of screens had been erected under the spreading oaks. They belled out in the steady northern wind. There was much activity around the cooking fires downwind.

At the entrance, they were greeted by two Heruli in the fine accoutrements of Alani noblemen. Both guards smiled, put their right palms to their foreheads.

One by one, they were announced. Somehow, Maximus's thoughts were still not sharp. He was the last. Waiting, he noticed

the screens were of fine linen and the sort of ornamented hangings the Greeks and Romans prepared for a wedding.

Inside, Naulobates sat alone on a couch at the far end. Two lines
of chairs, most occupied, ran the length of each side towards the
First-Brother. Maximus was given a silver cup to make his prayers.
He was not a man given to bothering the gods, but he knew what
was expected. He composed his face into what he considered a
suitably pious expression, emptied his mind and drank the wine
in one. It caught a little on the back of his throat and was unwelcome in his stomach. Thanks to the earlier livener, he neither
spluttered nor brought it back up.

A Herul showed him to where the Romans were seated. Ballista
was first, on the right of Naulobates, then Castricius, Tarchon,
Biomasos and Hippothous. Maximus was seated between the
Greek and the Herul leader, Pharas. Checking, Maximus could
see no obvious danger. He was only a few paces from Ballista, and
they were all armed. He must try not to get too drunk.

The space was lit by torches. Dark clouds scudded over the
swaying branches above. Maximus realized that Naulobates was
not alone. At one end of his long couch sat Andonnoballus and a
boy of about seven or eight. Looking at the opposite line of chairs,
Maximus saw Peregrim, the nephew of the Urugundi King Hisarna.
More startling, next to him was Aruth. The Herul looked thin and
badly sunburnt. Either Naulobates had shown uncharacteristic
clemency, or Aruth had survived nine nights and days in the cage.

A servant poured two cups of wine in front of Naulobates,
and took one to Ballista. The First-Brother and Ballista drank to
each other. The next cup went to Peregrim, the third to Castricius.
There were thirty men on the chairs. It went on a long time. The
cups passed out glittered silver in the wavering torchlight. Naulobates' was plain wood. Each guest downed his; Naulobates
merely sipped.

The toasts concluded, tables were set up and food put out. Again, Naulobates paraded his unconcern for luxury. On the wooden platter placed in front of him were some simple cuts of cooked meat. The guests ate elaborate dishes off heavy silver. The cooks had to be captives from Greece, probably from Ionia.

Maximus asked Pharas who the boy with Andonnoballus was. The Herul looked uncomfortable, and leant close to reply.

'It is a prophecy the First-Brother received on one of his daemon journeys. He was told that after he had sacked the city of Athens he would relinquish his rule of the Heruli when he was translated simultaneously into both master and slave. Andonnoballus would succeed him. When the latter fate befell Andonnoballus, the boy Odoacer would be the chosen, who would lead the Heruli to a better place.'

'What better place?'

Pharas shrugged.

'And Naulobates believes this?' asked Maximus.

'Naulobates believes this,' Pharas said in a flat voice.

'And you?'

'The First-Brother has the mandate of the deity.'

After the first course, there was another round of toasts. Maximus was feeling much better. He had no problem at all downing his cup to the First-Brother.

After the second course, there was no more food except nuts, cheese and dried fruits. There was a lot more drink. Maximus was warming to the occasion.

A bard stood in the middle and sang a song of the glorious victory of the Heruli over the Alani. The singer concentrated on the martial virtues of Naulobates, but included graceful compliments to his ally Hisarna of the Urugundi, and to Ballista and Tarchon. The slaying of the evil Saurmag was a good verse. The audience was rapt. Some Heruli were moved to tears.

Castricius and Hippothous, not knowing the language of Germania, appeared less involved. The little Roman had his eyes on the trees above, lost in thought. The Greek had his eyes fixed on a young Herul opposite. It had better be physiognomy, not lust, Maximus thought.

The song ended with a flourish. Naulobates took a thick gold band from his arm, and gave it to the bard. Then he stood, and the only sounds were the splutter of the torches and the snap of the screens.

'We have won a great victory, but not yet the war. Like a viper, Safrax has slithered back to his nest. We killed many, and many of his riders, but many remain. The Croucasis will see hard fighting. In the mountains, the great-hearted infantry of the Urugundi will come into their own.'

The Heruli cheered and *yipped*. Peregrim, although rather flushed, made a face full of dignity.

'But tonight is a celebration.' Naulobates paused, looking out over the hangings at the racing blackness of the night.

When he resumed, his voice was thoughtful. 'A man can have only three blood-brothers. It is our law. I have Uligagus, Pharas and Aruth.'

Naulobates gestured. Three armour bearers stepped into the middle. They carried a spear, a buckler and a *gorytus* bound in white leather. Behind them a man led in a great red horse. At the noise, the stallion rolled its eyes and tossed its head.

'It is permitted a man to have many sons-in-arms. Tonight I will give the honour to Dernhelm, son of Isangrim, son of Starkad.'

Maximus, along with everyone else, looked at Ballista. The Angle's face was completely without expression. Ballista got to his feet. He went to the stallion and, with slow, open movements, he took its bridle. Speaking softly, with no hurry, he calmed the animal. Eventually, he brought his face close to its nostrils, talking all the time he needed, letting his breath mingle with that of the horse.

Returning the bridle to the handler, Ballista stepped before Naulobates. He buckled the bowcase to his belt, the small shield to his arm, and took the spear in his hand.

Ballista got to one knee. He placed the spear upright in front, both hands around its shaft.

Naulobates cupped his hands over those of Ballista. 'From this moment, you are my son. Wherever you go, my daemon Brachus will watch over you.'

The horse was led out, and Ballista took his seat again.

Naulobates had not finished. A servant appeared, carrying a cup that flashed gold.

'Tarchon of Suania, you killed Saurmag, the would-be tyrant of your people, the crooked advisor of Safrax. When you drink, all will remember your valour on that day. It is a custom of our people.'

Tarchon stood and took the cup. Now Maximus could see it was a gilded skull – the skull of Saurmag.

Tarchon was beaming with straightforward pleasure.

Naulobates turned to Ballista and smiled. 'Your *gorytus* is bound in his skin.'

Ballista looked down at the thing on his hip. When he looked up, again no emotion was to be read on his face.

Later, much later, the Romans staggered back to their quarters. Everyone disappeared to their tents. Maximus did not. The blood was pounding in his head. He stood, leaning on the spear Ballista had planted, letting the cool wind play over him. Soon, he could hear the other three snoring inside his tent.

Maximus raked the ashes off the cook fire, exposing its glowing heart. He sat, cross-legged, by it and drew two knives from his boots. With exaggerated care, he fished out a bag, and put some of the cannabis on the flat of one blade. He held it down with the other blade. He held the daggers in the heat, then hunched over, inhaled the aromatic smoke. He repeated it, until his head was light, buzzing.

The wind fretted at the ropes of the tent, tugged clusters of sparks from the fire. Up above, glimpsed between the clouds, the moon continued its near-eternal flight from the wolf Hati. Maximus laughed, recalling the very different reactions of Ballista and Tarchon to their grizzly gifts. Soon, they would be gone from this mad place.

A noise – not the wind – made Maximus turn. He half overbalanced. A figure was approaching; tall, spectral, only part of this world.

Maximus got to his feet unsteadily.

Hippothous moved as if in a trance. The Greek's face was white, immobile.

'The horror,' Hippothous said, 'the horror.'

Maximus had a knife in each hand.

Hippothous took a step forward.

'What?' Maximus said.

Hippothous started, as if realizing where he was.

'What?'

'The Heruli . . . I found them. They were . . .'

'What?'

Hippothous balled his fist, thumb between index and middle finger, to avert evil.

Maximus noted the Greek's other hand was also empty.

'Pharas was there, Andonnoballus too. They were . . .' Hippothous struggled for the right words. 'They were fucking a donkey. They laughed when they saw me; said it was the custom of the Rosomoni.'

A moment's pause, and Maximus started to laugh. After a

335

time, he found he could not stop. The Heruli were not as other men.

Water was slopping from the Fountain of Trajan, running down the street. He stood in the Sacred Way of Ephesus, irresolute, afraid. Above, swallows darted, their wings flashing in the sun. There was a single line of cloud, straight as if drawn by a pencil.

Small figures crawled like ants over the debris of the terraced houses the earthquake had collapsed down the hill. A man was herding two blond children into the shelter of the Temple of Hadrian. He knew he should have killed the boys too.

The mob spewed out from the commercial agora. Like a huge predatory beast, it sighted him. He turned to run uphill. His legs were not working properly. The Sacred Way reared in front, impossibly steep. The noise swelled. They would break him up like a stag.

He woke, full of apprehension. He forced himself to look.

The daemon was standing at his feet. She was a little girl, no more than five or six. She looked as he had left her; the white tunic bloodied, mud in her golden hair. The daemon never spoke. She just regarded him, almost dispassionately. As she had on that night, she held her hands out in supplication.

Hecate, all the chthonic deities, all you Olympians, make it leave.

As if in answer, the daemon turned and went out.

He raised himself and looked around the tent. The others were sleeping, the scribe snoring hoggishly. He lay back, heart pounding in his chest.

He had made a terrible mistake with the girl in Ephesus. She had been innocent. He should have mutilated her. The unjustly killed cannot walk if they have been mutilated. He had not made that mistake again. If he had only wiped the bloody blade in her hair, he would have been spared this recurring horror.

What he had done, all of it, had been the gods' will. It was a war on vice. In all wars, the innocent suffer. You should not suffer blood-guilt in a war.

Outside, he could hear men moving. It must be the last watch of the night, near dawn.

Why had the daemon returned now? It had been months since the last visitation. The gods of the underworld must have let her walk for a reason. He had let his work lapse while they were here. In truth, he had been scared of the Brachus of Naulobates. If he had continued his work, Naulobates' daemon would have caught him. Of course he was not scared to die. The demonstration with the trees was laughable in its barbarian crudity. But if he were killed, the work of the gods could not be carried out, the Scourge of Evil would end.

The gods had sent her to recall him to his duty. They would leave this place soon, and then it would be time to take up the struggle again.

There was no fanfare when Ballista finally led the mission out of the camp of the Heruli. Naulobates had ridden south with the majority of the nomad warriors three days after the feast. The First-Brother intended to join with Hisarna and his Urugundi and, although it would be late in the season, together they would take the war to Safrax in the Croucasis.

Now, two days after the departure of the horde, the few remaining men and the women and children were packing up the great summer camp ready for the annual trek back down to the winter grazing on the banks of the Tanais. Ballista had received word that he and his men were free to begin their long journey back to Lake Maeotis and then on to the *imperium*.

He pulled his horse out of the line, and shaded his eyes as he looked back into the rising sun. The column was in order so far. There were seventeen riders, including himself. Maximus, Calgacus and Tarchon rode point at the front with the guide provided by the Heruli. They were followed by the surviving members of the staff: Biomasos the interpreter, the scribe and the messenger, and Amantius the eunuch. It was odd seeing the latter in his red cloak and white tunic; odd that he was alive, when so many obviously tougher men had died.

The pack animals came next. There were twenty of them. The Heruli had been generous. One thing they did not lack was ponies. Roped into two strings, they were led by the two remaining slaves. Who owned these slaves was a moot point, given both Mastabates and Hordeonius the centurion were dead.

Castricius and one auxiliary cavalryman were on flank to the north, Hippothous and the other trooper to the south. The two freedmen brought up the rear. These ex-military slaves had the worst of it. Anyone riding drag got to eat the dust raised by the rest.

Their course lay west of south-west across the sea of grass. They would come to the higher reaches of the Tanais on the second day. There was a crossing place. Then they would take a direct line to the town of Tanais. Rudolphus, the guide, said it would be twelve days' easy ride. Ballista saw no reason not to trust the Herul. Behind the swirling tattoos, Rudolphus had an open face. He had lost three of the fingers on his sword-hand, which accounted for why he was with them.

That first day, they rode under a burnished sky, empty except for the occasional vulture or rook. They plodded along the open land, the sweat running down them. Rudolphus had said they did not need to wear their armour. They were unlikely to run into any serious trouble. Given the heat, they were all glad of that.

In the afternoon, they saw great pulsating clouds of dirty yellow dust off to the north and rolling down towards them. One of the outlying Heruli herds, Rudolphus said. An hour or so later, from a slight rise they saw the ochre plain up there dotted with the tiny black shapes of cattle, hundreds of them. Like the main body of the nomads, these were making their way south. It would be a long journey. Rudolphus told them the herds – sheep, goats or cattle – if grazing as they went, usually travelled at no more than five miles a day.

They came to the Tanais, before noon on the second day. The land here folded up a little more. They saw the trees fringing the river, and smelt the water before it came in view. The river was wide, but mainly shallow. Rudolphus led them straight into the water. They waded their horses out to a narrow island with a line of trees, then across to another. They had to swim the animals the last part. Ballista kept an eye on Tarchon. The Suanian would never make a natural horseman. It was quite a stretch, but the current was slow, and nothing bad happened. In retrospect, the crossing seemed easier than scrambling up a gulley in the higher western bank.

They saw to the horses, lit a fire, dried out themselves and the baggage, and ate lunch. Afterwards, while most rested in the shade of some willows, Maximus inhaled some hemp with Rudolphus. The Hibernian had grown to love that stuff.

Hot and dirty, and not in the mood for narcotics or company, Ballista walked back down the gulley to the Tanais to bathe. Down by the water were the remains of a tiny settlement. The jambs and lintel of the doors of the two huts still stood. Their four-square solidity was strange against the rest. The walls were sagging or gone, and above the roofs were partial skeletons of joists and beams. The wattle of the stock pen wall had fallen and unwoven. Its warped sticks were strewn across the dust, while the sets of twin posts that had once held it upright stuck up at crazed angles, white like bleached bones.

Ballista walked through it, held by the common human fascination for desuetude. How did this happen? Where did everyone go? Any portable possessions had long ago been robbed out. The dust sifted grey and fine on his boots. There was no sign of burning, but somehow he had no doubt violence had been involved in its

340

abandonment. There were fish in the river, wildfowl would flight here, the soil was fertile. He had a vision of two hardworking families, models of rustic virtue. Maybe one had a daughter to betroth to the son of the other. They would sacrifice a specially fattened calf for their bucolic nuptials. And then the riders had come. They had steel in their hands, and quite likely they had red tattoos.

The country beyond the river, while still flat, was not feature-less. It was patterned with dry watercourses. The sides of these dropped down suddenly, as if they had been cut by the spade of a giant. Greyish shrubs grew in them, back flush to the level of the surrounding grass. They curved like dark tattoos across the face of the Steppe.

That night, Ballista lay watching sheet lightning on the northern horizon. Rain would come soon, Rudolphus had said.

The third day, the Steppe reverted to type, a flat run of brown-black grass as far ahead as could be seen. The north wind had brought down the clouds. Black and without a break, they slid south low overhead. As the travellers rode south-west, it was as if they were trapped between two solid planes, like the hemp between Maximus's blades.

By noon, it was dark enough to be evening. The thunder welled up in the clouds. The sheet lightning accentuated the gloom with its sporadic flashes of pure white. In one of these Ballista saw three men on ponies riding parallel to them in the south. A quarter of a mile away, half a mile? It was impossible to judge.

'There are many broken, tribeless men on the Steppe,' Rudol-phus said. 'More now, after Naulobates' victory; many Alani, riders from the Sirachoi, Aorsoi, their subject tribes.' The guide shrugged. 'Heruli too. Fear made some of the brothers slip away from the fighting. They were fools. It is better to stand up to the arrow-storm and the steel for an hour or two, better to take the wound'

– he held up his right hand, with the truncated digits – 'better even to die, than live as an outcast. It is a hard life; bad for the soul. Those men have seen our horses and pack-ponies and the baggage. They may try to steal them. But, unless there are many of them, they will not try and fight us for them.'

They made camp early, under a loud, angry sky. Ballista decided they would set pickets. To keep them sharp, prevent any falling into a routine, they would be chosen by lot each evening. After dinner, Ballista and Maximus took the first watch. They sat, cloaks pulled around them, at either end of the horse lines, to the west of the camp.

Ballista could sense the rain in the storm. Nine more days to Tanais, some of them would be wet. A day or two in the town hiring a boat, another day or two crossing Lake Maeotis. Would there be an imperial official with new orders waiting for them in the Kingdom of Bosporus? If so, they might have to winter in Panticapaeum again. If not, they should be able to get passage across the Euxine to Byzantium before the weather closed the shipping lanes. If no *mandata* awaited them there either, he was minded to journey on by land. The weather would be bad, but he still had *diplomata* to use the *cursus publicus*. They could use the imperial posting service up through the Danubian provinces, across the Alps – if the snow had not closed the passes – and report to Gallienus at Mediolanum, assuming the emperor was there with the field army.

He was not unduly worried how Gallienus would receive them. True, he had ransomed no Roman prisoners, and had failed to turn the Heruli against the Urugundi and the other Goths. Yet there was war on the Steppes. Having fought in the Caucasus, he did not think Naulobates and Hisarna were likely to attain a quick victory over the Alani. The remote passes and upland pastures were studded with forts and made ideal terrain for ambush. That was three tribes too occupied to raid the *imperium*. And half the gold with which he had been entrusted was returning.

The thunder and lightning were spooking the horses.

Time was passing since Ballista had been forced briefly to assume the purple. Gallienus had not had him condemned in the immediate aftermath. There was no reason to think the emperor would do so now. Unless . . .

Lightning illuminated the whole Steppe with a fleeting brilliance that had no perspective, and was gone in a moment. The blackness after was impenetrable.

Unless there had been an outbreak of usurpations, and the *consilium* thought a purge was necessary to reassert the authority of the central government. Ballista had been away from the imperial council for a long time. He had never fully understood its inner machinations. Undoubtedly, he had enemies there. Yet he also had friends. The last he had heard, Aurelian and Tacitus still stood high in the favour of Gallienus.

Lightning tore across the sky.

Ballista wondered how Rutilus had got on in his embassy to the other Gothic tribes, the Borani and the Grethungi. Being yoked with the old consular Felix would have been no joy.

Halfway along the line, a horse reared against its tether. Ballista got to his feet, stretching the knots out of his muscles. A figure was at the horse's head.

'Maximus?'

A gust of wind snatched the word away.

Ballista walked down the line of white-eyed horses.

There were two men by the plunging horse.

'Maximus!' Ballista threw off his cloak, drew his sword. 'Horse thieves!'

Ballista ran at them. One figure swung up on to the animal, the other holding its head.

'Maximus!'

The second man jumped up behind the first. The horse bolted.

Something warned Ballista. He turned, weapon ready. A blade sliced towards his head. He parried, and riposted. But the man had leapt aside, and was running off into the darkness.

'Maximus!'

A dark shape in front. 'Is that you?'

'Of course it is fucking me.'

Other men were running up from the campfire.

'They just got the one.'

The next night, the storm returned, but still the rain did not fall. About midnight, someone shook Calgacus awake.

'Enough, enough, you ham-fisted fucker.'

Tarchon stopped shaking him. 'Your turn with the pederast.'

Calgacus clambered to his feet. His shoulder hurt. It seized up when he slept. He yawned, coughed, hawked, spat and farted; all as loudly as possible, inspired by a half-realized resentment at others sleeping when he was awake. The noises were lost in the clamour of the storm.

Hippothous was waiting by the fire with one of the soldiers. Sparks whirled away to die in the darkness.

The change of pickets was shite. Calgacus would tell Ballista in the morning. If both men on watch came in to rouse their replacements, it would not take the most intelligent horse thief in the world to work out when to strike. Although if any of the fuckers were out on a night like this, good luck to them.

The horses were tethered in two lines running north–south out to the west of the camp. Between the lightning flashes, it was so dark they were barely visible from where the men slept around the fire. Hippothous disappeared off to the northern picket.

Calgacus walked through the lines to the southern post. The

horses shifted and whickered at him as he passed. He liked the sweet smell of them. He muttered soothing things. A Herul pony tried to nip him.

Out beyond the shelter of the animals, the wind buffeted him. There was no cover, so he sat with his back to it. He pulled his cloak around him. Since they had been there, he had never liked the night on the Steppe.

Up above, the storm roared. There were no stars. All the constellations, the Pleiades, the Eyes of Thiazi – whatever different men called them – were gone. The moon had vanished as surely as if Hati the wolf had devoured him.

It was Ragnarok weather. At the end of days, Fenrir the wolf will break his bonds, Jormungand the serpent rear up from the sea, the dead rise from Hel, and Naglfar – the ship made from dead men's nails – bring doom to gods and men.

Calgacus wondered if he believed it, any of it. They were the first stories of the gods he could remember. The Angles had seemed to believe. But it had been made very clear he was not an Angle. He was a *nithing*, a Caledonian slave.

He had grown up an outsider in Germania. All these years with Ballista, he had remained an outsider among the Greeks and Romans. When the traditional gods were always beings other people worshipped, it made his own belief in any of them improbable. Those religions he had encountered which offered a new identity – Manichaeism, Christianity – struck him as the self-evident results of human ingenuity.

Something warned Calgacus. He shifted, and peered out from under his hood. Hippothous was ghosting down the horse lines. He had a sword in his hand.

No daemon then; all the time, just a man's murderous insanity.

Calgacus did not move. Under his cloak, he eased his sword in its scabbard. He watched out of the corner of his eye; waiting,

waiting. As Hippothous closed, Calgacus rose, turned, drew his weapon and thrust in one fluid motion.

Caught by surprise, the Greek sidestepped. Too slow. The edge of Calgacus's blade scraped down his ribcage.

Hippothous stepped back. He seemed not to feel the pain. In the lightning, his eyes were mad.

Calgacus roared as he cut at Hippothous's head. Sparks as Hippothous blocked the blow, countered, and was blocked in turn.

They circled. Intense concentration made it hard for Calgacus to shout. Hippothous led on one foot then shifted his weight to the other and launched a flurry of blows.

The heavy impacts jarred up into Calgacus's shoulder. The steel rang against the thunder. The horses were calling, fighting against their tethers. That would bring the others. Just stay alive.

Something turned under Calgacus's boot. He staggered. Hippothous struck. Calgacus brought his sword across. Not quick enough. The breath grunted out of him, as the steel punched up into his stomach.

As the blade was pulled out, Calgacus doubled up. He used his sword to push himself near upright, drew the long dagger from his right hip, got it out in front. The blood was running hot down his groin on to his thighs.

Hippothous stepped in, chopping down at his head. Calgacus met it with the dagger. The force almost drove him to his knees. Movement, shouting off towards the fire. Just stay alive.

Like an animal seeking the warmth of his blood, the steel cut at him again. He blocked – slower, the pain hindering his movements.

The horses were rearing as men ran through the lines.

Hippothous looked over his shoulder, then turned and ran into the darkness.

Calgacus felt his knees give. He was face down, the grass coarse under his cheek. The blood was hot on his hands pressed to the wound.

How long would it take the fuckers to get here? From a great distance, he heard yelling, above the howl of the wind.

With surprise, he realized he was not thinking of Ballista, and not of Rebecca and Simon. He heard the crash of waves on rocks, caught the scent of a peat fire, glimpsed a woman's half-remembered face.

XXXI

'There!' The Herul guide Rudolphus pointed.

Ballista shaded his eyes, though there was no sun coming through the low, fast-moving clouds. The air was misted with dust and debris picked up by the north wind. He could see nothing else.

'To the right of the three barrows, well beyond.'

'I see it,' Maximus said.

Ballista screened the right-hand side of his face to try to keep out the grit. His eyes were watering. A thin smudge of more solid dust, glimpsed for a moment, then merging back into the general obscurity.

'How far?' Ballista asked.

The Herul considered. 'Four miles, maybe a bit more.'

'A fair distance,' Ballista said.

'Not far enough.' The Herul nudged his pony on, and the other two did likewise. 'He has made bad time. We will run him down today.'

How had Hippothous hoped to get away with it? Maybe, if he had caught Calgacus unaware and had managed to kill him with no outcry, he might have tried to pass it off as the work of horse thieves. Not trusting in that outcome, Hippothous had untied a horse from the line, saddled it, and left it tethered out in the darkness of the Steppe.

And that had been his fatal mistake. The Greek had not learnt from his time on the Steppe. He had taken one horse. The three men pursuing him had nine; eight now that one had gone lame and been turned loose.

Not that it would have done them any good without Rudolphus. How the Herul had tracked Hippothous west for the last two days amazed Ballista. The surface of the Steppe was baked too hard for hoof prints. Now and then, Rudolphus lost the line, and had to cast around. He would drop from his mount, peer at the scorched grass and feel the dirt. Eventually, he would grunt in satisfaction, and swing back into the saddle. Only once – a pile of horse droppings – had Ballista been able to detect any sign.

They rode on at a fast canter. Each time the thunder cracked, the red Sarmatian Naulobates had given Ballista flinched and laid his ears flat. The Heruli ponies gave it less mind. The rain would fall at any moment. By the look of the clouds, it would be heavy.

Back at the camp, there had been chaos after they had found Calgacus. Chaos, then hard decisions. Holding the old man's head in his lap, Ballista had lost his temper, yelled at the others to be quiet – shut the fuck up and let him think.

A lone rider, even with only one horse, would outrun the column. Only some could give chase, and they had to have spare mounts. Ballista had known right away he needed Rudolphus. And he would not be without Maximus, not now of all times.

Tarchon had begged to come. He had ranted. He had failed in his duty. He had to redeem his honour. His passion led him to revert to his native Suanian. No one else understood the words, but his meaning was still clear.

Ballista had remained adamant. The column could not be too

stripped of its fighters; the Steppe was full of broken men. Besides – he had told the Suanian – one of them had to stay with Calgacus.

Ruthlessly, they had thrown away baggage, and taken six of the ponies as remounts. Castricius had been left in charge. He still had two auxiliaries and the two ex-military slaves, as well as Tarchon. Six armed men should be enough. The interpreter Biomasos had shown spirit. They should be enough to see off any but the most committed or desperate bandits.

Castricius had taken instructions from Rudolphus. These amounted to little more than to keep on south-west. Eight days' easy march, and they would come to Lake Maeotis, if not straight to the port of Tanais itself. The interpreter spoke all the local languages. There was water along the way, and they had ample provisions. Ballista had few fears on that score. A man like Castricius – a man who had survived the mines, the sack of Arete, and whatever else had happened to him in Albania – was unlikely to fail.

Ballista felt guilty for the times he had thought Castricius might have been the killer. A much greater guilt tried to force itself up into his thoughts. He stamped it down. Time enough for that when this chase had run its course. Allfather, all these years and he had never bothered to ask what funeral rites Calgacus wanted.

The first drops of rain dimpled the dust of the plain. Soon it was falling hard, beating in at an angle, running down his face, sluicing off his riding cloak.

Ballista called over to Rudolphus. 'There will be no dust to follow.'

The Herul turned, squinting against the downpour. 'There will be tracks. His horse cannot hold out for much further.'

They changed mounts, and ate some dried meat and drank milk. The Herul stepped from one pony to another, not bothering to dismount even to urinate. When they moved off, Rudolphus had them spread out across the plain.

Riding alone on the right flank, Ballista remembered something Julia had said years before. The dead do not suffer; that is for those left behind.

Calgacus had been alive when he reached him. But with eyes beyond hope, mouth beyond speech ... Ballista began to cry again.

Down in the darkness of the tomb, Hippothous waited. They would not be long now. He had seen them coming from the top of the *kurgan*. Three riders, each with a string of ponies on a lead rein. There had been no mistaking them, even through the rain at that distance: Ballista, Maximus and the Herul guide.

Hippothous hoped they had seen him silhouetted on the skyline. He had tethered the horse right outside the opening to make sure they knew he was here.

It was a story from Polemon's *Physiognomy* that had started him on the long journey to this dark place. There was a woman in the city of Perge in the land of Pamphylia. The women there go veiled – as decent Hellenic women should – you can only see the eyes and nose. It had been enough for Polemon. 'What a great evil is about to descend on this woman,' he had announced. The sign was that her nostrils had darkened, and her eyes widened and turned green. Her head moved much, and as she walked her feet knocked together, as if from fear. To the astonishment of Polemon's companions, someone ran up, shouting that the woman's daughter had fallen into the well at their house and been drowned. The woman ripped off her veil, tore the front of her dress and threw off her clothes – even her loincloth of Egyptian or Greek linen. Naked, she fell on her face, sobbing for her beloved daughter.

It had been the first step on Hippothous's journey. Physiognomy not only let you look into someone's soul, it allowed you to see their future.

Polemon had also met a man from Lydia. His colour was dark, tending to redness, as if he had drunk wine or were angry. He was strong, his ankles were thick, the digits of his hands and feet were short, and in his voice was an ugly hoarseness. Of course, his eyes were evil. Often, he bared his teeth, like a wild pig when it turns on its hunter. It was evident to Polemon that the man was full of tyranny and enmity, often threatening evil; a killer, and a shedder of blood. Yet no one but Polemon was aware of the horror the man would perpetrate.

The man's neighbours were celebrating a festival. The man sent them a basket of food. The basket was put among the offerings, and opened. On top were saucers of oyster shells. But underneath was a severed head.

The story had been a revelation to Hippothous.

The neighbours had cursed the killer, the polluter of festivals. Polemon had been among those who cursed him. As long as the physiognomist lived, he had not neglected to continue to curse him. Yet that was all Polemon had done.

The gods had put Polemon's story in Hippothous's hands. He was sure of that. Unlike Polemon, he would not stand by supine, and let evil men do the things their perverse natures drove them towards. Why had the gods given man the science of physiognomy, the ability to know the future, if not to prevent such horror? As Hippothous read the story, the Hound of the Gods had been born. For years Hippothous had laboured – alone, and in secret – to perform the necessary and dangerous work of the gods. He was their Scourge of Evil.

Even in the depths of the burial mound, the thunder could still be heard. Hippothous grinned. It was all suitably apocalyptic. The *kurgan* was perfect. He had lost a lot of time checking the ones he passed, but this was absolutely perfect; its perfection only visible once inside.

He did not want to kill Ballista. The signs of his physiognomy were conflicting. But it might well be necessary. If it was, the least he would do would be to wipe the blood on his head. The full mutilation – the entire ritual from the *Argonautica* of Apollonius – would be safer. One of the last things Hippothous wanted was to be haunted by the northern barbarian's daemon. The little girl from Ephesus was bad enough.

Maximus was a different case. With the thick, dark hair of a savage animal and the never-still eyes of the enemy of truth and the lover of false conjecture, he needed killing. Any physiognomist could tell, if he was left alive, untold suffering and the deaths of any number of other people would result. For much of this journey, Hippothous had been unsure if he should kill him or the old Caledonian first.

The Herul did not much matter either way. Since witnessing the disgustingness with the donkey, Hippothous realized that all the Heruli were rotten, less than human, close to the beasts with which they mated. Conveniently, Rudolphus was missing most of the fingers of his right hand – which would make him easy to put down.

Hippothous had no fear of death. But he had no intention of dying here in this subterranean dark. The gods would not want it. They had held their hands over him in many bad places. They would do so again. Their work must continue. They would lead him back into the light.

Back in the *imperium*, back in civilization, he would move somewhere new. North Africa appealed, maybe a big city like Carthage. Or perhaps Syracuse in Sicily. Ballista's estate at Tauromenium was just up the coast. The Hound of the Gods had unfinished business with others of the barbarian's *familia*.

He would change his name and alter his looks. The thought of such reinvention made him feel curiously dislocated; as if his life so far were somehow unreal, the product of his own artifice or sleight of hand.

People said the gods sent insanity down on a murderer who stood on sacred ground. He had killed the girl, and had been in temples since, but the gods had spared him. It was their work he was doing.

Nevertheless, as soon as he reached Hellas, he would undergo purification. He would be rid of the daemon of the girl. It would be hard to find a priest who would be willing to proceed, once he had been told what he had done. That was no insuperable problem. Jason had been purified by Circe. But Hippothous would purify himself. He was closer to the gods than Jason had ever been. All the ritual, all he needed to know, was in the *Argonautica* of Apollonius; that invaluable work.

First, he had to rid himself of the three approaching men. The wound the old Caledonian had given him hurt. It would slow his movements. He needed to summon all his courage. If *andreia* alone did not prove enough, the gods would help.

XXXII

The horse was at the foot of the *kurgan* on which they had seen Hippothous. It was tethered by the opening.

Maximus remained off to one side, watching the horse and the opening from a distance. Ballista and Rudolphus scouted all around the *kurgan*. It was a huge burial mound, big in circumference and tall as a three-storey house. Bald grass on top, it was overgrown with thorns on its lower slopes, although not enough to conceal a man. The only tracks were those going to the top and back, and quite a few around the opening. Hippothous had been in and out several times. There were no other tracks, no other place to hide. He was in there now.

'I will get his horse,' Ballista said.

'I will come with you; cover the opening,' Maximus said.

All three dismounted. Maximus and Rudolphus each knee-hobbled the horse they had been riding, leaving the others on the lead. Ballista tied his spare mount to the string of Maximus. He got back into the saddle and waited for Maximus to get ready.

The two lines of riderless horses turned their backs to the rain. A couple pulled at the grass, the other five stood in head-down unhappiness. The thunder crashed above them.

Maximus untied his bowcase from his horse and strapped it to his belt. Hunched over to protect it from the rain, he checked his bow and selected an arrow. He held the arrow in his right hand and put the flap of the *gorytus* back over the bow and his left hand, which he left resting on the weapon. He walked along the base of the *kurgan* until he was standing just to the left of the opening. He nodded at Ballista.

With pressure from his knees, Ballista got the Sarmatian moving. Taking it up to a canter, he hooked his left leg around the left rear horn of the saddle and leant right forward along the right side of the animal's neck.

Hippothous's horse made an ideal ambush. It was right in front of the black opening. All too easy to imagine an arrow whistling out at anyone who went to untether the beast.

Ballista reined up and rolled down on his feet as he came to Hippothous's mount. Keeping the animal between him and the opening, he cut the tether, grabbed the bridle, and ran, pulling the horses with him as shields. When the angle was too acute for a man to shoot without emerging from the tunnel, Ballista stopped.

Nothing had happened.

Ballista remounted and, leading the Greek's horse, rode all around the *kurgan* to rejoin the others without passing the menacing opening.

He got down and added the horses to the strings. Hippothous's was exhausted, but it was not lame. It could have gone a bit further before foundering. The Greek had decided to make a stand.

'You could wait him out,' Rudolphus said.

'No.' Ballista and Maximus spoke at the same time.

'You will need torches,' Rudolphus said. 'I will see to it.' The Herul stomped off into the bushes on the mound.

'I would be happier if we had bigger shields,' Maximus said, looking at the small nomad buckler in his hands.

'These may be handier in a tunnel. Should we take bows?'

Maximus thought it over. 'Might be worth the second man having one.' He began to unstrap the *gorytus* from his hip.

'I will go first,' Ballista said.

'No.' Maximus looked straight into Ballista's eyes. Both were blinking from the rain. Maximus was one of a handful who knew of Ballista's fear of confined spaces.

'I will go first,' Ballista said.

'I use a *gladius*; the shorter sword is more suited than the *spatha* you carry.'

'Calgacus has been with me all my life.'

'A fair bit of mine too,' Maximus said. 'If one of us gets killed, who would your boys mourn most?'

Ballista snorted, but said nothing.

'You would not send a man who could not handle heights first in a storming party up a wall.' Maximus put both hands on Ballista's shoulders, drew him close, spoke in his ear. 'If you go first, you endanger both of us.'

Ballista still did not speak. After a moment, he nodded. They embraced, kissed on both cheeks and stepped apart.

Ballista strapped on his *gorytus*. If Maximus was killed, Ballista knew he would not forgive himself. This was cowardice. Some men were naturally brave: Maximus, Calgacus. Courage was something Ballista had to steel himself to display its image. It had always been a test. This was the test he had failed. No matter what happened, he would always feel worse about himself. Someone had once said to him that courage was a treasure house from which you could take things, but never deposit them.

They were either side of the horrible mouth of the tunnel. Swords drawn, they carried the torches Rudolphus had improvised in their left hands. The Herul was back with the horse strings.

They looked at each other. Maximus mouthed, *'One-two-three.'* He started to move. He was gone.

Allfather, Deep-hood, hold your hands over me. Ballista forced himself to follow.

Maximus was moving fast.

Ballista had to crouch. *Do not think, just act.* The tunnel ran down steep. The circular band of the light of Maximus's torch was racing ahead. Ballista blundered after; helmet, elbows scraping the earth.

The tunnel opened into a chamber. Ballista saw Maximus go left. Ballista went right.

A large, domed space; the soil of the walls very light in the torchlight, a chalky paleness. There were many skeletons. The legs of one sprawled obscenely. It lay next to a decayed cushion, from which spilled desiccated eelgrass. *Concentrate – do not think, just act.* There were two other openings off the chamber. Maximus was flattened against the wall next to one. Ballista went to the other. He was fighting to get his breathing right.

Ballista looked across the chamber. They would enter the tunnels at the same moment. Maximus mouthed, *'One-two-three.'*

Torch and shield thrust out, Ballista threw himself into the entrance. This was higher, some sort of corridor. Age-rotted wood splintered under his boots. A bone snapped as he trod on it. Fifteen, twenty steps in, it ended in a wall of rubble; a burial shaft that had been filled.

Ballista ran back, across the chamber and into the gap through which Maximus had gone. Another corridor, this time faced with wood. Another chamber at the end; weird dancing shadows visible in it.

Something tripped him. He fell forward, skinning his elbows, grazing his face. The torch rolled away. He was face down in the remains of a centuries-dead fire, cooking utensils around him. He scrambled to his feet, snatched up the torch and pressed on. He realized he was panting out monotonous obscenities: *fuck, fuck, fuck*.

Another round chamber, hollowed out of the pastel-coloured, almost white loess. Just one exit, Maximus back to the wall against it. Ballista joined him. He was gasping for breath. He knew it was fear. Although a long way down, the air was not stale.

'Fucking rabbit warren,' Maximus whispered.

Ballista tried to grin.

No noises except their rasping breathing and the hiss of the torches as their flames shifted.

'Has to have gone up here,' Maximus said. 'Take our time, get ourselves set.'

Ballista managed to grin.

Suddenly, a crash of thunder echoed around the chamber. Odd, this far from the entrance.

Ballista very much wanted not to be here. If only they could just retrace their steps; get out of this subterranean hell and not have to face the steel of a madman lurking in the dark.

'You ready?'

Ballista nodded at Maximus. The Hibernian's face was sheened with sweat.

This was the tunnel of a graverobber. Low and narrow – little wider than Ballista's shoulders – it climbed sharply. They had to crawl, wriggle up it. Ballista had to hang back to avoid burning Maximus with his torch. It was slow going. The tunnel twisted. The excavation was crude. There were no pit props, nothing holding the roof. Loose soil sifted down. Ballista tried not to think what that might signify.

A much louder roll of thunder. A gust of fresh, wet air. Maximus was swearing. He was fighting his way out through a thorn bush. He was back on the surface.

It took Ballista a time to join him. Maximus held back some of the branches of the thorn as he hauled himself clear.

'Not good,' Maximus shouted over the rage of the storm. 'Far from fucking good.'

They were out among the scrub on the side of the *kurgan*. The storm raced all around them. At the foot of the slope, Rudolphus lay dead. The horses were gone.

They worked their way up and around the mound. From the summit, they could see the two strings of horses and the lone rider leading them. They were headed south-west at an easy canter. In the flashes of lightning they appeared frozen, and almost close enough to touch.

The trail would be easy enough to follow. The rain had stopped, and nine horses left more than enough traces. But there were things they had to do before they could leave the *kurgan*.

They had no food except the small bag of air-dried meat Maximus always had about him. But they had Ballista's bow, and could hunt as they went. There was game, and wildfowl on the watercourses. More worrying, they had no water. If the Steppe continued well watered, things would not be too bad. However, their flasks and skins had been on their saddles. With nothing to hold water, it could be serious if the walk between streams was long. They went down into the barrow to see if there was anything useable among the grave offerings. There was not; all the cooking utensils were either broken or shallow bowls which would be too much trouble to carry without their contents slopping out. As Maximus said, they might as well try to carry water in their helmets.

Their helmets and armour were another problem. Ballista guessed it was at least three days' walk to the shores of Lake Maeotis. Somehow, neither had any doubt that was where Hippothous would be headed. The war gear would weigh down men on foot. Mailcoats, helmets and shields were left in the first burial chamber. It would be a lucky traveller who found them; good coats of ring mail were expensive beyond the dreams of most men.

Obviously, there was no question of abandoning their swords, daggers, Maximus's various concealed knives, or Ballista's *gorytus*. Both knew the straps would rub their shoulders raw within a couple of days.

And there was Rudolphus. The Herul lay curled around the arrow in his gut. The two in his back must have finished him off. They searched his body. He had an *akinakes* and a dagger, which they left, and some coins from the Bosporus, which they took; but nothing of real use. They had not the time to burn or bury him, but could not just leave him on the Steppe. They carried him down into the *kurgan*, and left him with their armour. Ballista closed his eyes and put a coin in his mouth for the ferryman. He was not sure the latter was right for a Herul, but it could do no harm.

There was only an hour or two of daylight left when they set out. They walked on the virgin grass to one side of the muddied path the horses had left. They did not hurry. There was no point. They had a long way to go.

They had not gone four miles before they saw the vultures. It was Hippothous's horse. It had been unable to go on, and he had killed it. There was a deep stab wound in its throat. It had bled to death. It was still saddled and bridled, but Hippothous had taken anything of use from its packs.

Although it delayed them, Maximus cut meat from the carcass, stowed it in one of the packs and improvised straps from the leather of its tack. As they walked on, the vultures returned.

When darkness came, they did not stop. There was a line of trees a mile or so ahead. The trail was there when the moon showed between the ragged clouds of the rearguard of the storm.

At the stream, they got a fire going, eventually. The damp wood smoked, hissed and spat, and gave little heat. The horse-meat was raw inside a charred crust. They ate it, and drank water. Far off to the south, the storm flickered and grumbled beyond the horizon.

They did not speak of what had happened, or what might happen. They hardly spoke at all. Wrapped in his cloak, Ballista tried to empty his mind. With every thought came memories of Calgacus. He repeated Julia's words to himself: the dead do not suffer, that is for those left behind. At last, he slept.

Maximus woke him. The sun was not yet up, the sky just paling in the east. The fire had gone out. Ballista was cold, tired, and his stomach was uneasy. They tried to eat the raw horsemeat. It made Ballista's gorge rise. He persevered. He would need the sustenance.

The dawn came up behind them as they walked. Their shadows, canted and misshapen, marched ahead. The sky was clear. That was something. If it had rained as before, the trail would have been washed away.

With the warmth of the day, the Steppe came to life. First in patches, then in great swathes, the grass turned green again. Miraculous yellow flowers opened. It was as if the storm had turned back time, ushered in a second springtime. Birds sang, plovers swooped around them. There were butterflies, yellow like the flowers. All of it was superficial, false to Ballista's eyes. It did not lighten his mood an iota.

They could not go wrong. The trail was the only thing to

follow in the immensity of the plain. Ballista kept his eyes on it, a few steps in front of his feet. To look up was to accept the scale of the Steppe, to invite the admission of the futility of what they did.

They crossed small streams with banks that had been swept by flash floods from the storm. Their soil, where it had been undercut, was red; sometimes hanging like bloodied stalactites.

The north wind sang across the Steppe.

That evening, they halted early at a place where a stream broadened out into a mere. They concealed themselves in the cover around the edges. When the ducks had flighted and were on the water, in the lingering light that remained, Ballista shot one. The others rose up, clamorous in their fear.

Ballista lit a fire. Maximus plucked and dressed the bird. Cooked, it was an infinite improvement on the horsemeat.

Ballista did not want to talk about Calgacus. He could tell Maximus did not want to either. There was nothing else to talk about.

There were a few clouds that night, coming down from the north. They gave the moon a fugitive air, as if any one of them might conceal the wolf. Of course, some peoples did not think the moon was masculine, or that it would one day be eaten by a beast. For the Greeks, it was Selene; a goddess riding for eternity in a chariot drawn by shambly-footed oxen. He wondered what Calgacus had thought when he looked into a moonlit sky. He wondered what view Calgacus had held of an afterlife. They had never talked about it seriously. They never would now. It would be a comfort to believe he would be reunited with the old Caledonian, in Valhalla or somewhere. But it was hard to give it credence. This life was unforgiving; no reason to think the next would be better. If it existed.

The third day was much tougher. Ballista's feet were blistered. He took off his boots and bandaged them. The bandages slipped, chafed, soon did no good. Maximus was walking badly too. The only advantage in their slower pace was the time it gave them to find the trail; it was getting harder to follow as the rejuvenated grass sprang up.

Twice – once to the north, once the south – they saw herds dotted and indistinct in the distance.

The Steppe stretched on, pitiless in its enormity. But they knew they were getting closer to Lake Maeotis. The smell of it was in the air, and the streams they had to cross were much fuller, broadening out into real rivers. Each of the latter was somehow shocking in its sudden declivity, as it brought trees and wildfowl, and a reflection of the sky, things near forgotten and almost unimaginable in the previous hours of their absence.

They cut thin branches to use as walking sticks.

They walked all day. They had nothing left to eat, and did not stop to hunt. As the sun began its final descent – they moved like old men now – they heard the sea birds. Looking up, Ballista saw the overgrown earthworks, and ditches full of brambles and thin trees of some long-abandoned fortification. Beyond, there were reed beds, and beyond them the open water of some quiet inlet. There was the thatched roof of a lone cottage. Off to the right, eight horses grazed in a water meadow.

Dogs hurtled out, three of them: vicious-looking, snarling, eyes popping.

The horses stamped away to the far end of the meadow.

Ballista and Maximus stood still, leaning on their walking sticks.

The dogs circled.

An elderly man clad in rags appeared out of the reeds, an eldritch figure with the low sun behind him. He whistled, and the dogs fell back a little. He put his right palm flat to his forehead.

Ballista cleared his throat to speak.

The old man spoke first. 'He has taken the only boat. He made my son sail it.' He used the language of Germania.

Neither Ballista nor Maximus said anything.

'He said you would come.' The aged fisherman held his hands out placatingly. 'It is not our fault. Do not blame us. He was armed; a man of violence. What could we do?' He fell to his knees.

'When?' Ballista said.

'Yesterday morning, just after first light.'

Ballista felt as if something was broken inside him, something that had been keeping him upright.

'How far are your neighbours?' Maximus said.

The old man pointed to the south-east. 'Near Tanais.'

'How far?'

'A long day's walk.'

'The other way?'

'Further.'

Ballista spoke. 'The horses are ours.'

'Yes, of course. He said you would want them. We have looked after them.' The old man showed his teeth like a dog which fears a beating. 'We had no choice.'

'Get off your knees. Do you have any food we could have?'

'Yes, yes, of course.' The old fisherman scrambled up, started backing towards the cottage. 'Fish stew, and bread, good bread.'

'And chain up those dogs.'

'Yes, right away, *Atheling*, right away.'

The dogs winding around his legs, the old man went to the cottage.

'When we have eaten, we can ride to Tanais,' Maximus said. 'Keep the water on our right. We should be there before morning. Good chance of hiring a boat there and then.'

'No,' Ballista said. 'The wind has been set in the north. It would have been on his quarter. He would have reached Panticapaeum some time last night. If he did not stop, by now he could be across the Euxine. It is over.'

'If the gods ever let me find him . . .'

'Yes.' Ballista felt unutterably weary; vaguely sick, but hungry. 'Would you check the horses?'

When Maximus was gone, Ballista stared at the dying sun, and tried not to think too much about anything.

Appendices

Historical Afterword

Title

The working title of this novel was *The Nomad Sea*, and it was referred to as such in the Historical Afterwords to previous novels in the series.

History and Fiction

As in all but one of the *Warrior of Rome* novels, the surface story – here, Ballista's mission to the Steppe – is fiction, while the background in all its forms is as historically plausible as I can make it.

The Roman empire of the AD260s is a profoundly obscure and uncertain place, and the Pontic Steppe in antiquity seldom is anything else. Some trust can be put in the map of the Roman empire in AD263, but that of the Steppe is a contentious product of guesswork and inference.

Places

Kingdom of Bosporus

The standard work (in German) on this fascinating kingdom centred in the eastern Crimea (Greek in origin, heavily influenced by the Sarmatians, and a client of Rome, but one that at times in the third century AD is found providing shipping for the Gothic raids into Roman provinces) is V. F. Gajdukevič, *Das Bosporanische Reich* (Berlin and Amsterdam, 1971). For this period, two useful works in English are N. A. Frolova, *The Coinage of the Kingdom of Bosporus AD242–341/2* (Oxford, 1983); and M. Mielczarek, *The Army of the Bosporan Kingdom* (Łódź, 1999). Not being able to read Russian is a constant limitation in researching the kingdom.

A reconstruction of Bosporan history in the third century AD mainly has to be based on the coinage of the monarchs which can be dated. Rhescuporis V minted AD242–76, with gaps between AD258–60 and AD268–74. Coins also survive for other kings: Pharsanes AD253; Teiranes AD266 and AD275–8; and Sauromates AD275.

For the novel, I have reconstructed things as follows:

Pharsanes, Teiranes and Sauromates were sons of Rhescuporis (possibly with different mothers, who may have been from different tribes – Kings of Bosporus married women from various local tribes: see Lucian's *Toxaris*, which may be an ancient work of historical fiction, but was intended to be plausible to its original audience). In AD251, after the defeat of Rome by the Goths at Abritus, the emperor Gallus withdrew the annual Roman subsidy which the King of Bosporus mainly used to pay his troops and bribe surrounding tribes not to attack (interestingly, the lack of Roman coins in the eastern Crimea suggests it was paid in bullion, which was not the normal Roman practice). In AD253 the Goths attacked the Kingdom of Bosporus. Rhescuporis elevated Pharsanes to be joint king, but the latter was killed in battle. Rhescuporis was then forced to let his subjects 'connive' with the northern tribes by providing vessels for the northerners' first seaborne descent on Roman territory, which ended in defeat for the northerners at Pityus on the Black Sea.

Renewed war with the barbarians brought chaos in AD258–60. Rhescuporis, with tribal help bought with money from the pretenders Macrianus and Quietus (AD260–1), regained his throne and a little measure of stability in AD261. As Rhescuporis had recognized Macrianus and Quietus, relations between him and the emperor Gallienus may have remained strained for some years: Bosporan coins featuring two emperors begin in AD261, but continue well after the fall of the Macriani, until AD264.

It must be stressed that the above is a background story necessary for this and the next novel, *The Amber Road*. While it is inspired by the coins, other sources and wider events in the empire, as a historian, I have no faith in it whatsoever.

The Kingdom of Bosporus fell under the military sphere of the Roman governor of Bithynia-Pontus. However, in this novel, the auxiliaries with Ballista have been sent by the governor of Moesia Inferior, because they have come with imperial functionaries from Byzantium, which, while part of Bithynia-Pontus, was defended by the former.

Panticapaeum

Most of the ancient city is buried under the modern town of Kerch on the eastern Crimean peninsula in Ukraine. For introductions to the archaeology (in English), see G. R. Tsetskhladze in T. H. Nielsen (ed.), *Yet More Studies in the Ancient Greek Polis*

(Stuttgart, 1997), 44–9; and V. P. Tolstikov in D. V. Grammenos and E. K. Petropoulos (eds.), *Ancient Greek Colonies in the Black Sea, volume II* (Thessaloníki, 2003), 707–8.

Tanais

The ancient city of Tanais lay to the west of modern-day Rostov on Don, where the Don met the Sea of Azov. On this town, see B. Böttger in G. R. Tsetskhladze (ed.), *New Studies on the Black Sea Littoral* (Oxford, 1996), 41–50; and T. M. Arsenyeva in Grammenos and Petropoulos, op. cit. above under *Panticapaeum*, 1047–102. Both stress the complete abandonment of the settlement for a century or so after its sack by the Heruli/ Goths. I have given it a little more life.

The Steppe

Our bit of the Steppe – north-east of the Black Sea, north of the Caucasus and west of the Caspian and the Volga river – lies at the edge of the focus of two monumental works of scholarship. It is at the western end of C. I. Beckwith, *Empires of the Silk Road: A History of Central Eurasia from the Bronze Age to the Present* (Princeton and Oxford, 2009), and the eastern of R. Batty, *Rome and the Nomads: The Pontic-Danubian Realm in Antiquity* (Oxford, 2007) areas of study. Useful introductions to the Steppe can be found in E. H. Minns, *Scythians and Greeks: A Survey of Ancient History and Archaeology on the North Coast of the Euxine from the Danube to the Caucasus* (Cambridge, 1913); and R. Rolle, *The World of the Scythians* (Eng. tr., London, 1989).

Peoples

Nomads

The essential comparative work on pastoral nomadism is A. M. Khazanov, *Nomads and the Outside World* (2nd edn, Wisconsin and London, 1994).

On nomadic warfare, see P. B. Golden, 'War and Warfare in the Pre-Cinggisid Western Steppes of Eurasia', in N. di Cosmo (ed.), *Warfare in Inner Asian History (500–1800)* (Leiden, Boston, and Köln, 2002), 107–72; also useful for its concision and illustrations is A. Karasulas, *Mounted Archers of the Steppe 600BC–AD1300* (Oxford, 2004).

Heruli

The Heruli (also spelt as Eruli, and several other variations) are deeply obscure. There are various problems with our literary sources. They are all written long after the third century. They all work within the classical ethnographic tradition, which on the one hand makes all nomads the same and on the other allows for considerable invention of detail. Our main source, Procopius, is extremely hostile to the Heruli. Archaeology is not much help. Nomads leave few archaeological traces. Contrary to modern popular ideas, it is often impossible to match archaeological artefacts to ancient peoples or political groups (i.e. we are often unable to tell if an artefact from the right time and place belonged to the Heruli, Alani, Sarmatians or Goths).

The most influential modern study, A. Ellegärd, 'Who were the Eruli?', *Scandia* 53 (1987), 5–34, takes a very reductionist line. To my mind better is M. Scukin, M. Kazanski and O. Sharov, *Dès les Goths aux Huns: Le Nord de la Mer Noire au Bas-empire et à l'époque des Grandes Migrations* (Oxford, 2006), 31–6. The reconstruction of the history and social and political structure of the Heruli in this novel largely follows the latter, and runs as follows.

The Heruli originated in Scandinavia, in modern Norway or Sweden. In the early third century AD, the tribe divided. One part moved to the North Sea coast somewhere east of the Rhine. The other migrated – as a tribe, accompanied by at least part of one subordinate tribe, the Eutes – to the Steppe north-east of the Sea of Azov. Here they subjected local tribes (some of the Sarmatians and others) and took on local culture (including nomadism and cranial deformation).

The Heruli elite was the 'clan' of the Rosomoni, who tried to mark themselves off from the rest by attempting to monopolize various (to us) weird cultural practices (e.g. cranial deformation, red tattoos, bestiality, sharing their wives and voluntary immolation). Below them were the ordinary Heruli, descendants of those of lesser status who had migrated from the Baltic, and locals incorporated on 'good terms'. At the bottom were the 'slaves', locals incorporated on poor terms and people captured in raids. The novel's assumption of quite a lot of upward social mobility via prowess in war comes from Procopius on Heruli slaves, and a famous individual with the Huns recorded by fifth-century diplomat and historian Priscus.

Politically, the Heruli are seen as rudely egalitarian by Procopius. Picking up on a suggestion by H. Wolfram, *History of the Goths* (Berkeley, Los Angeles and London, 1988), 87–8, I have pictured Naulobates attempting to install a charismatic kingship, partly based on his monopolization of the flow-through of trade from the Urals and the Volga.

A central theme of this novel is culture shock. For the preconceptions of those travelling from the *imperium*, I have employed Pseudo-Hippocrates, *Airs, Waters, Places*; Herodotus; Strabo;

and Lucian, *Toxaris*. For men brought up in classical cultures, I believe, this is historically plausible: their thinking about the Steppe was shaped by reading just such books as these. For the realities they find, I have assumed Procopius's ethnography of the Heruli is historically true – of course, this is a naïve and improbable assumption. I have then proceeded to import to the Heruli various things attested for other nomads: cannabis use from the Scythians and wife sharing from the Agathyrsi, both found in Herodotus, and scapulimancy and cranial deformation from the Huns.

Other Nomadic Tribes

Not all nomadic tribes are as under-studied as the Heruli.

On the Sarmatians, see: T. Sulimirski, *The Sarmatians* (London, 1970); I. Lebedynsky, *Les Sarmates: Amazones et Lanciers Cuirassés entre Oural et Danube VIIe Siècle av. J.-C -VIie Siècle apr. J.-C.* (Saint-Germain-du-Puy, 2002); and R. Brzezinski and M. Mielczarek, *The Sarmatians 600BC–AD450* (Oxford, 2002).

On the Alani (who, most probably, were a Sarmatian people), see: B. S. Bachrach, *A History of the Alans in the West: From their first appearance in the sources of classical antiquity through the early middle ages* (Minneapolis, 1973); V. Kouznetsov and I. Lebedynsky, *Les Alains: Cavaliers des Steppes, Seigneurs du Caucase* (Paris, 1997).

Goths: Migration and Ethnogenesis

Quite deliberately, I have included two types of migration in this novel. The Heruli moved as a tribe, with their women and children and dependants – a *Völkerwanderung*, as scholars tend to call it. In the case of the Urugundi, a small war band of warriors moved and then incorporated others to expand to a tribe, which is one type of tribal formation often referred to as ethnogenesis. Neither case necessarily happened that way.

For a robust defence of the whole idea of migration, often summarily dismissed by scholars (e.g. Ellegärd, op. cit. above under *Heruli*), see P. Heather, *Empires and Barbarians: Migration, Development and the Birth of Europe* (London, 2009).

Individuals

Naulobates

A leader of the Heruli called Naulobates is recorded in the time of Gallienus by the Byzantine chronicler Syncellus (p. 717). Unlike some scholars, I have decided he was not the same as the Herul Andonnoballus recorded by the sixth-century historian Petrus Patricius (fr. 171, 172) in the reign of Claudius II.

The messianic Naulobates of this novel owes something to two real men – a lot to Baron von Ungern-Sternberg of the Russian Civil War from J. Palmer, *The Bloody White Baron* (London, 2008), and a little to P. Short, *Pol Pot: The History of a Nightmare* (London, 2004).

Biomasos

The interpreter Biomasos might be the son or grandson of Aspourgos, son of Biomasos, an interpreter of Sarmatian from the Kingdom of Bosporus, whose tombstone (*IG XVI* 1636) shows that he died accompanying an embassy to Rome, probably in the late second/ early third century AD. My thanks to Rachel Mairs of Brown University for bringing him to my attention.

Miscellaneous

Freedom

This is the second main theme of this novel. The best book I have read on the subject in antiquity remains C. Wirszubski, *Libertas as a Political Idea at Rome during the Late Republic and Early Principate* (Cambridge, 1950). The debate was widened in a review of Wirszubski by A. Momigliano in *Journal of Roman Studies* 41 (1951), 146–53.

Murder, Mutilation and Pollution

The killer's modus operandi of cutting off the extremities of his victims, tying them on a string and packing them under their armpits, licking up and spitting out their blood three times and wiping the blade that killed them on their heads, derives from a description in Apollonius of Rhodes, *Argonautica* IV 467–84; with additions from the *Suda* E 928; Aeschylus, *Choephoroi* 439; and Sophocles, *Electra* 445. There is a useful modern discussion in R. Bardel, 'Eunuchizing Agamemnon: Clytemnestra, Agamemnon and Maschalismos', in S. Tougher (ed.), *Eunuchs in Antiquity and Beyond* (London and Swansea, 2002), 51–70.

For forensic matters, I drew on the wonderful D. Starr, *The Killer of Little Shepherds: The Case of the French Ripper and the Birth of Forensic Science* (London, New York, Sydney and Toronto, 2011). A medical friend, Andy Peniket, told me how to remove human eyeballs.

For classical concepts of blood guilt, I relied on R. Parker, *Miasma: Pollution and Purification in Early Greek Religion* (Oxford, 1983).

Blood River

That Calgacus gives the name Blood River to the battle around the laager by the river in Chapter XX is no surprise. It is modelled on the battle of that name between the Boer *Voortrekkers* and the Zulus, as recounted in O. Ransford, *The Great Trek* (London, 1972).

Poetry

When Anglo-Saxon poetry comes into characters' minds – *The Wanderer* in Wulfstan's in chapters VI and XVI; the same poem in Ballista's in chapter XXII, and *Beowulf* in chapters XI and XIX – as ever, in these novels, it is the splendid translations of Kevin Crossley-Holland, *The Anglo-Saxon World* (Woodbridge, 1982). When Ballista thinks of Beowulf in chapter XIX, he reinstates the original *wyrd* for the modern English *fate*.

The Homeric verse recited by Ballista in chapter XVIII is from Richard Lattimore's unrivalled modern-verse translation of the *Iliad* (Chicago and London, 1951).

In chapter XX, Hippothous quotes Sophocles, *Oedipus the King*, ll. 1303–6 in the translation of E. F. Watling (London, 1947).

Sparta

Ballista in chapter XI might somewhat overemphasize the role of the *Gerousia* (the council of elders) in classical Sparta.

Philosophical Works of Consolation

Some may consider, and with some reason, that Ballista in chapter XXII is unfair to the works of consolation written by classical philosophers. But it should be remembered that Ballista was forced to read them many years earlier. When he thought of them more recently, in *Lion of the Sun*, they brought him little comfort. He does not remember the works clearly and is prejudiced against them. The former deficit is shared with the author, who deliberately did not re-read them. This could be the authorial equivalent of method acting.

Among surviving works are Seneca, *To Marcia, On Consolation*; *To Polybius, On Consolation*; Plutarch, *Consolation to his Wife*; Dio Chrysostom, *Melancomas* I and II, and *Charidemus*.

Battue

Almost everything about the hunt in chapter XXIV is drawn from T. S. Allsen, *The Royal Hunt in Eurasian History* (Philadelphia, 2006), a superb example of *longue-durée* history and anthropology, although nomads actually often did employ nets. The classical philosophizing about hunting is examined in H. Sidebottom, *Studies in Dio Chrysostom on Kingship* (DPhil thesis, Oxford, 1990), 156–66.

Physiognomy

As noted in *The Caspian Gates*, the modern study of ancient physiognomy has been put on a new level by S. Swain (ed.), *Seeing the Face, Seeing the Soul: Polemon's Physiognomy from Classical Antiquity to Medieval Islam* (Oxford, 2007).

Previous Historical Novels

Each *Warrior of Rome* novel includes homages to other works of fiction.

The *yipping* of the Heruli is borrowed from the Mongols in Cecelia Holland's enthralling *Until the Sun Falls* (1969).

While editing this novel, I chanced upon a novel I read as a child. Re-reading *The Year of the Horsetails* by R. F. Tapsell (1967), I realized where my interest in nomadic warfare began, and, with Bardiya Tapsell's siege engineer, outsider hero, something of the origins of Ballista. Tapsell was a superb historical novelist, and some enterprising publisher should put his works back in print for a new generation.

In *The Wolves of the North*, the assemblies of the Heruli draw heavily on those of the Cossacks in a much older historical novel: *Taras Bulba* by Nikolai Gogol (1835, revised 1842), in the splendid translation by Peter Constantine (2003).

Behind everything in *The Wolves of the North* lies the Steppe itself, and behind every description of it lies Anton Chekhov's story 'The Steppe' (1888).

Thanks

Every year, a new novel, but I am always delighted to thank almost all the same people.

First, my family, for their love and support. In Woodstock, my wife, Lisa, and sons, Tom and Jack. In Suffolk, my mother, Frances, and aunt, Terry.

The usual set of friends: Peter Cosgrove, Jeremy and Kate Habberley, and Jeremy Tinton.

At Oxford: Maria Stamatopoulou at Lincoln College, John Eidinow at St Benet's Hall and Richard Marshall at Wadham College. The latter deserves especial thanks for his help compiling the List of Characters and the Glossary.

Finally, the publishing professionals: at Penguin, Alex Clarke, Francesca Russell and Claire Purcell; for copy-editing, Sarah Day; and at United Agents, James Gill. This book is dedicated to the latter, whose relationship with the author is not entirely a matter of percentages.

Glossary

The definitions given here are geared to *The Wolves of the North*. If a word or phrase has several meanings, only that or those relevant to this novel tend to be given.

Ab Admissionibus: Official who controlled admission into the presence of the Roman emperor.

Abasgia: Kingdom on the north-east shore of the Black Sea, divided into an eastern and a western half, each with its own king.

Accensus: Secretary of a Roman governor or official.

Acropolis: Sacred citadel of a Greek city.

Aetna: Mount Etna, volcano on the island of Sicily.

Agathyrsi: Nomadic tribe living on the Steppe.

Agora: Greek term for a market place and civic centre.

Akinakes: Short sword used by the Scythians. Also the name of one of the two Scythian gods.

Alan (plural, *Alani*): Nomadic tribe north of the Caucasus.

Albania: Kingdom to the south of the Caucasus, bordering the Caspian Sea (not to be confused with modern Albania).

Alontas: River in the Caucasus, the modern Terek.

Alsvid: In Norse mythology, one of the two horses that pulled the sun across the sky.

Amber Road: Name for a series of trade routes leading south from the Baltic to the Mediterranean.

Amphora (plural, *amphorae*): Large Roman earthenware storage vessel.

Anarieis: Form of impotence said by Herodotus to afflict the Scythians; the 'female disease'.

Andreia: Greek, 'courage'; literally, 'man-ness'.

Anemos: 'The Wind'; one of the two Scythian gods.

Angles: North German tribe, living in the area of modern Denmark.

Anthropophagi: Greek, literally 'man-eaters'; a tribe of the northern Steppe thought to be cannibals.

Aorsoi: Nomadic tribe living on the Steppe; subjects of the Alani.

Aphorism: Greek, a wise, pithy saying.

Aphrodite: Greek goddess of love.

Apodyterium: Changing room of a baths.

Apollo Iatros: 'Apollo the Healer', an aspect of the Greek god.

Apotropaic: Intended to ward off evil.

Aquileia: Town in north-eastern Italy, where the emperor Maximinus Thrax was killed in AD238.

Arelate: Modern Arles, a city in the Roman province of Gallia Narbonensis.

Ares: Greek god of war.

Arete: Fictional town on the Euphrates, modelled on Dura-Europus, scene of the action in *Fire in the East*.

Argippaei: Nomadic tribe of Scythians, living on the Steppe.

Argo: Mythical ship of Jason's Argonauts.

Armata: Latin, 'the armed one'; in *The Caspian Gates* the name of a warship.

Arsacid: Dynasty that ruled Parthia 247BC–AD228.

Arsyene: According to Galen, a Greek physician, a dry white wine.

Artemis: Greek goddess of hunting.

Arvak: In Norse mythology, one of the two horses that pulled the sun across the sky.

Atheling: Anglo-Saxon for lord.

Augustus: Name of the first Roman emperor, subsequently adopted as one of the titles of the office.

Aurvandil the Brave: Figure of Norse mythology whose frozen toe was said to have been broken off by Thor and thrown into the heavens as a star.

Autokrator: Greek for sole ruler; used as translation of the Latin *imperator*.

Auxiliary: Roman regular soldier serving in a unit other than a legion.

Aviones: German tribe from the area of modern Denmark.

Azara: Town situated on the eastern marshes of Lake Maeotis, the modern Sea of Azov; in this novel given the Greek nickname Conopion, 'mosquito net', from an unidentified place on Azov.

Bacchus: Roman name for the Greek god of wine, Dionysus.

Barbaricum: Lands of the barbarians. Anywhere beyond the frontiers of the Roman empire, which were thought to mark the limits of the civilized world.

Barbaritas: Barbarian, uncivilized; literally, 'bar-bar', the sound Greeks heard when non-Greek was spoken.

Battue: Technique for driving game into a killing circle.

Bay of Naxos: On the eastern coast of the island of Sicily.

Bithynia et Pontus: Roman province along the south shore of the Black Sea.

Borani (also *Boranoi*): German tribe.

Borysthenes: Greek name for the Dnieper river.

Bosporus: Latin, from the Greek *Bosporos*, literally 'ox-ford', the name of several straits, above all those on which Byzantium stood and that in the Crimea; the latter gives its name to the Roman client kingdom of the Bosporus.

Bouleuterion: Greek, 'council house', where the *Boule* or council met.

Budinians: Nomadic tribe of Scythians, living on the Steppe.

Buticosus: From the Greek *buo*, 'to stuff', made into a Latin name; mockingly bestowed on a slave with a large erection depicted in a mosaic pavement from Ostia, outside Rome.

Caesar: Name of the adopted family of the first Roman emperor, subsequently adopted as one of the titles of the office; often used to designate an emperor's heir.

Caledonia: Modern Scotland, or the Highlands.

Carpi: Tribe living north-west of the Black Sea.

Carrhae: Town in northern Iraq, scene of a disastrous Roman defeat at the hands of the Parthians in 53BC.

Carthage: Capital city of the Roman province of Africa.

Caspian Gates: Name given to the passes through the Caucasus mountains.

Cataphracti: Heavily armoured Roman cavalry, from the Greek word for mail armour.

Centurion: Officer of the Roman army with the seniority to command a company of around eighty to a hundred men.

Chi: Fourteenth letter of the Greek alphabet, shaped like an 'X'.

Cilicia: Roman province in the south of Asia Minor.

Circesium: Town on the Euphrates.

Clibanarius (plural, *clibanarii*): Heavily armed cavalryman, possibly derived from 'baking oven'.

Cohors: Unit of Roman soldiers, usually about 500 men-strong.

Cohors I Cilicium Milliaria Equitata Sagittariorum: Double-strength auxiliary unit with a cavalry component, originally raised in Cilicia, modern south-eastern Turkey, now stationed in the province of Moesia Inferior, abutting the Black Sea south of the Danube.

Colos: One of the fantastical creatures said to live in Scythia.

Colosseum: Largest amphitheatre in the ancient world. In the centre of Rome, it was used for gladiatorial combats and took its name not from its size but from a colossal statue standing close by.

Comitatus: Latin, literally, 'a following'; name given to barbarian war bands.

Consilium: Council, body of advisors, of a Roman emperor, official or elite private person.

Contubernales: Latin, 'comrades'; from *contubernium*, a group of ten or eight soldiers who shared a tent.

Corrector Totius Orientis: 'Overseer of all the Orient'; a title applied to Odenathus of Palmyra.

Croucasis: Scythian name for the Caucasus, means 'gleaming white with snow'.

Cursus Publicus: Imperial Roman postal service, whereby those with official passes, *diplomata*, could send messengers and get remounts.

Cybele: Eastern mother goddess adopted by the Greeks and Romans.

Cynic: The counter-cultural philosophy founded by Diogenes of Sinope in the fourth century BC.

Daemon: Supernatural being; could be applied to many different types: good/ bad, individual/ collective, internal/ external, and ghosts.

Demeter: Greek goddess of the harvest.

Dictator of Rome: Magistrate with sole authority elected in a crisis; in theory held power for a fixed period, but the time limit was often abused.

Dignitas: Important Roman concept which covers our idea of dignity but goes much further; famously, Julius Caesar claimed that his *dignitas* meant more to him than life itself.

Dionysus: Greek god of wine.

Diplomata: Official passes which allowed the bearer access to the *cursus publicus*.

Disciplina: Latin, 'discipline'; the Romans considered that they had this quality, and others lacked it.

Dominus: Latin, 'lord', 'master', 'sir'; a title of respect.

Draco: Literally, Latin, 'snake' or 'dragon'; name given to a windsock-style military standard shaped like a dragon.

Ecbatana: Capital of the Medes, in western Iran.

Eirenarch: Title of chief of police in many Greek cities.

Empusa: Shape-shifting monster of Greek folk tales, associated with Hecate and witchcraft, although often in a comic context.

Epicureanism: Greek philosophical system, whose followers either denied that the gods existed or held that they were far away and did not intervene in the affairs of mankind.

Essene: Ascetic Jewish sect.

Eumenides: 'The kindly ones', a euphemism for the terrible furies from the underworld that pursued and tormented wrong-doers.

Eumolpos: In Greek mythology, son of Poseidon and Chione, who settled in Thrace; claimed as an ancestor by the kings of Bosporus.

Eupatrid: From the Greek, meaning 'well-born'; an aristocrat.

Eutes: Nomadic tribe that migrated to the Steppe from the area of modern Denmark.

Euxine: From the Greek *euxenos*, literally, 'kindly to strangers'; ancient name for the Black Sea.

Fairguneis: Thunder god; one of the most important deities of the Goths.

Familia: Latin term for family and, by extension, the entire household, including slaves.

Farodini: North German tribe.

Fasces: Bundles of wooden rods tied round a single-bladed axe, symbolizing the power of Roman magistrates to punish lawbreakers.

Fenrir: In Norse mythology, a monstrous wolf that will break its chains at the end of days, Ragnarok, and devour Odin, father of the gods.

Ferryman: In Greek and Roman mythology, rows the souls of the dead across the river Styx to the underworld; required a toll, thus the practice of leaving coins in the mouths of the dead.

Fimbulvetr: In Norse mythology, a series of severe winters that foretell the end of the world, Ragnarok.

Flamen Dialis: The Roman high priest of Jupiter, subject to numerous taboos.

Frisian: North German tribe.

Frumentarius (plural, *frumentarii*): Military unit based on the Caelian Hill in Rome; the emperor's secret police; messengers, spies, and assassins.

Gallia Narbonensis: Roman province roughly corresponding to the French regions of Provence and Languedoc.

Gauti: Scandinavian tribe.

Gepidae: East German tribe.

Germania: Lands where the German tribes lived; 'free' Germany.

Gerousia: Institution of the Spartan government; a small council whose members had to be over the age of sixty; responsible for capital punishment and submitting proposals to the citizen assembly.

Gladius: Roman military short sword; generally superseded by the *spatha* by the mid-third century AD; also slang for penis.

Goltescythae: Tribe from the Ural mountains.

Gorytus: Combined bowcase and quiver.

Gospel of Light: Religion propounded by the eastern mystic Mani.

Goths: Loose confederation of Germanic tribes.

Graeculus (plural, *Graeculi*): Latin, 'Little Greek'; Greeks called themselves Hellenes, Romans tended not to extend that courtesy but called them *Graeci*; with casual contempt, Romans often went further, to *Graeculi*.

Grethungi: Gothic tribe living on the Steppe north of the Black Sea.

Gudja: Gothic priest.

Gymnasium: Exercise ground; formed from the Greek word *gymnos*, 'naked', as all such activities were performed in the nude.

Gymnosophist: Greek, literally, 'naked wise-man'; a member of an ascetic sect of Hindus who were supposed to contemplate philosophy in the nude, having renounced all interest in earthly possessions.

Hades: Greek underworld.

Haliurunna: Gothic witch.

Harii: Germanic tribe living between the headwaters of the Elbe and Oder rivers.

Haruspex: Roman priest who determined whether the gods approved a course of action by inspecting the entrails of sacrificed animals; a custom originally adopted from the Etruscans.

Hati: In Norse mythology, the wolf that chases the moon, causing it to flee across the sky.

Hecate: Sinister, three-headed underworld goddess of magic, the night, crossroads and doorways.

Hel: The underworld in Norse mythology, reserved for those who do not die a warrior's death.

Hellenes: The Greeks' name for themselves; often used with connotations of cultural superiority.

Helots: Serf-type underclass in classical Sparta.

Heracles: Heroic man translated into god, popular among Greeks and Romans; known to the latter as *Hercules*.

Herul (plural, *Heruli*): East Germanic tribe living to the north of the Black Sea, having migrated from Scandinavia in the early third century AD.

Hibernia: Modern Ireland.

Hippodrome: Greek, literally, 'horse race'; stadium for chariot racing.

Humanitas: Latin, 'humanity' or 'civilization', the opposite of *barbaritas*; Romans thought that they, the Greeks (at least upper-class ones), and, on occasion, other peoples (usually very remote) had it, while the majority of mankind did not.

Hybris: Greek concept of pride, which expressed itself in the humbling of others.

Hypanis river: Flowing east to west in the North Caucasus region, the modern river Kuban.

Hypocaust: Underfloor heating system, relying upon hot air from fires.

Ides: Thirteenth day of the month in short months, the fifteenth in long months.

Imniscaris: Tribe living around the river Volga.

Imperium: Power of the Romans, i.e. the Roman empire, often referred to in full as the *imperium Romanorum*.

Ionia: Area of western Turkey bordering the Aegean, settled by Greeks.

Iota: Ninth letter of the Greek alphabet, the smallest and simplest to draw.

Jormungand: In Norse mythology, the world serpent which lay in the depths of the ocean waiting for Ragnarok.

Kalends: First day of the month.

Kataskopoi: Greek, literally, 'an around-looker'; a scout or spy.

Keryneia: Town on the north coast of Cyprus; its ancient name is still in use.

Kindly sea: From the Greek name *Euxine*, the modern Black Sea.

Kurgan: Name for a burial mound in the Slavic or Turkic languages of the Steppe.

Kyrios: Greek for lord, master, sir; a title of respect.

Langobardi: Tribe living on the banks of the river Elbe in central Germany.

Legate: Latin, an ambassador, or a high-ranking officer in the Roman army, drawn from the senatorial classes.

Legatus extra ordinem Scythica: Extraordinary envoy to the Scythians.

Legion: Unit of heavy infantry, usually about 5,000 men-strong; from mythical times, the backbone of the Roman army; the numbers in a legion and the legions' dominance in the army declined during the third century AD as more and more detachments, *vexillationes*, served away from the parent unit and became more or less independent units.

Legionary: Roman regular soldier serving in a legion.

Lesbian: From the Greek island of Lesbos; their wine was highly praised in antiquity, and was sometimes mixed with seawater.

Lesser Rhombites: Ancient name for the river Kirpilli, flowing into the eastern shore of Lake Maeotis, the modern Sea of Azov.

Libation: Offering of drink to the gods.

Libertas: Latin term for freedom or liberty; a political slogan throughout much of Roman history, though its meaning changed according to an author's philosophical principles or the system of government that happened to be in power. More technically, the state of being free as opposed to being a slave.

Libitinarii: Funerary men, the carriers out of the dead; they had to reside beyond the town limits, and had to ring a bell when they came into town to perform their duties.

Liburnian: Name given in the time of the Roman empire to a small warship, possibly rowed on two levels.

Logos: Greek philosophical term meaning 'reason'; in many ancient theological systems, the mind was said to govern the universe.

Loki: In Norse mythology, the trickster, bad god.

Lustral: Pertaining to a religious ceremony of purification.

Lycia: Region on the south coast of modern Turkey.

Lydia: Kingdom in Asia Minor, conquered by the Persians in 546BC.

Macrophali: Greek, literally 'long-headed', peoples who practised head-binding, leading to an elongated skull.

Maeotae: Group of peoples living in the area of the Maeotian marshes, found on the eastern shores of Lake Maeotis, the modern Sea of Azov.

Maeotis: The Sea of Azov.

Maiestas: Latin, 'majesty'; the majesty of the Roman *imperium* was a core component of imperial ideology, and maintaining Roman prestige among barbarian tribes was central to foreign policy; offences against Roman *maiestas*, personified by the emperor, were considered treasonous and punishable by death.

Mandata: Instructions issued by the emperors to their governors and officials.

Manichaeism: Religion founded by the 'prophet' Mani (AD216–76); a mixture of pagan, Christian and Persian beliefs, which opposed good (identified with the mind) against evil (identified with matter).

Manichaeans: Followers of the religious leader Mani (AD216–76).

Manumission: In Roman law, the legal act of freeing a slave.

Massilia: Roman port on the southern shores of Gaul; modern Marseilles.

Mediolanum: Roman city in north Italy; modern Milan.

Menog: Persian word for spirit, immaterial; the spirit plane.

Middle Earth: In Norse culture, the world of men, as opposed to Asgard, the realm of the gods.

Miles Arcana: Latin, *miles*, 'a soldier', *arcana*, 'secret', so in English, 'secret soldier'.

Milesians: People of the city of Miletus, in Ionia.

Mithras: Eastern god popular among Roman soldiers.

Mobads: Persian priests of the Zoroastrian religion.

Moesia Inferior: Roman province south of the Danube, running from Moesia Superior in the west to the Black Sea in the east.

Mordens: Tribe living in the region of the river Volga.

Mural Crown: Roman award for valour, for being the first over the wall of an enemy town; in the principate, reserved for officers.

Museum: Temple of the Muses in Alexandria, an institution that attracted leading intellectuals from all over the Greek world, who came to study in its vast library and would lecture in its precincts; origin of the modern word 'museum'.

Mycenae: Seat of the legendary King Agamemnon in the epic poems of Homer.

Naglfar: In Norse mythology, a ship made from the finger- and toenails of the dead, which will carry the armies to battle with the gods at the end of days.

Navarchos: Greek, literally, 'ship commander'; the commander of a squadron of ships.

Nemausus: Town in Gaul (modern Nîmes); possibly the birthplace of Castricius.

Nerthus: Germanic earth goddess.

Nervii: Germanic tribe feared for their fighting skills, originally from the area of modern Belgium.

Niflheim: In Norse mythology, the underworld for those who do not die in battle.

Nithing: Germanic word for coward, wretch; highly derogatory.

Norns: In Norse mythology, the three goddesses responsible for weaving the destinies of gods and men.

Novae: Town on the south bank of the Danube; successfully defended from Gothic attack by the future emperor Gallus in AD250.

Obol: Small-denomination Greek coin.

Olbia: Town near the mouth of the Dnieper river.

Omega: Last letter of the Greek alphabet, shaped like a curving 'U', with longer cross-pieces to the top which project at either side.

Ordo: Latin term, meaning a social or professional class.

Ornamenta Consularia: The 'ornaments' of a consul; often used by Rome as a diplomatic gift to foreigners.

Oxygala: Greek sour milk or yoghurt.

Palmyra: Now-abandoned city in central Syria; in the chaos of the third century AD, its ruler was put in charge of the Roman provinces of the east by the emperor Gallienus.

Pamphylia: Region on the southern coast of modern Turkey.

Panticapaeum: Greek, literally, 'all-cradling'; a trading city at the eastern end of the Crimean peninsula, now modern Kerch.

Paraclete: Greek for advocate, go-between; became a religiously charged term for someone able to intercede with the divine.

Paradise: Persian for garden or game reserve.

Parthia: Empire centred around north-eastern Iran, conquered in AD224 by Ardashir I, founder of the Sassanid empire.

Pataroue Point: Headland on the eastern shores of the Sea of Azov.

Patronus: Latin, 'patron'; once a slave had been manumitted and become a freedman, his former owner became his *patronus*; there were duties and obligations on both sides.

Patronymic: Ancient practice of taking a father's name as part of the personal name.

Pepaideumenoi: Greek, literally, 'those who have been educated'; members of the intellectual elite.

Perge: Regional capital of Pamphylia, an area on the southern coast of modern Turkey.

Phanagoria: Town on the eastern shore of the straits of Kerch, leading into the Sea of Azov.

Pharos: Greek term for a lighthouse.

Phasis: Town on the eastern shores of the Black Sea.

Phoibos: Title of the god Apollo, literally, 'the Radiant'.

Physiognomy: Ancient 'science' of studying people's faces, bodies and deportment to discover their character, and thus both their past and future.

Pileus: Felt cap, given to freed slaves as a symbol of their new liberty; adopted by French revolutionaries in the eighteenth century, and still worn by some modern personifications of France.

Platonic: Pertaining to the philosopher Plato.

Polis: Greek, a city state; living in one was a key marker in being considered Greek and/or civilized.

Poseidon: Greek god of the sea.

Praeco: Latin, 'herald'.

Praenomen and *nomen*: Latin, 'forename' and 'family name'. Slaves were given only one name; if they were freed, they adopted the forename and family name of their previous masters, giving them the three names symbolizing a free Roman.

Prefect of Cavalry: Senior military post introduced in the mid-third century AD.

Principate: Rule of the *Princeps*; the rule of the Roman *imperium* by the emperors.

Procurator of the Hellespontine Provinces: In Roman imperial government, a procurator oversaw the collection of taxes and goods; the Hellespontine provinces bordered the northern shores of the Hellespont, the modern Dardanelles.

Prometheus: Divine figure, one of the Titans; variously believed to have created mankind out of clay, tricked the gods into accepting only the bones and fat of sacrifices, and stolen fire from Olympus for mortals. Zeus chained him to a peak in the Caucasus, where an eagle daily ate his liver.

Proskynesis: Greek, 'adoration'; given to the gods and in some periods to some rulers, including emperors in the third century AD and foreign potentates. There were two types: full prostration on the ground, or bowing and blowing a kiss with the fingertips. Barbarian princes merited the lesser form.

Psessoi: One of the tribes of the Maeotae living on the eastern shore of Lake Maeotis, the modern Sea of Azov.

Puer: Latin, 'boy'; used by owners of male slaves, and by soldiers of each other.

Ragas: Tribe living along the banks of the Volga.

Ragnarok: In Norse paganism, the death of gods and men, the end of time.

Res Publica: Latin, 'the Roman Republic'; under the emperors, it continued to mean the Roman empire.

Reudigni: Germanic tribe from the north.

Rha river: The Volga.

Rhombites: Ancient name for the modern river Yeia, flowing into the eastern shore of Lake Maeotis, the modern Sea of Azov.

Rogas: Tribe living to the north of the Caucasus mountains.

Rosomoni: Elite clan of the Heruli tribe; their name perhaps means 'Red ones', either referring to the colour of their tattoos or the dyeing of their hair.

Rune sticks: Sticks marked with runes and thrown into the air; the patterns they made were used by the northern tribes to read the future.

Sacramentum: Roman military oath, taken extremely seriously.

Sarmatians: Nomadic peoples living north of the Danube.

Sassanid: Persian, from the dynasty that overthrew the Parthians in the 220s AD and was Rome's great eastern rival until the seventh century AD.

Saturnalia: Roman festival in honour of the god Saturn, taking place over several days around midwinter, marked with feasting and gift-giving.

Saxones: North Germanic tribe.

Scadinavia: Ancient name for the southern part of the Scandinavian peninsula, thought in antiquity to be an island; also called Scandza.

Scapulimancy: Practice of telling the future from the cracks in burnt shoulder blades, known as *scapulae* in Latin.

Sceptouchos: Greek, literally, 'sceptre-bearer'; a high office in the Persian empire and the title of a noble in the region of the Caucasus.

Scrithiphini: Scandinavian tribe.

Scythia: Term used by Greeks and Romans of the lands to the north and east of the Black Sea, roughly bordered by the Danube in the west, the Volga in the east and the Caucasus to the south. Its nomadic peoples were a source of fantastical tales for ancient geographers and began to take on a terrifying aspect from the frequent raids they made on the Roman empire. Raiding increased in intensity throughout the third century AD.

Scythians: Greek and Latin name for various northern and often nomadic barbarian peoples.

Seal of the Prophets: The religious leader Mani claimed that his coming was foretold in the New Testament, and that he would be the final prophet sent from god.

Selene: Greek moon goddess.

Senator: Member of the senate, the council of Rome. The senatorial order was the richest and most prestigious group in the empire; in the third century AD, suspicious emperors were beginning to exclude them from military commands and imperial offices.

Sirachoi: Tribe living on the north-western edge of the Caucasus mountains, subject to the Alani.

Skalks: Gothic, 'slave'.

Socratic dialogue: Literary genre taking the form of conversations on philosophical themes, popularized by Plato's more or less imagined discussions with Socrates.

Sophist: Highly regarded public speaker who specialized in display oratory.

Spatha: Long Roman sword, the normal type of sword carried by all troops by the mid-third century AD.

Spolia Opima: Roman generals who personally killed the opposing commander in combat were allowed to strip the armour from their enemy and dedicate it to the gods. The honour was so potent that Augustus, later to become the first Roman emperor, blocked the claim of one of his generals on very spurious grounds to avoid being outdone. Only known to have been won three times, the last in 222BC.

Stipendium: Latin military term for a soldier or sailor's pay.

Styx: In Greek and Roman mythology, the river marking the boundary of the underworld. The spirits of the dead had to pay to be ferried across.

Suania: Kingdom in the high Caucasus; included the modern district of Georgia called Svaneti.

Subura: Poor quarter of the city of Rome.

Suebian sea: Ancient name for the Baltic.

Syzygos: Greek, literally 'yoked together', so consort. In ancient mystical religions, a term for a companion angel.

Taifali: Germanic tribe settled around the river Danube. Ammianus Marcellinus reports that their boys had homosexual relationships with older men until they had made their first successful hunt.

Tamga: Term for the tribal or family symbols used to differentiate the nomadic peoples and clans of the Steppe.

Tanais: City at the mouth of the river Tanais (the modern Don), located on the extreme north-eastern shore of the Sea of Azov.

Tanais river: The Don.

Tarandos: One of the fantastical creatures said to live in Scythia, the size of a cow with the head of a deer.

Tarpeites: One of the tribes of the Maeotae living on the eastern shore of Lake Maeotis, the modern Sea of Azov.

Tauma: Persian, literally, 'twin'; a spirit double.

Tauromenium: Town in Sicily (modern Taormina), where Ballista and Julia own a villa.

Teiws: God of war worshipped by the Goths.

Tervingi: Gothic tribe living in the region between the Danube and Dnieper rivers.

Thiazi: Giant in Norse mythology, whose eyes were placed in the heavens by Odin.

Timeo Danaos et dona ferentes: 'I fear the Greeks, even bearing gifts.' A much-quoted line from Virgil's epic poem, the *Aeneid*; origin of the saying, 'Beware Greeks bearing gifts.'

Toga: Voluminous garment, reserved for Roman citizens, worn on formal occasions.

Toga Virilis: Garment given to mark a Roman's coming of age; usually at about fourteen.

Trapezus: City on the southern coast of the Black Sea, sacked by the Goths in AD258.

Trierarch: Commander of a *trireme*; in the Roman forces, equivalent to a centurion.

Trireme: Ancient warship, a galley rowed by about 200 men on three levels.

Tumulus: Latin term for a burial mound.

Urugundi: Gothic tribe settled along the Don river.

Valhalla: In Norse paganism, the hall in which selected heroes who had fallen in battle would feast until Ragnarok.

Varini: North Germanic tribe.

Vesta: Roman goddess of the hearth.

Vir Egregius: Knight of Rome, a man of the equestrian order.

Vir Ementissimus: Highest rank an equestrian could attain; e.g. Praetorian Prefect.

Vir Perfectissimus: Equestrian rank above *Vir Egregius* but below *Vir Ementissimus*.

Woden: High Norse god.

Wonders Beyond Thule: Novel written in the second century AD by Antonius Diogenes, taking the form of a fantastical travel book in 24 volumes, now known only via an epitome. Thule was an island thought to lie in the extreme north, beyond Britain.

Wyrd: Anglo-Saxon, 'fate'; one of the *norns*.

Zereba: Stockade of thorn bushes made by African tribes.

Zirin: Cry of the Scythians, said by Lucian to signal a person's status as an emissary and prevent the caller from being harmed, even in the heat of combat.

List of Emperors in the
Third Century AD

AD193–211	Septimius Severus
AD198–217	Caracalla
AD210–11	Geta
AD217–18	Macrinus
AD218–22	Elagabalus
AD222–35	Alexander Severus
AD235–8	Maximinus Thrax
AD238	Gordian I
AD238	Gordian II
AD238	Pupienus
AD238	Balbinus
AD238–44	Gordian III
AD244–9	Philip the Arab
AD249–51	Decius
AD251–3	Trebonianus Gallus
AD253	Aemilianus
AD253–60	Valerian

List of Characters

To avoid giving away any of the plot, characters usually are only described as first encountered in *The Wolves of the North*.

Achilles: Greek hero of the *Iliad*, Homer's epic poem of the Trojan War.
Aegisthus: In Greek mythology, he seduced Clytemnestra, wife of Agamemnon.
Aeschylus: Greek tragic playwright of the first half of the fifth century BC.
Agaetes: Semi-mythical king of Scythia.
Agamemnon: Leader of the Greek forces in the Trojan War.
Agesilaus: Agesilaus II, King of Sparta, *c.* 445–359BC. Said to have ensured a favourable omen before battle by inscribing VICTORY backwards on his hand and pressing it on the entrails of the sacrificial victim.
Ajax: Greek hero of the Trojan War.
Alaric: Outcast from the Taifali, now a war leader for the Heruli.
Albinus: Decius Clodius Septimius Albinus, *c.* AD150–97. Appointed Caesar by Septimius Severus. When the latter elevated his own son Caracalla to be Caesar, he sent messengers with orders to assassinate

Albinus. When the plot failed, Albinus declared himself emperor from his base in Britain.

Alexander the Great: 356–23BC, son of Philip, King of Macedon, conqueror of Achaemenid Persia.

Aluith: Young Herul, from the Rosomoni clan.

Amantius: Publius Egnatius Amantius, an imperial eunuch originally from Abasgia.

Ammius: Leader of a war band of Heruli.

Anacharsis: Scythian philosopher who settled in Athens in the sixth century BC, sometimes numbered among the Seven Sages of Greece.

Andonnoballus: Chief of the Heruli, from the Rosomoni clan.

Aordus: Ex-slave of the Heruli freed for courage in battle, now a full member of the tribe.

Aoric: Deceased King of the Urugundi, father of King Hisarna.

Apollonius of Rhodes: Third-century BC writer, author of the *Argonautica*.

Apollonius of Tyana: Greek philosopher and holy man of the first century AD, said to perform miracles.

Apsyrtus: Brother of Medea. In some versions of the myth, he was murdered and dismembered by Jason, but in others by his own sister, to delay pursuit by their father's men.

Artemidorus: Greek from Trapezus, captured and enslaved by the Heruli. Later freed, and appointed a leader among the nomads.

Aruth: Chief of the Heruli, from the Rosonomi clan.

Augustus: First Roman emperor, 31BC–AD14.

Aurelian: Lucius Domitius Aurelian, a Roman officer from the Danube, one of the *protectores*. A friend of Ballista at the court of Gallienus.

Aureolus: Once a Getan shepherd near the Danube, now Gallienus's Prefect of Cavalry, one of the *protectores*.

Ballista: Marcus Clodius Ballista, originally named Dernhelm, son of Isangrim the *Dux*, war leader, of the Angles; a diplomatic hostage in the Roman empire, he has been granted Roman citizenship and equestrian status, having served in the Roman army in Africa, the far west, and on the Danube and the Euphrates (*Fire in the East*); having defeated the Sassanid Persians at the battles of Circesium (*King of Kings*), Soli and Sebaste, and killed the pretender Quietus, he was briefly acclaimed Roman emperor (*Lion of the Sun*); the year before this novel takes place he served as a Roman envoy in the Caucasus (*The Caspian Gates*).

Bauto: Young Frisian slave purchased by Ballista in Ephesus.

Berus: Herul of the Rosomoni clan.

Biomasos: An interpreter attached to Ballista's embassy. See note in the Historical Afterword.

Brachus: Spirit-twin of Naulobates.

Calanus: Indian ascetic who attached himself to Alexander the Great's army. Falling ill, and not wishing to be a burden on others, he immolated himself.

Calgacus: Marcus Clodius Calgacus, a Caledonian ex-slave, originally owned by Isangrim and sent by him to serve as a body servant to his son Ballista in the Roman empire; manumitted by the latter, now a freedman with Roman citizenship.

Caligula: Gaius Julius, Roman emperor AD37–41, as a child nicknamed 'Little Boots' (Caligula), because his father had him dressed in miniature soldier's uniform.

Callirhoe: Prostitute met by Ballista's companion Maximus. Her story may have been 'borrowed' from the novel of the same name by Chariton of Aphrodisias.

Cannabas: Said to have been a king of the Goths in the mid-third century AD, though perhaps a Roman joke about nomadic drug use from the Greek form of his name, Cannabaudes.

Castricius: Gaius Aurelius Castricius, Roman army officer risen from the ranks, was Prefect of Cavalry under both Quietus and Ballista, served as Roman envoy to the king of Albania, now Ballista's deputy in the mission to the Steppes.

Censorinus: Lucius Calpurnius Piso Censorinus, *Princeps Peregrinorum* under Valerian and the pretenders Macrianus and Quietus; now serving as deputy Praetorian Prefect under Gallienus.

Circe: Mythical witch, who delayed Odysseus's homecoming from the Trojan War.

Cledonius: *Ab Admissionibus* to Valerian; captured by the Persians with the emperor.

Clytemnestra: Wife of Agamemnon; was unfaithful while her husband was fighting at Troy and, on his return, aided in his murder.

Corbicius: In some unsympathetic accounts of Manichaeism, Mani is said to have originally been born a slave boy named Corbicius.

Datius: Ex-slave of the Heruli freed for courage in battle, now a full member of the tribe.

Decius: Gaius Messius Quintus. Ruled AD249–51, killed in battle by the Goths at Abritus.

Demetrius: Marcus Clodius Demetrius, the 'Greek boy', a slave purchased by Julia to serve as her husband Ballista's secretary; manumitted by the latter, now a freedman with Roman citizenship living in the household of the emperor Gallienus.

Demosthenes: Son of Sauromates, a metalworker of Panticapaeum missing a slave.

Dernhelm (1): Original name of Ballista.

Dernhelm (2): Lucius Clodius Dernhelm, second son of Ballista and Julia.

Diogenes: Cynic philosopher, *c.* 412/403–*c.* 324/321BC.

Euripides: Fifth-century BC Athenian tragic playwright.

Eusebius: Imperial eunuch originally from Abasgia; when sent back there as part of a Roman embassy, he attempted to kill the king, but failed and was himself killed in a terrible way.

Felix: Spurius Aemilius Felix, an elderly senator; defended Byzantium from the Goths in AD257.

Fritigern: King of the Borani.

Gallienus: Publius Licinius Egnatius Gallienus, declared joint Roman emperor by his father the emperor Valerian in AD253, sole emperor after the capture of his father by the Persians in AD260.

Gallus: Gaius Vibius Trebonianus Gallus; a successful general on the Danube, he defended Novae from the Goths in AD250; emperor AD251–3.

Hadrian: Publius Aelius Hadrianus, Roman emperor AD117–38.

Hannibal: General of Carthage in the Second Punic War against Rome (247–183BC).

Heliogabalus: Derogatory nickname for the emperor Marcus Aurelius Antoninus, AD218–22. Said to be remarkably perverse.

Herodotus: The 'Father of History'; fifth-century BC Greek historian of the Persian Wars.

Hippocrates: Greek physician and medical writer of the fifth to fourth centuries BC.

Hippothous: Rough Cilician, claims to be from Perinthus originally; *accensus* to Ballista.

Hisarna: 'The Iron One', King of the Urugundi, son of King Aoric.

Hordeonius: Centurion of Cohors I Cilicium Milliaria Equitata Sagittariorum.

Idmon: Mythical seer from Argos, joined the Argonauts even though forewarned he would die on their journey.

Iphigenia: Mythical daughter of Agamemnon, sacrificed in return for a favourable wind to Troy.

Isangrim (1): *Dux*, war leader, of the Angles, father of Dernhelm/Ballista.

Isangrim (2): Marcus Clodius Isangrim, first son of Ballista and Julia.

Jason: Mythical leader of the Argonauts.

Julia: Daughter of the senator Gaius Julius Volcatius Gallicanus; wife of Ballista.

Kadlin: Woman of the Angles, to whom Ballista has been emotionally attached.

Khedosbios: *Eirenarch* of Panticapaeum.

Laocoon: Mistrusted the wooden horse left by the Greeks, but failed to persuade his fellow Trojans not to take it into Troy; killed with his two sons by two great sea serpents.

Loxus: Greek physician of the third century BC, author of a work on physiognomy.

Lucian: Satirical author of the later second century AD, writing in Greek.

Lycurgus: Legendary founder of the constitution of Sparta.

Mamurra: Ballista's *Praefectus Fabrum* ('Prefect of Construction') and friend; entombed in a siege tunnel at Arete.

Mani: Religious leader whose teachings, drawing on Christianity and Eastern religions, inspired Manichaeism (AD216–76/277).

Mar Ammo: Manichaean missionary, known to have been active in the third century AD.

Marmaryan: The mother of Mani. Claimed to be descended from the Arsacid dynasty, rulers of Parthia until the first quarter of the third century AD.

Mastabates: Imperial eunuch originally from Abasgia; served with Ballista in Suania the year before this novel takes place.

Maximinus Thrax: Gaius Iulius Verus Maximinus, Roman emperor AD235–8, known as *Thrax* ('The Thracian') because of his lowly origins.

Maximus: Marcus Clodius Maximus, bodyguard to Ballista; originally a Hibernian warrior known as Muirtagh of the Long Road, sold to slave traders and trained as a boxer then gladiator before being purchased and then freed by Ballista.

Medea: Colchian princess and sorceress who helps Jason win the Golden Fleece.

Mithridates: Mithridates VI Eupator the Great, King of Pontus (134–63BC); having failed to commit suicide after his defeat by Rome, requested that his Gallic bodyguard kill him.

Morcar: Son of Isangrim, war leader of the Angles, half-brother of Ballista.

Narcissus: Slave purchased by Hippothous in Ephesus.

Naulobates: King of the Heruli.

Ochus: Herul of the Rosomoni clan.

Odenathus: Septimius Odenathus, Lord of Palmyra/Tadmor, appointed by Gallienus as *corrector* over the eastern provinces of the Roman empire.

Odoacer: Prophesied king of the Heruli.

Olympias: Greek woman, captured by the Heruli at the sack of Trapezus.

Orestes: In Greek myth, the son of Agamemnon and Clytemnestra.

Ovid: Roman poet, concentrating on mythological and amorous themes (43BC–17AD).

Pattikios: Father of Mani.

Peregrim: Son of Ursio; nephew of Aoric, the King of the Urugundi.

Pericles: Son of Alcibiades; a retainer of the King of the Tarpeites, sharing his first and second names with two famous Athenian politicians of the fifth century BC.

Phanitheus: Friend of Naulobates' father.

Pharas: Herul of the Rosomoni clan.

Philemuth: Sickly Herul of the Rosomoni clan.

Plato: Athenian philosopher, *c.* 429–347BC.

Plutarch: Prolific Greek writer of philosophy and biography, *c.* AD45–125.

Polemon: Marcus Antonius Polemon, *c.* AD88–144, famous sophist and physiognomist.

Polybius (1): Slave purchased by Ballista in Priene.

Polybius (2): Greek historian of the second century BC, writing about Rome.

Porsenna: Marcus Aurelius Porsenna, *haruspex*.

Postumus: Marcus Cassianus Latinius Postumus, once governor of Lower Germany, from AD260 Roman emperor of the breakaway 'Gallic empire'; killer of Gallienus's son Saloninus.

Potamis: Slave-trader on the Dnieper river who bought and sold Wulfstan.

Pythagoras: Sixth-century BC philosopher.

Pythonissa: Daughter of King Polemo of Suania; a priestess of Hecate.

Rebecca: Jewish slave woman bought by Ballista.

Regulus: Roman herald.

Rhescuporis: Rhescuporis V, King of the Bosporus (*c.* AD240–76), client of Rome.

Romulus: Legendary founder of Rome.

Roxanne: Concubine of Shapur, captured by Ballista at Soli.

Rudolphus: Herul guide.

Rutilus: Marcus Aurelius Rutilus, Roman army officer, Praetorian Prefect under both Quietus and Ballista; a Roman envoy to the King of Iberia the year before this novel takes place.

Sabinillus: Roman senator; a follower of the philosopher Plotinus.

Safrax: King of the Alani.

Sallust: Roman historian (86–43BC).

Sarus: Leader of a war band of Heruli.

Sasan: Founder of the Sassanid house.

Saurmag: Fourth son of King Polemo of Suania; after a failed coup, an exile among the Alani.

Seneca: Roman philosopher (*c.* AD1–65).

Septimius Severus: Lucius Septimius Severus, Roman emperor AD193–211.

Shapur (or Sapor) *I*: Second Sassanid King of Kings, son of Ardashir I.

Simon: Young Jewish boy owned by Ballista.

Solon: Law-giver of the Athenians, *c.* 600BC.

Sophocles: Athenian tragic playwright of the fifth century BC.

Starkad: Chief of the Angles, grandfather of Ballista.

Strabo: Greek geographer of the Augustan age.

Suartuas: Father of Naulobates, King of the Heruli.

Sulla: Dictator of Rome (*c.* 138–78BC).

Sunildus: Great-grandfather of Naulobates, King of the Heruli.

Tacitus (1): Cornelius Tacitus, *c.* AD56–*c.* 118, the greatest Latin historian.

Tacitus (2): Marcus Claudius Tacitus, Roman senator of the third century AD (most likely) of Danubian origins; one of the *protectores*; may have claimed kinship with or even descent from the famous historian, but it is unlikely to be true.

Tarchon: Suani rescued by Ballista and Calgacus.

Trajan: Marcus Ulpius Trajan, Roman emperor AD98–117.

Turpio: Titus Flavius Turpio, army officer and friend of Ballista; executed by the Sassanids.

Uligagus: War leader of the Heruli.

Ursio: Brother of Aoric, King of the Urugundi.

Valerian: Publius Licinius Valerianus, an elderly Italian senator elevated to Roman emperor in AD253; captured by Shapur I in AD260.

Videric: Son of Fritigern, King of the Borani.

Virgil: Roman national poet (70–19BC).

Visandus: Grandfather of Naulobates, King of the Heruli.

Vultuulf: Gothic *gudja* (priest), attached by Hisarna to Ballista's embassy.

Wulfstan: Young Angle slave purchased by Ballista in Ephesus.

Zalmoxis: Sources disagree as to whether he was a god or a mortal. Said to have been worshipped as a god by the Getae for teaching them religious rites, but was thought of as a law-giver by the Thracians.

Zarmarus: Indian ascetic who immolated himself at Athens before Augustus in 19BC. His motives are unknown to the sources.

Zeno: Aulus Voconius Zeno, a Roman equestrian, former governor of Cilicia, and *a Studiis* to Gallienus, now a Roman emissary to the tribes near the mouth of the Danube.

Author photo: www.jameshawkinsphotography.com

DR. HARRY SIDEBOTTOM is best known for the Warrior of Rome series of novels, including *Fire in the East, King of Kings, Lion of the Sun, The Caspian Gates, Wolves of the North,* and *The Amber Road,* all published by Overlook. He teaches classical history at Oxford University, where he is a Fellow of St. Benet's Hall and a Lecturer at Lincoln College. He has an international reputation as a scholar, having published widely on ancient warfare, classical art, and the cultural history of the Roman Empire. Visit readswordsandsandals.com.

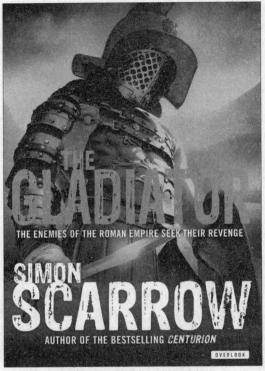
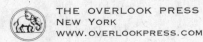

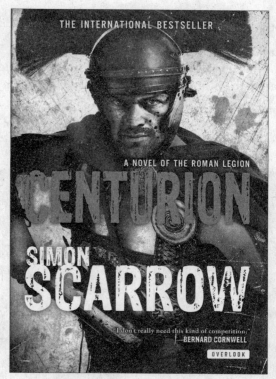

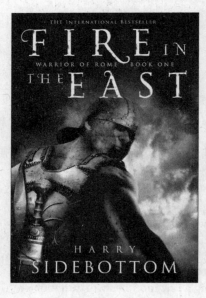
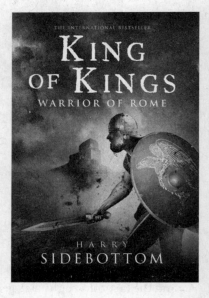
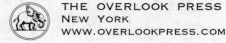

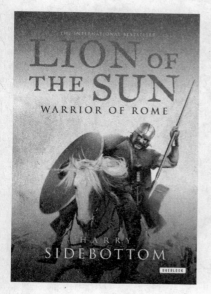
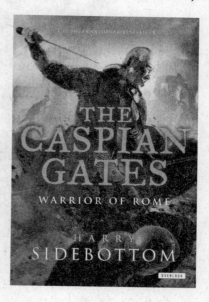

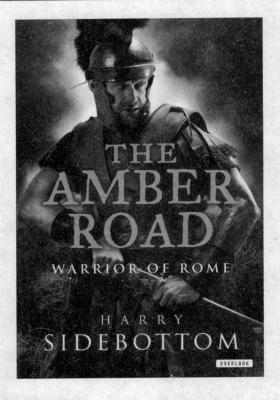